Rhapsody of Moon

By Roy Baldwin

Creative Gateway

To Aliyah Marr

*For encouraging and providing
the creative inspiration
and inspired creativity
to design the Rhapsody themes
and complete the fifth novel
in the series*

Perihelion—Chapter One

A whirlwind of unexpected experiences with gorgeous triplets, Magdaline, Eveline and Geraldine had severed a well trodden routine during the hectic seven days of her first week at home. That enduring myth of the calm, decisive and maternally unencumbered nuclear scientist, Lauren Hind, had vanished inside a frantic jumble of nappies, bottles, creams and assorted paraphernalia, as she struggled to find some semblance of normalised routine with three constantly hungry tiny babies. The initial euphoria and media exposure after their successful birth out in the Congo jungle, and a reuniting with husband Philippe finally released from a Siberian prison, already felt like a distant era. The logistical difficulty of feeding, sleeping and keeping them and herself clean had surprised even her highly ordered and organised self. But she was rising on top of it and felt confident that by the end of week two this erratic loop process would succumb to the usual rigors of scientific discipline she implemented in all other walks of her life. The girls would not be treated differently from either inside her laboratory or the board room. In any case, she needed to ensure she could return to work in three months time. Systematised routines needed to be established fast. She had a global company to run.

Marie had been wonderful, adopted as both a full time housekeeper and nanny, but Lauren already realised that once she returned to her office at the Cassini Cyclops Centre, additional help would be necessary. Furthermore, she decided to buy Marie some new furniture, including a decent writer's desk and a king sized luxury bed for the small caretaker cottage at the back of the garden. Keeping Marie happy and comfortable would be a wise investment.

Best of all she was amazed with how Philippe, inveterate wanderer from domestic routine, family stress and long-time addict of the next big business deal, was rapidly settling into quiet domesticity. Without doubt a spell of breaking rocks at the Krasnokamensk labour camp on the Chinese border had moved his mind rapidly towards a 'better the devil you know' orientation—the devil of course being her. Philippe was prepared, with no fuss or complaining in the middle of the night, to feed one triplet with expressed milk whilst she suckled the other two, providing fatherly comfort to enable her to get more extended sleep. At least the girls were on an almost three hour between feeds routine, which she happily encouraged. They already liked the time predictability, definitely, she decided, displaying characteristics of nascent budding scientists. Even Philippe's nappy changing was expertly executed with a constant happy gurgling from Magdaline, who had howled with dismay at his initial fumbles. Since seeing him for the first time in months, skinny and stumbling badly behind the fast strides of her son-in-law, DG, when they finally found her in the jungle being looked after by Vega the gorilla, Philippe's stated and unexpected commitment to enjoy domestic bliss with a newly found wife and beautiful, freshly made daughters had grown daily. This was more than she truly expected given the bizarre fracking catastrophe in Russia and his extraordinary affair in Novosibirsk with Olga, the maniac gas engineer. Now that Olga was exiled forever, lost on the run for good from Russia and on the top wanted list of the FSB, she could rest easy. Any lingering thoughts of Olga had magically vanished. However any thoughts he might be having of celebrating his new marital bliss would have to wait. She was still sore from top to bottom, although the special cream which Edward Jones her gynaecologist had prescribed, with an infusion of natural remedies including witch-hazel and aloe vera, was doing wonders. But although she had quickly mastered the technique of expressing her own milk by hand, then carefully refrigerating bottles and rotating two at once plus a bottle, which they loved, it was already too time consuming.

Freshly changed and fed, the triplets were quietly asleep in their cots and she sat down for a well needed breather and herbal tea. She was preparing mentally before the next feed for an assault on a complex fusion paper to be jointly written up with Juliette, her Research CEO. Lauren was hugely satisfied that her mind was on fire again with mathematics; the entire fuzzy brain period had departed thank goodness. She was feeling confident that Cassini was on the cusp of a breakthrough with Bhavika's new figure-of-eight modified stellerator design, to contain the ends of the hot plasma and enable the working of a commercial prototype fusion reaction. They had decided after secret internal discussions to start small in contrast to their JETR partners who were building a massive huge building and complex to house their enormous tokomak trial alternative. Maybe if they were lucky, the Cyclops Centre prototype might only generate ten to twenty kilowatt of energy, but it would be sustainable fusion energy for the first time, with more coming out than going in, the first tangible fusion generation to take place. Ramping up would subsequently be much easier to solve the engineering problems of scale. She thought of the enormous energy of the sun being released every second from the conversion of eight hundred thousand tons of hydrogen into helium and that rate would amazingly continue for at least four and a half billion years more before finally slowing down, as red giant stage commences. Then of course the Earth would be frazzled out of existence by the expanding sun. Whether anybody liked it or not, no matter what religion or otherwise they may believe in, man on planet Earth has an eventual shelf-life in this solar system, a scientific certainty beyond any power to rectify. The timescales and the amount of solar matter being burned up were almost beyond comprehension for day to day dealings, even for her highly attuned mathematical capability.

She seriously wondered whether human life would still exist in five hundred years time let alone four and a half billion. Surely by then, and a lot sooner, other life-forms on habitable exoplanets, whirling around stars elsewhere in the universe would have been found and the technological means established to escape planet Earth if any irreversible catastrophe happened? However there was certainly, as far as she was concerned, nowhere else in the existing solar system where man could run. All planets and moons were far too inhospitable for life, despite the speculations and fantasy colony ideas—certainly one can practically forget Mars and the Moon for the foreseeable future. Wouldn't it be nice instead to create a tiny fusion star, locked up and contained safely in the corner of her research workshop to power her new reactor?

Suddenly, dreamy reveries of stellar physics were jostled from her mind as the door opened briskly and Marie walked in.

"Lauren, I've just taken in a rather large parcel addressed to you. I have a feeling it may be the equipment you ordered from Edward Jones's clinic? Shall I open it up?"

"Gosh Marie, that was quick. I only rang Edward yesterday. Yes please, bring it in here and let's take a look."

As Marie carried the box in and began carefully cutting through the wrapping tape, Lauren was calculating the time efficiencies and increased comfort this device, if it worked satisfactorily, would provide. She was all for using as much technology as feasible, whilst ensuring her babies gained from the best maternal care she could provide. Edward Jones and his team had just patented a new design and he was keen for Lauren to be the first customer. Together they pulled open the box and she carefully took out the components and instructions for assembly. Separate, in another box, was a lithium battery power supply. She had the lot assembled in an instant, and they gazed at a new portable electric pump, to aid expressing her milk. Edward Jones reckoned it would do the job better than anything on the market and provide a filled bottle in ten minutes.

"Wow, that looks very high-tech," Marie remarked.

"Yes, made from the latest easily cleanable polymers," Lauren replied, fingering the container and immediately scrutinising the specifications which Edward had supplied, knowing her technical curiosity. "As well made, I would say, as one of my own nuclear reactors. Well almost! Not cheap, but if they start to sell, which I'm sure they will, the manufacturing costs will come down. I'm quite excited. I want to try this now."

She began unbuttoning her blouse. Marie strolled into the kitchen to find a freshly cleaned and sterilised bottle and returned as Lauren adjusted the input and output tubes and started the motor to hear how it sounded. A gentle whirring filled the air as the special and very quiet magnetic motor came to life. She liked the sound; probably similar in electromagnetic construction to some of the pumps inside her reactor vessels.

"Gosh Lauren, your left nipple still looks a bit sore. I'll just fetch a tube of ointment you can use afterwards."

"Fine. Here goes."

Suction device now firmly secured over her right nipple, she switched on and the pump gently kicked into action. Marie returned to see Lauren, a big grin over her face, looking very pleased and relaxed.

"Mmm ... this gentle sucking feels quite divine, so much better than by hand. Almost orgasmic. Look at the flow into the bottle—it's quite amazing to be able to do this. I feel like one of Amélie's cows in her milking shed."

Marie laughed. "Honestly Lauren, sometimes you are too much."

"Well, I've just calculated that this bottle should be filled in nine point four minutes. This will make our life so much easier. I was concerned about being able to produce enough milk for three. Well I'm not that ample am I, but Edward insisted that female bodies are geared up to produce to demand and that three or even four babies is not a problem. So far, he's been spot on. This device will give me a lot of flexibility, especially as I'm determined to breastfeed my own milk for at least six months and longer if I can—all the evidence points to happier babies and long-term physical and intellectual development."

"Especially if you want to get back to work soon."

"Absolutely, and that remains non-negotiable, whatever Philippe may think. There are so many babies suddenly appearing amongst the senior management team, that I've asked Hermann to do a feasibility report on financing a suitably equipped and staffed crèche, both here and in Brussels, to be in place by the time I go back."

"I admire your approach and determination to ensure your female workforce is properly looked after, Lauren."

"Makes economic and business sense, that's where our real talent lies in Cassini. We have a much higher number of female engineers than any comparable nuclear company and it shows in results because they get things done—no macho posturing and bullshit like we had in Philippe's day."

"He ran Cassini once? Really? I had no idea."

"A long story Marie. One day over a pumping session, I'll tell you all. Yes he ran the show—that was until I turned up!"

They laughed loudly again when the door at the far end opened.

"What are you two finding so amusing this time of the morning?" Philippe queried, looking puzzled. "Jesus what on earth is that weird mechanical contraption?"

"Just castigating men as usual."

Marie giggled.

"This piece of Edward Jones kit, dearest," Lauren continued, waving his gaze down to her bare breasts as he blushed, "will make my life and especially yours, when you give the girls their bottle in the middle of the night, so much easier. Now I've finally become a genuine production line. What do you think? I'm done in one point two-seven minutes."

"Impressive ... I assume they're fast asleep? Now when you're finished, I want you to come outside and see your surprise of the day."

She wiped some ointment over her left nipple, did herself up and linking his arm walked happily outside into the clear air of a warm and calm, sunny day. The skies were bright blue. Only a few wispy clouds gently floated across the horizon, as she gazed intrigued at the side of the large, dark blue truck parked on the driveway.

"What on earth have you driven into the yard, or should I say why?"

"Come and have a look?"

As she walked to the rear, she suddenly realised what all the knocking and banging in the stables had been all about over the last few days. Surely not—this was too impulsive for the measured and predicable Philippe? He undid the bolts and pulled open the truck door, and a bundle of hay fell out to reveal two beautiful, gleaming horses, tethered carefully inside, standing quietly and majestically, steam pouring from their mouths.

"What do you think? I thought you might be pleased? DG tipped me off that a guy Orlando had met in the fish shop had two Arabian male horses for sale. We may as well make use of the stables, and we have the space. They're only a year old."

"They are absolutely lovely. I assume, darling, you're not planning to cavort off again to the far reaches of the globe shortly? Someone needs to look after these two ... and I'm a bit limited for the moment."

He grinned and kissed her on the lips with a quick passionate slurp. "Of course not. I'm here to stay and going nowhere, despite DG's continuous protestation of lucrative fracking work in Poland. I'm rather taking to this lifestyle already, fuck oil and gas."

"Even when your favourite, Magdaline cries and poos in your arms?"

"Definitely—hey I don't have any favourites amongst my four closest females—they're all equally gorgeous, especially this one," giving her another lingering kiss on the mouth.

She giggled. At long last being married to Philippe felt like she always wanted the sensation to feel ... and she was going to make the most of it.

"I'm assuming from your murmurings on the plane about horses when we flew back that you want the black one?"

"Yes please. I want to call him Vanya, after my Uncle Vanya who taught me to ride when I was a young boy on his farm alongside a big lake in Voronezh, which is south of Moscow. It was an idyllic setting for a child to grow up in."

"I suppose I should call the other one Chekhov?"

"Eh?"

"Never mind, I think my knowledge of Russian literature is infinitely better than yours. You must, incidentally, tell me more about your childhood, No more male reticence although I know a fair bit from your big daughter. The other one is beautifully spotted, he's a piebald. See, I remember my horses from a child. My father taught me well too. No, I shall call him Pi, that's pretty obvious I reckon. Pi and Vanya, I like that."

"Do you never stop thinking about mathematics?"

"Only when I'm having sex. I can see that glint in your eye. You will have to remain patient for a while yet, darling, I'm afraid, I'm far too sore still."

"I know, but it doesn't stop me thinking."

She laughed. "We can roll in the hay when it's time and Marie is in the house with the babies—don't want them getting ideas so young."

"No, it'll be bad enough when they become teenagers; three in one go all hormones raging at the same time. I shall have to be even stricter than I was with Svet."

Lauren laughed—not if she had anything to do with it, which she will.

"Anyway," he said, "They've got reins around them. Are you going to help me take them into the stables? I reckon you'll be pretty impressed with my handiwork in there. Took a bit of sorting but Orlando and DG helped when you were down at the clinic. I'll just get these bales of hay in there first."

Lauren jumped into the horsebox and gently patted first Pi and then Vanya. They stayed calm and relaxed. Arabian horses could be fiery but she remembered that when trained they also had a wonderful temperament for riding and even show-jumping or perhaps to race. What a lovely thought and a genuine surprise from Philippe, although she winced again thinking about getting into the saddle, but shouldn't be too long hopefully. She was pleased he was displaying tangible reasons to be sticking around and still couldn't get over the fact he wasn't indeed off to Poland—she must have a quiet word with DG not to encourage him. In fact it was time to see daughter Charlotte and have a long face to face chat, now Charlotte was feeling more herself with newly born Arthur-George. She would give Charlotte a ring and take the babies over there tomorrow. It seemed odd that she, with triplets should have had such a relatively easy time but that poor Charlotte, with just one, had gone through a very difficult birth, including a section. Thank goodness DG had provided Charlotte with top notch care throughout, but on the phone she sounded much better and was adamant she was healing up well, although not ecstatic about the long scar down her stomach.

Carefully, Lauren led each horse out and into the stables. She gasped seeing what Philippe had actually constructed. The interior was totally rebuilt and set out professionally with tethering areas and a feeding and drinking block, fresh hay plentifully strewn around. The horses whinnied the moment they saw their new home and commenced eating voraciously, whilst Philippe forked more bundles of hay into place and filled up the trough with water from a hose he had installed. She watched his industrious activity with interest, placing a mild bet to herself on how long it would last, although she was feeling more confident by the day that this really was a new emergent Philippe, and about time.

"I'll join you soon, helping out with the horses," she shouted over, patting Pi gently along his short mane. "Once my muscles are back to normal. Marie has been showing me some great exercises which I've just started. I'm desperate to get into shape as soon as possible, I'm not keen whatsoever on this mummy-tummy but Edward Jones is amazed how much slimmer I've already become, considering what was inside."

"Yes, me too, absolutely. But don't overdo it. Has Marie got any friends here yet? She seems very self-contained; I suppose it goes with the territory her being a writer?"

"What do you know about writing? Perched on a bar stool, prattling all day with a phone in your ear is more your image?"

"Don't be too sure. I had a lot of time to reflect in that goddamned awful prison. When I was at school, I won the prize for literary essay of the year. I was seventeen. There are literary figures, all Russian of course, in the Dubois family. Don't forget my intelligentsia heritage darling—I'm thinking of writing a memoir on Russia, how it really is day by day since the fall of the USSR."

"Mmm ... I thought you would have had enough of Russia for good this time ... I'd stick to pitchforks, suits you more, get those muscles back. It's nice to see you filling out already."

"All that wonderful cooking of Marie. I mustn't over-indulge on her speciality French pastries, but they are so ... mmm ... moreish, don't you think?"

Lauren laughed and pulled one out of her bag to sink her teeth into, when her mobile began to ring. "Shit ... oh gosh, it's Amélie. She must have delivered her twins!"

Philippe, seizing the moment of distraction, grabbed the pastry playfully from her hand and walked back to the feeding area. "You can't eat and talk to Amélie at the same time, shame to let good food go to waste!"

Lauren swiped across the call bar. "Hello there, the one and only Lady Westvale, so tell me the good news. Boys, girls or mixed? And who is the father?" she whispered, glancing across at Philippe who was now well out of earshot.

"I don't know who the fucking father is yet, Lauren. My waters have just broken and I've already gone into labour. Will you both fuck off out of here? I don't need all this damned fussing."

Lauren heard a clattering and a door slam.

"Sorry Lauren, I don't mean you; I can't be doing with medics all over me constantly. It's been overbearing hell all week in this clinic. You've got to help me, take me though what to do ... please ... I'm desperate and scared and I think this is going to be quick."

Lauren grimaced at the frightened tone of Amélie's voice and began to walk back to her study. This was not the together, calm and collected best friend she always knew and loved. "But where's Rufus? He's supposed to be there holding your hand? It sounds like your nurses have just cleared off—I do remember your top-blowing veracity!"

"Fuck them. And, Rufus as usual is never where he should be. Jesus, Lauren there's been an almighty disaster back on the estate. The substation I built got flooded out after the nonstop torrential rain we've had for the last three days. The river burst its nearside bank and the whole fucking building exploded sky-high and the critical circuitry vaporised, so neither the house not the milking sheds have power."

Amélie stopped and panted, between contractions. "Rufus doesn't know I've gone into labour. He and Giles are desperately trying to make the old backup generators work and get the power on. All the staff had been given a day off in lieu of the last festival we ran. So there's only my best friend to turn to. Bloody hell that twinge hurt. The nurses are back at the door looking through the glass, wary. You've got the tee-shirt for multiple births, so take me through it. I remember you said you were quick too."

"That was because I'd already had a child but you could take hours yet Amélie so …"

"Listen Lauren, no time for explanations but I had a baby when I was nineteen. She was stillborn, fuck knows who the father was, and as I'm late anyway, I just know—I can feel it. This one's a quickie—they are quite desperate to see some light and fresh air. Talk me through. I've put my bluetooth headphones on so I'm hands free; get going please … imagine you're Edward Jones. Oh my God, that pain has started again; these two are coming out natural, come hell or high water. I've just waved the nurses Susie and Elsinore back in—now get going will you—at least I'm not in a fucking jungle."

Lauren quietly closed the door of her study and sat down. "Shit Amélie, this can only be happening with you. Okay, you're getting the Vega gorilla routine for multiple births. Now, how often are the contractions? Bloody hell, they're not far now."

"I know. Right, I'm squatting like you did Vega style. No, you two, I don't want to see sight of Mr Ahmed, you keep that idiot out of here. No, how many times do I have to say it, will you pay attention. No epidurals, no pethidine, no anything, got it? My best friend on the end of this phone had triplets in the jungle, if she can do it so can I. This place is like a fucking jungle."

Lauren got her fast brain into analytical gear and methodically continued, trying as she knew well to visualise Amélie lying there remotely. This situation felt no different from analysing the inside of a nuclear reactor about to blow. In between the explanations, she stopped to allow Amélie let rip a series of piercing screams and shouts, when suddenly she heard a loud roar.

"The first head is coming out Lauren, bloody hell, with blonde hair. Rufus is the father at least of this one."

"Push Amélie, just push hard. The nurses will cut the umbilical cord. Keep pushing, and breathe hard in, out, in, out, in …"

Amélie screamed again, an almighty piercing yell, making Lauren jump. She desperately wished she was there. This situation was just too surreal to be true.

11

"Shit Lauren," Amélie groaned, panting hard. "The second one is coming now too, also blonde hair. Sorry Vaag, if you're watching from the flames, you didn't shoot hard enough."

"Jesus, Amélie, what will the nurses think?"

"Who fucking cares, they're out Lauren and you did it. Thank you so much. You delivered my babies and they are wonderful and so perfect and gorgeous. Lady Leonora Lauren de la Ville and Lady Caroline Charlotte de la Ville, that's a nice aristocratic mouthful. Don't mention the other to Rufus will you."

"No, of course not. Oh Amélie, I'm so happy for you. I can hear them crying, they'll want feeding now."

"Yes, I know, at least I am all prepared for that. Oh my goodness, would you believe the errant father has appeared at the door with his faithful assistant, both holding spanners and looking worried. Come in both of you. Sorry but the show's all over thanks to Lauren who delivered them over the phone here. Meet Lady Leonora and Lady Caroline, who definitely, Rufus, have your nose, but I can categorically say both have my eyes, don't you reckon? Sorry but these nipples now have more pressing tasks darling. Giles sit over there please, you don't have to look so embarrassed. You've seen enough pigs suckled, and this is no different."

Rufus took off her headset and picked up the phone to Lauren. "Of course all this drama is so typical Amélie but thank you so much Lauren for helping her through the labour, which must have gone extraordinarily quickly. The little darlings are ten days overdue and she was supposed to be induced tonight, but by the look of her and the relieved faces of the nurses, 'au naturellement' seems to have gone down fine. We had no idea of their sex, Amélie had refused all tests—but I love girls. Are you and the triplets keeping well?"

"Yes, all fine here and Philippe too. We look forward to you two bringing the tribe over as soon as they can travel. Plenty of room in the villa. But Rufus, I'm going to love you all and leave you now, I think you've got plenty to talk about and celebrate."

"You bet, see you soon Lauren. Bye ... and a wave from Giles too."

Lauren felt a warm glow though her tummy thinking again of the delicious Giles ... mmm ... Philippe had better keep up his new found domesticity. She closed off the call and sat down as Marie knocked on the door, carrying in a tray.

"Are you okay Lauren? Fancy a tea and some cake?"

"Yes please, come and share it with me. Philippe is getting down and dirty outside with the new horses he brought back, you'll love them. My best friend Amélie has just given birth to twin girls—I've never played midwife before over the phone. That was the strangest experience ever, almost as odd as giving birth in a jungle."

They giggled loudly when a familiar noise of simultaneous crying started up in the background. "Oh, oh, the big feed is about to start again. I can hear that triple crescendo of wailing for food. Do you want to do the bottle Marie? I think it's Eveline's turn, they almost fight for that now, would you believe?"

"Yes of course, no problem Lauren. I'll just go and fetch them in."

"But we'll have this freshly baked lemon drizzle cake of yours first."

Chapter Two

With the art work tightly secured into his specially designed easel, Henri-Gaston Landry looked back with pleasure at the large pen and ink drawing, completed from his photographs of Charlotte and newly born grandson, Arthur-George, down at the clinic in Nice. He had selected a specially absorbent paper and decided to apply a couple of special washes to the drawing, similar to a technique he had used often in the past, which Rembrandt utilised whenever he painted lions to emphasise the contrast between supple skin and heavy manes.

He began to carefully mix a small amount of green acrylic paint with water, the same shade as the baby room, and loaded up his wet brush with copious amounts of the paint pool, applying the wash carefully in layers over much of the surface. Once dry he would add a couple more washes in yellow and red. The phone in the hallway began to ring continuously and he called out noisily for his housekeeper to go and answer it quickly. Interruptions at such a critical stage made him angry, always balanced precariously at the end of a short fuse which prevailed whenever he became creatively absorbed. Then he remembered she had gone out with Charles to do food shopping. Cursing wildly, he shot out of the room and down the stairs, brush still in hand dripping onto the bare wood, and finally grabbed the phone.

"Yes," he snarled.

"Hi Henri, it's Charlotte. Sorry, I've obviously caught you at a bad time. I'll phone tomorrow."

"Ah non, ma chérie. It is no problem at all—I love to hear your voice always. I think this is perhaps serendipity, you calling me right now."

"I'm sorry, I'm not sure what serendipity means?" Charlotte replied and laughed. "But I hope it's not catching."

Henri laughed back loudly. For some reason he had an immediate flashback to a fleeting and very happy time long ago—how similar in humour and voice Charlotte was to Lauren. So many years ... and it felt like yesterday. He was looking forward to seeing Lauren at Charlotte's dinner party she had arranged.

"No, no, I am preparing a little surprise for you for when I come to your house next Sunday to meet err ... your husband DG, and of course my other grandchildren, Alexis and Katherine."

"Henri, you must call them Lexi and Kat. They hate their full names these days. Actually that's what I'm calling about. I still don't feel very well and I am totally exhausted. I think I was a little hasty arranging that dinner, so I've decided to put it off for a while. I'm so sorry to postpone at short notice but we will fix up something in due course. I do want you to meet the family, I really do."

Henri fell silent. He was disappointed. And Charlotte knew instantly why. She was desperate to divert him. Yes, she did want him to meet her family but not all of them. Since seeing Henri last time, she had given much thought to the tricky scenario of Lauren and her father meeting again after all those years and felt increasingly edgy and unsure. Eventually she conversed with Mila and Amélie on the matter. For a change they were both vehemently of exactly the same opinion. 'Dynamite ...whatever, don't do it.' She also had to first tell the children and DG about discovering her biological father and was far too befuddled and distracted with Arthur-George, who quickly had become a very demanding baby. She was too concerned with her own health to be bothered with more family distractions and difficulties. In fact Mila, now temporarily acting CEO of Cassini and throwing herself fully into all of Lauren's day to day business with the usual Mila high octane approach, including scaring the life out of all the staff, had suggested an ideal solution to keep Henri-Gaston Landry at bay for the time being.

Charlotte continued, attempting to sound cheerful and matter-of-fact. "Actually, Papa, something has come up so the arrangements were going to have to change anyway. Lauren has flown over to Siberia to join her husband, Philippe in Yakutsk, for at least the next three months, possibly six. She'll be out of contact and fully engaged leading some delicate business operation. They have won a major contract to build a series of new reactors in that area of Russia."

At least that part she did know was true, even though the news was only a day old. "But I'm sure you will of course meet my mother eventually."

He grinned down the phone. Charlotte had called him Papa for the first time which was far more important than anything else. Well, almost everything else. He was certain his daughter was lying to spare him embarrassment, and whatever Lauren's circumstances were it was obvious that contacting or meeting her was not turning out to be a good idea. In any case he had a new and serious distraction, Lauren's stand-in CEO, Mila. And, he never believed it would ever be possible after Lauren, but he was genuinely convinced he was in love again for the first time in twenty-seven years.

Mila of course was the world's best for keeping up secrets and unleashing a whole barrage of diversionary tactics that suited her. Neither Charlotte not Lauren had any idea of her new relationship with Henri-Gaston, a diversion she wanted to keep that way, but was unexpectedly growing to like.

"Not a problem, Charlotte," Henri replied. "I really do understand and the main priority is for you to feel well again and choose a date and time which totally suits you and your family. I am happy to wait. And if you prefer, when you are finally back to full energy, meet me again on your own if you like, as we have done to date. I have plenty of work coming up shortly in China to occupy me, a series of important architectural contracts to fulfil in Shanghai, so will also be out of the country too for a while. Charles sends his love. He too is keen to see you again soon. He loves having a long lost older sister and will also be happy eventually to meet his young nieces and baby nephew. And thank you, it means so much to me."

"Sorry?"

"Papa, I think it has a definite resonance as the English say, don't you?"

Charlotte laughed and felt hugely relieved that he was not unworkably negative. That was a good tactic but she too liked the resonance. "Yes, Papa, definitely."

"Ring me again in a few days. I shall be gone for three weeks middle of next week for the first leg of my China work. It will bring in masses of cash. I am thinking too of moving house. I am terribly restless so I intend to look for a different place sometime."

Charlotte hesitated and wondered. "Where? In France I assume?"

"Not necessarily. I am thinking maybe of fresh pastures new ... possibly ..." but then he bit his lip. Compelling thoughts of Mila were filling his mind again including things they had recently chatted about in bed after a torrid session of lovemaking all night in her swish, luxury apartment in Cannes. Mila was a sophisticated and cultured woman, unbelievably compelling, who was obviously at home in any part of the world, and he could be too, with her if he chose, although she was insistent that there would be no discussion whatsoever of Lauren between them. Business and pleasure were strictly separated for Mila. Charlotte was not to know of their relationship either. He was fine with all that, and he had to thank Mila for being the only woman who could impart a compelling sensuality to totally distract his constant wandering thoughts of women here there and everywhere, and especially from his obsession with what may have been in the past. Lauren was a married woman with a serious international business career and a life vastly moved on since their heady, secretive days when she was a stunning sixteen year old schoolgirl and he was a twenty-eight year old budding artist, and not long married. Mila was a distinctly unique woman for orientating his thoughts to a world of sensible reality. Lauren was to be permanently off-limits and now, all of a sudden, he didn't care.

He and Charlotte finished their conversation, uttered pleasant goodbyes, and he returned happily to his painting, realising that he had to venture out and buy some liquid frisket and rubber cement so he could more carefully control the next application of washes. Then he would hand it on when dry and finished to Pierre André, his artisan frame-maker, for something very special to be carved in genuine ebony. The high cost was immaterial; his daughter was worth every euro.

Charlotte put down the phone and contemplated for a minute. The can had been kicked down the road once more for a while, but at some stage she simply would have to deal with it. She gathered up a pile of nappies before checking on Arthur-George who was still sleeping peacefully in his cot for a change instead of giving out that incessant howling whenever he was hungry, which like his father was far too often. Oriane was interviewing some potential nannies later that day; hopefully she could find one suitable applicant, preferably living locally. Some extra help would be really welcome, although, unlike Lauren, she had no intentions to return to work. The stay-at-home mum plan she unexpectedly fancied and she could afford to do so for some time to come yet.

On impulse she decided to ring Lauren and invite her round for a quiet dinner on Sunday anyway. Kat and Lexi were dying to see the triplets again and they could all have a stress free family catch-up. She really wanted to get back to normality as soon as possible.

"Hello, Professor Hind's residence, how may I help you?"

Charlotte was thrown for a second by the formality and then immediately realised who was speaking. "Hi Marie, Charlotte here. I assume Lauren has popped out? Everything okay?"

"Yes, no problems. We're quickly getting into a manageable routine with the triplets. Lauren is remarkably focussed and organised, I can see why she has a stunning and successful career. Ah ... I can just see her now in the garden walking back to the villa. She's been outside with Philippe; they're enjoying themselves with the new horses they've just bought. I'm just waving to her to come into the study."

"Horses? Really? My, I'm definitely feeling jealous now. I miss riding, something I did a lot of on the ranch at Texas. Although the way I'm stitched up like a kipper, I can't see myself on a horse for absolutely ages."

"My best friend in the army had a caesarean and she was back outdoors and doing physical stuff after a month. You'll be surprised how quickly you heal up."

"I hope so, Marie, but I don't feel well either and I'm exhausted all the time."

"I'm just handing the phone to Lauren, Charlotte. Hope you feel better soon, bye."

"Hello Charlotte, what a pleasant surprise. Philippe and I were just talking about you and DG and wondering how you are. Would you like to meet up? I can pop over, but will be accompanied by the tribe, I'm afraid."

Charlotte took a deep breath. She had decided to mention Henri-Gaston and get it over with; she was tiring of the deception. "That would be wonderful. There's something I want to tell you ..."

"Yes?"

But Charlotte again wavered. Mila was right, bad idea. She just had to sit on this thing. "Err ... I should be getting a nanny soon, Oriane is interviewing today. If I get some help then maybe I can relax and feel better more quickly. And I'm very jealous of your new horses. I didn't know you and Philippe could ride. I'd really love you all to come over. Can you make Sunday lunch? We can sit out on the big patio. Just me and DG plus the twins and of course Arthur-George, who I'm sure, will be yelling the house down as usual."

"Yes, that would be great. Philippe is a veteran rider, and I learned as a child and had a horse as a teenager. So we're looking forward to riding together with Pi and Vanya. Are you still not feeling so good?"

"Better, but it's slow and I feel so tired. I assume Pi is your horse! It sounds fabulous that Philippe has quickly settled down into that elusive togetherness at last. You must be feeling so much happier. My doctor said I was a little anaemic, so I'm taking some iron and vitamins and now going for walks every day around the estate. Arthur-George loves being outdoors like his dad. At least the gorgeous environment makes up for it."

"Yes, I'm amazed at Philippe's overnight change and I am making the most of it, believe me. I still can't decide yet whether the situation may suddenly vanish like a mirage, but the triplets have been a hugely steadying force, as has the experience of a Russian prison. So yes, life seems to be settling to a pleasant normality. But I do want to get back to Cassini soon, definitely by three months. I miss the work and the buzz so I have a plan sorted already."

"I'm going to enjoy motherhood this time ... and no pressures."

"Charlotte, I know where you're coming from but in the end you're like me ... you need the buzz too ... you need to be occupied with something else, intellectually challenging and physical. I reckon, once you're back on your feet, you'll want to do something. And you have the means of course to buy in as much help as you need. It doesn't mean you have to neglect Arthur-George and his development or the twins, although Kat and Lexi seem to be growing up so fast, they're becoming quite independent for their age."

Charlotte sighed. Her mother had a point but she would see in due course. "Yes, the girls are like ten going on seventeen already. Heaven knows what they'll be like in two or three years time ... a handful I suspect, especially Lexi."

Lauren laughed. "So was I at their age. Sorry, but it probably runs in the family. Anyway, Philippe and I would like to teach them to ride sometime, I reckon they would love it."

"That's a lovely offer. Of course. Tell them on Sunday. I must talk to DG about getting some horses ourselves. We have the space, but would need to construct a small barn. Somewhere near the guesthouse would be suitable. Anyway, time for me to lie down and have a nap again. Then feeding time."

"Tell me about it! Okay, see you Sunday at lunchtime, take care. Bye Charlotte."

Lauren breezed into the bedrooms and placed Magdaline, Eveline and Geraldine carefully into their cots. They had been quiet after their last feed and were now sleepy again. Suddenly Geraldine turned her head towards the picture of the gorilla on her wall and making an effort to point, she began to gurgle and burble a big smile across her face.

Lauren laughed loudly. "Geri, you clever little girl. You remember don't you, being held in those hairy arms of Vega, the first one out as I struggled with your two sisters? Gosh, I'm amazed. I can see not only are you the extrovert one like your Aunt Mila, but perceptive too. There aren't many little girls who've been held by a gorilla. And that was when Daddy appeared as if by a miracle and Vega handed you to him. Do you remember Daddy too?"

Geraldine grinned and gurgled some more, then her eyes closed as she began to go to sleep. Lauren kissed her gently on the forehead, followed by Magda and Eve, as Marie came in. "They look beautiful, Lauren."

"Don't you want any yourself some time Marie? Sorry, I shouldn't be so presumptive."

Marie smiled. "Yes of course. I love children, but not just yet. I've still got some life to lead first, more books to write and eventually travel again and more adventure. I need to keep feeding the muse. Sorry, I sound like I'm ready to disappear as quickly as I came. That's far from the case, I truly love it here."

Lauren patted her arm gently. "Yes, I can see that, and Philippe and I are so grateful and hugely impressed with all you do which is a huge amount. But I've been thinking. You really must get a bit of a social life and have more free time. These three are turning out to be hugely demanding, presently. I would be happy to bring in some additional help; we can easily afford it, and it would take some of the pressure off both of us. I'm thinking ahead too Marie for when I go back to work ... and security issues for example will start again, a key reason also why you are here anyway."

"Actually Lauren, may I make a suggestion if it doesn't sound too premature? Funnily enough I've been talking a lot to my younger sister, Jesse, on the phone who's living in London. She is actually a top trained special nanny, presently living in with a Russian oligarch family but not terribly happy with the environment ... she's fending off the groping husband rather too much to be honest. She would love to come here and could live with me, we get on really well, always have."

"How old is Jesse?"

"Almost twenty, but she has a lot of experience and qualifications for babies, including multiples which she originally specialised her training in.

To be honest, she asked me if there might be a job as it sounds perfect for her. I could concentrate on the housekeeping, cooking and security again."

"And you could resume writing, Marie, which I know has been difficult and is hugely important to you. This sounds like a good possibility. Let's do it properly. Can you speak with Oriane, who will invite and gather Jesse's CV and references formally? Then I'll go through them objectively and make a decision."

Marie's eyes lit up and she smiled warmly. "Yes, of course. I'll get onto it immediately, once I've finished our evening meal. Chicken Kiev done with a special chilli recipe, which Marcie gave me, has a kick like a Louisiana mule so she said."

"Mmm ... sounds great. Philippe just loves your cooking Marie, and he isn't easy to please, I can tell you! Okay, deal. I look forward to hearing more about Jesse in due course. Now, I think I'll get back to that fusion paper for an hour. Something shot into my consciousness as we were talking. I have to solve some rather tricky exponential equations fast before I lose the plot."

Lauren walked back into her study, pulled across the white board and began scribbling all manner of complex mathematical ideas over the surface. Gulping down a large glass of iced Perrier water, she looked out of the window to see Philippe riding back into the yard, having taken Vanya down to the sea for half an hour to accustom his horse to the new environment. She smiled. He had that serious and determined look about him, dressed in his short sleeve, smart shirt and tight jeans, which always made him look sexy and inviting, at least for her. Life was good at last, and the coming weekend she would definitely pull a saddle over Pi and ride out with him too.

Chapter Three

Admittedly the setting was one of her more unusual choices for a business meeting, a forest clearing behind the sandy beach along the coast. But two months had gone by since the triplets emerged, blinking into this world, and Lauren was eager to move forward preparations for her return to her desk at Cassini the following month. As she finished tacking up, she reflected deeply on her global nuclear services company. She was enormously pleased with Mila's holding job as temporary CEO, standing in for Sonja now settled into her well earned maternity leave, having gone earlier than planned on Lauren's insistence, sensing that Sonja's health was more delicate than she was letting on. Eva, Sonja's PA, also another declared mum to be, had hinted a few weeks back, without breaking any confidences or appearing gossipy as Eva never did. Nimi, Lauren's research executive, was making great strides with accelerating a record number of research projects into demonstrators, surprising everyone with her determination and assertiveness to make things happen. Lauren was pleased with the way Nimi was fast growing into that newly designed role, exactly as she wanted. But she still missed Eva as her true P.A. Nimi was not a people person and missed the nuances, shifts and allegiance changes which Eva always picked up on and subtly reported back. Johann, joint CEO with Sonja, and also now Sonja's husband, was stationed temporarily in Russia for the next two months outside the Siberian city of Yakutsk to lead the first installation of their most advanced Xenostra fast reactor. This was another reason she had decided to put Mila in day to day charge, although the contrast in approach and personality between Mila and Sonja was undoubtedly being brutally experienced inside head office, where Mila spent four days a week in Brussels. At least for Johann it wasn't the middle of winter, although he was complaining constantly of mosquitoes. But Lauren had insisted that he must return and hand over to Jacques, his engineering deputy, nearer the time Sonja was due to give birth to their first child.

Lauren's recent meeting with the Russian Prime Minister had gone better than expected. The deals took place on DG's super yacht, quietly and inconspicuously moored well outside the bay of Nice. This was the last part of the secret agreement with the Russians to secure Philippe's full release from his Siberian jail, and she had been determined to see that through to the end. In any case, the financial rewards for investing their expertise in Russia were far too significant to ignore any longer, so a confluence of events was proving expedient all round. Although how the battalion of Russian security had embarked onboard the yacht without being noticed was anybody's guess. She didn't ask DG and she didn't want to know. Philippe of course was kept in the dark and well out of the way. Only when the energy deal was sealed did she break the news to him, quietly a few days later over a nice meal together at their favourite Italian restaurant on the port seafront. He was angry, but for a change pragmatic and controlled his rage better than she had ever seen. She and the family really did mean more to him than anything else. Without doubt, DG's usual hospitality this time in the form of a glut of best Siberian vodka accompanied by lashings of arctic caviar had decidedly oiled the wheels of reconciliation with the Kremlin. A bevy of scantily clad women, escorted onboard surreptitiously from a fast speedboat halfway through the proceedings, she discretely ignored. She also knew DG had paid a substantial sum of US dollars into an obscure Liechtenstein bank, and Ivan, the Russian Prime Minister with whom she got on extraordinarily well, considering what had gone on, confirmed that the Russian President would now be buying a substantial London home, replete with security for his two daughters who were intent on studying engineering at Imperial College, London. One unmentionable which stayed that way was the wayward renegade gas engineer, Olga. Although Lauren learned from a secretive backchannel, well it was her friend Rosie Li of course who else, that Chinese intelligence had located Olga well and truly disappeared inside the jungles of South America and was staying that way. She breathed a huge sigh of relief at that news.

Moving into a canter, they headed down the long and quiet coastal bridle path towards her intended destination. She gently tightened her knees into Pi and whispered some choice commands recently taught into his ear. He shot off immediately into a fast run. Lean, intelligent and fit, he was definitely bred from racing stock, having a lithe and perfect gait and loved to run hard. She glanced back and smiled at the forlorn expression as she began to leave Mila further and further behind on Vanya, a more pedestrian and steadfast horse. Mila was a good rider but Lauren on this occasion felt especially elated. She could beat Mila at something physical for a change. Approaching the clearing, she slowed down to a fast canter allowing Mila to gradually catch up. Soon they trotted alongside and Lauren pointed to an area between the trees further ahead. This was a spot she had discovered by accident a few days prior out riding, enticingly quiet and desolate with a fantastic view over the sandy beach and out over the sea. The curved bay was hemmed in comfortingly, with shrub-covered cliffs rising up at either end. The wind had died down. The air was calm and almost eerily quiet but she loved the isolation, feeling the warmth of the sun on her tanned face. The spot was difficult to get to, certainly by car, glancing up at the cliff towards the east and knowing that around the other side was a busy and frenetic tourist front with plenty of sunbeds, umbrellas and cafes along Kat and Lexi's favourite beach.

The ambience reminded her of Annabella's little island off the coast of Palermo, where they had first made ... She stopped. Her thoughts were suddenly running away with her and there was serious Cassini business to be done.

Dismounting, Mila turned and grinned. "I knew when you walked out of that front door wearing a stunning soft-shell orange jacket and matching black breeches that we were in for one of your more unusual meetings. Where did you learn to ride like that? More to the point what brands are that gear and those boots? I must get the same ones. Mind you, a horse might be a good starter. You look stunningly gorgeous ..."

Lauren laughed and touched Mila's lips gently. "You were going to say *again* weren't you, don't deny it? Are you not amazed how quickly my figure is coming back? It must be those genetic taut belly muscles kicking in again, and becoming tauter by the day when I hear some of the rumours of what you've been getting up to lately at Cassini headquarters?"

"You mean the AK47 shooting match, Seb and I had around the lake?" Mila replied innocently. "Well, he shouldn't have challenged me to a duel, and of course I won yet again. Mind you, poor old Herman jumped into his car and shot out of the car park. He wouldn't come back until Helena gave him the all clear on his mobile. He was quite white ... but honestly Lauren, it won't happen again. Sometimes I forget I'm not out in the Louisiana swamps, so I will revert to being a sophisticated, calm and collected CEO, I promise."

"Honestly Mila, only you could do that, and I've had to pick up the pieces and spend all night dissuading Herman not to give in his notice as you frighten him to death."

"So?"

"So what?"

"When are you getting back to work? You have that gleam in your eye, Lauren. I know you better than anyone even Lady Muck in the wilds of Anglo-Saxonia."

"You mean Amélie ... she doesn't call you names," Lauren replied with a grin.

"Mmm ... not what I heard. I still have my spies but I like Amélie really and I was the first to congratulate her on her new brood, *and* I sent her some lovely expensive jumpsuits, both pink of course. I heard you were a dab hand playing at virtual Edward Jones with a touch of jungle style midwifery thrown in. Actually Lauren that was pretty amazing. I would never have believed it, but then after what you've been through anything is possible."

"Ha, ha, anyway before we get down to business, you will want to know that the jacket, breeches and the boots you have been ogling are all made by Yamamah, a top equestrian outfit in Italy. Annabella tipped me off."

"Of course, the lovely Annabella, I might have guessed. I must say the material looks pretty high-tech, light, cool and suitable for all weathers."

"Well you knew it was a soft-shell. The fabric is shower-proof with a windproof membrane and very breathable, allowing moisture out but keeping the temperature regulated. The cuffs are neoprene, so ingress of cold and water is prevented and that scooped hem protects your lower back from the cold in the saddle. The breeches are similar but made from a new Kevlar based fabric and extremely hardwearing. Of course being Italian they look beautifully fashionable."

"I'm impressed ... hole in the bank balance a bit?"

"Well ... I suppose so but who cares, especially now I've sold three reactors to the Kremlin. But don't mention that to Philippe, it's like don't mention the war." Lauren replied, pulling off her tight boots with a grunt. "I'm glad he has nothing to do with Cassini now to be honest. In fact he's developing a new interest in, would you believe, local politics and the community ... energy never gets a mention these days. Homely domesticity suits him."

Mila, as ever, dwelt for a moment, her thoughts wandering. She wasn't necessarily convinced. Then she came back in a flash before Lauren, sharp as a razor, spotted the nuance. "Good, excellent, obviously the triplets are just what Philippe needed. Anyway, one advantage of losing the race to my boss was the magnificent view of her taut and prestigious rear, bouncing up and down, definitely back to its old, sexy self."

Lauren sidled up closer and ran her fingers through Mila's blonde, spiky hair and whispered. "So does that rear look as good as it did when naked and slung over a chair in Palermo one fateful night some time back? When someone unmentionable took a quick video?"

Mila uncharacteristically felt a volley of emotional disconnect zapping through her body. Why was Lauren suddenly becoming irresistibly frisky and compounding her own inner guilt she was keeping well down—that she was mercilessly shagging Henri-Gaston, Lauren's great historic love of the past and father of Charlotte. "We've got some serious business to sort out, especially as you didn't deny you're hurrying back to your laboratory very soon, and I can't be CEO forever. The natives are becoming restless with my crackdowns."

Lauren's eyes narrowed as she deliberated. Her lips broke into a sly grin. "A delayed Amélie effect is getting to me."

Mila looked uncharacteristically mystified. "Pardon?"

"Twelve months ago Mila you would have jumped at this opportunity. But now I remember exactly what you said on the plane coming back from Kinshasa about contemplating having a man back in your life ... the notion made Philippe laugh ... but something tells me someone male and sensuous has indeed been creeping into the Mila psyche. Ready to tell all, alongside a digest of the accounts and quarterly sales figures?"

Mila was trying very hard to appear non-plussed, but a slight reddening of the cheeks had started. Surely Lauren couldn't know? Her mind ran at lightning speed through cause and effect and concluded the answer was no. Charlotte certainly didn't and neither did anyone else, even Sonja. But this was getting awkward in so many ways.

But before she could concoct a suitable answer, Lauren, still grinning, had turned and walked over to her horse, opened the nearside saddlebag and pulled out a large, linen tablecloth wrapped around cut glass wine glasses. From the other side emerged a bottle of chilled Sauvignon, carefully encased in thick bubble wrap. "Don't worry. I can sense the secret discomfiture, Mila. You don't have to reveal all yet, but I'm sure the experience is good for you. You look very happy and it can't all be Cassini or having walking access to Luddite from my office, and going by the look of those expensive Prada jeans and jacket, your raised clothes allowance is not dormant either. If you look in your saddlebag you'll find a nice picnic, which Marie and the girls made earlier ... see we've been busy before you even came."

Mila breathed in a contented relief, smiled and began to poke inside the bag seeing carefully wrapped up baguettes, a bowl of mixed salad, fruit and a flask of coffee. "Jesus Christ Lauren, you're pretty remarkable, no wonder this horse was slow." As she fished around deeper she spotted something else and pulled them out carefully. A pair of brand new and gorgeous side-tie hipster bikini briefs with matching crop top in a jazzy orange and blue pattern. "Fuck, Lauren, these are nice, and my size. I'm astonished you remembered."

Mila turned around and her eyes went on stalks. Lauren was bent over, laying out the tablecloth, completely naked and deliberately taking her time, knowing Mila would be taking everything in, which she did instantly. Her cheeks began flushing red with unabated lust. This was no good. No matter how guilty she felt about Henri-Gaston, her love and desire for Lauren always trumped anything and anybody else. It had been so long since she had seen that truly unencumbered rear.

Lauren turned and slowly began to walk towards Mila, slightly swaying her hips, the only thing left around her soft neck being the special amber pearl beads she wore last time she and Mila confronted each other this way. Mila remained silent and stunned. Lauren's body looked as perfect as before in Palermo. Nobody in a million years could have guessed she had had triplets nearly three months before and was still breastfeeding. This was not at all as planned, especially because the seduction table had been completely turned three hundred and sixty degrees. Taking the lead was always her prerogative and the newly assertive Lauren flummoxed her totally.

"Yes, I think I am remarkable Mila. In fact, Marie's Special Forces exercises have done wonders for me, don't you think? But you know all about that of course," Lauren replied softly. She met Mila face to face and wrapped her bare arms under Mila's jacket and tee-shirt and up her back, pressing her bare breasts against her chest softly.

Mila looked down as Lauren deftly unclasped her bra.

"My nipples are going a bit darker, have you noticed?"

Mila, now very hot bothered and unsure had noticed and much more.

Lauren continued in a whisper, staring into Mila's eyes. She had waited so long for this moment to come along again and was not going to let it run away, like in Palermo. "Philippe knows about us, he's known ever since you and I met. We've discussed it openly and he's cool about everything ... He even confessed he had held back from talking because his former wife, Lyudmila, was also bisexual and she left him for a woman after he handled that situation badly. Svet of course doesn't know. Olga was bisexual ... Philippe understands my needs and now I have no guilt or need of restraint ... and you and I have held back far too long since

Palermo. Pleasure first, business later, I promise. You know me, the perpetual Professor Serious?"

Their lips met and their eyes closed. Mila was in another world, immersed again within their first encounter inside her apartment in Luigi's hotel. She too had waited for so long. Their tongues began to explore each other's mouths, searching every crevice, exactly like before, and their passions rose quickly as Lauren reached down, fumbled around Mila's crotch and undid her jeans before wriggling them down Mila's thighs. Without hesitation she pushed her fingers deep inside Mila, wet, shaved bare and gushing, as Mila reciprocated the pleasure with a loud groan.

"Be careful Mila, my breasts are tender of course and I'm still a little sore, but I can feel that sensation again. I know it won't take long, it never did with you."

Mila pulled off the rest of her clothes, lowered her jeans fully and stepped out of them carefully, as Lauren looked once more at Mila's gorgeous, naked body. Her insides were pounding wild with desire. Mila gently lay Lauren onto the grass, pulled her legs slowly apart, ran her hands up the insides of each of her long and smooth tanned thighs and with a deep sigh wrapped her mouth around Lauren's wet folds, licking and sucking gently ... It didn't take long for Lauren to scream uncontrollably as she climaxed in sharp bursts, one after the other, exactly like when she was with Rosie, only much deeper. They eventually came to, side by side for a breather, both panting hard with the release of such pent-up desire.

Lauren grabbed a bag by the side of the rock next to her. "Now Mila, the ultimate finale—this has been far too dormant in the making." She pulled out a pink contraption, carefully selected from memory of that amazing time when they first fucked, and strapped it on, settling the insert on optimum position. She had practised assiduously for this moment, as Mila gazed, wide-eyed at the size.

"I promised, when the time was right, to give you the ultimate experience that you asked for, remember? You wanted it more than anything else and only with me and we agreed to hold off. To remind you of the best time ever with your husband? Now is the right time isn't it?"

Mila looked at the appendage, and almost blurted out that it was larger than Henri-Gaston, but when she looked inside Lauren's eyes, the love that they had kept occasionally strained and often subdued but always there had risen to the surface of her entire being, lighting up her emotions like the warm glow of a beckoning new sunrise. She was gripped with an insatiable desire, more than with Luigi, Henri-Gaston or the myriad of other men she had fucked since the crucifixion of her husband during the Bosnian war.

She nodded and Lauren roughly shoved Mila's thighs up, and wide open, straddled her and entered forcefully with one thrust. Both yelled hard with the enormity of finally doing this secret thing, a long pent-up frustration which had begged itself for so long to be let out and savoured forever. As Lauren pumped in and out, faster and deeper, they gripped each other tightly and Mila began to moan, a deep and meaningful wail, unlike anything Lauren had heard, rising in pitch and crescendo until she screamed into the air hysterically. Shaking viciously as Lauren held her down, Mila tore her long finger nails down Lauren's back who squealed with the instant pain-pleasure. It was over. She withdrew gently and they held each other close, side by side, with Mila quivering constantly during the gradual come down.

"This is some senior management meeting—haven't experienced one quite like it before, definitely beats shooting the board room up," Mila murmured, Lauren's head resting on her breasts, and a swathe of long blond hair tickling her side pleasurably.

Lauren giggled. "A new experience for the worldly wise Mila ... Now that is something refreshing isn't it? I still love you and I always will."

"Me too. Good job the place is deserted in this neck of the woods isn't it?"

"You betcha."

"So," Mila replied, stroking Lauren's head gently. "Do you really want an in-depth analysis of Herman's boring old financial spreadsheets? There are plenty of seven figures with lots of noughts at the end, that'll do won't it?"

"The boss, I'm afraid, wants everything precise and detailed as usual and nothing less than two decimal places please ... but in a minute. Let's savour this glorious sun. Then we can get our bikinis on, open that wine and talk serious business over the food, especially about my return in a month's time. I'm starving."

Lauren cogitated happily over today's milestone with Mila—but she realised the time was coming to say yes to Philippe, although now she felt ready for him too.

Unknown to both however, the surroundings were not quite as deserted as they presumed. Peering surreptitiously over the ridge with a long distance lens, the voyeur, who had happily enjoyed the spectacle which just unfolded, carefully repacked the high powered equipment and quietly moved off back into the woods. All the evidence and more had been gathered.

The two horses were quietly munching grass on their long tethers. Lauren sat up, spying a small river flowing slowly into the sea near the edge of the trees, perfect for where they could have their business picnic and waved her matching style bikini in front of Mila, replete with black and white interlocking triangles.

"Like my mathematical bikini? I bought them to cheer us both up knowing your style, so no expense spared because you're worth it and don't moan."

"Okay, I do appreciate it. They're both lovely. Actually I've never heard of SoundSélect before. I can see they're an expensive brand but do they do nice dresses?"

"Absolutely. SoundSélect is an obscure but highly coveted small French fashion house. And they design long evening gowns too. I haven't worn a glitzy frock for ages. Time you and I went to some sophisticated parties in this opulent stretch of coastline and had fun."

Mila winced inside ... she thought again of Henri-Gaston ... She had already been indulging recently in some Côte d'Azur wild party excesses around Marseille. She had to resolve this tangled mix of emotions because Henri-Gaston was also becoming rather special and he wasn't going to be so easy to cast off, nor did she presently want to cast him off either, which had deeply surprised her.

Fairly soon they were sitting cross-legged around the tablecloth, the river splashing gently alongside, stuffing themselves happily with Marie's best prawn and salmon cucumber baguettes, washed down with the dry Sauvignon. Mila ran through all the latest sales figures in detail as Lauren returned to her mercilessly focussed business mode and grilled her relentlessly. Both agreed the overall outlook for the coming year with rising sales pipelines was looking good and there could even be another bumper bonus which Lauren desperately needed. She had spent so much money becoming established down in Nice.

Interestingly, Mila with Rosie's help was planning some discussions in Africa and outlined a strategy to engage with the President of the Democratic Republic of the Congo, who had been well pleased with the way Mila, Rosie and their female swat teams had forestalled a potentially catastrophic international disaster. He acknowledged that if there had been Cassini expertise in safeguarding and making the defunct nuclear facility economic again then the disaster would not have happened in the first place. A joint Sino-Cassini approach to developing Congo energy improvement alongside further mineral extraction for the Chinese was on the cards. Lauren was well pleased with Mila and Rosie. She would also return there once Cassini was onboard.

Mila moved onto the pressing personnel issues looming. "We have Sonja on maternity leave and not likely to be back for at least six months. Helena is due in two months time and so is Eva. Janine, who runs all the IT systems, is also due in two months."

Lauren looked puzzled. "Who is Janine?"

"Herman's long term girlfriend who is an absolute whizz with computers, as good as Bernie and Anya in my New York security office. I promoted her immediately after the former IT manager was removed when I found out he was dealing drugs onsite, following a tipoff. Unfortunately he tried out some rather nasty and sarcastic threats in my face. I'm afraid Bella had to find the wheelchair in reception immediately afterwards and get rid of him to hospital when he accidentally slipped down the stairs.

Seb has instituted court proceedings. I didn't want to bother you with all that, you've had enough on. For me the incident was trivial but the difference Janine has been making is huge."

Mila fumbled in her bag and pulled out a folded sheet of paper. "With Sonja, I've made some recommendations for temporary internal maternity cover promotions. We're all nicely taken care of if you approve."

Lauren looked through the list, impressed with the choices. Both Sonja and Mila had highly refined instincts for choosing the right people. She nodded. "Perfect. Actually all this has been giving me more food for thought. I'm thinking through a longer term plan of relocating the whole company down here eventually. If we do well this year, I could offer good packages for everyone ... Hey who wouldn't prefer being on the Côte d'Azur rather than dreary old Brussels? After an investment recommendation from Philippe's new political contacts, I've taken a holding option on a large chunk of development land down the road from Cyclops, which could become the new Head Office."

"Gosh Lauren, there's no holding you back is there. But don't forget the pull of families, not everyone would want to relocate. Eva is very close to her mother."

"I would relocate her mother too—maybe I need to sleep with the Russian Prime Minister ... don't grimace, I'm only joking. But Russian business is likely to grow significantly if Johann pulls the final deal through successfully and I've every confidence in him to succeed."

"Yes, me too ... so go for it ... why not. The build I mean, not Ivan the Terrible!"

They laughed, Cassini business finally concluded. It was time to head back and see how the triplets were doing. She had enough milk in the fridge for Marie to bottle feed all three for the afternoon, all well planned in advance as she needed the time today ... and it had been very well worth it.

Chapter Four

Walking across the wide gangplank onto the enormous, gleaming silver and white yacht, Philippe felt insanely impressed and jealous. The full length must have been well over five hundred feet. He looked up and the helicopter pad immediately caught his eye over towards the far deck at the front. This was some toy, even for a big guy like DG. Various deckhands and other crew members were wandering around doing assorted jobs. Philippe knew DG was planning to set sail for his first extended trip around the Mediterranean in ten days time, so work was being hurriedly undertaken. He, Lauren, Charlotte and all the family, including Marie, Orlando and Marcie, the joint tribe of babies, twins and Oriane and her husband had been invited for the inaugural voyage. Everyone was looking forward to it.

DG had summoned him to come and inspect the yacht. Arrangements were now being finalised for the big trip, or at least Philippe thought they were. A commotion at the top of the stairs for the middle deck caught his attention. The unmistakable booming voice of DG roared across the long gangway. He looked over to see DG with a group of contractors, holding up and pointing to large plan sheets, waving his arms in the air and pacing up and down. Even from that distance Philippe could see DG's angry red face and the genuine look of fear amongst the group he was tearing a strip off in what appeared to be a typical army style bollocking. DG's huge six foot seven inch frame was shaking with anger.

Philippe stood next to a lifeboat and waited until the confrontation died down, then he saw the captain or someone obviously dressed to be in charge have a quiet word with DG, who waved his arms in a grand finale and stormed off down the stairs in his direction.

Approaching at a fast pace, a large khaki sunhat perched on his huge head, DG waved and smiled as Philippe got up off the seat and walked along to greet him.

"Hey little old Philippe, how ya doin' buddy? I'm real glad you could make it. Sorry about the row up there. Damned idiot contractors who were supposed to finalise the renovation of the last ten cabins to a particular specification I demanded, before we set sail off yonder. The job looks like shit, so I've told them to rip it out and start again or nobody gets fucking paid. One guy who got ornery almost ended up over the side head first, but I kept my cool."

Philippe embraced his friend and mentor. "You kept your cool, DG? Fuck, I wouldn't like to meet you when you really were angry!"

DG roared laughing. "Just blew off a little steam, my friend. Anyway, we should be fine for a week on Friday. I assume you and Lauren and those tiny varmints of yours are still up for a cruise?"

"We sure are. Lauren sends her love. She's popping over with the girls to see Charlotte and cheer her up. They plan for a ride into Nice and do some shopping. I understand Charlotte's still feeling under the weather."

DG scowled and wiped his brow. "Yeah, I'm sure darn grateful to Lauren for the way she and Marie are keeping an eye on the old girl. Not really physical anymore, Charlotte's fine now health-wise that way; it's more sort of mental, like a gloomy depression has been getting to her. Can't understand it. She's got everything she would ever need. The twins have been a godsend helping out with Arthur-George, and Charlotte loves the villa and the environment. But it's like this black dog suddenly comes over her, no warning, and she don't want anything to do with anyone, especially AG. I got a special shrink, a real Texan girl living in Cannes, coming round daily, started this week, name of Bethany, who's been doing some good work on pulling her out of it most days. Cost me an arm and a leg, like this old tub we're sat on, but I don't care. Lauren says it's a form of post natal depression, whatever that is, but Beth is confident Charlotte is making good progress now. I'm so pleased Lauren's around. Shit Philippe, she and you have enough on your plate anyway with those three little girls, I don't know how she does everything. And, I gather she's preparing to go back to work soon too, and keeps writing papers. Lauren really is a superwoman reincarnated."

"Has she said that? Back to Cassini already I mean?"

"Darn Philippe, my great big mouth again. You'd think at my age I would have learned not to put a size twenty boot in it. Sorry, I assumed you knew. Lauren's mentioned it a number of times to Charlotte. Seems like next month's gonna be her big day. Tomorrow she's picking up Marie's sister, Jesse, who'll concentrate on looking after the babies, a fully trained nanny I hear."

Philippe went quiet for a moment and reflected. He had no idea Lauren was returning to work, but why hadn't she mentioned it? And he had no idea either about this person Jesse, although the proposition sounded a good idea. He was far less taken with the notion of Lauren resuming so quickly back in Cassini. Then it struck him ... probably she had been in Lauren's usual way, purposefully and quietly getting on with her career and company plans, perhaps sensing that he would be negative or questioning ... especially as his new life of community work and local political activity was as alien to Cassini and energy as he had now seemingly become too. Life was moving on ... and he had been so busy the last few weeks getting to know key people down at the NST party headquarters, but she didn't seem to mind, in fact very much encouraged him.

"Sorry DG, yes of course. All this running around the NST lately, I forgot for a minute. Time moves on and it slipped my mind how near to three months on we are. Jesse will be a welcome addition to the household. Doing everything has been a bit much for Marie especially when Lauren finally returns back to the office. I'm glad to leave all the Cassini stuff behind to be honest."

"I can see that now little feller, just like you said back in the Congo when we all left town for home. I didn't believe you then, but I'm hearing on the old grapevine that the local Mayor thinks very highly of you, making an impact already I'm told, so good for you. I'm sure you can make a good fist of the old politics. Say, I don't miss that shit either!"

They both laughed warmly, walking in the hot sun. DG directed him down another flight of steps towards his personal cabin which had already been finished properly. They walked through the door and Philippe drew in a sharp intake of breath at the grandeur of the room. Great views led out to sea through two large windows, a huge couch and matching chairs, big coffee table, onboard TV and a range of drinks cabinets, book shelves and other assorted paraphernalia filled the room. The ceiling had been raised, not just to more comfortably accommodate DG's height, but to house another unexpected visitor in the corner. The old black grizzly had resurfaced but in a new seafaring capacity.

"So, what d'ya think Philippe? Impressive quarters here, I'm well pleased. And yes, that old feller has certainly got around a lot. Decided to make a deal with Charlotte and get him outa her way. She never really took to Boris cluttering up the sitting room and I spend a lot of time down here these days, the yacht is sorta my new office."

"A bit of a splendid bolt-hole DG but a very nice one I have to say. I make do with the stables. I love looking after the horses and am in there quite a bit especially when Magda starts her yelling. She's louder than the other two combined."

DG smiled, he felt the same. "Yeh, I empathise. This boat kinda makes up for loafing around the old ranch on horseback which I used to do a lot and really do miss. A man always needs his own space to chill out in."

"But this lot must have set you back a fair bit, DG?"

"Yeah, suppose so, but I can afford it, although I had to raid the piggy bank for a quarter of a billion bucks. Hey don't tell Charlotte or Lauren. Net worth went up another quarter last Christmas tax end, despite the hit after the old Olga fiasco in the darn USSR. Say Philippe, you ain't keeping in touch with that whore still are you?"

Philippe winced. Sometimes he did miss Olga but that feeling was gradually disappearing week by week. He had no idea where she was and had no intention of finding out."

"No way DG. One lesson well and truly learned. That's an episode of my life long past and forgotten already."

"That's what I like to hear. Now how about a drop of some ripe old Jack Daniels?" DG sauntered towards one of the drinks cabinets but then suddenly stopped. He began to breathe heavily and sat down clutching at his chest.

Philippe hadn't noticed as he was still staring out of the other porthole windows to the quayside, watching a pair of good looking French women walk past and realising the red haired one was the owner of the NST party building, obviously out with a friend. He contemplated before turning around. "Yes please DG, love a shot of your best ... Jesus, are you okay? You've gone quite pale ... shall I get the captain?"

Philippe ran across the room and put his arm carefully around DG's bulky shoulders who was panting heavily on the couch.

"Fucking pain in my chest again, no, no, don't bother Simeon. Pass me that bottle of pills on the side there, it'll go away."

Philippe walked back with the small brown bottle as DG took one out and carefully placed it under his tongue. In less than a minute his colour had returned and the pain had obviously subsided. Philippe sat down on the chair opposite watching DG's breathing return to normal. He recognised both the symptoms and the medication.

"Suppose I'd better own up," DG started. "Had this darned angina now for nearly a year. Didn't want to bother Charlotte with any of it, doesn't happen often and only when I get worked up. Probably all that bother earlier with those idiots set me off again. To be honest little feller, it's another reason why I've wanted to take my foot off the pedal and wind off the politics and fully fronting the oil business. It's a great environment here for bringing up the family and relaxing. Gotta watch the boredom mind, although the yacht is a nice distraction, I miss the action still, oddly, back in the army."

"Know what you mean there DG. I think when you've been in Special Forces it never really goes away does it."

DG roared. "Sure as hell no. Rescuing Lauren in the jungle and you in the prison brought it all back to be honest ... nice bit of escape that lot. Anyway, what I wanted to tell you, but keep this quiet too, pains have been getting kinda worse of late. I suppose it's all the heavy drinking, loads of food, smoking and no exercise worth talking about, and I could lose some weight. All in all I'm just plain rotten bad."

Philippe laughed as DG continued.

"I know I've gotta do something about all those things, I'm a walking time bomb if I don't, but I am trying. Nevertheless, I'd like you to come with me—to see a specialist in Monaco. Oriane has helped me find someone I like the sound of ... an American top heart surgeon, expensive but what the fuck. Get a thorough checking over and a prognosis. Are you game for that? Quietly of course. I'll let you know when Oriane has got an appointment sorted."

Philippe felt concerned, but on the other hand he understood why DG wanted to keep this heart condition quiet with no fuss. He would be exactly the same. "No problem, just tell me when. I'm pretty flexible these days so should be fine."

"Great ... I'll charter a chopper for us, we can fly from here."

"I noticed you have a pad ... don't you want a chopper yourself?"

"Na ... gotta refill the old piggy bank first or Charlotte will definitely have my hide. The maintenance of this boat is enough. Have to budget for around twenty-five million dollars a year, but that includes all the staff. Hope them fracking stocks are still rising."

DG tipped his whisky into Philippe's glass and handed it to him. "Better get me a Perrier and start where I mean to go on ... for today anyhow!"

He roared his giant laugh and they proceeded briskly out onto the balcony before Philippe was taken on a guided tour, with the captain in tow.

Chapter Five

Sat alone at the bar with a gin and tonic, listening intently to the blonde jazz pianist work her way through more Sinatra, Henri-Gaston finally moved to his special round table in the cosy alcove near the front window in the Restaurant La Lune d'Or. He looked at his watch and dabbed his forehead with a tissue quickly. Never a man to normally feel nervous waiting for a woman, but tonight could or rather would be very special. He had decided and finalised his master plan with much scrutiny. The manager walked across to the table and beckoned over the head waiter who brought a small vase of red roses and placed it carefully in the centre, smoothing down the thick, orange tablecloth. The best silverware of the house was then laid out methodically for two. It was beginning to go dusk and the lights, subdued and easy on the eye, came on as the manager lit a candle to create an intimate atmosphere.

"Is this to your satisfaction Monsieur Landry? Would you like an apéritif whilst you wait for Madame?"

"It looks lovely André, thank you, a Perrier please with a dash of ice and lemon." Henri smiled with some satisfaction, gazing at two of his recent oil paintings hanging on the rear wall. Gifts for past services rendered in the restaurant private quarters, all above and beyond the normal duties of the *maître d'hôtel* but he definitely felt those days were now firmly behind him, despite the humorous teasing of disbelief by his son Charles, who once again was dating his previous girlfriend. However Nicole, to be fair was half his age, about the same as Charlotte his daughter. Charles was at least acquiring the benefit of learning from an older and experienced woman for a change, and he had become tired of the Renault Clio taunts from his staff. The door suddenly opened and he gasped as a tall and very beautiful woman walked in, as ever commanding in appearance, expensively dressed and extremely sure of herself. Male and female heads

41

across the whole restaurant swivelled to gaze and admire her poise and elegance, but the regular diners all knew Henri-G and his taste for special women. However this particular person excelled even for him. The manager grabbed the door promptly, and after hanging up a sleek mustard coloured coat, led her over to Henri-Gaston's table and pulled up a chair next to him. She sat down, smiled warmly and crossed her long legs, catching his gaze deliberately as her short, black, sleeveless dress hem rode high up her bare, tanned thighs.

"Make that two gin and tonics please, André," he said to the manager who placed some à la carte menus on the table. Henri's gaze remained fixed. He stared, hypnotised, into her almond eyes, as she leant forward and kissed him gently on the lips and held his hand.

She spoke quietly, he adored her unusual accent and after quickly realising her English was much better than her French, he soon adapted to communicating as if once more *de retour à Londres,* which still came *naturelle* to him.

"I must say," she began softly. "In the past Marseille has never been high on my list for eating out, but this little gem of a venue is worth all the hassle of parking which was fairly atrocious. How did you find it? Sorry I'm late. A few technical problems came up at work."

"And as CEO, of course you must deal with any situation without question," he whispered and continued to fondle her long, delicate fingers. "This is one of my old haunts from yesteryear. They know me well and I can vouch that the food is excellent."

She looked around and immediately noticed his two street paintings on the wall. She pondered and smiled.

"Old haunts but young conquests?" she commented with a sly grin.

He slightly reddened. This was a woman of the most acute perception on so many things. It was almost as if she could work out his every move two steps in advance and always had an answer ready. He knew so little of her background. She was reticent to talk of her past, and he wasn't interested anyway, always a man to seize the present and the opportunity here and now. But there was something deep and mysterious which lurked behind that beautiful smile. Why was she so innately knowledgeable, particularly about him? But that was a key part of what had instantly drawn him to her, along with those intense eyes penetrating and taking in every nuance. "Shall we choose our food? I can recommend the special on the board, roast duck for two, cooked and served in an unusual and oriental way whilst retaining *caractéristiques français délicates* as we say. Snails to start? And, as it is your birthday, I have asked André to search out the cellar for the most expensive Pinot Noir in the house."

"That will be exactly to my tastes and desires tonight. Thank you darling and for remembering my birthday," Mila purred and kissed him again delicately on the lips, feeling his body slightly tremble. Exactly as she liked her man; nicely ensnared.

"All your desires?"

"We shall have to see," she replied smiling demurely. But she was surprised he knew her birthday, she couldn't recall telling him. She wasn't the only one to discern a few secrets. Walking from the car, she had checked her phone to see if anyone else remembered. Only the usual text from Sonja still under the weather but wishing her a special night. Lauren of course had completely forgotten. Today, with Henri, she had decided to break a strict rule that ladies never reveal their age.

"Actually, I'm impressed that you never ask how old and normally I would never tell you anyway," she began with a laugh, caressing his hand again.

"But that is because I'm a true Frenchman, who would never expect a woman to divulge her secrets. And in your case age is simply a set of numbers. It is your fire of life and your burning soul of intensity which drives my passion for you every minute."

"You really are a man of poetic words and hidden emotions, I'm beginning to warm to you I must admit," she responded coquettishly, her skirt riding even higher as she re-crossed her legs. Anyway, the numbers are a little more significant ... having reached today the big four-zero. So there it is."

Henri gaped in disbelief. She enjoyed that. He began to question in his mind whether he was actually losing his grip on guessing a woman's age. Having seduced so many in the past five years, he was normally accurate to a few months. Mila looked at least ten years and more younger. Perhaps because all his girlfriends had been relative babies, they all appeared that way now. Whatever, he was surprised and pleased. Moreover, the age gap between them was pleasingly realistic for what had been gelling relentlessly in his mind all week. "You are so young, *ma chérie*. You still have time for everything possible in life that you want and will cherish—money, fame, and family, whatever it is, with me besides you."

Mila smiled and wondered.

André suddenly reappeared with the bottle of expensive wine and after a grandiose performance uncorking it, poured out a small glass for Henri to sample. He instantly swapped wine glasses and insisted that it must be perfect only for Mila ... he had actually guessed already from comments over the week that she was quite a wine aficionado and wanted to test her out.

He wasn't disappointed. She swirled, sniffed and went into a long diatribe about origins, grapes and age, exactly the way she had shown off to Lauren when they had first met in her Palermo hotel. Henri had no idea about Mila's advanced culinary skills either, something to impress him with in due course ... She was not at all sure what was happening to her with Henri-Gaston Landry, handsome and sophisticated playboy man about town, bon viveur and rich, world famous cultural entrepreneur. This feeling for a man was new, intense, unexpected and made her wake up with a smile. But being fearful of how to handle it further was for the first time uncharacteristically receding. What really bothered her intensely was Lauren ... she really needed to think hard about how to deal with their special relationship if she continued dating Henri.

Having munched their way through a tasty bowlful of escargots à la bourguignonne, which looked more like a pleasing fondue to Mila, they began to work through the oriental duck, replete with a huge range of vegetable and rice accompaniments. Mila skilfully continued turning the conversation constantly back to him; she knew he couldn't resist talking. Soon he was openly pouring forth all kinds of interesting and valuable titbits about his family life, his five sons and of course his physicist wife of twenty years who had sadly died of breast cancer five years before, as well as his art and creative achievements. She remained subtly generalist and diversionary. He was given access to the knowledge she was Serbian and had lived in Rome for many years and had done a lot of management and turnaround consultancy, but the focus on security, espionage and intelligence was strictly withheld. Something significant would need to move on in their relationship before he even got a tiny hint of that integral part of her life. But Mila was assured, clever and capable to set the agenda between them at exactly the pace *she* wanted. What she was pleased about was the uninhibited information cascading forth at that moment, enabling her to assess Henri as a desirable and worthwhile man, or not, with more critical precision. She had of course done all the personal background checks and risk assessment on his life and financial history already. That was easy, and surprisingly she had found no awkward skeletons ... except one, Lauren, which needed a decidedly different assessment in this mix of emotions and possibilities. If she was going starry-eyed she would do the whole job properly, which for her was ensuring expert management and total control. His cluster of former and existing celebrity girlfriends were irrelevant, she could outclass them all. Certainly the sex with Henri-Gaston, also uninhibited, was exactly as she liked it and had received a high A-plus mark all round. His reputation, appetite and drive out and about on the female celebrity street had genuine justification, which was a promising opening.

As they chatted, the door opened with a clatter and Mila glanced up to watch six men walk inside. No matter where she was her instinctive situational analysis always kicked in. She quickly assessed them as Eastern Europeans, likely Belarusians by the Russian accent combined with bad French, mixed with more Pidgin English. For a prestige establishment they looked slightly dishevelled and out of place. But they were waving wads of money, mainly fifty euro notes, and because it was midweek and there were a few unreserved tables they noisily demanded one. It was clear that manager André was trying to avoid a scene as diners nearby began to stare. He reluctantly waved them to a large empty table and his acolyte of waiters began to attend to them carefully and attentively. The racket died down and the East Europeans began to loudly order drinks and a variety of appetizers as food orders were quickly taken, given the time of night.

Henri had his back to the table a few rows further down but turned to see and caught the gaze of one of the more unsavoury ones in the group. He stared back in disgust then returned his attention to Mila, muttering a variety of disparaging remarks in French to her. Unfortunately, the lively murmur and chatter had died down in the discomfort amongst the rest of the diners, and Henri-Gaston had one of those imposing, and clear, deep voices which Mila loved, but carried in the silence. She looked up and assessed that the individual who Henri had perused had not only heard but understood the French by his decidedly unimpressed expression. The guy turned to his associates and they began to chatter loudly in what was indeed Belarusian. She couldn't catch the exact discussion, but from their faces guessed the sentiment. They were not exactly scintillated.

Her internal alert automatically went up a notch as Henri continued chatting amiably, but soon another bottle of wine and a plate of delicious desserts made them forget the intrusion, as vast quantities of spicy meat and rice were quickly brought to the Belarusian table accompanied by more bottles of the best house vodka and they settled down, albeit noisily, to themselves.

Half-way through their meal, one of the more drunk Belarusians started a heated argument and viciously swiped a glass and a full bottle of vodka off the table, breaking into tiny pieces to scatter across the tiled floor and distracting once more the rest of the remaining couples from their intimate tête a tête, including Henri. Silence swept across the room. He waved André across as a couple of young waiters hurried towards the mess with a broom and brush. One of the gang of six yanked the broom off him and threw it angrily across the floor, shouting a variety of obscenities whilst the rest joined in with loud laughter and insults.

"You shouldn't have let that scum in here André," Henri protested in French, annoyed his special evening with Mila was being spoiled. "They're not in the slightest fit to be in this establishment. Those fuckers should be downtown in a Rue Anglais Turkish cafe, amongst the whore houses where they belong."

His comments once more were louder than desirable as the Belarusians stopped and the big and ugly one, who Henri had last stared at, spoke quickly amongst his friends. Mila flinched and began to quietly assess the environment. She sensed this was no longer looking a good situation. They laughed and hollered, drunk and out of their heads with excesses of vodka and heaven knows what else before or during their meal in the restaurant.

Henri turned back to her, his shoulders hunched up and his face tense. "I'm sorry *ma chérie*, but these idiots are ruining our evening. I'm going to give them a piece of my mind. Don't worry, I'll protect you, I'm pretty good with these fists."

Mila was not concerned about the Belarusians, but she was very bothered now about Henri and put her hand firmly over his. He was obviously keen to show off and impress her with some misplaced display of peacock manliness, something she neither needed not wanted right then or ever for that matter. "No, darling, ignore them. They're vulgar idiots and not worth a breath of your time. They look like they're finishing anyway and I noticed your friend André was on the phone, probably to the police. It really doesn't bother me. Let's order a cognac."

He looked into her eyes, breathed a deep sigh, calmed down and nodded, as the Belarusians, now finished, rose from their seats. Whether they were actually going to pay or not was a visibly debatable issue but that was not her or Henri's concern. But in an instant the biggest one and obvious leader, sprang across the room towards Henri and grabbed him around the neck, pulling a small handgun from his jacket which he jammed against the side of Henri's skull. Screams erupted from a number of the female diners. Everyone stood still. The jazz singer burst into tears.

Mila sat motionless and calm, staring into the dark eyes of this burly Belarusian, who was sweating profusely. His blue suit, although expensive, had certainly seen better days. But she had already clocked earlier and surreptitiously analysed that unlike his rowdy friends, this fucker had stayed relatively sober and his movement and approach indicated he was no ordinary street criminal or dealer either, a likely hitman, trained and carrying a bruised ego, a dangerous combination. She looked at the gun, a Sig Sauer P238, a nice piece, US made, light and accurate and not cheap.

She glanced at the others, weighing them up and was less impressed. They were still stood around their table smirking at the boss. Yes, this brute was a definite pro ... her assessment began to rapidly formulate.

Henri was shaking and had gone pale but stayed still. "What do you want? Money?" he whispered in English, not taking his eyes off Mila.

"That's an idea, you pompous old shit," the assailant replied in a Russian accent but with a slight American drawl to it. He immediately slid his hand down into Henri's inside jacket pocket and pulled out a wallet. "Mmm ... nice Gucci leather, plenty of notes. You have style my friend. You see, we scum, and fit only to be Turkish dogs, can also appreciate the nicer things in life. This will compensate for disturbing our meal tonight. So you and me are making progress now, perhaps I don't need to blow your head off just yet."

He shoved the wallet into his pocket. Pointing to his table, he nodded to André, stood rigid at the side along with his petrified waiters. Nothing like this had ever happened before in this exclusive neighbourhood or in his restaurant. "On the house, yes?"

The others laughed and did up their coats ready to go.

André nodded. A few bottles of vodka and a pile of kebabs and rice were the least of his worries right then.

"Finally," he continued, "I would like an apology to my scum friends here for such an unacceptable and rude disruption to our meal. Then I can leave you alone, shithead. Say it, and say it out loud so everyone in this room can hear. Not so fearless now my friend are we?"

Henri winced. This was a form of humiliation he resented badly ... he stayed silent but then he heard the gun mechanism cock and the cold barrel was pressed harder into the back of his head.

"I think I said say it? You are not understanding well."

"I'm so sorry sir," Henri blurted out between clenched teeth but the fear inside was overwhelming, his pride battered especially in front of Mila who he had to protect somehow. "It won't happen again."

"Good, and one final thing?" the man whispered, shoving the gun harder making him wince, the sweat pouring from his brow.

"What?" Henri muttered, wishing it was over.

"Your gorgeous Slav whore sat there with the giveaway cheekbones."
He looked into Mila's eyes who stared back impassively. "My friends and I
would like to see a little more of her before we go. You, Serb slut, on your
feet, now. You know what to do, start from the top."

Mila didn't move. An immediate flashback zapped through her brain.
She was back in Bosnia, 1993, in that awful prison camp for women
again in Srebrenica and she had a distinct aversion to being called a Serb
slut.

"No, you can't, no, I beg you, please, we had a deal," Henri shouted,
a great wave of dismay running up his body as the man grasped him
tighter around the neck with massive burly hands and he began to splutter
uncontrollably.

Mila knew exactly what to do, but it would not be what this thug or
his friends were expecting. He moved away from Henri and with a leer he
began to tilt the handgun towards her, but she was so incredibly fast, a
blur in the air, as she unexpectedly sprang forward from her seat like a
missile directly at him. Following a well aimed blow to the lower kidneys,
she grabbed his gun hand and with a flick and a sharp crack broke his
wrist, twisting the gun downwards which went off with a loud bang as he
shot himself in the testicles. Screams echoed around the room as a number
of people near the door ran out. The man fell with a piercing roar and a
hard shove from Mila, head first into their heavy French oak table,
breaking his front teeth, as Henri, incredulous, dived out of the way, the
gun clattering underneath.

The five stared in disbelief at their boss and then at Mila, totally
disoriented for a moment. Then, knives out, they began to run across the
room towards her, shouting crazily, their faces contorted with rage. They
would cut her into tiny pieces. But that second or two delay was all Mila
needed. In an instant she dived across the floor and picked up the broom
handle, always her favourite hand to hand weapon of choice. She whirled
it around expertly in a Catherine wheel of circular and lateral movements
as they came for her and then ran hard at them. They froze. It was all over
in an instant as each one dropped into a writhing heap on the floor, her

carefully placed blows ensuring they sustained severe broken bones but would live to tell the tale.

The rest of the diners remained motionless, in shock and disbelief but also their faces displaying huge relief and gratitude. Henri too was in shock, in even more incredulity. Who on earth was this woman he had fallen head over heels in love with? Never in a million years would he have believed what he had just witnessed. Outside, everyone could hear sirens wailing as a group of squad cars from all directions approached the restaurant, lights flashing everywhere. He stared silently at Mila, who strutted across to André.

"Good timing, the police will take care of them, André. They'll live but will be very uncomfortable in custody. I'm sure these undesirables are well known local criminals. As for that one?" She smiled, pointing to the toothless leader curled up in agony on the floor, blood oozing from his crotch and surrounded by waiters, who had removed the handgun and Henri's wallet. "He won't be fucking any Serbs for a long time or anyone else for that matter."

Police, guns drawn, and paramedics rushed in but instantly assessed the trouble was over and began carting off the semi-conscious miscreants quickly on stretchers into waiting ambulances. The waiters rushed around and rapidly began to clear up the mess, which considering what had happened was remarkably little. Mila was surgically precise when necessary. André implored the remaining diners to stay and began seating new ones who walked in wondering what all the fuss had been. He was insisting that the panic was over, with all meals and drinks for the whole evening on the house and waved the jazz singer to continue playing. A loud cheering and applause spontaneously erupted, directed towards Mila from the diners, most of them regulars who knew Henri-Gaston well as they all retook their seats.

Fully recomposed, following a quick application of her favourite red lipstick, she walked over to the dazed and uncharacteristically mute Henri still sat staring on his chair and kissed him gently on the cheek. "I think we can finally enjoy those cognacs now, don't you?" she whispered.

"That was the most incredible scene I have ever witnessed in my life. Who are you Mila? You're a killing machine. Will you marry me? I love you."

Mila looked hard at the police commander who had walked in and was speaking immediately to André. She turned to Henri. "The police chief? Do you know him by any chance?"

"Yes of course, I know everyone worth knowing in this town, Commander Jacques Trousseau. We are in the same ... err ... club. He is an old school mate. Why?"

"Excellent. I suggest you, me, André and the Commander pop into a private room now. I will do any talking."

Commander Trousseau walked over, breaking into a laugh as he approached and held out his hand. "Henri-Gaston, you seem to have got yourself into an even bigger pickle than normal, my friend. But I understand your ... err ... companion ... ably fended them off. We've been tailing this new mafia gang for months, muscling in for a takeover of the key drugs and prostitution rackets. A few of their Russian compatriots already had their heads blown off last week. Sadly Marseille is not the city it once was. They will all be going away for a very long time and off the streets for good. Your name, please madame?"

"Her name is ..." Henri began but Mila had been unexpectedly anticipated. André interrupted Henri instantly and insisted they all follow him into his private sitting room inside for a chat, out of ear's reach.

As Henri and Mila followed behind Trousseau and André, she whispered with a smirk. "Remember, darling, you say nothing and know nothing, got it? And the answer to your question?" She put her fingers gently across his lips and strode on ahead into the room.

He turned, not knowing what to do except grin inanely then nodded in pursuit. On this rare moment out with a woman, Mila had become the boss ... and she knew it.

The head waiter brought in a tray of rare eighteenth century porcelain cups and an old silver pot of black coffee. He silently left them on the table before withdrawing and closing the door with a distinctive clunk. André began to pour and Commander Trousseau pulled out a small notebook.

"My father taught me a little self-defence when I was in my teens," Mila began. "On this occasion it definitely came in handy. I think I was fortunate with the timing, but they had much more to drink than me, Commander. Those drunken men, they had become so very slow. Just as well. You are happy with me speaking in English? My French is so bad, I'm afraid."

"*Oui sûrement*, of course."

Henri looked across and stared. Mila was talking blatant untruths for whatever reason, and in a quite unfamiliar accent. But he had to keep his mouth well and truly shut, that much he at least realised. He knew one thing for sure. Mila was extraordinarily special. On that, his instincts were right, but now he was very much out of his depth and his comfort zone. Silence was as they say, *le meilleur du moment*.

"My name is Catarina Della Lucia. I am Italian businesswoman from Milano, not as those oafs thought, Serbian. I write software for Swiss banks."

Trousseau nodded. She was, he mused, certainly an impressive and individualistic woman, tall, beautiful and had an aura of high intellect and presence. To be expected from Henri-Gaston, as ever, but even Henri was excelling this time with his new lady.

"You have identification Signorina Della Lucia?"

Mila fished deftly inside her handbag and handed him a passport, which was indeed for the very one and only Catarina. She was relieved she had brought one of her many aliases out with her, a sixth sense once again. But this time she took a rare chance and inside the passport she surreptitiously placed a tiny photo-card, before handing it to Trousseau. If her instincts were correct on the situation in this room, then Trousseau had the appropriate background. Watching him walk, his manner and the way he observed his surroundings had already convinced her.

Henri walked to the table to grab another much needed coffee. Caffeine was high on his needs right then. The Commander peered at her name and picture then perused the card inside and smiled. He glanced over the Hebrew and read the English—special operative with Israeli diplomatic immunity. The colour of the Star of David and the specific stamp over her picture he recognised. Catarina reported directly to the Israeli Prime Minister. She was top Mossad with the highest status. This would not be going any further, and certainly not to his police committee back at base. Also he owed Henri a favour or two, because without Henri's pulling of some political strings in the Town Hall he would not be holding the top police job."

"Well Signorina," he replied with a smile. "Your credentials are perfectly in order. Now, Henri?" he shouted across to his friend, sipping the hot coffee and gazing aimlessly at the nude painting on the wall, still in a daze. "*Écoutez, mon ami.* We will not need to proceed any further with you or Signorina Della Lucia. All the Mayor has been interested in these last few months is getting that despicable scum off the streets and locked up. How we do it he wasn't over-concerned with. I suspect we will quietly deport them anyway once they've been patched up ... Minsk has expressed a particular interest in the inept one who shot his own dick off. He has other strings to his bow which we can well do without in Marseille. Enjoy the rest of the evening both of you, I must return to headquarters and complete my report. Henri—I'll see you down the beach club next week. André, I assume you'll be there too?"

André nodded and smiled.

"Fine, Jacques, much appreciated," Henri-Gaston replied, a relieved expression billowing across his face. "I feel better now with that coffee. I think we have a meal to finish off don't we Catarina?"

"Yes, I think we definitely do?" she replied grinning.

"Ciao Signorina," Trousseau replied, shaking her hand. She immediately felt his subtle but distinctive grip and a faint touch of the thumb against her palm. She was right. Former Shin Bet in a past life long ago. He departed promptly with his crew.

"Just going to pop to the gents, then I think we can order those brandies at long last, don't you Catarina?" Henri said to Mila.

"Definitely," she replied and looked at him tenderly. It wasn't often she got a formal marriage proposal ... in fact she'd only ever had one before, from her husband murdered way back in the Bosnian conflict. It had been a long time and she wanted Henri-Gaston Landry. She dwelt momentarily on her turbulent life and in particular on her two young children who also died at the hands of those brutes who she later killed in revenge. She pondered. There would be conditions for any marriage that of course she would set.

"You shall have a bottle of our best Napoleon vintage brandy, on the house, with my compliments, Catarina. Thank you so much for all that you did. We are very grateful," André insisted, as Henri sidled out cheerfully through the side door to relieve himself.

As they walked back down the corridor towards the restaurant area, Mila turned quietly to André. "You know of course. Foreign Legion?"

He smiled, expecting this. "Yes. I know of very few people with the skills you exhibited today. You are a true master of hand to hand combat. Discretion and secrecy comes with the territory we inhabit and a given. I shall continue to call you Signorina."

She laughed. Again she was right and pleased by the evening's efforts because she really thought she was slowing up and losing it after that ridiculous error of being hit on the head when rescuing Lauren in Kinshasa and then allowing herself to be strung up naked on a high pole by Olga and her Russian mercenaries. Being rescued by Rosie had evened up the score between them ... and she was happy with that. On the other hand, this day was a milestone. She was reaching an age where many of her contemporaries do hang up their frontline boots on the special agent circuit, and maybe it was time to change her life. Henri-Gaston had become delectable serendipity if she thought about it meaningfully ... and cogitated about the conditions she would require.

"Henri-Gaston confided in me earlier that he has serious plans for your relationship, Signorina. In my humble opinion you two would make a wonderful couple. He is decidedly smitten, which I have never seen in all the twenty odd years I know him. He needs your strength and vitality, but equally he is a good and interesting man."

Mila turned. "Yes, I agree. Thank you André for the endorsement."

After a personal refresh of her own, she sat back down at the table. A large ancient looking bottle of old brandy and gorgeous blue balloon glasses awaited them, just as Henri-Gaston returned, slightly breathless and definitely unsure of his next step. Mila had indicated 'yes' but equally, being a woman and they were all fickle, she could change her mind, as he had asked in the heat of an extraordinary moment. Everywhere around was back to normal, with mainly couples sat quietly chattering. The lights were dimmed as a plethora of tiny candles in intricate holders flickered romantically on the tables.

Henri poured out generous measures of brandy and they sipped slowly, saying nothing, simply watching each other's deep expression with mutual interest. He suddenly fished into his jacket pocket and brought out a small box. She suspected what this might be but was quite stunned by the size of the beautiful diamond ring emerging from inside which he placed gently onto her finger, a little tight but that could be easily rectified. They continued in silence, before she leaned forward and kissed him on the lips for a full minute.

"If I say yes, I will mean it and then there will be no going back for either of us. Understood? Thank you Henri, this is a most beautiful ring," she said fingering her huge diamond possessively. "But I want this to be cherished only between us for the moment, and nobody else to know, please."

"Something tells me Catarina that a life with you will never have a dull moment. You don't need to tell me anything about your past and I don't care what your conditions are. I will do whatever it takes and go to the ends of the Earth with you."

That may very well be the case she thought dreamily, already planning some life changes. "Good," she purred. "Because I won't be telling you anything anyway. You are such a traditional French romantic, Henri-Gaston Landry and I love it and you. Now that our large bill is taken care of but I can't guarantee to repeat the exercise at every future meal out, I think we should catch a taxi to my apartment and celebrate properly. Cassini security will pick up my BMW tomorrow."

He took her hand as they both rose from their seats and André wrapped her mustard coat carefully around her shoulders. Hand in hand, they walked slowly through the door into the night air for a stroll in the fresh sea air along the promenade, to a great cheer from André, his staff and everyone else inside.

However her mind was ablaze, painting a new canvas of radical long-term plans ...

Chapter Six

Philippe slowly wound up the heavy water hoses in the barn following a lengthy cleaning session with Pi and Vanya, when he heard the familiar chugging of Marcel's old yellow moped coming up the hill. Today he should find out once and for all. He walked across the yard to the front gate in anticipation, feeling the warmth already building up in the bright early morning sunshine.

"Good morning, Marcel, how are you doing today," he called out cheerily in French to the young postman who had stopped sharply in a cloud of dust, as Philippe began pulling a few large weeds from Lauren's delicate sunflower seedlings poking though her array of grand pots surrounding the gate.

"*Très bien, Monsieur Dubois,*" he replied, rooting furiously through his small trailer attached to the moped, amongst a great mass of letters and packages. How Marcel could sort anything sensible out of that pile was beyond Philippe.

"For Madame Lauren only today," he uttered, pulling out a couple of US custom franked book parcels from Amazon. He handed them over as she strode across from the house and snatched them promptly out of Philippe's hand.

"Good, my research books on synthetic biology. Thank you, Marcel."

He gazed at her with affection, in her short yellow summer dress. "Why do you need those, darling? What on earth has synthetic biology, whatever that is, got to do with nuclear fusion?" Philippe replied, puzzled.

"If you spoke a little more to your big daughter instead of spending all your time in that smoky club for aging male politicians, you would find out that Svet is writing a rather novel thesis for her final year degree project. And it's given me some ideas—heard of the death of Moore's Law?"

He screwed up his face. Everything Lauren did was way beyond him these days, but he really didn't care anymore, especially after their dusk escapade the previous night running *déshabillé complètement* down the beach, followed by a first-time catch-up behind the deserted groyne. Almost a year, it had felt a very long time, mostly of course his fault. Something, he thought, seemed to have gotten big time into Lauren's psyche again. She was suddenly very hot and sexy, hotter than ever she'd been before. It must, he concluded, be the horse riding together. But to feel that their physical relationship had finally got back to normal was especially good ... he vaguely heard her voice again sounding in his ear.

"No, I thought not. Anyway, no time for banter, darling. My first day back at Cassini tomorrow. Three months on the dot and I have a mountain of agendas to go through for Exec, and I must talk to Svet later ... She doesn't know yet but her work at Harvard with Sergei has genuinely sparked a few wild ideas. So has it come then?"

Philippe looked glumly disappointed, but Marcel wasn't to be beaten. He fished deep into the recesses once more and suddenly pulled out a large brown envelope. "*Eh bien.* This may be what you are looking for Monsieur Philippe, I suddenly remembered. I must improve my sorting techniques."

Philippe perked up distinctly. Marcel kick-started his old moped and trundled off towards Charlotte and DG's villa.

"Well? Are you going to open it?" she cried, impatiently. "I hope after all that time preparing, writing and working Oriane's network of government contacts that the result has been worth it."

He tore open the government envelope and pulled out the thick wodge of official letters and papers. Glancing quickly over the first page, he immediately saw what he expected. Oriane had already dashed his optimism with a realistic assessment based on a tightening of the rules through terrorism fears.

"I can see it, plain and clear, exactly as I expected— a great big *non.* I'm sure their fucking dislike of Russians overrides any other supporting case whatsoever, no matter how economically well it's presented," he grunted, hugely annoyed and disappointed.

"Here, give it to me," she said, snatching the papers off him as he paced in circles around the gate. Reading through the French fine print quickly, using her well-honed speed reading techniques gleaned through years of fast absorption of scientific papers in all kinds of languages, by the tenth page she had come to her own conclusions. And her French was immeasurably better than his, although she had to admit his conversation had improved significantly with the intensive tutoring Oriane and her husband, Director of the local American International School, had given him. "I see the old, hard-wired Philippe aversion to detail remains alive and kicking," she shouted to him.

He stopped pacing and squinted at her shiny blonde hair, reflecting in the sunlight.

"I'm afraid this actually says a great big *oui*. The *non* simply refers to having dual nationality with Russia will not be permitted," she finally replied with a big smile.

"Really? You mean I'm now a legitimate Frenchman? Wow ... fuck Russia. I never wanted to fill that section in anyway, DG forced me into it—'fire all the chambers, little feller.'..."

"*Vraiment, ma chérie*. Here's your legal document."

Gloom turned immediately to elation. He rushed forward, the envelope and papers scattering on the ground, and gave her a big hug and a long sloppy kiss.

She felt all quivery in that tight fitting dress and looked into his eyes with affection. "So the great and enduring love for the eternal motherland is well and truly over then? I would never have believed it," she purred softly, her arms wrapped around his burly shoulders. His body mass and muscles had significantly recovered, especially with all the riding and his daily workout and weightlifting sessions in their new gymnasium he had built in the basement. Sadly, for her, the wine cellar had now become somewhat more shrunken.

"You betcha darling, I never want to go near that damned border again. I'm done with everything Russian."

"Including the magnetic allure of mysterious gas engineers?" she replied, stroking his beard gently which she now rather liked. It did suit him, although not quite as D.H Lawrence as Amélie's Giles.

"Especially, gas engineers!" he said with a laugh. "Hey, fancy another session down the groyne?" he murmured, feeling her bottom and the profile of her underwear.

"Mmm ... methinks it depends what groin you're talking about. Sadly, it is actually broad daylight, in case you haven't noticed and the beach will be heaving with tourists. Exhibitionism isn't my thing anymore darling, especially not with my picture on the front of magazines in every dentist around. I have to stay professionally demure and respectable and besides, I have very pressing work to do."

"Later, when Marie goes to her book club?"

"I'll think about it," she responded playfully and prised his firm grip from her rear, before heading briskly back to her study. She was more excited by tomorrow. Her big return to the helm of the Cassini ship full time, and she was taking the triplets along with Jesse, to be sworn in as the first official occupants of the newly opening company crèche at the back of her research laboratory. She intended to cut the ribbon in the morning, alongside Juliette. Mila was still busy in Africa, negotiating with the President of the Democratic Republic of the Congo and would not be back until the end of the week, but she had Mila's report. The rest of the Executive would be arriving from Brussels, most importantly Johann. The main agenda would be business development and sales. Although Philippe had clearly become quite xenophobic about his former birthplace, she on the other hand was keen to embrace the old USSR as much as she now could, thinking of a further build of her very latest Xenostra Two advanced plutonium fast reactors. These money making monsters incorporated her patented cooling design using a unique and stable blend of sodium, lithium and potassium metals, liquid at room temperature but having a much greater neutron absorption than any other coolant on the market. So, feedback from Johann on progress with the Kremlin alongside a feel for the cache of foreign dollar reserves from Russian oil and gas waiting to be spent on her was critical. She also had another proposition but wanted to work that through first with Nimi, her Research Executive. She could sense the time was right for wider commercialisation of more of Juliette's research activities. Nimi's latest feasibility report, which only she had perused, had swung it. She had been radical and daring once with Sonja's appointment and the splitting up of Cassini into two divisions. Now she would create a third, with a quite different focus ... and initially head that up herself and intensively groom a successor within six months. She had the perfect person in mind, hand-picked, who had shown the tenacity, insight and bloody-mindedness over the last three months to be perfect for such a role. It simply had to be Mila ... she dwelt on that thought with a large inner smile as she walked inside ...

Standing besides Dr Juliette Curwen, CEO of Cassini Research, Lauren cut the ribbon with a flourish and surveyed with much satisfaction the newly built and furbished crèche, with its bright blue and yellow walls and a plethora of playthings and educational amusements. Jesse, alongside a group of nursery assistants of the same age and Joan the manager were busy looking after their charges, including the triplets. She counted eight babies and twenty children, some as young as two, who had been divided into small groups and taken care of individually. There had been a higher interest than anticipated and Juliette had built for a capacity of forty, but already it was apparent that a number of female researchers had returned full time and more were expected within the next month. The cost to employees was zero including meals for the children. Juliette had convinced her after a recent visit to Seattle, that the enlightened employee perks of numerous US tech giants heralded a sound investment to facilitate good morale and loyalty. Lauren needed to retain as many of her highly skilled researchers from escaping into the clutches of her competitors as possible and she had asked Bella to do more research on the factors which improve staff retention, motivation and productivity. Decent and above the norm pay levels she had introduced from the start, when Cassini was reborn under her leadership.

She glanced once more at the happy atmosphere before indicating to Juliette that she would head for her office and finalise the Executive agenda for their early afternoon meeting. Then she would leave with Jesse and the triplets at four pm on the dot, when Marie picked them up. The girls were settling into a manageable routine of feeding and sleeping and she would maintain that for the next three months and then review.

Walking through the glass doors, she felt a palpable relief that she was back. Boredom with the babies or her new found domesticity and marital bliss with Philippe was not the issue, she loved every aspect. However the desire to return to her fusion research and the cut and thrust of Cassini business had been overwhelming. She needed the testing challenges desperately, mentally and physically. And she finally had Mila around, in more ways than one, and smiled naughtily. Plonking down on her orange covered couch, she immediately remembered something Irena had said, a long time back, when they first met at her husband's the then UK Prime Minister's official residence at Chequers. *There's still plenty of time. You can have it all Lauren. I do and I look after five children and two psychiatric practices in London and Moscow.'*

The notion then had terrified her and seemed so utterly improbable as to be statistically ruled out completely. How much had changed dramatically in eighteen months. She was indeed having it all, and she could include Mila too in the mix whenever the urge took her. She was pleased that Irena had fully recovered, apart from occasional cold weather twinges, from the shoulder shooting injury incurred at Kinshasa. Irena was also apparently, at long last, working miracles down at her London clinic with Amélie's nemeses, the psychotic Rufus half-siblings, Cordelia and Simon. Sighing with genuine contentment, a knock preceded a breathless and red in the face Nimi who walked through the door, having run from robotics at the other end of the site.

"Sorry Lauren, I'm late on your first day back which is inexcusable. I'll get the coffee on. I've just been playing with Buster."

"Buster?" She screwed her face up, thought hard and then remembered in a flash and grinned. "Ah Buster ... our unique robot dog that walks about with cooling rods in his mouth. Of course ... and Buster had a rogue progeny, Razz, I seem to remember? The forty mile per hour, backpacking, robotic puppy dog? You were convinced of some commercial potential, were you not? Oh—I'll have a large cappuccino please."

Nimi laughed. "I've kept this information for your ears only for today, Lauren. As I suggested, we have the first non-nuclear commercial licensing of a spin off from our research labs. I've just negotiated a cracking five year deal with the Pentagon who are keen to make a few hundred super-Razzes for immediate trials in the Arizona desert, and with more to come if successful. In the end, after a protracted beauty contest, they much preferred him to another concept version which one of the US tech giants had put together, especially as Razz could run faster and carry more. It's all in Bhavika's legs."

Lauren laughed heartily. "I'm sure Bhavika's legs have a lot to answer for. Now, what about the legalities of this bit of personal entrepreneurship, which Nimi, I'm totally all for and very pleased about? I did tell you to think about it before I disappeared and you've obviously done a lot more. An excellent initiative to start my first day."

Nimi blushed. Her successful sister was so embarrassingly extrovert, even Lauren had noticed. "Sonja went through all the paperwork with a fine toothcomb and double checked with the Cassini legal team who added a few riders, but otherwise they were happy. She approved and signed it off. It was the last thing Sonja did before she went on maternity leave."

"So, we really do have some legitimate business with the military then?"

"Absolutely, and I have a few more projects I'm working on in lasers which could follow."

"Right. All rather timely because I've been thinking a lot more about this concept, having had plenty of time breastfeeding the tribe and simultaneously to daydream commercial ideas into action. We'll talk about my ideas later. I want to discuss a plan with you in detail first before floating it anywhere else. But our priority for the next few hours is to finalise that Executive agenda for this afternoon, and then fill me in on the gossip. Don't look so shocked Nimi. Gossip is as necessary as management by walking about. So pull up your chair, grab the diaries and let's get to work ..."

Pondering alone in the cafeteria in her time honoured fashion, she ran systematically through the good and bad points of her first day and concluded that on balance it was pretty good all round. Sales were effectively up and Russian business was a knockout, only some niggling engineering leakage issues on Xenostra 2 which had now been prioritised by engineering for remedial action fast. The Board endorsed the progress made in the Democratic Republic of Congo by Mila, and Juliette confirmed that the joint Cyclops research work with Israel continued apace, despite political concerns again in the Middle East and especially with Iran.

She needed to do some urgent work on Iran and still retained a dream of landing there and doing radical business. Sadly, everything was so very tricky right then with more US and European sanctions on the horizon. But most importantly, a successful day one, and whilst she felt quite elated she realised she was totally exhausted. She really had to pace herself better and not try rushing about like a demon until she was back into the flow of her hectic job. Needing an energy boost, she eyed with love the large, sugary iced bun being brought over with her afternoon coffee. The most important and unexpected gossip was that Juliette was dating again, and it was a man ... a divorced CEO of a tech start-up in Silicon Valley who she had met briefly on her last visit. It sounded to Lauren like a distinctly long-distance relationship, but Juliette was very happy and perky and even more focussed, so from that perspective she had no problem but would ask Mila to quietly check out the background of the said Dan Morino of Light Wave Altruism.

Her phone suddenly rattled vibrate only on the table. She didn't recognise the number but that didn't matter as the voice wailed out in time honoured fashion, loud and clear into her ear before she had a nano-chance to say anything.

"You haven't forgotten have you as I've now booked the flights?"

"Haven't forgotten what?"

"That I'm coming this weekend with the tribe for the great Côte D'Azur social event of the year on DG's famous yacht that I keep hearing about from Charlotte."

"Oh shit, got the date wrong ..." Lauren muttered before relenting as a long string of expletives rattled down the airwaves ... She laughed. "Only winding you up, of course not. I see motherhood hasn't dulled the formidable temper. You're still as fiery as an Icelandic volcano, Dr Helgudóttir."

"Fuck, you worried me then. This is my first outing to climes further than Preston since the great emergence. Sadly the Earl of the palatial pad is embroiled in some deep skulduggery over the weekend down in the House of Lords. Somebody is trying to reform the old codgers and make them extinct or do real work for a change ... so he's fomenting a palace revolution or something.

"That's a shame, we were all so looking forward to seeing the redoubtable Rufus again, especially DG so he can indulge in another Havana smoking contest. Maybe next time?"

"Well knowing you would be devastated, I've managed, at great personal cost you'll understand, to arrange a pitch substitute, but you have to promise to keep your hands off him."

"Pardon?"

"Forgotten already, such is the life of the roving, global chairman. Your latent love affair with D. H. Lawrence reincarnated? Still brain dead are we?"

"What, you mean the delectable Giles? He's coming with you? Without Rufus?"

"All the way—well maybe not quite so literally, anyway he'll do wonders to revive your libido and Charlotte's. I needed someone to carry the babies."

"I can't speak for my daughter but mine's bubbling along nicely these days."

"Mmm—obviously lots of grit for your best friend to tease out of the purest nuclear oyster. You can save all the worst bits for white wine and pastry delicacies alone on your terrace when Giles plays tennis."

"With who? Anyway how do you know I've got a tennis court?"

"The delectable Marie from what I hear. Sorry but my spy network, even in upper Anglo-Saxonia remains alive and kicking."

"Now I know who has been typically spilling the beans but to you I'm truly amazed. I always said she loved you really. Anyway, the miscreant is away in darkest Africa presently, hopefully making me even more money. Some of us have to work still, Lady Westvale. My first day back today and I am so pleased I can't tell you. I love the kids and him indoors but I desperately needed that kick in the brain again and it's returned big time. Business in Russia is booming but don't mention that to Philippe, the new rising star local politician— although now he's been officially adopted as a true Frenchman. Finally got his citizenship papers through."

"It really is odd, whenever I don't see you for a few months, suddenly we're silently orbiting Sirius. I find that truly hard to take in, although logically I suppose having the crap kicked out of you in a Russian prison would break most xenophiles, even him, and he had a double dose with Murmansk. Sounds like you finally have your marriage in the good place you always wanted it ... and you deserve it Lauren. Actually, you've just reminded me, now Rufus has become all aristocratically political, he has revised my formal status amongst his conspiring peers, amongst whom I was paraded out in full bloom last week at our social ball for the great, rich and the socially godly. His father never liked such formality and wouldn't allow its use, but he was a tad zany, as you probably guessed from the deviant family behaviour of many years ago, unlike Rufus."

"What status? I haven't a clue what you're on about Amélie, but that's nothing new. Keeping up with you in conversation is making my tired brain ache ... bring on some fusion equations."

There was a timed silence. "I'm married to an Earl ... so officially in the hierarchy of lording over the local oiks, I'm a Countess ... but you can still call me Lady if you prefer," Amélie replied with a laugh.

"Bloody hell. The Countess Amélie of Westvale ... that takes some beating ... only one more heave and it will be Queen."

"Not quite ... Duchess still to go yet, but I reckon that title has much frumpier connotations somehow—Countess is far more exotic, don't you think? Sort of racy and foreign?"

"With you, anything is possible, and you are foreign remember. Anyway, after your spell of exotic amongst the badlands of Chechnya and the lucky escape from being a statistical blip amongst Vaag's vast list of progeny, exotic may be better avoided. One can't keep pushing one's luck forever, Countess, so Giles is well out for both you and me.

"Actually, I was really thinking more about Charlotte? Especially, as I believe she requires a manager for her new vineyard?"

"Eh? What vineyard?"

"Oops, I've put a great clodhopper in it again … I should never assume you know anything. That saves embarrassment all round. When are you seeing her?"

"Actually I've just decided. Right now! And I can hear Marie and Jesse coming down the corridor with the triplets."

"Don't shout at her—shoot the messenger, me, as ever. Anyway like mother like daughter again. It appears that Charlotte is desperate for something challenging but different, so she's just bought a large vineyard and olive grove for cash, her own apparently, which came up for sale behind the villa, which she's apparently been eyeing up ever since they moved in. I'm sure she will be dying to tell you."

"Mmm … I've known all along she's been keeping some big secret from me for ages. Now I know what it was. Good for her. To be honest, I've suspected for a while that she would want to pick up something to work on. I must go Amélie, here they come, and Marie is driving us all back. I'll pick you, the twins and Giles up personally from Nice Côte d'Azur International, text me when you leave the UK, don't forget."

"Well there you go; I thought you might … that's great. See you then. Bye Lauren."

"Bye and thanks, really looking forward to seeing you and the twins, bye."

Amélie put the phone down gently. She frowned hard, realising with dismay that Charlotte's true big secret had yet to be revealed— she really had to be extra careful not to put her foot in it again, that may never be forgiven. The factoring in to Charlotte's life of Henri-Gaston Landry was very much her fault, having encouraged Charlotte in the first place and then providing the detective work in the shape of her ex-husband, to successfully track Charlotte's long lost father down. She decided to give Charlotte a quiet ring before she left for France. This running sore issue with Lauren really had to be resolved …

Walking at a fast pace past the swimming pool, Lauren kicked Lexi's ball hard which sailed right past both her and Kat who desperately dived across the grass to try and catch it, missing Orlando cutting the lawn. The ball landed with a great splash in the middle of the water.

"Grandma, look what you've done?" Lexi cried, wailing miserably, as she gazed disconsolately at the ball bobbing about. I'll have to find Orlando's big net he uses for cleaning.

"Never mind that now," Charlotte shouted. "You can both go into the pool later. I want us to show Grandma our new purchase."

"Great Mom, it's really cool over there. Come on Kat, I'll race you to the gate. Last one there is a sissy."

Lauren turned to Charlotte. "Why didn't you mention it? I heard all about this mystery vineyard from Amélie, who as usual is forever uncannily ahead of the game where I'm concerned, whenever something interesting is going on."

"Not all the games?" Charlotte replied, immediately biting her lip, because she had just heard an impossible to believe rumour from Oriane, who mixed a lot amongst the top, affluent cultural networks of the coast as an amateur art collector. The rumour had made her numb with shock. Amélie's phone call now made her doubly uneasy because she knew inside her own heart that the revelation of Henri-Gaston coming into her life needed to be faced with Lauren and all their family … but the right moment simply hadn't come up and DG was so distracted with his yacht, she hardly saw him which didn't help.

"What games?" Lauren replied sharply, her eyes narrowing.

"Sorry, nothing Lauren, just a figure of speech. Anyway, it wasn't that I didn't want to tell you but Philippe wanted the purchase kept quiet because of the politics involved. He had intervened directly on my behalf with the Mayor as there was some local and well-connected family sensitivity, and I didn't know fully until two days ago and the final legalities were signed over."

Lauren stopped and stared, incredulous. "You mean Philippe has been involved in the deal making?" She continued, now angry. "He's said absolutely nothing. I really felt he and I had got over all that old Philippe secrecy nonsense and had finally become fully open with each other on everything. Although, I must say, he's looked decidedly shifty the last two days, especially when I mentioned it last night. I should have known he was up to something. He disappoints me ... again! You've said 'I' a lot of the time, Charlotte ... Does DG know you've bought this vineyard?"

"Also a large olive grove is included with commercial oil making presses and a wine fermentation building and storage. No. I wanted to surprise him on the yacht ... he was aware ages ago that I had put a small option on the land, but was never interested in the specifics or realised the opportunity to buy came up when the owner died. Philippe has been the driving force to make the whole thing happen. Listen Lauren, I'm really sorry. I've messed up in my quest to surprise everyone tomorrow, especially DG that I could do something new and enterprising here and independently, okay with Philippe's help. But he's been marvellous so don't blame him. Only the girls know and they've been told to keep quiet too. I didn't realise Amélie would mention it to you."

Lauren took a deep breath, pondered in a split second everything that had been said and concluded instantly that she actually understood her daughter way better than anyone else. It was now very obvious that Charlotte needed the same challenges and desires to be important and independent, outside of her immediate family ... and she had Cassini and was back at the helm in full throttle. Lauren realised that Charlotte was creating her own local business opportunity, exactly as she would have done in the circumstances. Chairing a business in Texas at a distance wasn't the same thing as managing something truly hands-on where her home is.

"Actually, I do understand everything and I'm very proud and pleased for you," Lauren replied jauntily. "To be honest this sounds much more fun than well-drilling!" She gave Charlotte a hug. "Also, occasionally I can't believe that Philippe has become a proper husband at long last and I keep pinching myself because the dream is going to end any time soon as abruptly as it happened."

Charlotte rubbed her arm and kissed her cheek as they resumed walking up the hill towards Kat and Lexi, waiting impatiently at a gate freshly made in the hedge on the outermost perimeter of their estate. "Thanks Lauren. There is no reason whatsoever to fall out. You and I are far too alike, and much as I didn't want to admit, I do need more in my life than Arthur-George, DG and the twins. Something that I personally own and control. And I have the means to do it. But my immediate challenge is to find a good manager as the former person retired when the owner died. There is a small workforce and I'm paying a couple of them to do essential maintenance, but effectively things are in a bit of limbo until I restart the business, which I must do in the next few weeks, as the summer starts. Also, from what Philippe has said to me, he's never been happier in his whole life, especially with you and the triplets. So you can dispel any nagging notion this is a fleeting display. Politics seem to suit him. Let's be honest, networking was always his big strength from what you said, and he gets on well with all kinds of people. Now becoming a French citizen, a whole host of doors are suddenly opened to him that he is unsurprisingly keen to exploit."

"Yes, you're right. I need to trust him and I do to be honest, especially with the demands of the triplets and now my going back to Cassini. I haven't paid much attention to his political interests ... and I should have done ... So time for me to turn over a new leaf. And I'm pleased that what he's done for you has paid off."

"Absolutely ... I've got a real father-in-law back again, now that the old father-in-law became my husband!" Again she bit her lip, wanting to add that she also had a real father back too, as an extra bonus. She had to do something very soon and tell her mother first before anyone else did.

Lauren laughed heartily. "Don't remind me Charlotte just how complicated our family is."

As they trudged up the hill, Charlotte continued thoughtfully. "Actually Amélie mentioned she might have a great solution to my manager issue."

Lauren stopped and smirked. "She hasn't told you then?"

"No. But by the look on your face, you know something I don't. Role reversal time ... anyway I deserve it. Well? What is this grandiose solution? I can't for the life of me see what Amélie can do remotely from the UK."

"The solution ... and I don't know the details yet ... are coming with her tomorrow. I suspect Amélie has been doing some wheeling and dealing for her own reasons ... but it could be a very good solution if my instinct is correct."

"Sorry Lauren ... I'm not with you whatsoever? Coming with her. What is coming with her?"

"Not what. Who. She's bringing Giles. Rufus sadly has had to give his apologies—he's wanted in the House of Lords all weekend."

"Giles? Who is Giles?

"He's Amélie's estate manager."

"So you've met Giles?"

"Yes."

"But you've never mentioned him?"

"No."

"You're being very monotone, Lauren."

"I'm saying no more ... If for whatever reason Giles is available ... you need to make your own mind up."

"Well, would you have him? Or is he some grumpy old English retiree she wants to get shut of who wants a quiet life in the French sunshine?"

Lauren smirked. "Possibly," she said impassively. "You really have to make up your own mind. Hey look, Kat has just opened the gate. I can see the path now leading into the olive trees."

Charlotte was still staring at her mother. "Possibly what? I can see you've gone into change the subject mode. You can tell Amélie that I am very severe with grumps and shirkers, and I am not having her estate cast-offs, even if she is a Countess!"

"Okay," Lauren replied staring ahead and stifling another smirk, in fact a great rollicking laugh.

"Grandma, we've been here for ages, hurry up," Lexi shouted back, as she and Kat started walking ahead into the olive grove, towards a large and modern green metal building further into the distance. "I want to see whether Louise managed to bottle the oil yesterday out of that huge wooden vat."

"Lexi, your mother and I have just had four babies between us ... we still need to get our energy back."

"Grandma, if having babies makes you as tired out as you two then I am definitely never having any babies, ever. Anyway I'd much rather play tennis. Quickly Kat—I can see Louise outside ... wave to her."

Charlotte grinned. "Ms Independent Minded again, sadly like you and me both. Since starting their international school, Lexi has really got into sport especially playing tennis with her American friends. Boy, she has quite a natural talent. I'm considering hiring her a proper coach next year. The twins are becoming much less reliant on each other now for company and developing their own social lives at school ... I'm not sure whether that's good or bad."

"It's good Charlotte. The twins will be eleven soon. Even though they're identical, they have their own diverging personalities, very much so, and children, especially girls, grow up fast."

"True. I did at their age. Eleven was a major turning point, periods, breasts, boys, the entire adolescent stuff."

"Gosh ... I was nearly fourteen before all that happened. Who is Louise?"

Charlotte smiled ... still thinking wistfully of Lauren ... because two years later Lauren had given birth to her ... a lot happened after her mother hit fourteen. No wonder her father, Henri, was continuing with an unending insistence to meet Lauren. She must have grown up precociously fast. "One of the two people I'm paying to carry on with the essential maintenance. Her brother Karl is keeping an eye on the vineyard. They are both in their mid twenties. Their father, a widower, was the former manager but he's now seeing his retirement out with other family members, an older brother I think, in Lyons. Now first I want to introduce you to Louise. She knows everything about olives you could ever want to know. Then we can look at the small plant inside, I think the engineering will intrigue you."

Louise had come outside with Kat and Lexi standing and chatting to her excitedly in English. She looked up and smiled warmly at Charlotte approaching with Lauren. An old sheepdog was lying slumbering in front of a kennel nearby. He opened one eye, yawned and went back to sleep.

"Bonjour Charlotte. I assume this is Lauren, your mother, who you told me about. Goodness me, you two are like sisters, the similarity is amazing."

Lauren laughed and held out her hand and they shook warmly. "Hello Louise, we've kind of gotten used to being told that now. I must admit some people never believe we are mother and daughter."

"And Grandma," Lexi added, looking her usual serious self.

"Yes and Grandma," Lauren replied, patting Lexi affectionately.

"But we never fail to adore the compliment," Charlotte added, "Especially my mother!"

They all giggled and went inside. Louise explained that her English was good because she had studied English and French at university, but decided on graduation to join the family work with her father and brother.

"Also Louise's mother was English, but sadly died suddenly ten years ago," Charlotte added as Louise blushed, slightly embarrassed.

Louise began to talk about the olive press. "I understand that like Charlotte you have an engineering background and would like to see the olive oil making process, Lauren. And for Charlotte and the twins it is also their first time. I had a barrel of olives left after the February harvest which we stored in brine—for bottling, but it is too late now for that. After my father retired we struggled a bit with the olive side of the business here. So I will show you, please come inside."

Lauren, always excited with technology and industrial processes, walked in first and gazed around at what looked like a small production line. She immediately noted the presses and grinding wheels and looked inside the centrifuge at the end. Unlike the complex machinery in her nuclear reactor environment, what she saw in front of her appeared almost timeless and quite mechanically simple but presumably effective. The black olives were in a basket at the beginning as Louise switched on some machinery, and they watched as the olives were carried up a form of escalator and discharged onto trays over which water flowed to begin washing them.

Louise continued. "There are essentially four simple processes here which have been applied the same way for thousands of years. I shall speed it up so you can see exactly what happens. First we wash the olives thoroughly. Soil especially must not be allowed in as the flavour can be badly affected. Cleanliness throughout is especially important. Now Lexi, you press that button please."

As Lexi pressed the next control, concentrating hard and wide-eyed, the olives began to move into a trough with the grinding wheels revolving slowly.

"The next stage is to grind them up into a paste. To maximise the flavours, normally they would stay inside for about forty minutes or so but I'll move them on so you can see what happens. Kat, press that other button please and Lexi, as the paste comes out of the opening there, spread the paste with the knife thickly and evenly onto that flat disk. Then Kat can carefully transfer the disk and put it over the hole in the press next to it. We can do two or three disks Lexi please with that paste."

As Lexi completed the final disk, they all stood back and she pressed the button for the press to start, which slowly descended on a hydraulic piston and compacted the paste under high pressure, forcing out oil and vegetable matter which was washed away by sluices of water into a centrifuge to separate the immiscible liquids. Soon there was enough mush for Lauren to turn on the centrifuge, creating a run off of a bottle of fresh olive oil. Kat and Lexi cheered, holding up the golden liquid.

Lauren and Charlotte stood side by side in silence, eyeing the whole process from beginning to end. Five thousand years of successful simplicity but still plenty of scope for some efficient technologies and innovation to be imported into the run, lots of challenges ahead. Both were individually ruminating, Charlotte from her oil and gas experience and Lauren from a nuclear perspective.

Kat poked Lexi and pointed to the pair, as they laughed. "Mom and Grandma's brains are really sizzling together, Louise," Lexi commented. "I think they both liked that demonstration."

"You betcha," Lauren hollered to more giggles. "When do you normally harvest the olives?"

"Green olives in September and black olives January to February, depending on the weather and temperatures," Louise replied. "Something like eighty percent is made into oil fairly quickly and the rest we sell and bottle for eating, so there will be a lot to do, Kat and Lexi, at certain times. The rest of the time we spend on pruning and looking after the trees, and there are many of them, some very old and gnarled, perhaps a thousand years and they produce a big crop still, and of course I mustn't forget packing and selling the oil. There is the vineyard too, which is also very busy throughout the summer."

Lauren smiled at Charlotte. "Quite a challenge, this lot but I can see you're up for it. There is indeed some fascinating engineering which I'm going to give some deeper thoughts to."

"You betcha," Lexi and Kat hollered back in unison to loud laughing and squeals as Louise took them into the kitchen at the back, with Ned the sheepdog, sensing food, ambling behind, for all to share a coffee and homemade Swiss roll cakes. Lauren deftly fronted the queue, as usual.

Charlotte felt very pleased all round, especially given the enthusiasm of the twins. If she could find that elusive manager soon, they could get started properly. She would see whether curmudgeonly old Giles would suffice as a starter but held out no real prospects on that score, but was grateful that Amélie had been looking out for her as a good friend.

Like Philippe, she really wanted a change of direction ... something else she and him had shared and discussed together, but she would choose a better moment to chat quietly with Lauren about what Philippe had talked about and unexpectedly confided in, which sounded quite a momentous decision. But Charlotte had not made it a two-way street, not with regard to her father, not yet. However, Philippe's supportive frankness had boosted her confidence and she decided that perhaps telling Philippe first about

Henri-Gaston and seeking his advice about Lauren would be a good step forward ...

Lauren slammed open her study door. "Shit Philippe. Why didn't you remind me? I'm going to be late now for Amélie. Philippe, where the fuck are you?"

She looked down the corridor towards his workroom but the door was firmly shut as a series of not too melodic musical chords could be heard being strummed behind. "Damn it, not that bloody guitar again," she cried out as Marie suddenly appeared briskly from around the adjoining corridor.

"Don't worry Lauren," she said quietly. "Actually I've just checked and there has been a delay in Amélie's connecting flight from Paris. She's going to be an hour and forty minutes late, so you've got plenty of time including their last feed before I put them to bed."

Lauren, feeling a huge wave of needed relief wash over her, kissed Marie on the cheek. "Thank goodness for that. I wouldn't know what I'd do without you, an oasis of calm. I think Philippe is in another universe, what with the politics and now his new found music obsession. Still, I'm not complaining. He sounds quite good already, considering. Can you ask Oriane if she knows any tutors? I'll pay for it!"

"I do actually, someone in Cannes who teaches beginner jazz guitar ... he's very good and a nice guy. I went out with him once ... but he caught sight of my 9mm pistol on the bed and left in a hurry, before I even got the handcuffs out."

Lauren giggled, she wasn't sure whether Marie was joking or not but didn't care. "We'd better keep him out of your cottage then. The Kalashnikovs won't rock his boat either!"

"Actually, I forgot to mention. Seb has invited me to a security refresher programme he's going on in Monaco, if that's okay. Big focus on new technologies and there's a shooting range. He's challenged me to a dual."

"Of course. Gosh, I thought Seb would have learned after his shootout with Mila around the Cassini lake ... he lost."

"Really? He never mentioned that, I think he's been practising."

"Yes, probably trying to redeem his lost esteem by beating another woman."

"He doesn't really know how good I am, Lauren. That might be a problem."

Lauren laughed. "Never mind. I'm sure Seb can take it. Anyway, with pending fatherhood coming for the first time, he has other priorities in his life. Eva is going on maternity leave next week, along with Helena. Fortunately I've just promoted some excellent temporary managers, but I think the Cassini crèche will definitely be filling up over the next twelve months. Mmm ... I can hear the loud lungs of Magdaline again. Oh-oh and there goes Eveline and Geraldine in harmony. No wonder Philippe has barricaded himself in with his Fender Stratocaster or whatever it is."

"It's a Gibson semi-acoustic actually Lauren," Jesse cried, running past with a bottle from the fridge to warm up.

"Right, breasts at the ready, I'm behind you Jesse. Marie can you put those papers on the table into my briefcase? I should have time now to finish the calculations at the airport."

"No problem, your BMW is outside ready when you've finished. I'll put them on the front seat."

Lauren, deep in further concentration and shutting out the general racket around her, glanced up at the flights board. It was very busy and warm in the airport and parking had been a real struggle, especially with her large SUV. Having landed, Amélie's flight had already progressed to baggage reclaim. Sighing, she pushed her papers down the back of her rucksack, checked her hair and makeup in her pocket mirror and headed towards the meet and greet area. She was especially pleased because this was the first day she had managed to prise into her best Prada blue jeans with four inch black Louboutin ankle boots, and chose a new mustard yellow-flowered matching top, showing more cleavage than usual, but then Giles was coming.

A troupe of people sauntered through, all ages many accompanied by children, when she caught sight of the unmistakable Amélie, pushing a twin buggy, tall, confident and commanding, her hair as usual short, spiky and coppery, just like in the old days when they did the night clubs every weekend in Paris. She sighed with a tiny remembrance of former husband nostalgia, then spied the trademark skinny Gucci jeans and bright red blouse and smiled. They were always uncannily in tune meeting up again with matching clothes; it was like some sort of spooky 'action at a distance' which Einstein first said about quantum mechanics. But then they were both high powered physicists so that wasn't so surprising. Lauren suddenly dwelt on their one thousand pound dress bet ages past, that Amélie would eventually return back to science, but immediately decided to remain wise after the event. The likelihood of the Countess reverting to former type and nuclear employment seemed to have radically diminished into a black hole. She certainly looked good with aristocratic motherhood.

Lauren waved and Amélie turned a sharp left, ploughing fearlessly with her wheeled tribe across the crowds who scattered out of the way. They hugged immediately.

"You look absolutely fabulous." Lauren burbled excitedly. She was so pleased to see Amélie again. "And these two are simply gorgeous," looking down at Lady Leonora and Lady Caroline, their distinctive Icelandic blonde hair very visible, both fast asleep, and dressed in matching pink and grey.

"You look amazingly good yourself. I like those jeans," Amélie replied, grinning. "Anyway, I don't do frump as you know but I must admit Charlotte's recommended exercise routine has done wonders for the big belly."

"You get on really well these days with Charlotte don't you? I expect you both share all kinds of dark secrets and lots of scurrilous gossip then?"

Amélie felt an instant inner twinge. She simply must not show any unease or hint of deception. "Of course, as ever," she replied jauntily. "Charlotte has become a good friend, but not my best friend," giving Lauren another hug, peering over her shoulder at the arrival exit door. Where the hell was he?

"But I thought Giles was coming with you?" Lauren queried, looking around again. "Has he bottled out?"

"Giles decided to pop into the duty free as we came through. He insisted on buying you a thank you present for putting him up. Oh, and that blouse button is undone. Still reminiscing are we of what may have been?"

Lauren felt herself stupidly blush and did up her button. "He shouldn't have, we love to have guests, plenty of room. Anyway most of the time will be spent on DG's yacht. Look, Leonora and Caroline are waking up."

They looked down as Leonora gurgled and Caroline opened her eyes and squinted. Lauren squatted on her haunches to hold their tiny hands.

"Hey you two," Amélie said, making them more comfortable. "Meet Aunt Lauren, your precious godmother, without whom you may never have emerged into this world."

"But I don't do God?"

"You never change, do you? Merely a figure of speech Lauren. I do know and church isn't obligatory. But you must promise to give them extra special attention as they grow up."

"Of course. They're so beautiful, exactly like their mother and father too. I can't wait to introduce them to Magdaline, Eveline and Geraldine."

"You've really taken to babies haven't you?" Amélie replied. Her eyes narrowed. "I'm quite surprised considering how anti you were before the big bang. Fortunately, despite the glares from all and sundry, I managed to feed them both on the way from Paris and Giles and I changed them at baggage so they should be fine for a while, no pongs. Ah, here comes the delectable miscreant. He's quite non-plussed now when I breastfeed, so you can legitimately get your tits out in front of him, Lauren."

"Honestly Amélie, it's you who never changes. As if all I think of is sex all day long."

"Well ...?"

They both giggled and Lauren looked across the airport lounge to see a tall and heavily bearded Giles ambling down the aisles, sporting a large grin and pulling two large suitcases with one hand whilst holding a large bottle of duty free in another. Lauren unexpectedly found her breathing take a deep inward lurch. Gone were the late autumn heavy country clothing, boots and Barbour jacket. Instead they'd been replaced by a tight and very smart red tee-shirt and matching well-fitted blue, wide belted, stonewashed denim jeans, which she immediately recognised as Dolce and Gabbana ... stylish no less. His hair was slightly shorter and nicely cut, but as she stared, mouth open, she understood how farm management work for Amélie had brought on a set of rippling muscles together with very desirable thighs. He was broad, sexy and turning her on unlike any man for a very long time. What on earth was the matter with her these days?

Amélie turned her head to take in her best friend's totally unexpected hot and dreamy red-faced reaction. "Jesus Christ, Lauren," she hissed. "Isn't him indoors back to five nights a week yet? You're forty-four, a global company chairman and mother of baby triplets, get a grip. For heaven's sake, it's only Giles. Admittedly a very delectable Giles these days but I do, as ever, have some influence on such matters. He's been a fast learner with my hints and tips to dress better."

"How old is Giles? Fuck, he could be ..."

"No, he isn't because both men you're thinking of are dead and buried, thank God. And he's far too young for you, even if that was the vaguest of possibilities which it plainly in a million miles isn't."

"Mmm ..." was the most Lauren could muster but as Giles approached she composed herself quickly, grabbing a baby-wipe off Amélie's buggy to dab her face. "Ridiculously warm in here, air conditioning should be on."

Amélie jumped up and walked briskly to meet him and took one of the suitcases, as they wandered back together chatting. Lauren got up, realising that even with her five inch heels, Giles was still a few inches taller, he wasn't far short of DG, which she hadn't really realised before. With a deft twist of her fingers she immediately undid her pony tail in an instant and flicked back her long blonde hair with both hands so it cascaded over her shoulders, receiving another glare from Amélie.

Approaching Lauren, he surreptitiously looked her up and down, which she was very happy with, and held his hand out in true friendly Brit style. But she was already a few moves ahead.

"Giles, how wonderful to see you again, it really has been quite some time over twelve months I think," she burbled aimlessly. "Now you're in Nice you must greet a lady in true southern French style. First a long kiss on the right cheek and then on the left please."

Lauren remembered instinctively that gorgeous Giles was a little shy and unsure of women and that made him even more desirable and in need of some mild female torment, something she hadn't done for so long ... not in fact since Luis ... oh God, why was he still locked inside her mind. That lurching feeling in her stomach felt oddly familiar again ... and she wanted it back, if only for a micro-second.

Amélie, irritated, folded her arms and watched the show contemplating. Was Lauren quite out of character being deliberatively provocative? Or did she and her have to have a long and very private chat, even sooner than she had reckoned on? Seeing Lauren close her eyes, breathe in his aroma and pull her arms around Giles's ample warm back and yank him closer, lingering longer than normal in polite company, she decided that the latter hypotheses was becoming an increasingly high probability, especially as she saw him whispering something in Lauren's ear which Lauren obviously enjoyed.

As they withdrew, Giles picked up the bottle of Russian vodka out of the buggy. "A present for both you and your husband Philippe. I'm very much looking forward to meeting him. Amélie mentioned he was once in the Russian Special Forces."

Lauren glanced at Amélie who looked away, wishing she had not let that slip after too many gin slings at their last country ball.

"A very long time ago," Lauren replied. "All that is long behind him now. Philippe's big consuming interest is rather *boring* local politics, especially now he has been granted French citizenship ... his family have a French lineage dating from the Napoleonic wars which is where his surname, Dubois, emanated from. I remember you like history Giles, but you're obviously not an army man yourself."

Amélie, now agitating inside to go before the twins woke up, watched quietly, taking Lauren's asides in with her usual analytical precision ... she was already drawing conclusions and reflected.

"Actually I am a little," he replied. "I've been active in the British Territorial Army, the reservists, for many years. I'm a Major and go on occasional weekend sorties, as long as Amélie and Rufus are not affected. I try and get things arranged well in advance."

"So you can shoot in a straight line then, Giles?" Lauren remarked with a smirk.

"A very straight line," Giles replied instantly with a loud laugh.

Amélie coughed wishing she had never tried that particular joke out on Lauren last time she was over. "Don't you have triplets to feed?" she said briskly. "I think we should get going before these two wake up and howl."

"Sorry Amélie, absolutely," Lauren answered, bringing her thoughts instantly back to reality. "I forget sometimes about babies, with Marie and Jesse, my housekeeper and nanny around."

"My word, I totally forgot," Giles replied instantly. "That is badly remiss of me, very big congratulations Lauren." He gazed again, first over her and then over Amélie. "I must say I would never believe you were a mum of triplets," he stuttered, blushing. "You've sort of like ... err ...and Amélie too ... both of you ... are so fantastically ... err ...

"Readjusted, is the word you're looking for," Lauren said with a large grin and made Amélie, uncharacteristically serious, laugh at long last too. "Wait till we tell Charlotte that one."

"Charlotte?" Giles remarked, puzzled.

"My big daughter, Giles." Lauren answered with a sharp glance to Amélie.

"I was going to mention her tonight, before we go to the yacht," Amélie murmured.

Giles glanced back to Lauren, clearly confused. "You have another daughter Lauren? I never knew. I presume she is still at school here then?"

"I think I would like to push my new godchildren ... you are both so gorgeous, exactly like your Mummy," Lauren chuntered, ignoring him.

They set off, Lauren happily pushing the double buggy, and soon reached the car park. She spotted her red BMW X5 and pressed her car key button, as the lights flashed and the doors clunked. Giles moved off quickly with the suitcases. "I'll just put these in the boot. I'm sure when I've folded up the buggy, it should fit in there too," he shouted back, contemplating the logistics.

Lauren turned to Amélie. "Quite the domestic little helper isn't he and still a bit of a charmer too?"

Amélie stopped. "Yes, I can see that," she hissed back in a whisper. "What the fuck has got into you Lauren? You're like that Congolese gorilla Vega, on heat. I would never have believed it, the way you've just reacted. A bit of a difference from last time you were at my place."

Lauren immediately realised, looking at Amélie's stern face. "I'm sorry, I don't know what's got into me ... Remember what you said about you and Rufus pre-birth? It's sort of hit me post-birth. I am getting a grip, honestly. I could do with a hair brush, forgot it in the rush."

"As usual, here," Amélie replied, thrusting one out of her bag into Lauren's hand, finally seeing the funny side and laughed as Giles returned and pushed the twins over to the car, unbuckling their individual carriers to put them inside. "When we're back then you and I are going to have a little bit of quiet time to ourselves and a long chat, for necessary confessionals and to indulge in some of Giles's vodka, never mind wasting it on Philippe."

Lauren smiled. "Yes I agree? And how come you've never mentioned Charlotte to Giles?"

"It was supposed to be a surprise, but meeting you again seems to have been enough for one day."

Lauren laughed and linked arms. "Come on. It won't take long and I know nothing impresses the Countess these days but I'm sure you'll adore my new pad, and you've got the guest bedroom with an amazing view towards the sea."

What Lauren didn't know was that Philippe had just returned home from a trip with DG on a chartered helicopter, to see DG's heart specialist in Monaco. The diagnostic results done there and then and the prognosis would mean that DG, on return, would simply have to tell Charlotte immediately. There was no way he could keep that news away from his wife any longer than necessary.

Chapter Seven

The early summer days were always Lauren's favourite time of the year in the south. Flowers poked their heads up in vigorous bloom and the birds singing their heads off once more woke her at five for the morning dawn. She gingerly levered herself out of bed, dressing gown wrapped tightly around and wandered down the stairs, quietly. All was very peaceful, triplets and twins were fast asleep. Philippe was completely dead to the world, snoring loudly which irritated her intensely alongside coming to bed drunk and amorous which she was not in the mood for. He and Giles had worked their way right through that large bottle of vodka, spending most of the night on the veranda, regaling each other with increasingly lurid tales of 'taking out' insurgents from Chechnya to Afghanistan. At least neither of them smoked. She wondered where DG had got to. Normally he would have been there with his Havana cigars at the ready. With Amélie and Marie, after dinner, she had walked into town and enjoyed coffees, a good gossip and a few brandy chasers on the seafront for an hour after dinner. Anyway, at lunchtime they and the joint tribe of babies would all head to DG's yacht for a tour, lunch and then a short trip down to Monaco where they would anchor and have dinner in a swish restaurant, with a huge family table booked in the evening, all on DG's expense account whatever that was. Oriane had arranged onboard nursery care so that everyone in both households could come, relax and have fun, a mega get-together for the first time since moving down.

As she opened the old kitchen door slowly to avoid the squeak, a dark staring figure hunched over the table made her jump badly.

"Giles? Bloody hell," she whispered loudly. "What are you doing here? I thought you'd be in bed sleeping off the night's excesses?"

He looked up and grinned sheepishly. "Sorry I startled you, Lauren. I'm always an early riser, long ingrained with the job even after all that booze. I do apologise. I only realised how much we had drunk when Philippe threw the empty bottle across the yard straight into the bin. Just getting a coffee ... do you have any aspirin?"

"Here," she replied, throwing a packet of paracetamols at him. He caught them deftly and she sat down demurely on a high stool next to him. He stared down for a moment when she realised her dressing gown was riding higher up her bare thighs than decorum suggested, and pulled it lower and tighter.

"Thanks," he said, taking two quickly. "To be honest I'm feeling better already after this amazing French coffee ... Apologies again, I helped myself using your machine. Normally I would be out in the fresh air now which takes away any bad head."

"That is what the coffee machine is there for ... and stop apologising please. I like my guests to treat this place like they were at home. You remember? I hate formality?"

"Yes, I do, alongside your liking for D.H Lawrence, one of the things very attractive about ..." He stopped and gulped his coffee.

"Giles, do you ride?"

"Of course, I love horses. We keep a few on the estate that I personally look after. Rufus rides too, usually for the local hunts, but we haven't been able to persuade Amélie yet."

"Want to come for a quick jog with me to the beach?" she ventured, her eyes flashing with excitement at the impulsive thought.

"When?"

"Now. I do this quite often on my own first thing. Helps me think through the day ahead, although today is scheduled no work and just plain old, simple fun, yippee. Well?"

"You have horses?"

"*Naturellement.* I'm not Amélie. Although best friends for a long time and we do share a lot, on some things we're totally different."

"I can see that," he replied grinning.

"See you outside in ten minutes ... you can get a shower later. Jeans and a tee-shirt is all you'll need, same as me."

"Great."

In a trice, Giles had the two horses expertly saddled up. After helping her on, they set off at a light canter down to the beach front. Everywhere was virtually deserted, a few early morning walkers were out but that was it. The air was crisp and fresh. Soon the colour was back in Giles's cheeks as she led him towards her favourite beach outside of town. This was sheer pleasure. She had not been out with Philippe for a while, especially since she had become engrossed again with returning to work. But as she was quick to acknowledge, equally he hadn't been around much either. They cantered briskly along the edge of the water, both horses enjoying the run as much as their riders. Giles had a very natural way with Vanya, almost an instinctive and immediate bonding. He was, she thought, a very knowledgeable and natural countryperson and obviously enjoyed the simple pleasures of the outdoors immensely. They rode side by side, and she found herself enchanted with his intimate knowledge of the surrounding nature, pointing out all kinds of things on the tide line … crabs, shells, jellyfish, even all the different types of seaweed. After half an hour they turned past the next headland towards the bay where she had ridden with Mila and stopped. Dismounting, she stared in a reverie out to sea as the sun began to poke up fully from the horizon, lighting up the blue sky in a blaze of yellow rays. Such wonderful nature and setting and so little enjoyed for so long. She felt an arm firmly placed around her shoulder and a bottle of water passed to share, which she gulped down thirstily.

"Do you fancy a dip in the water? Bracing but warmer than the Irish Sea and so good this time of day," he murmured.

"I should have brought my costume."

"You don't really need a costume," he replied softly.

There was silence for a good half-minute. She turned and looked into his dark brown eyes, sand caught in his beard and his hair blown out of place, and she was no better. Those eyes looked exceedingly naughty and her heart raced stupidly. Her quick brain suddenly flashed through all the occasions of late when she had ended up naked with bad men, as Amélie had put it in her usual direct way, but never in the end really did the deed. What about a reverse polarity effect, ending up naked with a good man and doing it? ... She thought of Philippe and Olga. The thought of the two of them making love all day long prancing around the Siberian forest had constantly lurked in her mind. She didn't want revenge, rather just a mild mathematical even-up of the dice.

"Why not, but you first and I'll consider how to follow."

He laughed loudly, kicked off his sandals then ran crazily towards the water, shouting and creating a racket, simultaneously pulling off his tee-shirt and dropping his jeans and boxer shorts, clumsily kicking them away onto the sand. She gazed, mesmerised, at the increasingly unclothed Giles until the sight of his bare but white and ample hairy rear, gave her another sharp intake of breath, before he ran into the waves and dived in headlong underneath the blue, clear water, finally emerging, spluttering and shouting. He had the most gorgeous legs; she hadn't quite seen the rest.

"Come on Lauren, it's really lovely in here."

She decided to do exactly the same and ran towards the water, shouting stupidly. She pulled off her tee-shirt and unhooked her bra, throwing them at the sand on top of his jeans. He stopped splashing and stared incredulous, not believing for a moment that Lauren would really do such a thing, when her skinny jeans and skimpy underwear followed suit, after an energetic wriggle. She grinned and felt amazingly empowered and powerful, exactly as she had done with Luis that time in Palermo in the secret room when she stripped for him. But then she was drunk and probably also drugged. Here she was quite the opposite. Sober, confident and she didn't care.

Giles was mesmerised. He had always suspected Lauren had an awesome body and had often thought happy fantasies of her, but was totally blown away by her all over tanned nakedness, actually there in front of him. She caught his reaction, loving it as ever with a man at that crucial point and vulnerable with desire. She ran in screaming too quick for him to gaze too long, as the sharp cold of the water caught her breath sharply, but then she threw herself over the waves and dived in fully underneath, swimming vigorously towards him, thinking immediately of that fun time she had once with Annabella.

They began frolicking and laughing. He started splashing her all over and she responded the same as they giggled and played like children in the waves, racing each other to a rock further out. He was a strong swimmer but she beat him, of course, much to his dismay. She had been a champion surfer and swimmer at university. Then she dived under the water as he frantically looked to where she was, before she emerged behind him and jumped onto his back, pressing her breasts into his neck. He reached back and grabbed her and they fell headlong under the water, laughing and spluttering before both came up for air opposite one another.

She pulled her long wet hair back from her face. In a split second they were locked in each other's arms. She pulled his head towards hers and their lips met with a passion she had fantasised about all night as Philippe was snoring noisily, keeping her awake. His hands were all over her body, feeling, and touching her bottom and thighs, his eyes wild, gazing avidly at her breasts and darkened nipples as she pushed her hands over his wet, hairy chest and into his heavy beard. She felt him instantly against her. He was big, hard, and erect. She grabbed down into the water with both hands and grasped him firmly, feeling him gently everywhere underneath, right back into his anus, fondling his balls as he groaned and closed his eyes.

"Now, Giles," she spluttered. "Shoot in that straight line. Fuck me."

She held him tightly around his shoulders and opened her legs wide whereupon he put his hands around her bottom and pulled her right up from the ground and around his waist. He needed no guidance. His aim was a perfect first time shot. He entered her in one deep thrust as she gasped out loud with the sensation, kissing him deeply, both pushing in and out gently, already in perfect rhythm, whilst she moaned and cried with the sheer and absolute pleasure of such a wild escapade.

Visions, like a continuous film reel loop gone mad, ran crazily through her brain, first of her former husband, then Luis, then Vaag, and Philippe, followed by Annabella and Rosie and back again, but she felt no guilt with Giles. Exactly as she had felt no guilt with Mila two weeks earlier, except Mila she loved as passionately as ever. Giles she just fancied like crazy. She felt him stiffen inside; the moment had arrived for him. He had been incredibly excited which made her the same, more than any man in such a short time, even Luis. Giles came full on inside her with a series of yells and deep thrusts, pumping every millilitre out for all it was worth. He had been too quick for her, but she didn't mind. Her curiosity and burning fire, ever since the airport, had been satiated.

They uncoupled and she kissed him gently, pulling his hair back. "That was perfect, Giles. I agree wholeheartedly—an early morning fuck in the sea is definitely good for the circulation. But I do think we'd better be getting back."

His expression suddenly changed as the enormity of what had happened struck him. "Oh God, Lauren. What have I done? I never intended such a thing except in my head, shit, all the consequences ... especially Amélie?"

Lauren put her finger gently over his lips. "I intended it Giles and I wanted it," she whispered. "We're two consenting adults. Right? We don't mention this to anyone, least of all to Amélie, whose friendship and love we both value greatly and who we don't ever want to hurt. This is our secret. It's happened, it was lovely and we just carry on as normal, like the friends we are. Got it?"

Giles grinned again, slicking back his dark, floppy hair. "You're right. I haven't done it for ages, which you probably realised. My long term fiancée and I broke up eighteen months ago and I'd almost forgotten how good it felt ... you are truly an amazing woman Lauren."

"Good. That's what I always like to hear a man say and that's how you and I will remain. Remember Lady Chatterley's lover?"

He laughed loudly. She took his hand and they began walking out of the water. "Now, as it happens I think I've got a large beach towel still in Pi's saddlebag. Grab your clothes, we get dry, and this time I've remembered my hairbrush. Then we head back quickly and start breakfast before they get up, all very normal, although Marie might be awake already and wonder where I am. I need to feed those babies of mine soon."

"I think I can manage that, Lady Lauren. I'm also in the Preston amateur dramatics society, so I enjoy acting and I'm good, so the Director says."

"Excellent. Then I don't have to advise you any further do I," she said with a smile, kissing him gently. Soon they were fully dried, clothed and well brushed up. Jumping swiftly onto their horses, they headed off at a fast pace. She thought instantly of Amélie, who would certainly not be surprised but very disapproving—this was one secret she would keep delectably to herself ...

However once out of sight, someone else quietly put away their high powered camera and slid off into the obscurity of the nearby woods ...

The gushing hot water of her shower continued for minute after minute whilst she scrubbed and washed everywhere, inside and out rigorously, removing every ounce of presence of Giles from her body as thoroughly as if it was nuclear contamination. It wasn't guilt or shame for what she had done, but some form of resetting the clock. Then she could face Philippe as naturally as possible and continue where she left off the night before without distracting contaminants present. Her inner scientist, always the haven of sanctuary and comfort when an unexpected hurdle in her life arose, had gone into autopilot. This seemed the most logical and sound possibility. Hopefully, Giles was as mature in his head as his body and realise this had to be a one-off for both of them, a necessary one-off for her ... and he would be as good an actor as his word on the beach. Her female instinct felt positive on all those issues. Thank heaven she and Philippe each had their own ensuite, either side of their bedroom. She opened the window to let out the copious steam, wiped the mirror, and gazed pleasingly at her naked body, almost back in pre-triplet shape. But it was obvious Giles had liked a little bit of tummy the way he had fondled her own.

But in a lightning flash she suddenly registered alarm. They had gone all the way, and neither in the heat of passion had used contraception, something she was going to sort out with Edward Jones next visit. Fuck, just say she became pregnant again or picked up some sexually transmitted disease? Her mathematical brain consoled herself with the probability of being near enough zero for both, especially conceiving with her age and past track record—although Giles certainly gave all the appearances of quite liking the idea of fatherhood and he had certainly discharged half a gallon of the facilitating medium. She smiled. Ten years previously she too would have thought differently. She opened a cabinet and grabbed a small syringe and bottle of spermicide she had bought from the local pharmacy in the week Philippe returned but had never used the stuff in the end. Inserting the nozzle gently, she sprayed copiously, allowing the excess to drain out in the shower. Crude but about as effective as she was going to get.

Peering out of the door, she realised Philippe had woken up and was in his bathroom, his electric razor whirring. He had walked in the previous weekend from the barber in town, unexpectedly minus the sexy beard she liked, claiming it felt hot on his face His head was shaved again, just like old times. She was ambivalent. Mainly because the Philippe as was, always making decisions without consulting her and generally going his own independent way, gave very mixed memories, some good, but too many bad. She wondered all the while how long the new domesticated Dubois would last, sensing instinctively that the old wheeling and dealing ways were slowly returning. He wasn't working either. She was keeping him, which of course wasn't a problem and he did have some savings. But she knew after he bought the horses and his pickup truck that there wasn't much left in the bank. For the Philippe of old, that equilibrium point was never going to remain tenable. Most of what he had disappeared into the pocket of voracious former Russian girlfriend Olga, who seemed to have acquired an adept skill at spending other people's money, Philippe and DG both, like water flowing down a drain or else accumulating illegally what she never earned. But Lauren loved him and most importantly Philippe loved and wanted to be with his gorgeous tiny daughters. No way was she going to hurt him with her spur of the moment morning fling.

Quickly she dressed in a different white top with matching black skinny jeans and began to carefully apply her muted pink lipstick and green mascara, when his door flew open. Philippe had emerged from the shower naked but definitely appearing worse for wear. Unlike Giles he was getting past taking the hard drinking of yester-year.

"Hi darling," he grunted. "That feels better, well at least my stomach definitely does; just the head throbbing a bit. Never again, I swear. But I do like Giles, a real man's man from the services, like DG. All those stories we batted between each other. Great fun don't you think?"

She slightly shuddered inside, forcing herself back into normality, but immediately looked down his body from tip to toe making instant and inevitable comparisons. Philippe still looked pretty good for his age, slightly flabby chest, but Giles was decidedly more ... No, she had to stop that, there and then.

"Do you feel like breakfast?" she asked gently. "Someone is up already and cooking bacon and eggs, I can smell it. A long time since I've had that."

"So can I, and it's making me very hungry. Where have you been? When I woke up a few hours ago you'd disappeared and the triplets were fast asleep."

"I'm just going to feed them. Actually I went for a quick ride with Giles, only down to the beach and back. He loves horses. He's also an early riser like me, goes with his job apparently."

"I know. I suggested riding to Giles last night, definitely good for him being an outdoor man. I can see you really enjoyed riding him, Pi I mean. He can hold his drink better than me too ... age sadly I suppose. Listening to his tales, he seems to have a lot of energy for everything young men should be doing." Philippe grinned and she squirmed inside even more, but maintained a smile. This conversation was not going the way she wanted. She had to find the triplets immediately.

"Must go darling, time for the big feed. You haven't forgotten the trip later to DG's yacht for lunch have you? Then I can introduce Giles to Charlotte too which will be nice."

"No of course not. Oh, shit. Listen. Shut the door. Fuck, I need to tell you something urgent."

"What?"

"Just shut the outside door first."

She closed the door and sat down quietly on the bed, perplexed and uncomfortable although why she wasn't sure, praying he hadn't suspected anything.

"It's DG. He's ... well ... sort of in a bad shape."

She looked up wide-eyed, the last thing she expected.

"How do you mean a bad shape? What's that supposed to imply? Just tell me the facts Philippe, quick, straight and logical," she replied brusquely, irritated that whatever it was Charlotte hadn't told her and as usual she was the last to know yet again.

"Okay, still the hard-hitting and unemotional engineer as ever aren't we?" he replied, biting his lip, his thumping head getting the better of him.

She stood up and started to walk out, no way was he speaking like that again but he jumped across and held her hand. "I'm sorry, totally uncalled for," he uttered, and kissed her on the cheek. "DG has a bad heart. He's had angina for the last six months and is on special pills. I went with him by helicopter to see a specialist in Monaco yesterday morning and he must have a triple bypass operation as soon as possible. They booked in some potential dates there and then."

"My God, Philippe. But why didn't you tell me yesterday? In fact you almost didn't today which could have been hugely embarrassing. And why hasn't Charlotte said anything? This is terrible. I would never have guessed it, he looks so well."

"Charlotte doesn't know anything, not even the angina. I only found out because he had a bad turn a while back when we were drinking on his yacht. At least she didn't know up to last night, but I implored him to tell her the moment he got back. But knowing DG he may still be keeping it from her. This bad health thing doesn't sit well with his macho self-image. Bit of a man thing."

"That's the least important factor he should be considering. For his family's sake, Charlotte needs to know."

"But don't you be telling her, it's up to ..."

She interrupted him sharply. "Listen Philippe, I'll say this just once. If I want to tell my daughter, I will tell her, I won't be asking your permission ever," she hissed in a loud whisper. "This isn't time for a

94

slanging match. We have guests and a big family get-together later. I think we should go down quietly for breakfast. Anyway you still could have told me, even about the angina, which you knew weeks ago presumably. Getting secretive again?"

He looked over warily, a combination of sheepishness and anger at the same time. Why did Lauren always catch him out?

"Sorry, it just slipped my mind. I've been very distracted lately with politics, especially with Gabrielle since..."

"Gabrielle?" Her eyes narrowed.

"Gabrielle Legendre. She owns the building our political group meet in and provides a lot of financial support for activists and volunteer agitators."

An unfortunate feeling of déjà-vu seeped immediately into her consciousness. "So who is this woman? What does she do?"

"Gabrielle doesn't do anything. She's an heiress, not as rich as DG but not far behind. She supports politics and the arts, but especially politics. Her late husband, much older than her, died last year apparently and made a ton of money from shipping and films."

"You were saying since?"

"Since Gabrielle proposed to fund and create a new centre right party with enough time to prepare for the next Presidential election. And ... she's asked me quietly if I would like to become leader, with our Nice group forming the core ... especially as I have a good chance of being proposed for Mayor in the autumn. I've told her I won't neglect my family, especially my ..."

"Daughters, I think you were going to say. As your wife obviously has so many other far more important priorities in her life like her business that supports your lifestyle presently, then deigning to talk to her about all this and DG was *way* down the list of priorities being around the rich and tarty Gabrielle. I assume Gabrielle suggested your new, or should I say recycled image makeover?"

"Gabrielle is classy and sophisticated, Lauren, as you might expect with her aristocratic background and wealth ... I decided I need to look ... err ... more professional again. Anyway I've apologised, but getting into politics is really important to me."

"Okay, I think we've said enough. I'm going to breakfast. At least I don't have to fund your political ambitions like the rest of your life. I suggest now we pull ourselves together; the girls will be hungry. We have guests to entertain and when we meet Charlotte later, we leave it to her and DG to explain at a suitable opportunity how he is and what he's going to do."

He nodded, and walked straight back into the bathroom.

She caught sight of her red face in the mirror, drew breath and wished she could make a restore point in her life to twenty-four hours before, like she did with her laptop when things turned ugly on the screen. After dabbing water on her cheeks and forehead she walked out, catching Jesse in the corridor racing to the bedrooms with three bottles of milk.

"They've just woken up, Lauren. I assumed you wouldn't want to breastfeed this morning?"

Lauren smiled, she wanted to breastfeed more than anything else. "Put all the bottles back in the fridge, Jesse. I must pump some more tomorrow actually. No, I'll see to them myself. I'm going to feed them all in the next three quarters of an hour. You go down to breakfast and relax. I think Giles is cooking. You haven't met him yet and probably Amélie will be up soon."

"Actually, Amélie is feeding in her room. I helped change Leonora and Caroline. They are such beautiful, well behaved babies and with the same stunning looks as their mother. I think Amélie is very impressed with the organisation in here around the babies after I told her what Marie and I do with you ... she says it's making her think. She said she'd be down in an hour. I'll go and join Marie."

Lauren reflected ruefully, wondering if she may yet win the bet ... she desperately needed to talk to Amélie one to one, about her instincts.

A second round of bacon and scrambled eggs with tomatoes, mushrooms and hash browns began to take shape as Marie and Giles, in a masterful union of culinary coordination around Lauren's giant Aga, began serving up large platefuls. Normality seemed to have returned. Lauren and Amélie were chatting happily at the large table, the five baby girls lying together in a huge playpen, gurgling happily, pointing and chattering as they obviously were already recognising faces, sounds and their surroundings. Marie was showing Philippe and Jesse the galley proofs and book cover designs for her latest novel, now near to final publication, comments flying around the table. Philippe tapped Lauren gently to catch her attention, pointing to the babies.

"That collection of tiny beauties are really taking an interest now in everything. I'm sure Magda was trying to have a conversation with me last night when I put her to bed."

"Yes, darling, something along the lines of 'when are you going to give up on putting my nappy on back to front, Papa, then I might stop crying?'" Lauren replied, with a grin, determined to dispel the earlier acrimony between them.

Amélie and Giles roared laughing as Jesse looked on, unsure what to make of the banter and deciding to stay quiet. Marie giggled; she knew the special relationship between Magdaline and her father.

"Tell you what Philippe, there's some combination of devastating brains and beauty with those five," Amélie remarked. "Just look at the way they eye each other and then coyly glance at you and Giles ... you'd better start saving up hard because your three are going to cost you a mint when they get to their teens, never mind the clothes and the horses. There will be a lot of hearts broken along the way by them all too, if their mother is anything to go by."

Lauren started to clap, shouting 'yes definitely' in agreement and the five tiny girls looked in unison and tried to copy with big grins, but rather mixed results, Geraldine was making the best effort by far with Caroline, next to her, not far behind, encouraged even more as everybody laughed.

"Talking of horses, I understand you were out on an early ride this morning, Lauren, whilst the rest of us were snoring peacefully?" Amélie suddenly chipped in.

"Well not quite everyone, Giles came as well. I caught him in the kitchen nursing his head over a glass of alka-seltzer and reckoned some fresh air would be better, didn't I Giles," she responded, desperately trying not to sound forced or wooden, knowing how astute Amélie could be on any nuance, expected or otherwise, especially with her.

"Yes, it was great," Giles replied. "Felt like I was back at home, the sea air did my head a power of good, which is why I'm on my second helping of bacon and eggs. And Marie, those hash browns are delicious, I have never tasted anything like them. Where did you learn to cook like that?"

"Afghanistan,"

"Really? You were on active service? There, in that hell hole? Gosh."

"Marie is a woman of many skills and might also have a few tales to tell, Giles, probably matching yours, even when you're sober," Philippe added with a smile. "I'll just make some more coffee."

"None for Lauren and me, Philippe. We're just going down to the local pharmacy, I need a couple of things," Amélie suddenly uttered, glancing at Lauren who knew that look immediately ... Amélie either knew, surmised or had put two and two together and was making five as she always did. But they needed to talk anyway. This was a good opportunity and anyway, she rethought quickly, there was no way anything untoward had been revealed so she could relax. Giles had been as good as his word.

They didn't need their jackets; the early morning chill had morphed into very pleasant warmth as they strolled out of the gate and down the path towards the town centre.

"Isn't this weather adorable? That was a good ruse to get us some time on our own. I know a lovely coffee shop on the front that does a mean cappuccino, exactly as you like it. We've got a couple of hours before we need to be ready for lunch with Charlotte, and I must tell you something, which needs to be kept secret."

"I know all about that actually Lauren and I agree it does need to be kept strictly between you and me."

"You do? Gosh, as always I'm last in line and I was pretty harsh on Philippe, but that's what I wanted to talk about anyway."

Amélie ruminated and then changed tack, realising they were likely at cross-purposes.

"We do need to go to the pharmacy first."

"Really? I thought you were joking. Okay, we need to take a right turn down that street, pharmacy is at the bottom. What do you need? Is it for the twins? I've probably got whatever anyway."

"No it's for you?"

"Me?"

"Yes, the morning after pill before you're too late. You fucked the backside off him didn't you—the last thing you want is a repeat right now, the unintended sequel Vaag Two. Well?"

Lauren fell silent and felt a flush of red blood run up her body from bottom to top. Shit. Why could she never fool her best friend? She'd really tried hard through the whole morning. "Yes," she muttered guiltily into the ground as they continued strolling.

"And was it good? And I'm not judging you either."

Lauren stayed silent for a moment before breathing deep. "Fabulous, raw and untrammelled in the sea naked."

They stopped. Amélie turned and grinned. "Really? Gosh. That even beats my mile-high on that plane to Stockholm!" She put her arms around Lauren and hugged her as they both laughed with the relief.

"I thought we were starting confessionals over coffee. How on earth did you know?" Lauren asked, still puzzled.

"Must admit, you were good earlier, very good, both of you. I would never have guessed except ..."

"For?"

"In the airport. Do you know the last time I saw that look on your face when you met Giles? When I fixed you up on your first date in Paris with your last husband. It took you three hours from memory to complete the task and for the next three days he walked around like a cowboy who'd lost his horse. A little bit of present day extrapolation and an unassailable hypothesis immediately locked itself into my analytical brain."

Lauren giggled loudly. "Fuck ... motherhood hasn't dulled your touch; you're as pin-point sharp as ever."

"Nor has it dulled your libido? This is your best friend at your side, never condemnatory or reproaching, well only occasionally. I may not have

Annabella's caring skills but I probably come a close second. I understand two things. Fucking Giles is a no-brainer. *I've* got too much to lose on the doorstep so good for you. But more importantly, I sense that Philippe certainly embraces adoring fatherhood, but some of the old ways have been creeping back? Her name?"

"Gabrielle Legendre, a local heiress, funding his new political party they are forming together. But that wasn't the reason I fucked Giles. I just wanted him badly. My instincts had however with Philippe been confirmed this morning as we got up, when he brought her up and I know that Olga look. Although I'm not sure he's having an affair, but I wouldn't be surprised anymore. I still love him, I let him back into my life and I really did believe it was going to be all roses around the cottage door, but deep down I still don't trust him ... and I never will ... and he has that restless look again, only this time it's not energy. Politics has become the obsessive deal making venture."

"For which Philippe may in fact become very successful. He's a consummate networker, arrogant, good looking, telegenic and he tells a good story. People like and respect him ... the perfect politician. My advice? Carry on with your marriage and the children as if nothing happened and continue to focus on your work, because after the knocks you and he have had then trust is something you'll both need to take on the chin. Sometimes it's good, sometimes not. Same with Rufus and me. You and I both have to be realists and enjoy as much as we can from what we have. None of it will ever be perfect. You've evened up the score with Giles, who cares? Philippe is certainly going nowhere that's obvious, he adores his new daughters and loves his settled life here."

Lauren thought and felt much better, and they'd reached the pharmacy. "I'd better go in and get that pill first. Actually, your Annabella caring bit is really quite good, I never would have thought of that. Thanks for watching my back. What you've said makes sense. I don't know what I'd do without you Amélie."

"Well someone has to ... Mila won't." She wished immediately she could have started that sentence again.

"How do you mean?"

"Only joking, a figure of speech—you know how I am with the Serbian sleuth. Then let's go and get that coffee. Now we can sit in silence and admire the view. Confessionals are done."

Lauren laughed. "Yes, but Mila's not all bad, believe me."

Amélie was not convinced in the slightest but this was not the time for even a hint of what she had heard from Charlotte.

The Café Marie Antoinette was already crowded with a mix of people. Tourists were downloading as much as they could on their laptops and phones with the free Wifi, old men in groups played cards and a noticeably affluent set of young people, obvious from their dress and the sports cars outside, relaxed and chatted. A group of cyclists took up three of the best tables. Lauren grabbed an empty table on the front balcony, facing the sea. The wind was very light in their sheltered spot and the growing morning heat was becoming noticeable in the strong sun. The waiter immediately raised the wide umbrella and took away Amélie's order of two large cappuccinos and a couple of French pastries, with Lauren suddenly adding a jug of iced water.

They both looked out to sea where the wind was stronger, sufficient for the local surfers to be out skating like crazy across the waves. Lauren had decided inside the pharmacist not to mention DG's potential heart issue. If Amélie knew or didn't know, being close now to Charlotte, it wouldn't matter because both of them knew enough of how each other thought and acted, especially after what they had shared in work and personal situations over the last twenty odd years. They implicitly understood that family discretion time was paramount when everyone meets up later.

As they began to devour their pastries, Lauren noticed Amélie was being atypically quiet and thoughtful and staring out to sea, always a sign of something significant about to be said, whether good or bad. She grabbed a glass of water and downed the pill in one gulp.

Amélie smiled. "That should do the trick. Anyway with your track record, my probability calculation is less than one percent of one percent even taking into account the likely mega-billion of tadpole output of the young buck."

"I put paid to a load of them too with a sluice of spermicide, so downgrade that estimate by another thousandth of a percent please." Lauren mouthed, tucking greedily again into her apple and cream pastry.

Amélie laughed loudly. "The things that two female mathematical physicists talk about on holiday would only ever be believed by ..."

"Two other female physicists of course. Good job Svet and Charlotte aren't here. Then everyone would be leaving fast!" Lauren added with a giggle. She began supping her hot cappuccino. "Anyway, what are you deep in thought about? Motherhood definitely suits the Countess. You're much more organised and confident than ever you claimed you wouldn't be."

"Yes, I suppose I've surprised myself and Rufus too, who is I must say in all truth, turning out like Philippe to be a very commendable father which was more than one would have said about the other potential phantom claimant, thank goodness. But let's be honest Lauren. Neither of us became CEOs because we couldn't get our shit together."

"True, so?"

"How are you going to feel about handling your conflict of feelings?"

Lauren stared. The ever abstruse Amélie was going into full flow again. Why was it that she could solve the most difficult mathematical problems in the world but when it came to her best friend, she was always way off the starting grid? "Sorry, but as usual I need a beginner for ten, and yes, I know I have a pea brain for emotional intelligence."

"Because ... I've agreed to a year's secondment if the body is pleasing?"

"Secondment of what?"

"Fuck me, Lauren. Forget the pea, ant size is more apt. One consequence you never thought of. Not what, but who. Giles or have we forgotten that I promised Charlotte I may have a suitable solution for her exotic estate management requirement?"

"Yes, of course I have. Hell fire. He could be around for some time if she likes the look of him."

"And is Charlotte not going to like the look of him?"

Lauren went suddenly very quiet and ponderous. There were times when she truly begged desperately for her heart not to rule her head and her logic, and think scientifically and carefully through cause and effect ... and this situation, very sadly, wasn't one of them. "Charlotte thinks Giles is some old and miserable retired codger and Giles thinks Charlotte is a speccy, studious little school girl at a French boarding school."

Amélie looked up, realised instantly what the pair of them had unwittingly unleashed and immediately looked down and quietly continued with her coffee and pastry. Lauren stared disconsolately out to sea, her mathematical brain kicking into gear. She needed a solution fast which she could manage ... or did she? Her lightning quick mind was running through all kinds of scenarios, none of them especially pleasant and some distinctly explosive. Then she realised ... the deciding variable, which made her equation either crash and burn all in its path or simply remain tacitly benign and insoluble. And that was her feelings for Giles. She had none, except for his large warm penis. She smiled with a very wide grin.

"Okay laughing girl, have you modelled every possible nuclear meltdown situation then?"

"Of course. But you did the decontamination earlier. The logical conclusion is this. Giles was a necessary one morning stand. Very nice, but that's it, all done and dusted and he knows and accepts that. If Charlotte likes him, well fine. He's a nice guy, reliable, hardworking, and enthusiastic and could really get her new business off the ground as he's done with your estate. So allowing him a year off is a great opportunity and a commendable gesture on your part. I'm sure he'll get on well with DG. Charlotte isn't like me ..."

"Complicated you mean?"

Lauren smiled. "Definitely not. She's loyal and committed to DG and simply wants a new work challenge to occupy her active mind, just as I believe you will too in due course. I've already chosen my Luddite dress incidentally. They're opening a branch in Nice, after some subtle encouragement by me and Mila. So the idea that I might be in some love triangle competition with my own daughter is so ludicrous as to be totally laughable; or more importantly not logically tenable. In the end Amélie, I learned one very important aspect from the Olga crisis, which I know you understand well. I'm a financially and if necessary, emotionally independent woman, with money and my own business. I don't need men, least of all Giles."

Amélie put down her coffee and smiled. "Well that's all sorted then," she replied quietly, looking straight into Lauren's triumphant gaze. "I do love your quick, firewalled, logical behavioural analyses, laid out like an incontrovertible Annalen der Physic science paper of Einstein."

"I can detect your cynical tone of old, Amélie," Lauren fired back laughing, "meaning you obviously know more and are not letting on. However, as far as I'm concerned this hypothesis is nailed shut. None of them can touch me in the end."

Amélie patted her hand gently. "I know. Me neither, and we have our tribes too don't forget. Seriously, now you've downed that pill, it is time to move on home and have some fun at lunchtime when Giles and Charlotte finally meet each other on the yacht."

"Actually ... you don't know do you."

"Know what?"

"About DG and his recently diagnosed heart condition. He may have to have a triple bypass, I find it quite terrible. How will Charlotte cope? I'm assuming she knows now, the news only became clear to DG with Philippe yesterday when they met a specialist in Monaco."

Amélie reflected carefully. She had no idea, but she was rather too familiar with triple bypass operations.

"No, I didn't know but both of us do understand how practical and organised Charlotte is and how she instantly rationalises and sorts out a clear working pathway when she meets a problem, exactly like you do. Anyway, I understand quite a lot about that particular malady. Rufus had a precautionary bypass operation in his early twenties. There's a congenital heart issue in the male side of the family and his father had a successful triple bypass in his fifties and he lived to nearly ninety, shagging everything under twenty on the estate that moved, before and after. And Rufus does pretty well too. Nowadays, with the way technology has moved on, such procedures are almost routine ... I suspect maybe you're making more of it in your head than you need to. I would assume DG has told her now ...

but he may not have yet ... I suggest we just let it ride. That's a private issue between them. But Charlotte will undoubtedly cope, believe me."

"Rufus? Gosh, I would never have known, I had no idea. That's what Philippe said too. I gave him what for, not telling me before breakfast. You're right."

Amélie breathed a sigh of relief. "One more quick decaffeinated coffee, then we'd better head back and feed. But first I want to hear all about Luddite and what you're going to wear to this yacht do. I've not brought much and am hugely annoyed now with myself, so I might have to borrow something, like I used to."

Lauren smiled and waved to the waiter. "No problem, I had a restock a few weeks ago after a blowout with Mila and Juliette and have a lovely Versace summer dress which you might now just about get into."

"Cheeky!"

Just before noon, they all tumbled out of Lauren's SUV and Philippe's pickup truck onto the quayside to wait for a motor launch to take them a few miles out to sea where DG had moored his yacht, well away from the crowds and the other boats. Marie and Jesse soon bundled the five babies, dressed in their best outfits, into the two buggies.

Lauren, her long, blond hair blowing in the breeze and Amélie, her extra coppery short, spiky hair, well gelled, wore complimentary yellow and red Versace summer dresses, and had decided to mix all the babies up, with Leonora joining Magdaline and Geraldine, whilst Caroline sat happily with Eveline, the three extroverts and the two introverts together. Marie and Jesse, in their smart trouser suits and pristine blouses looked equally stunning and made up, whilst the two males, in their new jeans and summer shirts, jackets over their shoulders as they had been told only smart casual, simply stood next to each and gazed in awe at the phalanx of gorgeous, busy women.

Philippe directed Giles towards the view of a somewhat derelict area and neglected frontage where groups of men stood fishing, a long way down towards the end of the busy quayside. "Our new party has made the transformation of that former trading zone into a new marina and tourist area; bring in some needed regeneration to this part of the town."

"Lauren mentioned you were active in local politics, what party is it? I'm not that familiar with the French system."

"You won't have heard of the Liberal French Democratic Party yet. We've literally just launched and I hope to be leading the LFDP from a local base in due course, once we firm up a more comprehensive manifesto. We believe in enterprise with compassion—there's too much dogmatic extremism in France presently, for lots of reasons but the effect of the socialists presently in government is catastrophic for the economy. Business is reeling from ridiculous taxation. Time to capture the centre right ground again."

"Yes, I can understand your motive, especially for small businesses. I don't get involved in local politics in the UK. Too be honest I'm a bit of an environmentalist, a green save the planet supporter, especially green energy, sort of goes with my job. Big oil and gas is becoming increasingly detrimental for our future climate in my view and the stuff should be left in the ground."

Philippe smiled, but said nothing. He was done with those arguments and preferred to forget his past. "In case Amélie forgot to mention it, but DG is an old fashioned oil man right down to his cowboy boots, that's where he made his money in Texas. He's a big guy like you and gets short tempered on environmental issues. Be tactful, Giles."

"Of course, appreciate the heads-up. I only surmised he was a very wealthy friend, owning a yacht. Tact and diplomacy, especially when working for a big aristocratic landowner, is something I've learned to be good at for many years."

"Excellent. I'm sure you'll like DG, another Special Forces man. He was a young US Colonel in Vietnam. But this time both you and I need to go steady because DG will drink both of us well under the table, as I know to my cost!" Philippe grinned and slapped his new friend lightly over the shoulder and pointed some distance out to sea, as a large boat slowly approached.

"Here, give me that lipstick quickly, I need a refresh already," Lauren whispered, also watching the motor launch approach with Amélie. "What did you actually say to Giles about Charlotte?"

"Nothing at all in the end. I only mentioned to Charlotte I might have some ideas concerning her manager problem. Giles had asked Rufus and me a while back about having the equivalent of a 'gap year' and to learn some new land management skills abroad if he could fix something up. He was willing to take a year off without pay, but once Rufus had quietly identified and was satisfied of a potential temporary successor, basically Giles's deputy, we agreed to pay his secondment anyway as if it were a full time course. Then interestingly, Charlotte reveals her vineyard and olive grove purchase and there you have it ... an ideal match and everybody wins. Giles doesn't know all this; I thought we'd surprise him here."

"What if Giles takes the job but doesn't want to come back?"

"You know the code Lauren that we've both adhered to throughout our careers. Someone may be desirable but is never indispensable. She looked at Lauren all over and grinned. "Even Giles."

"Don't you dare go there Amélie, case closed, agreed?" Lauren replied sharply, not wishing to be reminded yet again of her faux pas.

"Of course," Amélie replied, amused with Lauren's serious expression and kissing her on the cheek. "Your secret remains safe and sound with me," she whispered, mischievously.

"That's what worries me?" Lauren countered, finally breaking out in a wide grin deciding that what's done is done, so what the hell. "I vaguely mentioned Giles to Charlotte but she immediately inferred that he was a retired pensioner, you want to get shut of. Giles knows I have a daughter but assumed she was at school. He obviously has no idea of my age."

"Well there you go cougar."

Lauren glared mildly. "Actually, how old is Giles?"

"You really want to know?"

"Yes, of course I do."

"Well ... he's in his twenty-ninth year, almost the same as Charlotte. I assume from your face you thought he was somewhat older. I agree, he does have a rather more mature and experienced disposition with all that manly confidence and literary bushy beard, helpful sometimes." She burst out laughing again. "Sorry Lauren, honestly that's it, I promise. No more. Anyway the boat's coming in, I assume for us. We'll know very shortly what he thinks of Charlotte. Come on cheer up, it's a bit of a laugh now. You've sold your wild oats, satiated your curiosities and got over it. Now we move to phase two. I'm just going to grab the triplet buggy, you take the other two."

Lauren nodded. But inside her mind, those over-active neurons were once more running hell for leather through all kinds of illogical and heretical things. What if the jealously Venn diagrams did intersect? Emotional arrogance and waving her independence card were all well and good, but she knew she had gone way too far in a lapse of madness ... whatever. She had to row back the fantasies and not jeopardise, under any circumstances, her most important relationships she had worked so hard to secure ... her immediate family.

She suddenly felt a hand lightly touch her shoulder.

"Darling, something has come up really urgent. Gabrielle has managed to get Richard Devereux, the Minister of Interior Affairs, who is apparently desperate to resign and change political sides, into a meeting with the Mayor of Nice. See that two storey building at the far side of the roundabout? They're in there and she's just phoned me, desperate for me to come, she's feeling out of her depth. We should be able to persuade him to become a founder, with us I mean for the LFDP. This could be a real coup. I'll ask the boat to come back for me in an hour, that's all I need. Is that okay? No way am I going to miss the rest of today with all the family."

She looked at him warily, her demeanour inside ill at ease. He had that can't keep still air of old once again. Fuck Gabrielle, with the same sentiment as fuck Olga. She knew it was all returning but there was nothing she could do. She simply had to trust him and get on with her life. She glanced at Amélie, busy with the babies, Giles and Jesse getting them all onboard the motor cruiser. "Okay, go on then, I understand. But promise me, you'll be on the yacht as soon as possible?"

"Thanks. I promise darling. You know my persuading skills; I'll be in and out. See you soon."

She casually watched him run off towards the building, his expression turned immediately to the political job in hand. It was obvious he loved his daughters and probably her, but family life would ultimately, as it always had even whilst Svet grew up, be an irritation getting in the way which had to be managed as best as possible. Thinking he would change now was a pipedream; his character was encased inside his DNA. She had married an inveterate wanderer and she just had to get on with it, seeking compromises that would work for both of them. The best thing she ever did was to buy him totally out of Cassini ... that was hers and hers alone.

"Are you coming or what?" She turned to see Amélie next to her and everybody else on board waiting. "Where's he off to? Don't tell me, I think I can probably guess. Never mind that, let's go and have some fun with DG."

"He'll be back in an hour ... urgent politics, all a delicate time right now with the LFDP setting up."

"As ever Lauren, come on."

"Well little feller, it's a real pleasure meeting you," DG began in his booming Texan voice, stretching out his large hand to Giles. They shook vigorously and then DG realised as Giles stood up properly from the steps onto the deck. "Well, darn it all, Philippe was right. I should be calling you big feller from now on, almost my size young man, not many can say that." He looked at Lauren, Marie and Jesse bringing the babies across. "Say ladies, if you go into the big lounge there, that's where we'll be setting up for lunch and we can have a few pre-drinks first."

"Okay DG? Wow it looks lovely in there."

"Sure is Lauren, just got that lot refurbished, no expense spared," DG hollered back. "Will be hammering away at that old piggy bank again next week to pay for it all. Say, where's Amélie? Didn't fall in did she?"

"Not quite DG, she had to rush to the loo. The ride across was a bit choppy for her and she turned a paler shade of green! She hasn't got her sea-legs yet," Lauren replied with a smirk.

"Darn, but she'll be fine on this old boat, all computer stabilised and high-tech, smooth as a baby's bottom. We'll pick up little ol' Philippe later. He rang me to say he got a bit diverted. He's going down a storm Lauren with the local business people ... makes a better politician than an oil man, I can tell you." He roared at his own joke as Lauren joined in. She was determined to have fun.

DG turned again to Giles. "My wife has just gone to fetch Arthur George, born same time as those gorgeous triplets. Quite a tribe we got now on board, don't yer think? You like kids, Giles?"

"Sure do DG," Giles replied, already feeling at home in DG's company.

"Let's go join the ladies in the lounge now, and I'll fetch us a rather nice malt, all the way from Kentucky to start the day properly. You game? Philippe will have to wait 'till later."

"Yes sir, DG, absolutely," Giles replied, his eyes widening as he finally looked properly up and down the five hundred feet plus super-yacht with three main decks and even housing a helicopter pad. This was a man with a serious cache of money.

Everybody was soon sat down in the luxurious armchairs and chatting happily as Lauren took charge and handed out a tray of nibbles. They all began helping themselves to drinks, laid out ready with an ice bucket on the drinks cabinet. Marie set up the portable play pen in the corner and the babies were soon happy and contented, having fared far better than Amélie across the water. Her colour quickly returned along with her smile when she heard how smooth the voyage of the mother-ship would be, but the double breakfast helping of Giles's bacon and eggs and a gooey pasty to follow hadn't helped.

Whilst the general hubbub punctuated with DG's booming vocal chords continued, the door at the end quietly opened and Charlotte walked in, immediately setting down Arthur George happily amongst his five new girlfriends. Lauren looked up, as did Giles.

His mouth dropped like a stone as he gazed at Charlotte's face who had walked over to DG and given him a peck on the cheek. "My word, Lauren. You never told me you had a twin sister," he stuttered.

Amélie looked across, glanced at Lauren and smirked. She could read Giles's mind like a book. Lauren of course, was decidedly chuffed as ever with such a remark.

Charlotte turned, frowned and wondered immediately who on earth this guy was but DG caught her disdained look and intervened, realising she had no idea. "Say Charlotte, can I introduce you to Amélie's friend, sorry I mean he works for her. This is Giles, her estate manager."

Giles immediately appeared puzzled and confused, but he was matched equally by Charlotte who looked over at Amélie and then Lauren, totally unsure of who was what and where.

"Charlotte?" Giles uttered and held out his hand as usual.

"Giles?" Charlotte replied equally bemused.

Amélie decided it was her turn to intervene and stir the pot a little more. "Remember Giles, you're not in England."

He grinned, stepped forward, held her waist and kissed her gently on the right cheek and then the left.

"And I'm American and not French, Giles, but that was done quite exquisitely," Charlotte jested, her eyes flashing, and her sharp brain having cottoned on to the Lauren and Amélie joint conspiracy. "I thought you were a retired English pensioner, bald, no teeth and smoked a pipe."

Just as quick, his actor pretensions revving into overdrive, Giles responded. "And I thought you were a fifteen year old, pigtailed virgin, with thick bottle lens glasses and long white socks. Someone has been telling us both porkies."

Everyone in the room began to laugh uproariously. "Hell fire and damnation, that sure as heck sounds funny, but I'm at my wits end to know what on earth is going on," DG shouted, his voice booming over everyone's. "But by the look of it, I can see my mother-in-law and her best friend are the source of the plot, and anything these ladies cook up I sure as hell will be at the far end of the queue in knowing what it's all about, outwitted again. Even my own wife has worked it out before I even got an inkling!"

They roared even louder at DG's apparent discomfort from the wiles of his favourite women. The other door suddenly opened and ten year old Kat and Lexi, who had been playing on the small tennis court behind, ran in and hugged Lauren, begging to know what all the racket and laughter was about. Amélie shot a surreptitious glance over at Lauren and also realised, her earlier instinct had a validity she hoped wasn't going to materialise. Despite the forced laughter, she knew her best friend intimately for far too many years to be fooled. The eyes always gave Lauren away. And they were greener than ever.

Once the noise died down, Charlotte waved the twins towards her who scampered over and grabbed her tightly around the waist, grinning up at Giles who still had his mouth half open. "Giles, these are my two daughters, Kathryn and Alexis, so just to be clear, so you will never be confused again. I don't have a twin sister and Lauren is not only my wonderful mother but a fabulous grandma as well."

"You betcha, Giles, whoever you are," Lexi responded cheekily with a flirty grin.

"Hey Mom, I sooh like Giles's accent. He's real posh English like in Upstairs Downstairs we used to watch in Dallas," Kat chipped in, not intending to be outdone by her sister. More laughter resounded across the room.

"Okay you two, that's enough now," Charlotte replied sharply. "Giles may be coming to work for us, so behave please."

"Am I?" Giles uttered, now totally baffled and looked at Amélie for salvation, continuing to display no response.

Lauren however was boiling up inside literally and she could feel her face reddening and desperately was trying to dispel any sign. She really had to drive away all feelings of jealousy towards her own daughter. It was obvious the way Charlotte reacted that she found Giles highly attractive, most women would. He was innately that kind of man and didn't have to try. Shit, Giles was even the same age as Charlotte but earlier he'd just fucked Grandma. Holy hell, what had she been doing? Her left brain was

112

busy rationalising and ordering up all the long list of logical arguments she had cleverly enunciated earlier about why she wouldn't ever feel that way. Her right brain kept humming the same old tune over and over ... Giles was mine ... and I want more.

"DG, I'm just going to see whether our chefs, Raol and José, have done the lunch and then we can bring it over," Charlotte said, turning to her husband. "Marcie is with them. Looks to me like everyone is getting hungry."

"Sure thing honey bunch, me especially," DG shouted back and continued pouring out cokes for Kat and Lexi.

Charlotte beckoned to Giles as she marched out. "Come with me and I'll show you the rest of the yacht on the way down and we can have a chat."

Lauren's eyes narrowed, but Giles was up like a coiled spring and traipsed happily out of the door. "Lauren, it's feeding time?" Jesse whispered to her. "Charlotte has given me a bottle. Lauren are you okay, you've gone into a sort of daze?"

"Yes, she's fine," Amélie said, cutting in. "Me too Jesse, we can have a tribal eat-in I reckon. Lauren, are you coming?"

"Yes, coming." Lauren replied disgruntled. She wanted to continue with the girls for six months. She knew it made sense and she still had plenty of milk, but was beginning to question whether she had the patience. Three babies were definitely becoming wearisome at times. She also knew Charlotte had decided to stop breast feeding already as she was struggling with producing enough milk ... Arthur George seemed to be a chip off the old DG block and had happily taken to bottles.

Striding fast with his long legs, Giles soon caught up with Charlotte, admiring her svelte figure from behind in her short, sleeveless dress. They stopped under an awning to gaze over the Mediterranean to the horizon. The yacht, anchored in a quiet spot with sea all around them, was motionless but no boats or land could be seen anywhere and the breeze had nicely died down. It was a great setting to relax. He looked up at the sun loungers and umbrellas, laid out on the deck above. Charlotte caught his anticipating gaze, laughed and motioned to the bench.

"Let's grab a seat for a minute ... I want to ask you something whilst I've got the chance. If you want beach shorts for later, I'm sure we can find you a pair," she added, eyeing up his tan, obviously a man who likes the sun like her.

"Actually, I always sunbathe commando, don't need shorts just lots of oil," he replied then blushed, wishing he could kick himself for being idiotic and not thinking, a bad habit with women.

Charlotte was totally unfazed. "Now that would be interesting Giles. You'll tell me when won't you?" she said with a wide grin. "And my mother of course too."

His mouth dropped, not what he expected. Suddenly he thought of Lauren and then Charlotte on either side of him, the three of them ... he stopped. This was not appropriate and shuffled his position on the bench which had suddenly become uncomfortable and stared at the boards. Charlotte, as ever astute, was very happy with that response.

She had already decided the moment she realised what the huge joke was about earlier that Giles would actually be perfect and she would pay Amélie for the secondment too, despite her generous offer. Like Lauren she always needed complete independence. Giles, interestingly, reminded her of Lyell but with the missing bits filled in. He was as big and beefy, but sharp as mustard with an intelligent, attractive face, and she rather adored those twinkly English laughing eyes and that great bushy beard, definitely a rural loving dude.

Giles looked back and grinned sensing Charlotte was idly staring at him. He couldn't believe Charlotte was Lauren's daughter and struggled to tally her age with what he assumed was Lauren's although he realised he didn't actually know that either.

"I researched a lot about the eco-system and natural habitat of this area, and the Mediterranean, the fishing, the sea-birds and the struggling balance of man versus nature," he began. "It was my dissertation for a part time Masters degree in farm management. I spent a lot of time collecting data between Marseille and Montpellier. I was working for the Earl then, err ...

Rufus's father before he and Amélie got together." He talked in detail about the specific flora and vegetation of the region and the wild animals still in the forests inland.

Charlotte listened, fascinated. She wanted to hear more, a lot more from this desirable man. Suddenly she gently put her fingers to his lips. "Shush for a minute, you can continue later, we're running out of time. I must get this lunch sorted out. Would you like to work with me here for a year, Giles? The secondment that I know Amélie has promised you? I've just bought a huge rundown vineyard and olive grove behind my estate, near Lauren's place but up on the hill, and we could make it all happen again and become truly commercial. The land has got great potential. Doesn't that sound an exciting project?"

In an instant Giles realised that Charlotte had exactly the same wild enterprising spirit and attractive tempestuousness as Lauren. They were each intoxicating and together completely irresistible. How could he turn this opportunity down? Thank you Amélie, another amazing woman ... In the space of twenty-four hours he had rediscovered his ardour and passion for beautiful women, after so long since Yolanda left him. It had been like being out in the wilderness, dedicated only to work, but now the spark was reignited. He nodded but remained puzzled.

"I'll answer you very briefly," Charlotte began, almost eerily tuned into his thoughts. "Lauren had me in her early teens. It was a passionate affair with a much older man, an artist, which never gelled for many reasons, a tragedy perhaps of a different era than you and I know or understand. I was immediately adopted, given away to an American couple who were subsequently killed in a plane crash. I too had the twins in my teens, another passionate affair which ended tragically when their father accidentally shot himself. My mother and I independently pulled ourselves up by our bootstraps. We're clever, independent and individualistic women, Giles, with a murky past and an unconventional present. You see, DG is the father of the man who fathered my children and now I've just borne his child, so we're complex, unpredictable and temperamental. Do you think you can handle us both then?"

He immediately thought of his early morning tryst with Lauren and shuddered inside. What was he letting himself in for? "Yes, I reckon I can," he replied slowly, before giving her a large grin.

"Excellent, then we have a deal in principle. Now we must go and find that lunch?"

"Actually, I'll catch you up, I must pop into wherever that sign is pointing downwards that says gents."

She laughed. "Okay, I'll go up one flight on the same stairs then walk towards the stern of the ship. The smell of spicy cooking will direct you. I've asked them to do us a special Moroccan chicken tagine, with a Mediterranean salad buffet, so keep sniffing and you'll find me."

"Sounds delicious Charlotte, see you in a minute."

Relieving himself of a litre of DG's Coors light beer took longer than he thought. Once on the second deck he looked up and down the vast expanse of walkway. Which way was the stern or was it aft? And they were anchored. Boats were not his forte, he much preferred attack helicopters. He sniffed hard, probably they were cooking too far away so decision time loomed. He turned left around a corner when he suddenly tripped and stumbled hard over a sack of something left stupidly in the way. As he picked himself up, the sight flashing across his view changed all the parameters of his next move. A pile of blood was oozing steadily from the sack which in reality was a male in a blue uniform, curled up motionless against the railing. A chef's hat was lying next to the lifebelts. His military training kicked in immediately and he looked around quickly and furtively. No sign of anyone, nor Charlotte. He felt the man's pulse but his instinct was correct. He was quite dead, shot in the back of the head. Giles looked carefully over the side and further up saw it. A large, motorised rubber dinghy was floating at the side of the yacht and some kind of rope ladder secured to a rail on the first deck.

He made his way stealthily along the side of the second deck, using all his knowledge of close quarter surveillance in urban street fighting areas, which he had undertaken in Helmand. At most inside that rubber dingy there would be six to eight men, hopefully less. He wished he had some weapons. All he had was his mobile phone. He had to find Charlotte. A faint whiff of tangy food filled his nostrils. He couldn't be far and further ahead saw a separate cabin area lit up and vague movement was taking place through the windows, with voices percolating and low. Whoever was onboard, they were inside. There was nobody watching outside. Approaching, he crawled under a lifeboat tarpaulin and little by little edged along underneath, a slit of light at the bottom guiding him. Cleverly this should place him at window level opposite, to be able to see better inside. He got to the end and peered through a gap. Inside stood five masked men in black, two with submachine guns, the others holding knives and pistols. At the far end of the room he could see Charlotte with a gun pointed at her head standing next to a black woman. That must be Marcie or whatever her name was. A couple of other women were also there but separated with another male chef. He wondered where any other staff or the ship's security were? Possibly DG had given them time off as the boat was anchored, until later. These intruders whoever they were, must have known there was little or no protection—a likely inside job. But what were they demanding? Charlotte and Marcie were being made to kneel and their hands tied behind their backs, execution style. Fuck ... he looked at his mobile phone, a one bar signal was showing, just, but the only number he had relevant was the desirable Marie, who last night, after they all had too much to drink, had quietly given him her details. This was his only chance. He would send her a text, she was trained security ... he was desperately outnumbered on his own but perhaps DG had some weapons somewhere. He sent the message then continued watching, weighing up how he could do something if the situation took an even worse turn.

Marie, intruders at stern kitchen, Charlotte held but fine Code Eleanor Rigby.

Back in the lounge Marie, tidying away the buggies, heard her phone ping. She watched DG gazing quietly out of the window, pouring himself another scotch. The moment she saw the text, she took a deep breath and walked across.

"DG, read this," she whispered.

He scanned the brief message and scowled. "Fuck. Darn it, we've got a situation Marie." He walked to his desk and took out a large key.

"Outside, at the back of that seat there's a large box. You'll find what you need in there, then go and find Giles. Careful mind. You know the drill."

"Sure do, DG."

"I'll get all our ladies here into a secure area and then I'll come get those pirates, leave me an AK. I'll ring security now. Damnation, the one time I give all these guys a couple hours break on land, and we get this shit, whoever they are. Anyway, go girl, no time to lose."

Marie was off like a rocket, all her special training had kicked in; this was Helmand over again. Opening the box, she pulled out a couple of pistols and stuffed them into her belt, picked out a shortened AK47, ammunition and some knives and stun grenades and began to make her way to the stern, watching all directions like a hawk.

DG got onto his mobile. "Hey Doug, where the fuck are you? Get your arse over here quick with all the boys. We got boarders in the kitchen at the far end. I'm gonna try and contain the situation."

"On our way boss, we're in a bar in the town. Now I know for sure. That arsehole Jeb I fired last week, lazy son of a bitch, I knew he was on the take. I could smell it clean over the fucker."

"You're probably right. See you shortly but take care, these bums are armed apparently."

He walked into the lounge and marched straight over to Lauren and Amélie who were preparing the babies for sleep. "Where's Jesse?"

Lauren looked up, his face was red and his expression so pained she immediately froze. Was DG not well? Or was there some sort of major problem? He was never a flapper.

"Just gone to the loo, DG," Amélie replied also now sensing something wrong. "Why?"

"Good. Now I want both of you and Jesse to take all the kids through that small metal door over there in the corner. It leads down below, plenty of air and lighting, but you'll all be fine there. Darn safe room built for pirates, when this boat did the coast of Africa. We have a problem."

"What sort of problem, DG? Where's Charlotte? And Giles for that matter?" Lauren replied, anxiety racing through her body from tip to toe.

"Boarders—swung up the side from a motor raft down by the stern. Giles spotted them and has the varmints under surveillance. Don't know why they're here but Charlotte and Marcie are fine, on their way back up. We'll take care of them." He bit his lip ... there was no way he could say different, this could be find and kill ... Lauren needed safe containment in the hold, one problem at a time. He remembered Murmansk very, very clearly.

"I need to go with you DG, that's my daughter out there."

"And you have three more here, Lauren. Marie is over there ... she'll sort Charlotte out. You need to look after Lexi and Kat."

"Marie?"

"That's what she's trained for ... remember? That's why you hired her and she's good, way darned good, believe me. Trust me Lauren. Please get in the safe room. Remember the crap in Murmansk?"

"He's right Lauren. Neither you nor I are much use out there. Besides, the security team are on their way and won't take long. Let's go. Jesse, can you move the babies inside please."

"Nice work Amélie and I've called the police too," DG replied. "Now, I gotta go."

"DG, that door has a coded lock. What's the opening sequence to get out?"

"Shit, damn near forgot. Charlotte said she'd programmed the first six digits of Planck's constant whatever the fuck that is. Sorry ... hells bells ... should have written it down, there were a lot of sixes."

"Got it ... Hey, two of the world's top physicists are here." Amélie retorted. "As easy as pie, eh Lauren?"

Lauren smiled and nodded. "Fine, let's get in there. Good luck and take real care DG ... please ... you know why." She wished Mila and Rosie were here, but Mila was in Israel and Rosie had once again disappeared out of touch and out of reach into the depths of inner China.

DG looked hard at Lauren and immediately realised. Of course, she obviously knew about his dodgy ticker and he still hadn't told Charlotte which was bad, but he felt fine, all nicely pumped again. It had been too long since Murmansk. Suddenly he turned back as Lauren and Jesse disappeared with all the children in their carriers, Kat and Lexi now helping enthusiastically. He opened another desk drawer and pulled out a small handgun. "Amélie ... I remember, you could use one of these ... take it ... it's full of ammo."

She grabbed it and primed it up to check the workings. "You betcha, now go blow their brains out DG," seeing the short AK47 he was suddenly holding.

"Atta girl." He kissed her cheek, popped two of his heart pills in his mouth and set off at a pace. Where the fuck was that security team?

Giles remained completely still under the tarpaulin watching closely through the window. Charlotte had now been separated from all the others and he couldn't discern what was happening to her. He felt an arm around his shoulder and turned like lightning, seeing Marie who had crawled in next to him with her fingers to her lips. "How on earth did you find me? I was going to text you."

"Beat you to the draw ... actually the sole of a very expensive Diesel trainer sticking out gave the game away, you're bigger than you think!"

"Shit ... must try harder ..."

"You're doing brilliant, Giles. Don't beat yourself up. Everyone and the children are in a bomb proof pirate room. DG is heading this way with another of these and his security team and the police are on their way."

He looked down to see the AK47 as she handed him a pistol and a knife.

"Magic, Marie, you're simply amazing."

"That's what I like to hear, but not yet please. Now what's the assessment in there?"

She peered out through the crack with him as they watched Marcie, the remaining chef and the others being herded together as Charlotte was roughly pushed aside by a big individual, obviously by the way he was waving, the leader of the assailants.

"It looks like Charlotte is the focus of their attention," Giles began. "Perhaps they intend to kidnap her for ransom money from DG. Look,

120

quick, two of the six are going to take the rest outside, through that door on the left."

"Now we strike." Marie wanted to move before DG got there. She knew instinctively it would be an immediate Wild West shoot out, not helpful but that was his innate style. There were better ways. "I'll take out those two ... if DG's security and police are coming we need them all alive if possible so we know what's been going down. Besides, DG will want justice for his poor chef ... I saw the body. Remember the drill— Helmand?"

"Totally."

She handed him a stun grenade. "Take one of these. When I wave, I'll go through the left door and you go through the right and let them go, you know where. You take the big guy and get Charlotte out. The other three don't look pros to me, but the leader definitely is, the body movement shows the signals. They'll all be disoriented for those vital seconds and a piece of cake, especially as they won't be expecting this blitzkrieg."

Giles smiled. "I'm impressed Marie, you really were special - Special Forces as DG said."

"Save the gratitude till later, okay? I also do a mean steak and chips," she replied grinning and wriggled out stealthily, levering herself with a hand firmly on his delectable bottom, as he grinned back again. Marie could definitely grow on him. After a minute the left door opened and the designated two assailants marched the other five hostages outside and began walking them along to the stairs. Marie watched carefully, crept to the corner, timed it precisely then sprang around into their startled faces.

"Hi boys." Before they could blink they were each struck in the throat with a hand simultaneously, slithering slowly to the ground as she held each on the way down to ease them to the floor quietly. The hostages stood open mouthed.

"Lord above Marie, I would never have believed what I just saw. God is alive and well today," Marcie uttered her face pale.

Marie put her fingers to her lips with a quite shush. In an instant the two unconscious assailants were hand and feet bound with plastic straps, rags shoved into their mouths and taped up. She pointed to the gap leading away to the outside deck walk. "Go through there and back to the lounge, all of you wait for me and Giles there."

"Giles? Where in the Lord's name is he, child?" Marcie whispered.

"Charlotte—we'll get her, don't worry. Now go, please, quickly."

She crept back to the door. Giles was ready at the other side. He caught Charlotte's glance through the window as he put his fingers to his lips and then put his hands over his ears to signal. She looked petrified but didn't move, her fast brain working out something was about to happen; she had to be on rapid alert. In a microsecond three large bangs one after the other resonated inside, the room filling with disorienting smoke. Giles sprang like a tiger on top of the leader, knocking him to the ground, the AK47 relieving itself of a burst of round through the window and with one massive punch to the head he had done the job. Marie followed suit with the nearest one, staggering about and simultaneously shot the other two through the knees as they screamed mercilessly and fell writhing to the ground. She hated doing it but better than a shot in the eye and chest as far as they were concerned, certainly from her ... they'll recover as cripples. Giles ran to Charlotte who had thrown herself under a table, smoke and soot all over her face, and took her, disoriented and shaking badly, into his arms. She looked wild eyed into his face. But quickly she calmed herself and began a fast reorientation, her brain running again on overdrive.

"You're safe Charlotte," Giles whispered, holding her shaking body close, her head buried in his chest as he cut the rope from her wrists. "They're all down, it's over. I've got you. Everybody else is fine. We got Marcie and the others out too and Lauren, Amélie and the children are all safe in the pirate hold."

"Oh Giles, you're a real hero and Marie. You were both absolutely wonderful. I don't know how to thank you for saving my life." She stared into his eyes, wrapped her arms around his wide shoulders and kissed him passionately. He knew he shouldn't respond but his adrenaline was high and Charlotte's torn summer dress was open, revealing her light brown nipples, and he kissed her too, grateful she was alive.

Finishing off tying and gagging the last of the assailants, Marie looked on, understood and sighed to herself ... maybe another time. Looking outside, she spotted two boats approaching. One was definitely police, the other full of DG's shaven-headed security team, desperately sobered up. They could take this lot away and interrogate them now until the pips squeaked. She was equally intrigued about what was behind this heist, not convinced instinctively or professionally that it was an intended kidnap. She had much greater experience and she knew, from all the ongoing stages she watched, that Charlotte was likely to have been executed there and then, but why? However, Giles had been amazing for a TA officer, exemplary. He deserved a commendation and she would recommend it through her line of military contacts. And of course there was Marcie who hastily whispered 'damned Russians,' to her. Marcie had recognised the lingo because DG received lots of Russian visitors in the past.

Further along the other side of the deck DG was still making his way steadily down, checking each corner unsure of what was ahead, when that horrendous sharp pain gripped his chest, worse than ever before. "Fucking shit, not now old ticker, just hang on in there, gotta rescue Charlotte," he said to himself. He had to stop and rest for a minute. There was no way he could walk a step and he felt totally useless, irrelevant and hugely pissed off with himself that this was the physical state he'd gotten into, now of all times. Where was the security? And where was Philippe? He should have been back well by now. He'd said an hour and could have made a huge big difference to events unfolding.

He popped another pill under his tongue and breathed in and out slowly. The pain started to ease as he peered over the rail towards the direction of the coast and could make out two fast speedboats approaching on the horizon. He felt instantly better seeing them and the big nitroglycerin capsule had finally kicked in. He looked casually down to the water, ready to set off ... but froze instantly on the spot. There, unmistakably, but it could not be possible ... but it was, sticking to the side of the boat near the waterline. He stared harder and his insides went ice-cold. A very long time had elapsed since he had last seen one of those fuckers, not in fact since Vietnam. But he recognised the deadly shape immediately and the varmint was a big'un too. Some kind of modern designed limpet mine.

Holy shit ... what kind of people would do a thing like that ... he had to get going. "Charlotte, I do love you ..." he began to say to himself but that was the last thing he would have remembered. An almighty explosion ripped through the side, resounding heavily through the whole super-yacht, blowing him right up into the air, sky-high.

At the sound of the huge bang, Charlotte and Giles jumped apart. Marie looked outside, startled, and ran through the door to see what was going on. The rescue boats were approaching and uniformed people inside had begun waving madly. Then she felt the aftermath as did Charlotte and Giles. The boat began to jerkily list over starboard in sharp movements. Marie knew immediately. A hole had been blown in the side of the ship and the vessel would be sinking and fast. Giles followed her, leaving the groaning bandits to their fate whatever that was going to be. He too had worked out the severity of that sound ... he had heard mines going off far too often in Afghanistan. Rope ladders had already been thrown up over the lower deck railings and the first tranche of security and police were abseiling up.

"Marie, we've no time to lose, I calculate we've got about eight minutes looking at the list angle. Take Charlotte to the rescue boat and then get Lauren and everyone out of that safe room and onto a lifeboat. Quickly, run both of you. I've got to find DG."

"DG?" Charlotte wailed. "Oh God, where on earth is he?"

"Charlotte just go please, we're sinking," he hollered, commanding her belligerently as the ship suddenly listed over further. "I'll find him, he was on his way. Charlotte is there anyone else onboard? Staff down below in the engine room?"

"No. DG had given them all, including the captain, a break on land for a couple of hours whilst we were anchored to leave us in peace."

She ran towards two police officers who shoved a life jacket into her hands and helped her onto the rope ladder as DG's security guards roughly dragged the intruders, bleeding and groggy, along the deck and into one of the lifeboats, which was being slowly winched over the side. Marie indicated to some of the other police officers where the body of the dead crew member was and then began racing towards the other end of the ship for Lauren and everyone else. Giles grabbed two life jackets and a pair of binoculars and ran up to the top deck, quickly finding a good viewing vantage point. He leaned over the side and could see a wild flurry of water and foam half way along indicating where the water was fast entering, but no sign of DG anywhere, as he peered as best as he could from one end to the other. Perhaps the blast had knocked him out ...

Despite being heavily padded and insulated, inside the safe room, they heard the bang and felt the ship shake too. Kat and Lexi began to cry as Jesse cuddled them firmly.

"What the fuck was that," Amélie cried out to Lauren, but they had no windows, only ventilation inlets. I don't like the sound of ... oh my goodness, did you feel that lurch? We've starting to lean." They all stumbled and righted themselves for a few seconds, when a second lurch followed.

"We've got to get out of here," Lauren shouted. "My guess is the ship has been holed. Six, six, two six, shit, is it zero or three, next ...?"

Her mind had gone uncharacteristically and stupidly blank. Hell, she had only been teaching Svet about 'h', Planck's constant, eighteen months before. $E=hv$, the relationship between energy and the frequency of an electromagnetic wave.

"It's zero, six." Amélie replied in a sure-fire voice. DG was correct about the sixes. Now punch it in."

But the handle didn't move, the lock stayed stuck rigid. Lauren pulled and tugged, re-entered the digits but to no avail. The twins had immediately recovered and began helping, strapping in each baby with Jesse, preparing to go.

"Grandma," Lexi shouted, "Just outside towards the tennis court where we were playing. There's a lifeboat, we should head there immediately."

"And I've found a box of lifejackets," Kat shouted, dragging out a crate with bright orange contents from under the table. "We all have to put one on. Jesse, we can use the small ones for the babies. Quickly."

"Aunt Amélie, could it be another mathematics number?" Lexi shouted. "I'm sure Mom said the code started with a one, I wasn't supposed to be listening but I did."

Amélie grabbed a lifejacket for her and Lauren and pondered, but Lauren, her brain now fired into warp ten survival mode, had recalculated instantly in her head and re-punched in a new number: one, zero, five, four, five, and seven. The handle turned instantly, and she shoved the door open hard into the fresh air, sunlight pouring into the darkened room. She turned to Amélie, still puzzled. "It's not 'h', Charlotte's an engineer. She used the shortened form of the constant, 'h-bar', relevant to angular rotation. I had to divide by 2π."

"I need to get my brain alive again. Okay everyone," Amélie yelled. "Keep steady, the yacht is leaning badly now. Over there to Lexi's lifeboat."

They began to slip and slide along towards the tennis court, the cover on the boat now having slipped off. It had some sort of crane winch, but would it work, if all the power had gone? Lauren thought hard. Probably the mechanism was wired to a battery emergency pack with a manual override if necessary. A flurry of sound with someone shouting caught their attention. Lauren looked across to see Marie waving, with Marcie, stumbling behind and leading four other crew members. By now the babies were outside, laid but not strapped into their carriers, each one with a tiny life jacket on.

"Quickly, everyone," Marie hollered. "There are two …"

"Marie, where's Charlotte? Lauren shouted across. "And DG and Giles?"

"Don't worry Lauren, Giles and I rescued them. They're all safe at the other end now; the police and security are onboard getting them off. We must do the same, quickly, the yacht is sinking fast. There are two lifeboats here, enough for all of us."

Lauren hugged her. "Thank you Marie, thank you so much. What do we do?"

The boat lurched again, it was listing about forty-five degrees and they could see the surface of the water now through the railings.

Marie took immediate charge. "Jesse, Amélie and all the children. Get into the first one now. Marcie and crew into the second. Lauren—I need you to help me. I'll guide and steady the boats—you work the engineering winch. Okay, ready? Press the button. Hopefully the emergency batteries are charged up. It's like driving a digger."

Lauren had never in her life driven a digger but pulling levers, winches and handling small cranes had been all in a day's work for a nuclear engineer when she was in the thick of testing and maintenance of a reactor. She pressed the red button for the first boat. Amélie looked down nervously. "Have faith in a real engineer Amélie not some sledge hammer swinger," Lauren shouted back grinning.

Amélie waved back. Her best friend was in her element as she ordered everyone to hold tight.

There was an unhealthy stutter as dirt and corrosion on the contacts burned off and then the motor kicked into life. Lauren had already worked out how to steer up and forward and shoved the engagement clutch lever into the on position as the crane started to slowly winch and the chains tightened. With more judicious pulling and Marie's steadying, the boat and passengers were soon up in the air and heading towards the side.

"Well done Grandma," Lexi shouted as everyone clapped. Standing on the raised area, Lauren slowly let the winch and chain take the lifeboat into the sea, admittedly made easier and quicker by the angle they were at and the closer proximity of the water, which at least was fairly calm. Once floating, Jesse and the twins unhooked the chains and Amélie pulled the engine cord. It fired up instantly, thank Christ she thought, although there were oars. They could now see a speed boat heading towards them, not knowing Charlotte was on it, guiding them to follow which she did rapidly moving away from the disaster area. They all looked back to the super-yacht and could see where the huge hole was letting in water and the extent to which the ship had sunk. There were literally only minutes to go.

Lauren was already well on the way with Marcie's boat. They hit the water quickly and Marcie followed suit, fired up the engine and began to chug off in the wake of Amélie.

Lauren grinned at Marie. They'd done it, then her face turned to stone as she realised there were no more boats. "Christ, Marie, what do we do?" she wailed.

"No problem, I know you're a good swimmer. We take this and now. This yacht is going under. We must get away before the final swell drags us down with it."

Lauren stared at the tiny rubber dingy for two with a pair of oars fastened inside. Marie had already tied a long rope into a large ring on the dinghy, secured the other end to a railing, and threw the lot overboard. She had a second rope in her arms.

"SAS style, Lauren, you can do it. Abseil down the side and jump in. I'll follow. Quickly."

Lauren was petrified. Hopefully her gym arm muscles were still as strong as her stomach muscles. She shoved her mobile phone with her wallet and credit cards into the jacket zip pocket and looked down in the water. The rubber dinghy was bobbing away from the boat she would have to swim to it. Grabbing the rope firmly and wrapping it around her, she climbed over the railing, ignoring Marie's assistance, and abseiled down smartly, her feet carefully walking the painted side of the yacht initially, but then with the angle she was soon mid-air, and gripped the rope with her two feet tightly. This was something she hadn't done since those shared outdoor activities in Scotland with her former husband in their heyday. Thank goodness she had married him ... first the motorbike skills in the Congo and now climbing down a cliff face. All in all he had proved a lot more useful than Philippe of late. At the bottom she propelled herself hard away from the boat, landing in the water, and began to swim hard for the dinghy before finally clambering in, unexpectedly far easier than waterskiing. She untied the rope and paddled towards the side as Marie followed behind and hauled herself in out of the water. They took an oar each, watching in fascination as the boat took another more serious lurch, the water now cascading over the lower decks and filling everywhere fast.

"Go, go, go, Lauren, paddle hard."

They swept their oars furiously into the water, and moved rapidly, further and further away from the stricken yacht. A third boat was heading towards them from the distance. The Amélie and Marcie lifeboats with the children onboard were safely well away, surrounded at last by a cluster of rescue boats; six could be counted, including the big motor launch which brought them there.

"Are we far enough away, Marie?" Lauren shouted, panting with the exertion but pleased they were all off safely and very pleased at how fit she was becoming again, helped definitely by the riding. She thought instantly of Giles. Somewhere along the line in this sorry and dreadful saga, he had been a genuine hero.

"Yes, we're well out of danger. Do you want to stop and watch? I would say a further half-minute and then the whole ship will disappear under water. It's so sad and catastrophic but thank goodness we got everyone off." Marie assumed that Giles would have easily found DG on his way to the kitchens; they were all trained ex Special Forces.

"Yes, it makes me think what all those torpedoed sailors during the war must have gone through," Lauren replied. But she needed to do one further action urgently. Someone was missing who was supposed to have been there ... but as usual was characteristically absent without leave. She pulled out her mobile and dialled. The number was answered immediately.

"Hi darling, I'm really sorry, got delayed at the town hall. The meeting went on much longer than we expected but I'm on my way at long last in ten minutes. Are you having a great time?"

She gazed sadly with Marie, in awe and silence, at the last dying moments of the Nodding Donkey, as it gasped a final death rattle, lurched right over and began to sink under the waves in a great flurry of undignified spray, bubbles and swirling water. They hadn't known each other long. She took a last picture.

"Yes wonderful. I'm sitting in the middle of the Mediterranean Sea in a tiny rubber dinghy with Marie, both soaked to the skin and shivering with lifejackets on and we're watching the Nodding Donkey disappear, Titanic style, down into the warm watery depths. No gin and tonic sadly. There she goes, whoa ... all gone ... four hundred million dollars in the blink of an eye. We had pirates you see Philippe, then a fucking great shoot out and the side of the boat blown out by a mine, but in the end the cavalry came to the rescue. Marie and Giles routed the boarders and got us all safely off. Where the fuck were you? Been making films have we?"

There was a long silence on the line.

Marie stared embarrassed wishing the rescue boat in the distance would hurry up and looked away. She hadn't seen Lauren so angry, her expression deeply vitriolic. It wasn't Philippe's fault ... but, Marie realised, she probably didn't know everything about their relationship. Certainly if Philippe had been there the situation may have all resolved much differently ...

Half an hour earlier, gazing lazily up at the eighteenth century ticking grandmother clock on the wall, Philippe hastily levered Gabrielle away, her arms entwined tightly around his naked body, and jumped out of bed. He gazed at her long red hair, now loose over her shoulders as she stared dreamily up at him on her stomach, the cover having slipped off well before onto the floor. He leaned over and ran his fingers through her thick mane when she defiantly grasped his bare bottom, moving her hands deftly to the front. She wanted an encore badly.

"You're a very desirable woman Gabi," he chuntered, his release fully over, but inside his head those pangs of irrational guilt and desire to roll the time back twenty-four hours were nagging away already. He had to get a move on. He was an hour late for DG's party already and he had promised Lauren faithfully. What on earth had compelled him into Gabrielle's sumptuous flat? He should have guessed the obvious but his weaknesses were back. He really thought that stupidity was over with, but somehow the same thing had just happened again. But Gabrielle was not Olga. She was sophisticated, highly cultured and wealthy but just as rampant. Fuck. Sometimes it was a curse, like a breaker on his flywheel, having Lauren for a wife. They were diverging so much lately. She seemed to dislike his new political career and they appeared to have even less in common than ever. Why God knows, except for Magda, Eve and Geri of course.

"With or without my money Philly?" she purred, not releasing her grip. "Did you like the deal we cooked up today?" she continued, masturbating him gently. "Mayor for you in Nice will be a shoe-in and the national stage now beckons with our ex-Minister suddenly on board. Politics with benefits is so much fun isn't it? Don't you think?"

"Definitely," he murmured and kissed her large brown nipples one after the other as she groaned. He prised her hand away. "But I really must go; family celebration on DG's super-yacht and Lauren will be hopping mad if I don't get a move on."

"DG has a big yacht? I never realised that. Mmm ... another desirable hunk of a man and with serious money, my kind of guy ... I could fuck him senseless too ... When was the last time you went to a proper, grown-up party Philly? ... I haven't had a special one for quite a while. Bring Lauren and of course DG. My ex-first husband, who I always invite, would find her very desirable. She is extraordinarily pretty and he has a thing about fucking cute scientists with big brains and matching tits."

But Philippe was ignoring her as he tapped his phone into life. There was a text from Giles, what did he want? He began to read the detail and his stomach froze. But he had to remain normal, calm, and nonchalant and think ... think hard, very, very hard.

"Sorry Gabi, just got to read this, some important business has come in."

His fast business brain was calculating a range of realistic scenarios, exactly as he used to do in Cassini and long before that in the Russian military and he was always right. He was raking through all the likely probabilities of what, when and if they happened. What should he do? Go or not go? ... In fact what would he actually like to do in the inevitable circumstances? He decided—there was only one sensible political solution.

"Looks like Lauren says I'm not needed for another few hours. Fancy a bit of a re-run darling?"

Gabrielle grasped his erection again, now immediate and hot. "Mmm ... I rather like being called darling. More please, much more. I was a little concerned about this aging member but it looks like my worries are totally unfounded, don't they just. I'm a woman who needs a lot of nurturing and satisfying. Reckon you're up to it?"

"You betcha," he replied.

He slid back onto her giant bed and they rolled over into position, kissing passionately once more.

Chapter Eight

Charlotte was devastated. She couldn't blame Giles, she couldn't blame anyone. He had risked his life not only to save her but then in great danger had desperately searched the sinking yacht from end to end for DG, and he continued beyond when it was safe to leave, ignoring the loudhailers of the rescue boats below to leave the ship immediately. He went right to the wire and was almost sucked down in the swell as he finally dived in from the top deck, heartbroken with failure, as a police speedboat hauled him in with a boathook in the nick of time.

Despite an extensive naval search, joined by helicopters and other volunteers, including Philippe, not a sign of anything was found. No clothing, no body, nothing. In the end they all had to come to the obvious conclusion. DG had somehow gone down with his ship, doing all he could trying to defend his family. Either he was blown up by the mine or blown off the deck into the water and drowned. If he was to depart this world in any shape or form that was the way which would have suited him, certainly not by any slow and debilitating illness lying in bed for months on end, or even worse something like dementia where all reality had been lost. Charlotte had reflected long and hard into the night, helped by Lauren and Amélie. Lauren also found a quiet moment to phone Mila, who was equally devastated. She was still in Israel and working frantically to ensure the Cassini partnership was staying intact after some hot-head internal rightwing interference. Lauren forcefully persuaded Mila there was nothing she could do. The perpetrators were in police hands and at the highest levels all was being done to ascertain what had been the motive for such a heinous crime. Mila was told to continue in Israel until she was satisfied their joint work was back on an even keel. Reluctantly, Mila agreed. Lauren also phoned Svet who was beside herself, but again Lauren told her to just continue normally with her studies as there wouldn't be any funeral.

Orlando, who hadn't being feeling well with a stomach virus and hadn't therefore been on the trip was overjoyed that Marcie had returned safely, albeit very shook up. But both Marcie and he had been through so much terrible trouble and strife during the sixties and seventies with racial riots, abuse and lynchings in Alabama. Although devastated, having worked for DG for over thirty years, they immediately got to work to ensure the household was running as smoothly as possible so that Charlotte could find personal space to grieve and make new plans. Their daughter Sabrina was also flying over for a month to help all round, especially with difficult baby, Arthur George.

A full week elapsed and the authorities finally called off their air and sea rescue searches. There was only one inevitable and logical conclusion, which Charlotte mentally accepted. Amélie had delayed her UK return to help out alongside Lauren. Philippe was making a particular effort to try and be supportive and useful, finally suggesting he assist Charlotte personally with the legalities when the appropriate time came, surrounding DG and his assets. But Lauren was having none of that. She still felt angry about his absence that afternoon and a chill was in the air between them.

Charlotte however gently brushed Philippe off before another row engulfed him and her mother, having decided that with Oriane's help she could and would cope. Legal complexities were the last thing to ever worry her. Having her own money and assets anyway for the time being meant she could keep the house and family going satisfactorily. The main issue she was concerned about was the massive debt of the sunken yacht. Whether the vessel had been fully paid for was already looming, but the Nodding Donkey was now a thousand metres down on the seabed so wouldn't be going very far. She assumed DG at least had the yacht insured; the policy would be worth a lot. In the meantime local police had been intensively interrogating the hospitalised suspects followed by Charlotte on her own and then Marcie. Giles and Marie, also interviewed, were personally commended by the Mayor for their bravery and quick thinking, having saved so many lives. A formal ceremony was suggested.

Kat and Lexi were remarkably grown up and sanguine. Both loved DG, and whilst very sad they demonstrated their mother's extensive fortitude and strength of mind. They promised faithfully to Lauren to do all they could to help their mother come to terms with such a terrible loss, and especially to look after their baby brother, and insisted only they would be allowed to bully him when he got bigger. Lauren hugged them hard, reiterating how brave and valuable they had been on the day. She made herself a special promise to keep a close and watchful eye on their wellbeing and development as they grew up into adolescence and set up a secret trust fund in Monaco, she alone would regularly pay into for their future university education.

At breakfast Lexi was screwing up her face hard, deep in concentration. "Grandma? Do you think Giles might stay longer now that DG has died, cos Mom likes him lots and is always happier with a man around the house?" Her utterance was made very seriously, the unassailable logic and rationality having run through her brain in a quiet orderly fashion, exactly as Lauren would have thought at her age.

Lauren saw the funny side immediately and giggled. "We'll have to see Lexi. Giles has a life and a job to do back in England."

"Aww ... that's a real shame," Kat murmured. "Mom will have to sell her new vineyard and olive grove now 'cos she can't look after all of us and that on her own, can she."

Lauren hugged them again. "We'll see. One day at a time for your mom," she replied softly. "It's early days yet, we'll think of something."

Inside she was hugely conflicted over Giles and would forever remain so, despite all the logical hot air she had justified doggedly about her own emotions being well out of sight and under wraps ... She had already suggested to Amélie that given the circumstances she should take Giles back with her. She knew, if he hung around, she couldn't trust herself not to fuck him again.

Amélie had already come to the same conclusion without any prompting. Her well-worn acuity for sensing the subtlest interchanges was not only as sharp as ever but heightened heavily with the tragedy. There was definitely too much mixed up emotional tension in the air, zipping around in every direction from all quarters, which had all the self-destructive semblances of a nuclear pile rapidly overheating. An off-the-cuff remark made by Marie when they were quietly chatting in Lauren's kitchen, about Charlotte showing a more than usual expected appreciation to Giles immediately she was rescued, raised alarm bells. For a whole host of reasons, Amélie knew Charlotte was vulnerable right then, and there remained the issue of her father, Henri-Gaston, to also contend with. Giles returning back to the UK would be equivalent to dropping in the graphite rods to cool everyone off and readjust back to some normality. She was especially mindful of Lauren and Philippe. Whatever was bubbling again under the surface between them, they equally needed space and time to resolve it. She would instruct Giles to return back to the estate in the evening.

"Actually, I can confidently say to you all, they were not Russians," Charlotte uttered quietly out of the blue. She was sat in the orangery, drinking afternoon tea with Lauren, Amélie and Marie.

Lauren got up to fetch a large piece of pecan pie from the silver platter of welcome sweet and sugary comfort food that Marcie had left on the side-table. Dousing it with double cream, Lauren turned around puzzled. "But Marcie was insistent, and anyway the police have corroborated the same. Apparently not only do they speak Russian, the investigators have had to bring in interpreters apparently, and they had identity cards and Russian passports with them."

"Where's Philippe gone, Lauren?" Amélie asked. "I thought he was going to join us here after he and Giles returned from walking the tribe in their buggies down to the beach?"

"They're all back. Jesse is putting them to bed for their afternoon snoozes. No, Philippe and Giles have gone into Nice to see the regional police commander, someone who Philippe has got to know quite well. Philippe wants to find out why no information is still forthcoming. They've had long enough, Christ—the interrogators have been at the

136

hospital for the whole week. The thugs are all under armed guard. Philippe is adamant these men are connected to the oil and gas oligarchs who had their financial noses put out of joint when he was released from prison last autumn and they were seeking some sort of retribution."

"You mean they had boarded the yacht looking for him?" Marie replied, now intrigued and quite disturbed with the complications suddenly alighting from Novosibirsk into the Côte D'Azur. She was beginning to understand the reasoning to Lauren's unease.

"Conveniently of course, Philippe never arrived at the yacht," Lauren added, now sat under the large lemon tree, forking into her pie. "Gosh, it's beautiful in here. I do love all these tropical plants, some are about to flower already. This will be a gorgeous retreat in the summer, Charlotte, as long as the vents are opened."

Amélie looked sharply at Lauren who ignored her, detecting immediately the acerbic tone of her throwaway comment on Philippe. Lauren was clearly and conveniently in her head blaming him for what had happened. She turned to Charlotte. "Don't remain quiet. I can see you're very convinced that those men are not who everyone thinks they are. So why not?"

Charlotte looked up and smiled warmly at Amélie. "I'm glad someone is prepared to listen," glancing over at Lauren who was staring into the trough of flowering cacti nearby. "Because when I was separated from everyone, the big one, the leader, with the rictus grin, who shoved me to one side, then stuck a gun against my head? His foul smelling mouth near my ear began blabbering all kinds of lewd obscenities he really wanted to do to me, in his own language, assuming of course that I didn't understand Russian. He then ended by saying that sadly, American whore, his boss in Moscow had insisted only a clean shot in the back of the head, with photographic evidence."

"So he was Russian then?" Marie said.

"No Marie, because I noticed he had changed his accent. It was subtle but I picked it up instantly. He had reverted for a moment to his natural language ... and spoke Belarusian and not Russian, they are very similar. It then made sense to me, because when they spoke to each other in Russian it didn't sound quite right, one or two words were not correct."

Lauren heard and was so sick of herself because she really wanted this ordeal to land guiltily at Philippe's feet, especially as he hadn't even bothered to be there to save DG who had done so much to get him out of that fucking Russian labour camp. But she knew more than anyone how good Charlotte's Russian really was, not only during their Murmansk drama. She had been a top student at university having done a double major in the language with engineering. What Charlotte had cleverly noticed had other implications.

"I believe you Charlotte," Lauren called over and walked back to her chair and poured out more tea for everyone. "Did you tell the police? Because ..."

"This arc of motive has some unforeseen attributes." Marie had intervened, her lightning intelligence brain immediately seeing the implications. "Those guys could indeed have simply been after you ... it also explains why you were separated. Some sort of targeted revenge aimed directly at DG. They must have known you were his wife, and their aim was to eliminate you and make DG suffer personally. Blowing a hole in the side of the yacht was an added bonus, so financially he would also have lots of money pain."

"Shit, Marie, you've got it," Amélie added excitedly. "But the plan all went wrong, due to you and Giles, because Charlotte is here and they got caught and should now be talking, at least soon."

There was a silence. Everyone was thinking but on different tracks and perspectives. Lauren spoke slowly and softly, and like her daughter was precisely synthesising the evidence scientifically and coming to her own logical conclusions. "Sadly, it actually went right because DG is no longer with us. Whoever was behind this will know that now and still be very happy, not the way it was intended but acceptable to them ... any interest in you is of no consequence anymore. It does point to those Russian oligarchs, but who probably found out DG was the real fixer behind Philippe's release and whose methods of action and influence internally with bribes and politics had a far greater negative impact on them. Philippe was a nonentity enroute, an irrelevance of their anger."

"This is why I didn't tell the police or the senior superintendent who eventually interviewed me," Charlotte replied. "I had plenty of time in that rescue boat back to think everything through in minute detail and draw my own conclusion, which was exactly the same."

She giggled, stood up and hugged her mother. "Sorry, I should be sad and sombre. I am really grieving inside but Lauren, I'm so relieved to be alive and I don't want this thing to continue like an ongoing family feud with some Siberian warlord. We and the children all need to carry on living normally and get on with enjoying our lives." She immediately burst into tears and wept hard, crying for a good few minutes as Lauren quietly hugged and consoled her daughter.

Fuck Philippe, Lauren quietly thought, as Charlotte tight in her arms finally unbundled her locked in emotions and at last found a necessary release. They were so alike, mother daughter, sister and friend all in one. She counted up the amount of time since she had fallen in love with Philippe that had been taken up with a myriad of unhappy events occurring in their lives. Apart from the birth of their daughters the bad greatly exceeded the good ... it was as if no matter how hard she tried he couldn't help himself, stupidly hurting either her, Svet and now indirectly DG and Charlotte too. Something had to give. She had to extricate from her mind that he wasn't a serial liability to her future happiness or get shut, as Amélie had poignantly suggested numerous times before.

Charlotte finally pulled away and sat down, her eyes red and her face flushed, but inside she felt a great load of detritus had fallen away from her entire mind and body.

"Good," Amélie said. "That needed to come out, now you can begin to move forward."

Charlotte nodded.

"Marie?" Lauren began. "Charlotte is absolutely right. We should keep our conclusions to ourselves. It will serve no further purpose, and of course we should ensure the same with Philippe and Giles. I'll take care of Philippe."

"And, I'll do the same with Giles," Amélie immediately responded.

Marie nodded. "I agree. Knowing how this works, those guys will stay quiet. They'll have a story ready, probably a kidnapping for ransom money because DG was a wealthy man, and say very little ... they got caught and they'll have to take the rap, do time and be the fall guys. That's the unwritten code or they and their families will suffer brutally if they squeal any truth. Already, lawyers will be briefed to try and minimise their sentences and probably get them extradited back to Russia, on some diplomatic pretext, to serve their sentences in Moscow. The French terrorist and internal security officers will be leaned on from high, whether they know their true identities or not. The whole business will soon be forgotten."

There was another long pause; finally Lauren broke the icy silence. "Actually Charlotte I want to say something about the person we shouldn't forget about. He died doing what he always did, protecting and saving his family and his friends every possible way he knew how. He would never have done any different. You could trust DG one hundred percent to deliver ... and we're all here to tell the tale. He wouldn't have wanted it any differently, nor would DG expect us to be sitting around miserable and grieving forever. I suggest that at the weekend, before Amélie, Giles and her twins return to England, that we have a small family remembrance party here. A nice big steak meal and DG's favourite wine and beer and celebrate stories of all the good, funny and daft things DG has done to make our lives worthwhile since we knew him. I'll pay for it, I insist, and bring outside caterers in so that everyone, including Marcie and Orlando, can relax and enjoy it—I'm sure DG, looking down, would love that."

Amélie smiled. This was so very vintage Lauren of old, and such a nice thought, and she was right.

"Hot dog, Lauren that is such a wonderful idea. Goddam it, DG would sure as hell love us girls to party that way," Charlotte cried, in her best Texan mimic of her husband she could muster. "Thank you so much. He always said you were by far the best mother-in-law he ever had and promised you'd be the last too."

Everyone felt joyful again and Charlotte hugged her mother tearfully. Suddenly the door swung open.

"Hey Mom, what's going on here, why are you all laughing?" Kat shouted, with Lexi tripping along beside her carrying fishing nets and beach umbrellas. Orlando and Marcie trailed behind with the remains of the beach picnic they had treated them to.

Lauren wrapped her arms around her granddaughters. "We're going to have a little party on Saturday, girls, to remember DG, just like he would want us to."

Orlando and Marcie stood alongside Lauren and smiled warmly.

"That's a fabulous idea, Mom, cos DG was a great dad," Lexi shouted, very excited again. "Can me and Kat have fancy dress please, and also big balloons, cake and jelly?"

"Of course, little ones, we'll have all that sorted for you," Marcie replied, grinning at Charlotte and Lauren. "Now go and hug Grandma, then you girls must get changed and showered immediately please."

As they all walked back to the house, joined outside by Philippe and Giles who had returned from the police headquarters, Charlotte had decisively made up her mind on something else. This would be potentially far reaching and with ramifications she needed to expertly manage, but she would do that, whatever it took, exactly as she had consistently done with her whole life. She would never be a victim. Glancing furtively at Giles as he walked ahead, chatting to Lauren and Philippe, Charlotte reflected on what she had done earlier. Late morning she had taken the opportunity, once they were alone, to show her full appreciation to Giles for saving her life, outside in the quiet and still air of the vineyard. The way he responded and the way she unexpectedly felt confirmed exactly as she surmised when they kissed on the yacht. He was definitely returning to England, but he would be back and she would be waiting for however long it took. But the most urgent thing occupying her was to desperately find some antiseptic cream and relieve the pain of all the prickly scratches over her bottom.

However one eagle-eyed person had surreptitiously spied Charlotte's glance and in a micro-second was reformulating her own conclusions and potential ramifications, and she was never wrong either.

Oriane, accompanied by her husband, had again organised a fabulous party evening which included outside caterers as suggested and a free bar. Everyone came round, including a number of crew members and security from the yacht who happily stayed for the huge T-bone steak meal, cooked with Marcie's sauces that she had passed to the chef. Over drinks the family continued to tell all kinds of outrageous stories. Charlotte had everyone in stitches about some of the antics DG had got up to in Texas before they had married and the entire partygoers roared and laughed when she joked that the one good thing about the ship going down, which even DG would have agreed with, was that Boris, the old seven foot stuffed black grizzly he'd shot in his youth, had disappeared with him. Lauren and Amélie added some of the classic DG antics when they travelled from Stockholm to Murmansk in his hired pickup truck and Philippe relayed some of the oil and gas experiences they had shared when he first joined up with DG to chair Rubidium. Even Kat and Lexi joined in, relaying the time DG split his shorts apart in the swimming pool diving in badly, and they demanded twenty dollars each before they would throw him a towel to climb out.

Kat and Lexi were putting all the babies together who had woken up in the giant playpen, cooing and gurgling at one another. Lauren, who couldn't wait a minute longer, departed for the bathroom announcing she would be back with some more tales from her wedding day with Philippe in Paris. Marie and Jesse were sitting with Giles, laughing and joking whilst Amélie and Philippe continued to amuse Charlotte about Lauren's early days at Cassini and the wild board meetings they used to have. Everyone finally had relaxed for the first time since the sinking, coming to terms with his profound loss exactly how DG would have wanted it, by acknowledging a larger than life, generous person who could never be replaced.

Lauren, whilst sitting in the bathroom, contemplated how much of a shame it was that Mila and Rosie couldn't have been present for this party. She had phoned Mila a few days earlier, still in Israel with Johann repositioning their fragile Cassini fusion partnership after the mayhem of political infighting following the recent election. Mila had agreed the celebration was perfect to help facilitate some closure. They also shared a confidential chat which Lauren badly needed with Mila, trusting her totally over the conclusion of why the terrorists had committed what they did. Mila had unusually reacted with a long silence, before simply saying 'interesting' and leaving it at that. Lauren pressed no more. The police commander had concluded to Philippe and Giles that the evidence of a potential kidnapping gone badly wrong by a criminal Russian mafia gang was overwhelming, and that a trial would not be required because all the gang members had willingly confessed, guilty. Long jail sentences of at least twenty years each would be the minimum expected in a few months time, although three of the five had major injuries which would take a long time to heal up. Exactly as Marie surmised, the first expected scenario stage was shaping up as they thought ... it would be interesting to see if and when the criminals ended up back in Moscow.

The large sitting room was continuing to buzz with noise when the end door suddenly opened quietly. A tall and elegantly dressed man walked in slowly carrying a large bunch of flowers, with Marcie behind, holding her hands up to indicate the man had been insistent. Only one person knew immediately who he was and she froze solid inside her stomach. This could not possibly be happening. Philippe and Giles looked up simultaneously, both puzzled.

Lauren had gone into the kitchen to fetch the three baby carriers and marched in through the other door, struggling with the three. "It's getting bedtime for Magda, Eve and Geri," she shouted unaware, in the direction of Charlotte. "I'm happy if my babies sleep over here tonight ..." She stopped mid sentence. The room had gone deathly silent, as she heard the distinctive and deep voice.

"I apologise Charlotte for the lack of notice. I heard about DG and just had to come immediately. I'm so terribly sorry." He turned to look at the six babies in the playpen who Marie and Jesse were now attending to, clearly perplexed.

Philippe was mystified and so were Kat and Lexi. Amélie remained silent, taking the situation in knowingly. Giles gorped aimlessly before he turned and caught Lauren's face, realising that something hugely significant was manifesting. He immediately tensed to protect Charlotte if necessary.

The man turned again and faced Lauren's intense, relenting stare, dumbfounded. He looked again at the three triplets, now separated.

"Henri-Gaston Landry, after all these years you suddenly appear," Lauren announced in a loud and belligerent voice. "What the fuck are you doing here, you bastard? This is a family gathering."

The silence ensued with all eyes turned to Lauren.

"I'm so sorry Lauren," Charlotte spoke in a loud whisper, rising mortified from her seat and wishing the floor could open up and swallow her whole.

The end door immediately opened again. Kat and Lexi continued to stare mystified, their mouths wide open, saying nothing as everyone turned. Philippe was finally beginning to understand, his own mind in a great whirl of its own as he thought through the enormity of this unannounced and unscripted encounter. Mila walked in, uncharacteristically silent, dressed in a stunning and short pink Prada summer dress. Henri-Gaston immediately took her arm gently and led her to one side.

Amélie immediately became conscious of the obvious and was instantly hugely dismayed. Never in a million years would she have guessed ... but on this occasion the revelation of the chemistry between Mila and Henri-Gaston had flashed across Lauren's senses even faster. Her eyes narrowed in disbelief for a micro-second until she spied the huge diamond engagement ring prominently displayed on Mila's left hand. Then the final evidence, no longer possible to hide, a small baby bump. Mila was at least two months pregnant.

Lauren felt her cheeks flush cherry red like a bright beacon illuminating the room. Her mind was in absolute turmoil and she reacted, her emotions blowing sky-high like an explosion of one of her own nuclear reactors. "You fucking pair of perverts," she screamed staring hard at both Henri-Gaston and Mila.

"Lauren, this is not the time to ..." Philippe called out, rising from the chair towards her, but she swiped him hard across the face, to a series of loud gasps, as he sank right back down into it, silently, rubbing his cheek.

"Don't you dare say nor do anything you piece of good for nothing Russian shit. I hate you." He had never seen her look so angry. He couldn't believe the venom in her eyes, everything, all the distressing feelings that had lain buried for months and years about him had finally come to the surface in a fireball, and he knew.

Lauren turned again slowly and stared directly into Mila's amber eyes, her face cold and unyielding. A large tear rolled down Mila's cheek. This was not the way it was meant to be.

"I never, ever, as long as I live, want to set eyes on you again," Lauren uttered slowly, her voice cold as ice.

Then, seeing Charlotte, whose own dismay was turning palpably to anger at her own father, Lauren's emotions unravelled as she cried out in abject pain. "My own daughter, who I've loved more than anything in the world for so long, and it was all finally so perfect again. How could you betray me with such unforgiveable treachery and deceit with this grotesque piece of low-life?" pointing to Henri-Gaston who was frozen with shock.

That was not how it was meant to be either.

Lauren finally screamed out loudly. "I can't bear this damned place any longer," and ran maniacally out of the door, sobbing loudly, as Philippe jerked back into life, leapt out of his chair and ran after her.

Charlotte turned sharply to her father and Mila. "Go, now both of you. I never want to see you either, there out the back way."

Orlando and Marcie beckoned Henri-Gaston as Mila took his arm and shoved him, stumbling, through the other door, the flowers still in his hand.

Giles, visibly shaken, stared at Charlotte's ashen face as she walked back across the room to comfort Kat and Lexi who began to cry. He turned to Amélie, still silent but pondering very hard. "What in heaven's name was all that about? Have you any idea."

"Yes, the nightmare I never believed would ever happen."

Philippe reached the front door and ran out into the entrance area, peering around everywhere in the darkness. The security lights for some stupid reason were not working. He never believed anyone could have run so fast, least of all Lauren. Then he heard the engine fire up behind him.

Lauren had jumped into her BMW X5. She slammed the auto into drive and shot forward towards him, headlights full on. His survival instinct on high alert, he dived headlong out of the way, rolling onto the grass as she hurtled past, straight out of the drive and up the road at great speed into the distance.

"Fuck it all," he muttered, dusting himself down and staggered back to the entrance, noticing a white Lexus at the far end quietly start up and disappear immediately through the other entrance causing the security lights to suddenly light up. The characteristic blonde bob of the driver with the man beside her was enough to conclude that Mila and this Henri-Gaston Landry, whoever he was, although he now had a pretty clear idea, were also sensibly vacating.

Once inside, he beckoned Marie and Jesse to gather the babies so they could all go back home to bed, confidently sure that Lauren would be home already, hopefully now cooled off. Then they could talk for as long as it takes and resolve all this business sensibly after a good night's sleep and reflection.

"Mom," Lexi began, drying her eyes, with Kat standing quietly next to her doing the same. "Why is Grandma so terribly angry and upset with Aunt Mila, and who is that strange man who caused all the shouting?"

Charlotte steadied herself, but there was no option now. "That man, both of you, is your grandfather, your true biological grandfather."

But all she could think about was what DG would have done if he had been present, which if ever there had been a situation she desperately wished he was there right then. She smiled. He would have calmly said, 'So what, I'm Lauren's triplet's step-grandfather brother-in-law and the world had gone darn crazy, so everyone best calm down and have a glass of fine malt instead.'

Lauren however didn't go home. She carried on driving. There was only one person left in the world she needed who would understand, and she had a very long road ahead.

Aphelion—Chapter Nine

Some years on, in Villefranche-sur-Mer: It was definitely a good time to reclaim the weekends back again. Strolling casually through a maze of cobbled streets in the old town, Lauren gazed nostalgically at a beautiful, dark-oak, eighteenth century coffee table in Losander, her favourite antique shop. She would return later and negotiate a deal on the thousand euro asking price. The warm, tangy breeze gently wafting across the bay made her breathe in deeply before she headed towards the Dolce Vita Café, a perfect venue for a morning coffee with Charlotte. The sun was already high in the sky on a lovely July morning and she settled down under a straw umbrella on the seafront patio, with an unencumbered view of the whole beach.

"Professor Hind, what a pleasure to see you. Have you been away? We've missed you these last three months."

She turned to Emil, the young and attentive Belgian owner manager with the arresting smile and hunky body, especially in his summer shorts and tight tee-shirt, who came over immediately to serve her personally.

"Yes, business in Iran needed me full time sadly, with constant shuttling between Tehran and Washington. Now that sanctions have been eased, openings we would never have thought possible in my business six months ago are actually turning feasible. In fact it's become quite a Wild West gold rush out there for technologists. You have to be ruthlessly quick off the mark to get the good deals."

"But I assume politically sensitive still?"

"Decidedly so. I did manage to get home a few times; I really missed the children but ..."

"Business is business, Professor Hind, I fully understand. You must be glad you can rely on Marie and her sister to keep the household running well. Usual cappuccino and a slice of apple cake?"

She nodded with a warm grin. She was always predictable with her food and he never forgot. She looked out into the distance towards the edge of the shoreline, watching Magda, Eve and Geri, playing and shrieking happily on the beach together with Jesse splashing them with water. As she tucked into her cake, Emil's remarks made her contemplate what she still missed ... after nearly seven long years without Mila. Certainly high on the list was DG. It was a strange time when he died. She only found out quite some time later that Charlotte had been resigning herself to DG slowing down markedly. He was spending most of his time latterly on that yacht or socialising down the US Consulate Club in Nice. He had even been writing his Colonel's memoirs about the good life leading his Special Forces division. But the sinking of the Nodding Donkey and subsequent upheaval, compounded by some of his clothes oddly turning up further down the coast on a Marseille beach, raised all kinds of unwarranted speculation about what really happened on that fateful day.

Everyone was shocked of course, once word got around. Charlotte had a year of hell. But a body was never found and Oriane managed in the end to secure a court order splitting DG's assets for the next seven years, after which he would be legally declared dead, a time very imminent. The reality of DG's assets also metamorphosed starkly into unwelcome visibility with an unexpected sting in the tail. The billions of dollars everyone assumed he had turned out to be wildly complicated with much of it backed up by debt. A variety of oddball oil and gas creditors from the US including Amélie's old company Rubidium and subsequently from other parts of the world began mysteriously appearing on the doorstep, and separating fact from fiction and real from imaginary became a legal and accounting nightmare which also proved hugely costly. DG had been immensely skilful and adept, playing off one creditor against the other and hiding accounts especially from the taxman, but for Charlotte she hadn't the strength or the desire to be bothered fighting and in the end settled out of court with all of them, including the yacht owners, who hadn't been paid nor insurance arranged. All in all a very hefty loss. However Charlotte still emerged a relatively rich woman and was determined to forget the trauma and finally enjoy her settled lifestyle in the South of France with her children. Texas became a fast receding memory, to where she had no intention of returning.

Suddenly Lauren was dragged from her reverie. Small tanned arms, sand and a mass of long blonde hair enveloped her from behind with a flurry of hugs and giggles.

"Momie, we have had a super time this morning, look at what I found," Magda shrieked, tipping a bucket of shells onto the coffee table.

"Yes, but Magda's not as good as me at building sandcastles," Geri called out excitedly not to be outdone, followed by a "nor me" from Eve who was jumping up and down.

"Okay you three ... calm down please," Lauren replied, smiling at Jesse as she approached. "Do you all want a small ice-cream?"

"Yes please," Magda and Geri yelled, dancing up and down again, as the other customers outside turned and smiled. Lauren turned to Eveline who now remained quiet and in deep thought. "And what about you Eve? What are you thinking about, *ma petite*?"

Eveline looked up with a wide grin across her face. "My lesson later of course. I have a new composition to play to my teacher, Maman."

Magda and Geri groaned, complaining they were now on school holidays so why did they have to do lessons as none of their friends did.

"Actually that isn't true Magda," Eve chipped in. "My best friend Lucille is starting the violin today, although I'm streets ahead of her. Anyway, I thought you two liked your extra lessons. Magda, if you play piano in accompaniment like you did the other night, the teachers will be very impressed."

"Yeh, Eve, you're right, but I'd rather stay on the beach today." Geri replied, "I love my ballet though, just as much as your violin and Mag's piano playing."

"You'll have plenty of time next week for the beach again," Lauren remonstrated. "We agreed that you would all keep up your special lessons in the summer or you will get out of practice. That's what I did when I was your age and it's only twice a week. Hey everyone, here comes your big sister with Arthur, and he's going with you as well today."

"Momie?" Magda began once more, looking very serious. "Sometimes it's very difficult at school when our friends see Charlotte and Arthur. When we say she's our sister and he's our nephew, they all snigger and laugh behind our backs. Why is that? And the boys make fun of us because we're identical triplets. Fortunately, we're all bigger than them so we biff them up when the teacher isn't looking."

"That's because Arthur's mother, your sister Charlotte, and his grandmother who is me, had babies at the same time, you three and him. It doesn't happen very often and neither do identical triplets ... you are very special. They just have to get used to it because it's true. And you must all stop bullying the boys—ignore them and walk away, understood?"

The triplets stood side by side, and looked glum.

"Sorry, Momie, we do understand the baby maths and we'll behave from now on, we promise," Geri mumbled as Magda and Eve nodded solemnly.

Lauren laughed—her little daughters were also a chip off the old block, multiplied three-fold. "Okay, now you can cheer up because here comes your ice creams and one for Jesse too," who she leaned towards and winked at.

"I'll take Arthur back home with them once they've finished, Lauren," Jesse replied. "Marie said she would drive them all to the Academy in Nice and then do some shopping and pick them up again later. She's trying to finish her new novel before the end of the month. Her publishers are suddenly giving her a lot of pressure. Someone is talking about a film commission."

"Really? That's amazing, I'm so pleased for her."

"What's amazing, Grandma?" a little voice piped up behind her.

Lauren turned and immediately hugged Arthur, standing with Charlotte, who raised her eyebrows back holding his hand. Arthur like the triplets was tall for his age and looked older, especially with the thick lens glasses he already had to wear. He was an introspective child, highly academic, precocious in mathematics, but loved to talk and constantly ask questions about everything imaginable. At that moment, he was a fanatical collector of rocks and seashells, immediately eyeing and categorising Madga's collection on the table with relish.

"I'm talking about Marie," Lauren replied firmly to him, rearranging his sun-hat which had gone wobbly, "who will be taking you to the Academy shortly for your lesson with the girls. Her next book she's writing may be turned into a movie."

"Wow, that's cool Grandma. I've been teaching myself to write in the last week, it's dead easy once you see the patterns. Kat and Lexi were impressed."

"Yes, but you can't read either as well or as quickly as us yet, can you genius," Magda burst out, stuffing the last remnant of ice cream cone into her mouth.

"Yes I can Mags, in fact I can also ..."

"Okay, that's enough. Arthur, off you go now with Jesse and we'll see you all later." Charlotte had promptly intervened as Lauren glared at Magda, who as usual fired off from her mouth before thinking, exactly like her father Philippe. Jesse grabbed a hand each of Arthur and Magda and they all immediately set off back to Lauren's villa, chattering away happily.

Charlotte sat down with a sigh. Lauren beckoned over Emil and ordered a glass of white wine each. Bliss. She quickly pulled out a mirror and applied a refresh of red lipstick. She looked pleasingly at her hair, freshly styled again by John Hawley who she flew down specially from Brussels the day after she came back from the great escape, six and a half years ago. He insisted then on demolishing her historic long locks for a revolutionary blonde bob, with lovely long bangs, carefully shaped shorter at the back. He insisted the change matched her new mood and determination. The style suited her oval face beautifully, although for many her new appearance was an abject shock. And all she had to do these days was pop into Nice for a refresh trim. John Hawley loved the Côte d'Azur client potential so much he never actually left, and now had a string of popular salons he built up along the coast from Nice to Monaco. He was a millionaire a number of times over. But he still always insisted on styling her hair personally.

"Some days that boy just wears me flat out," Charlotte began. "He never stops asking questions on everything imaginable with the tenacity of DG and the determination of his grandmother!"

Lauren laughed. "He can't help it. He's got an inquisitive brain like his grandmother too. Actually I was so pleased that the Nice Academy for Gifted Children opened up in the New Year. The four of them are doing well there and love the opportunity of being amongst their peers. Funny isn't it how Arthur has really got the mathematics bug and the triplets are all so amazingly musical. Although Geri is focused on ballet and dance, she has started really playing the clarinet well. The three of them practise together occasionally, it sounds wonderful, like having a mini ensemble living in the house, but they're still so very young."

Charlotte patted Lauren's hand. "I agree, Arthur's way ahead of his special Academy group even. Thanks to you, the Hind academic genes are well represented in my children."

"Yes, but Magda is so like her father; impulsive, reckless and far too sociable for her own good. Shall we go inside? The breeze is coming up a bit."

Charlotte sighed quietly to herself. They sat down at a new table by the window and ordered a Mediterranean salad lunch. She truly wished Lauren and Philippe's marriage had worked out ... well ... normally.

"Is Philippe not seeing the girls this weekend?"

"No, next week now. We changed it so that they could go to NAG today. Of course next weekend he stays with the irresistible socialite slut Gabrielle Legendre, whilst her new husband gallivants all around France at swinger parties. But her daughter, Lucille, is now Eve's best friend so I bite my lip. And I must say, all these years Philippe and I have been separated, he's been great and generous with the children. On that score I can't complain. On every other score, why did I marry such a fucking emotional loser full of bullshit? I should have listened to Amélie at the time. Although I have to say, living in his tiny bachelor pad in town suits everyone. He's out of my hair, Gabrielle fucks him whenever she's bored and he can shag everything else female that moves, which he does so I hear, regularly and unencumbered."

Charlotte sighed again. "I'm really sorry, Lauren. I wish DG was alive. You two got on so well and he always had a knack of cheering you up ... err ...don't you ... well miss ... like ..."

"Sex you mean?" Lauren replied nonchalantly. "After the Philippe and Mila disclosures all on that same day? To be honest, I enjoy my long celibacy so I can focus distraction free on my company, research, travel and most of all my immediate family, especially you. I never meant to be harsh on you that awful day, but I had no option but to run away, it was all simply too much. I simply shut down. It was so frightening; I never want to experience that again, ever."

Charlotte patted her hand affectionately and grinned. "I know, but I was worried crazy where you were and with DG dying and everything else—I think we had our annus horribilis and our emotional nuclear explosion at exactly the same time, didn't we. But at least you ended up with the best person imaginable at the time."

"Of course, we're too alike not to! But you're right. I was so grateful for Annabella. She took me in immediately for that whole month and nursed me back to life from that crisis. God knows what she thought when I landed on her doorstep at three am. I still clearly remember her sister Angelina, her face was a picture as well as my ex-husband who stood next to her as she opened the door. He's become larger and cuddlier like her, obviously from too much of her home cooked pasta, but Angelina still adores him. But, startlingly, we all got on incredibly well, including me with their children. That was an important part of my rehabilitation too then, getting rid of bad legacy. I still don't know how I had the wits to find them, driving all the way to Sicily. All I had were my credit cards. Something at least still functioned on autopilot. Everything else in my head had gone stone-dead. Annabella is an incredible, caring woman and will always be in my debt and my heart forever."

"And mine too, for resuscitating you back to normal. You've never really mentioned all that before."

"Actually, I've been thinking for some time and I want to tell you a number of things. Today is a good day."

Charlotte went silent. Suddenly out of the window, a group of men caught her attention. "Gosh, talking of Philippe, there he is over the road going into that bar. Who are those guys with him in suits?"

Lauren followed Charlotte's gaze, unimpressed. "Just look how fat he's become and that awful, slicked back hair. Once he was an attractive man. Remember when we first met, you, Lyell and DG in Dallas? All seems a lifetime ago. What on earth all those sluts locally see in him I simply don't know. I expect he throws his money about, and being Mayor and now the all powerful regional politician has an aura for some."

Charlotte said nothing ... then spluttered ... "Actually, with those guys alongside him he looks more like a gangster in an old film."

Lauren laughed. "You remember when Annabella and Luigi came to visit last year with her tribe? And then we all went out for a picnic with the children, including Philippe? When they were leaving for the airport, Luigi turned to me and said, 'I still get on well with Philippe but to be honest his appearance would even frighten Franco my younger brother to death.' Franco is a Sicilian mafia fixer in Palermo."

Charlotte looked silently and open-mouthed.

Lauren continued. "Franco is actually a great guy like Luigi. You wouldn't know he was mafia unless there is trouble. The last thing Philippe said to me before I kicked him out the day I returned was 'don't trust, don't fear and don't beg.' That aphorism apparently is what they all say banged up inside a Russian prison. I think that says it all about Philippe, definitely a metaphor of how he feels about me. And if you're wondering where he gets all his money to keep him in the lifestyle he always craved, then the company he keeps these days may give you a clue. Best not to ask questions. But since he's been Mayor, lots of new business properties have quietly gone up or mysteriously changed hands. His income certainly doesn't come out of my pocket and even less Cassini's."

"Why don't you just get divorced?"

"To be honest Charlotte, I can't be bothered. All the emotional acrimony and financial hassle and the children are happy the way things are, and so is Philippe. He only lives down the road and they can see Papa whenever they want, he's really very good like that. He even takes them to the Town Hall to meetings, and if they clash the girls always come first. They accept that we live separately in different houses. There's a lot to be said for them experiencing his company. They'll certainly grow up a lot less naive and more balanced about real life than I ever did."

Charlotte winced inside ... She caught the implication immediately, which is why they never talked about Henri-Gaston, her father, since that fateful day he turned up. The whole saga, especially Mila, had remained incredibly painful for Lauren. Nor, like Lauren, had she seen or spoken to her father either. But she kept in touch with what he was doing through Kat and Lexi, who wouldn't be deterred from getting to know their real grandfather by regular phone and subsequently Skype calls. Now the twins were seventeen, a showdown was looming because they wanted to fly to New York and meet him personally and stay at his palatial apartment, and Giles was in favour of allowing them. In any case she couldn't stop either once they reach eighteen and legally become adults.

Charlotte was hugely torn. On the one hand she had faithfully supported Lauren, but time and years had gradually passed by and much of that trauma had slowly healed up in her own mind. Lauren had been one hundred percent resolute about never wanting to hear about Henri-Gaston and Mila again. Charlotte had realised a long time back that the abject shock of seeing Mila as a pregnant love item of Henri-Gaston was the real trigger for her mother's temporary breakdown. Only she and Amélie understood Lauren's love for Mila and how devastated she was ... Henri-Gaston squarely got the blame and that was how it would stay. Neither of them, particularly Mila, had been seen, spoken to or talked about by Lauren since, a long six and a half years. It was as if Mila had been completely erased from the hard drive of her brain. Some careful attempts in the past to raise the subject of Mila and her father had been given immediate and very vocal short shrift.

She wondered whether Lauren had any idea of what had happened since Henri-Gaston and Mila drove off in one direction as Lauren drove off in the opposite one on that dreadful night with Philippe staring at the disappearing car lights of one car after the other. Certainly Lauren had been totally inscrutable since, but it was almost too incredible to believe she had no idea how much Mila had changed. Flying together straight to New York that week, Mila and Henri-Gaston were married shortly afterwards and now live in a ten million dollar luxury condo on the waterfront in expensive and lively Williamsburg, a mecca for the arts, culture and music. Apparently the enclave is also an important Jewish neighbourhood, with Mila significantly involved in the community. Mila had given up the security work, sold her business for a fortune and they were high-flying socialites in the centre of the cultural hub of New York, as much in the gossip magazines as Lauren had been in the past. And of course living with them was their six year old daughter, Adrijana. Fuck, Adrijana was her half-sister for Christ's sake and another baby-aunt for Arthur, poor boy. He probably wouldn't want to know. This ongoing nonsense of nobody talking to one another, complicated though it was, had to be resolved. It was time to break the silence and reconcile. Maybe their chat today could be a trigger ...

"Gosh Charlotte, usually they say it about me, going off in a far away daydream. What on earth are you thinking about grinning like a Cheshire cat?"

"What's a Cheshire cat?"

"You obviously never read Alice in Wonderland. I must get that book for the girls, they'd love it. Anyway, first thing I want to tell you is ... about Giles. Especially as you both now seem to be getting serious."

Charlotte, sipping a glass of apple juice, spluttered out loud. They had begun tucking into their salads, enhanced with a special hot quiche made from three local cheeses which Lauren insisted they both have. "He's been living with me for the last six years. I think we've been serious for some time, don't you?"

"But you don't want to get married?"

"No and neither does he. Giles has been the best thing that could ever have happened to me after DG's death. I know he's different, but he's been wonderful with Kat and Lexi, like the real dad they never had. And you have to admit, what he did to make that vineyard and olive grove productive defies imagination. Commercially it makes us a lot of money. I've never seen a man work so physically hard."

"Yes, I noticed you many times drooling when he was scything shirtless! I agree about Kat and Lexi too. His regular and unstinting tennis coaching with Lexi has turned her into an amazing champion, although regrettably her science interest has waned."

"Yes, but she still gets top grades without trying and will pass her Baccalaureate with distinction. Lexi is adamant, since she won the French Junior Open competition last summer, she wants to make tennis her career, but will continue her biological science academic study. Giles and I are looking at some top American tennis academies. She's keen on going back to the States. Kat of course has her heart set on the École nationale supérieure des Beaux-Arts, a top creative academy in Paris. She wants to eventually make computer animated films."

Lauren smiled. "Actually that sounds wonderful. They have talent and a fierce ambition, like both of us at that age."

"And beauty too! Those two turn heads. I try and keep strict with them though, no serious dating yet," Charlotte replied forcefully.

Lauren took a deep breath. Now it was time to get rid of one more guilty burden, which had been rolling around her head for far too long. "I want to tell you something about Giles, first."

"Well?"

Lauren winced, her sharp brain running through every nuance, angle and permutation of words to make it easy, but there wasn't one ... so it had to be straight and to the point.

"When Giles and I met, the very first day he flew over here with Amélie, the next morning out riding we sort of ... well, he kind of ...

"Yes I know, Lauren. I've known for the last seven years because Giles told me the day after DG died, immediately after he fucked me too in the vineyard before he left. He felt so guilty at the time, but that was the day I fell in love with him. It has never bothered me at all, *c'est la vie* as they say."

"You mean you've known all this time? It never happened again, I can assure you. But I must admit, Giles is a very attractive man and I'm glad you're both very happy together."

"Yes of course, and I would have known immediately if you had continued having a secret affair with him. You aren't very good at deception and let's face it neither am I. I'm quite rational and logical about these things, Lauren. Reminder, who do I take after?"

Lauren laughed and kissed Charlotte on the cheek. "Gosh, I feel like a big weighty stone has been untied from around my neck. Thank you big daughter."

Charlotte took her own deep breath. The moment had come to dive in deep while the going was good. "And equally I know about your bisexuality. Ever since Murmansk in fact, seeing as we're on a path of mega truth session. It didn't take much to work out. So I understand better than anyone why you were so traumatically affected that evening when my father and Mila turned up together. Seeing Henri-Gaston with no warning after all those years was bad enough for you and heaven knows I was so conflated inside about wanting to tell you I had met him beforehand, incidentally DG never knew. But it was Mila wasn't it who broke your heart that day?"

Lauren looked back silently. Her amazing daughter had depths of insight and understanding which were far better than her own. Perhaps Charlotte took some of that off her own Belgian grandfather too, he would have been pragmatic and sensible from day one. "Yes. Which is why I haven't been able to bear to see Mila or indeed talk about her. The pain is still so incredibly bad."

"Actually Lauren. Think also about Mila and how she too will have felt over all these intervening years. She must be as heartbroken as you. Listen, I understand you don't want to see Mila but would you like to know a little about how she's been doing at least? I know because Kat and Lexi have wanted to keep in touch with their grandfather and he with them, and they talk regularly by phone. I still haven't spoken to my father since that night. I knew what the reaction would be if he went and met you unexpectedly and he had faithfully promised he wouldn't do that. He broke that promise and look what happened."

"Yes, I really have no idea what Mila's been up to. Don't look so surprised, I can be exceedingly good at scientific compartmentalisation. Kat and Lexi were mindful never to mention Mila or their grandfather to me, I assume primed by you. Neither has anyone else, including Amélie, Annabella and especially Sonja. I've been happy to leave it that way too, but yes, after all you've said today I would like to know, Charlotte. And I have missed her dreadfully, even though I can't forgive her. I assume she had her baby?"

Charlotte spent the next ten minutes outlining everything she knew about Mila and Henri-Gaston, their marriage, their daughter and their luxury, cultural life style in New York. Lauren listened quietly, impassive but carefully taking in every word spoken, nuance and description.

She finally spoke. "Thank you, I really appreciate that. Actually, I'm pleased Mila has finally found the family happiness she always craved for after her first husband and children were executed in Bosnia. It's not the way I like it, but I'm pleased."

Charlotte looked up startled. "Truly? Mila was married previously and had children? I had absolutely no idea."

"Only one other person apart from me knows the detail—Sonja, who of course she lived with for some years. I've never before told anyone else. Mila had two boys when she was very young. Her husband was a teacher; they were very happy and had built a large house together. Then the Bosnian war came. Her boys were castrated and crucified along with their father, escaping to safety after a despicable village betrayal. They were eight and ten years old. Mila took her time. She had been secretly trained, years before, as a killer operative at university in Israel by Mossad and bided her moment for revenge. After a number of years she got herself captured and was put into a Serb women's prison, then decapitated the commandant, the person who murdered her family, with a cheese wire. She escaped to Italy, leaving his head on a desk. From there her life gradually evolved again amongst a like-minded group of sophisticated, professional women ... Sonja, Annabella, Kristina and others ... That was how I met her, as a manager and chef in Palermo, when I turned up at Luigi's hotel on a nuclear research conference. That entire dreadful trauma affected her life significantly. She became attracted to women in Rome, but she confided that all she ever wanted, deep down, was a normal, happy family. She seems to have finally achieved that now, in an expected Mila way, to include lots of fashion, glamour and money. I admire her; I just wish she had picked someone else as a partner." A couple of tears rolled down her cheek. She reached instantly in her bag for a tissue to wipe them away.

Charlotte, wide-eyed, kissed her on the cheek. "Heck, I understand much more now. And all that stays a strict secret too, especially from Amélie."

Lauren grinned. "Especially! Charlotte, I wouldn't worry about Lexi and Kat going to visit their grandfather, they've wanted to badly for so long. It will be good for them. I'm sure Gaz will spoil them and they'll enjoy his company very much."

"Gaz? Is that what you called him? And you knew already about Lexi and Kat didn't you? How did you find out?"

Lauren laughed. "Gaz was his pet name and he would call me Larry. We were the inseparable Gaz and Larry to our friends, mainly my friends. Of course my parents never knew all that, my mother would have been even more mortified, as of course she was when I became pregnant. It slipped out a few weeks ago when Kat, Lexi and I were all chatting, he must have dropped it into a phone conversation. Then they both became hugely embarrassed because they had mentioned Gaz again, after all those years, thinking I was going to go mental. Kat asked me why I had felt so upset that day he turned up. So I decided to tell them my story. About how I met Gaz, how in love we were despite the age difference and even though I knew he was married, what we used to do, and how bereft I was when he was 'disappeared' out of my life by my mother after I became pregnant with you. They were hugely interested to know the details and what happened subsequently and then how I got back into my studies, university and eventually my career. I felt it was right to finally talk about that period in my life and my feelings, especially to them, as they are now the age I was then. All of which I've kept bottled up for all those years. I hope you don't mind Charlotte, but talking about it is much easier and somehow more natural with grandchildren. I have to say, they were quite enthralled and extraordinarily quiet."

"Of course I don't mind, I'm so glad you did. It's good for you and definitely them ..." Charlotte giggled. "Giles and I wondered why they had suddenly become much better behaved and less stroppy over the last ten days! Actually, something else you won't know. Henri-Gaston had five sons one after the other, immediately after his affair with you."

Lauren's eyes widened. "Really? I had no inkling, but then again I knew nothing of him whatsoever afterwards and didn't want to."

"Henri-Gaston also had no idea, only vague suspicions about me, until the day I turned up at his door in Marseille unannounced. Four sons are marine engineers living very independently and remain staunchly single. All of them live around Asia, but the youngest, Charles, who is twenty-six now, is a designer and remains in France. He was also at home that day and was even more shocked than his father that he had a big sister. I've kept in touch with Charles over these six years. We get on really well, which is also how I know what my father and Mila have been up to. Charles took over the family house when Henri and Mila moved to New York. He lives there with his girlfriend, an artist."

"So perhaps now you can tell me how you found your father in the first place?"

"Okay, but ... promise you won't shoot the messenger will you."

Lauren grinned. "Not an Icelandic nuclear engineering Countess is it by any chance?"

They both giggled softly. "I might have known!" Lauren spluttered, supping her glass of water. "Any trouble, Mila is guaranteed to be in the thick of it, but any intrigue, gossip and secrets you can be sure Amélie will have a hand in wheedling out every tiny minutiae. Shall we order a plate of profiteroles and live dangerously? I could do with something sweet and chocolaty; we can worry about our figures next week." She waved Emil over.

Charlotte then proceeded to explain, after all that time, how and why she wanted to meet her father ...

Chapter Ten

Waving a large brown envelope in the air, Lauren rushed down the corridor and walked straight into the music room where a great wail of musical noise had been billowing throughout the whole villa.

"Okay everyone, you can stop playing, I want to tell you some good news."

"But Grandma, I'm just in the middle of explaining the mathematical ratios of music tones to Magda and Eve so they can play better," Arthur shouted, as Eve and Geri were re-tuning together. "It struck me earlier that the seven pitches of any diatonic scale can easily be found using a link of six perfect fifth notes, so Magda's seven notes on the C-major scale of her piano can be worked out from a pile of perfect fifths beginning with F. It's so easy Mags; don't screw up your face."

"Momie, we get Sushi the genius here but he doesn't seem to understand because he's such a nerd, that we don't need maths to tune up. We just have perfect ears, unlike his of course, which look like jugs!" Eve replied solemnly as her sisters laughed and Arthur's face reddened dramatically.

"Sushi?" But her girls just giggled together. Obviously another of their esoteric secret pet names they keep concocting with each other. Lauren pondered.

She stared at them all. How old are these children? "Arthur do you really understand the mathematics behind musical ratios?"

"Sure, Grandma, it's real fun applying maths like this. I love it. Momie is going to get me some new books on the subject."

Magda raised her eyebrows to her mother who grinned back.

"Now, I have a surprise," Lauren continued. "Do you all want to visit Aunt Annabella in Sicily next week?"

162

"Yes please," the four shouted and danced around.

"That was so much fun last year," Gerri added, "But don't you have work next week Momie? So will we have to go just with Marie again?"

"No, not this time because I'm taking a well earned holiday for three weeks. And, we are going to look at four horses, one for each of you including you Arthur, because Aunt Annabella thinks she's found the ideal ones."

He screwed up his face. "I don't think horses like me much. At least that's what Giles said."

"Don't be such a wimp, Sush, we'll show you how to ride properly, won't we Gevie?" Magda retorted with a wicked smile, as the other two grinned.

"Gevie?" Lauren asked, puzzled

"Sorry Momie, that's our secret shorthand for Geri and Eve, sort of makes talking simpler," Magda replied, now looking angelic.

"They must have two other names Grandma," Arthur immediately chipped in. "A permutation of two out of three possibilities where the order doesn't matter."

Lauren sighed. "Some days it would be nice to have a normal conversation with you children. Take no notice of Giles, Arthur. Your mother and I have made up our minds. Girls, Papa has finished extending the barn and getting it ready and he wants to then take you all out riding too, so won't that be fun? But you'll also have to learn to look after them properly."

"Wow," Magda cried. "Yes please. What day are we flying out?"

Lauren smiled. "Surprise number two—we're not flying anywhere. Inside this envelope is a signed contract, like a big letter. Charlotte and I have just bought a yacht together. She is not a huge yacht like Charlotte once had, but is around forty metres long and has five large cabins for sleeping in, a lovely kitchen and two modern bathrooms."

The girls began to dance up and down happily, singing their latest Irish folk song they had just learned from Jesse.

"Grandma, does the yacht have a powerful diesel engine?" Arthur began, "and can I also ask whether ...

"Just take this brochure to read, Arthur, no more questions," Lauren replied, thrusting a glossy publication of the new yacht technical specification into his small hand. His face lit up with sheer bliss.

"Momie? Who's going to steer the boat? Is Papa coming too?" Geri asked

"Well now that both Charlotte and I have just passed our sailing examinations then we can take it in turn. And Marie will be coming too. Papa has a lot of work to do this weekend so he can't come, but will do next time, he promised faithfully."

"That's a pity," Eve replied. "But I'm so looking forward to next week, aren't we Magie? When can we see the yacht? Can we give it a name?"

"The Fusion Queen is just being fitted out with some new furniture and beds for you four. Then we'll sail on Thursday to Palermo in Sicily where Aunt Annabella lives."

Marie suddenly opened the door.

"Okay all of you," Lauren said firmly. "You can go to the beach later this afternoon instead. Marie is taking you shopping to Nice first for some new clothes. Off you go—a kiss each please."

They trooped out after Marie as her phone rang.

"Hi Charlotte, they've just gone," Lauren answered.

"Great. Giles and I need to do some urgent repair work in the vineyard. That wind last night caused some damage. Hopefully not too serious because we should get a good yield this year of Hind Sauvignon, the grapes are looking very good."

Lauren laughed. "Save me some bottles won't you? I assume Giles is okay not coming next week? Anyway, we'll be back by Tuesday."

"He's fine. To be honest he wants to complete the installation of the new olive presses. Philippe said he would help him over the weekend."

"Mmm ... the girls asked whether he was coming too. I'll be surprised if Giles sees sight of Philippe. It's bitchfest weekend. I doubt whether he'll have the energy to prise his fat rear out of her bed, let alone turn a spanner."

Charlotte laughed. "You want to see the inestimable Geraldine Legendre. I spotted her in the health clinic the other day. She's gone and dyed her great mane of hair bright orange. What does Svet think of all this?"

Lauren sighed. "The everlasting fetish never went away. Svet remains polite on the phone to him and they talk pretty regularly, but now she's engaged to Sergei, she really doesn't have the time or inclination to be overly concerned about her father. She's quite philosophical about his character and her research work takes priority of course."

"Mmm ... well, I'm looking forward to the break next week. Haven't had a holiday for ages with all the work we've been doing here."

"Me too. Are you coming to the Hole in the Wall tonight? I'm singing a medley of Ella Fitzgerald with Helena's quartet. Probably be a full house."

"No, we've got some friends of Giles round for dinner. I wish he liked jazz more, you were pretty amazing at the last gig there."

"Oh well, maybe next time. I really love singing with Helena's band, it has definitely given me a whole new musical interest. Oh yes, some gossip before I forget, but last week she said that Edward has finally decided to relocate and live in Cannes with her. It will be really nice if they finally get together again. Bringing up their child on her own and being my Director of Personnel, especially with the new Cassini restructure, has been hard going but she's doing an amazing job."

"You mean Mr Edward Jones is finally leaving his wife in London and their two children?"

"The two boys are coming with him. I'm going to fix them up at Lexi and Kat's school. They're almost sixteen apparently and want to do medicine like their father. I was quite shocked. I always got the impression his children were much younger. He and Helena are going to buy a house and he's setting up a new gynaecology practice. Apparently wife Peggy has run off with one of his hospital senior managers. There will be plenty of rich female French clients to make his new business a success, I'm sure of that. To be honest it will be reassuring to just see Edward back around, and I'm sure he will rejoin the jazz group; they really need a decent guitarist. Gosh my work mobile's going like crazy. Hope there isn't another crisis down in the lab again. Have to go, bye Charlotte."

"Bye—see you later."

Lauren grabbed at her other smartphone just as it was about to vibrate off the table. Glancing at the number, she failed to recognise any part of it ... she pondered then answered terse and tentative. Calls to this phone were highly restricted. "Professor Lauren Hind speaking, how may I help you?"

"Before you start shouting, Eva gave me this number as I've lost your personal one. She sounds very contented down there. Motherhood and the South of France obviously suit her."

Lauren drew breath for a second then realised. They hadn't spoken for months and months, time really had flown by. She had been so engrossed with complicated Cassini business.

"Your ears must have been burning. Charlotte and I were only discussing you the other day, Ms Sleuth of Secrets. Sorry I've been quiet, dealing with another revolution at Cassini."

"Mmm ... that all bodes ominous. I would wager a sizeable slug of Prada dress-relevant euros that you and your lovely daughter have been sitting in the confessional box discussing other sleuths and men. Is this progress I hasten to ask?"

"Maybe. Gosh Amélie, I've only had this new Blackberry two weeks and I can hear a faint echo, there must be some feedback fault in the circuitry. Anyway, how are things up in Westvalia? Still peeling grapes and opening the occasional fete?"

"Of course. Countessing, the children and Earl Westvale are very much alive and well. However, your Blackberry is actually a good judge of a slight rift in the warp and weft of space-time."

"Where are you phoning from? I don't recognise the number?"

"Actually I'm just eating breakfast and phoning from my new luxury apartment in Boston, with a wonderful view over the river, and later on this morning will start day one of a three month intense visiting professorship in plasma physics at Harvard. I just thought I'd phone you and make you jealous, especially as someone close is only a few blocks down the road from me."

Lauren gaped. It was almost guaranteed, but whenever they had a long break from each other a mini-revolution broke out. But normally it was her who was life-disruptive not Amélie. "I don't know what to say, I'm flabbergasted and hugely jealous. I'd love a taste of academia again. But how? Why? Ahh ... you owe *me* that Prada dress. I said you would be back in the firm once aristocratic boredom set in."

"Sorry Lauren that was in the first twelve months, so I'm afraid our bet isn't valid now. Okay it has taken me seven years but who's counting? Although, if you come over here we could both make up for lost time and have a great big blow-out. The shops here are sooh decked out with the most wonderful summer Versace dresses. A girl could become positively spendthrift. Actually, in between opening fetes I have quietly kept in touch and even wrote a few papers in the last twelve months which have been published. Apart from nuclear bomb making, plasmas were my fulsome speciality, remember, in the riotous days of you and me at the Pierre and Marie Curie University in Paris?"

"All I remember is you blowing apart their special and expensive van de Graf generator straight through the laboratory window and causing a campus wide evacuation ... Honestly? You've been publishing academic papers? You never said."

"To be truthful I was testing the water and now I've stepped back in, the ambience is truly warm and lovely. Rufus is surprisingly supportive but he does have his new right-hand man Tristram, Giles's old deputy and even dishier I would add, to run the estate which is really doing well, and Rufus is very immersed now in Conservative Party politics and mega fund raising. I am required to be here, full time, three months a year plus guest visits and of course research and the teaching of postgrads virtually ... they are so geared up to online learning, who needs a classroom. So we decided to invest in a small but classy penthouse pad with three bedrooms and Rufus and the twins can come over whenever they want. I already have a working study, fully set up."

"Sounds great," Lauren sighed, even more jealous, but then she thought about what she was achieving at Cassini now and perked up again. She was certainly making a ton of money, a good future legacy for the girls and her pension when she gets fed up. "But what about the twins? Won't you miss them?"

"We talk every night on Skype, not a problem. I have a wonderful live-in nanny from Reykjavik called Prudence Sigurðardóttir, who is coping admirably with Lee and Carrie. They are turning out precociously arty and linguistic exactly like their doting father. Both of them are already trilingual in Icelandic, French and English. There isn't a mathematical pi-bone in their bodies, bless them, so I have nobody to teach advanced physics to. And, would you believe, guess who is back home and managing the thriving cultural, art and film location events, which make a stack of loot nowadays?"

"Good heavens Amélie, surely not? ... Cordelia?"

"Indeed. You wouldn't recognise her. Well you would—she looks just as gothically weird as ever, but since Irena got to miracle work on them over the years with psychotherapy, reorientation and anti-manic medication, Cordelia has made great strides to normalise. Alongside her is Simon, finally released from Irena's institution. He is even marrying the woman who originally had him locked up in the first place. She dropped criminal proceedings after they dragged on for years and fell back in love with him. Rufus is so pleased and so am I. His siblings are both very clever and talented individuals, and at long last they can lead relatively sane and useful lives ... thank goodness for modern antipsychotics. So now you can see how the seeds have been sown for me to dabble in the old black arts again."

"I'm so pleased for all of you and I will come over to Harvard soon, I promise. Just need to complete the next restructure. Everything is located down here in Cannes since we opened the second new head office building on land behind Cyclops. I've finally sold the old Brussels base, and paid a fortune to incentivise and relocate as many personnel as possible, including some immediate families, like Eva's mother. Most staff didn't need persuading when they saw the new location and the housing subsidies I offered. We've kept almost ninety percent of the original Brussels staff and the only Executive we lost is Bella, who decided to retire, but I promoted Helena to her post and she has been wonderful."

"Very sensible move. I'm amazed at your retention of staff ... presumably business in China has been good?"

"Exceedingly, another three reactors ordered ... PRC is the mainstay of our business in many ways but we continue to diversify. Nuclear has become harder since Fukushima. To be honest my one downside is the commercialisation of our fusion reactor which is still very slow. The challenge remains the effective containment of the hot plasma, as you will undoubtedly appreciate. We had a difficult situation a month ago which nearly resulted in a major explosion; we have to move forward slowly."

"Absolutely, but I believe Cassini is still way ahead of the game worldwide. Who said creating your own personal sun was ever going to be easy? ... Now I may know someone who could advise you on those plasma challenges ... toroids anyone?"

"Mmm ... Do you remember the last consultancy Dr Helgudóttir? You nearly blew Brussels train station and half the city into oblivion with your suitcase of esoteric dodgy contents. But it would be fun actually if you did a bit over here again with me. Let's discuss when I come over."

"Well at least I don't need the money now, but I would really relish the intellectual challenge."

"Me too and Nice is pretty good at blow-outing too."

They laughed ... old times again. Although Amélie was certain, merely from her far happier phone demeanour, that Lauren had been revisiting her recalcitrance with Charlotte over the no-go areas of Henri-Gaston Landry and the redoubtable Mila Krstic. But she wasn't going there ... yet. "Great, sorry but must go. I have a University Provost to meet, he's quite dishy too, in fact rather Giles-like I would say. There must be something about geologists. Speak soon, and I'll let you know how I get on. Oh, before I forget, I'm interviewing my first potential postgraduate student this afternoon who is researching on high energy plasmas for her PhD in astrobiology - her name is Svetlana Dubois."

"What!!"

"Phone her Lauren. Your step-daughter is dying to chat about proper science to you and is heartily sick of Philippe and his politics every boring weekend he calls her. Bye for now."

The call instantly ended. Lauren, still holding her phone away, stared blankly out of the window and sighed. The bombshell about Svet was just too much, but then Amélie always was. How they remained best friends for so long defied belief. But she had to get to work and promised to pick up Sonja on the way so they could discuss the appropriate location of the expanding military department, which had been steadily commercialising a range of research developments under Juliette's watchful eye into increasingly important sales to selective governments. Lauren herself had been overseeing negotiations, ensuring that she retained responsibility at the top of the company for the most ethically acceptable uses. It had been a deliberately long gestation, with Nimi, her Executive Assistant, undertaking day to day control and project management with a small team of young graduates who Nimi was managing. Now the second major Cassini reorganisation in the eight years of her ownership and leadership was in the throes of completion. The time had come to let go, and she wanted Sonja's agreement on the business proposal she had worked on solidly for a full week alone.

She drove slowly down the wide Nice coast road boulevard of Halévy Street, enjoying her loud Wes Montgomery music and looking for the almost concealed side entrance to the reserved parking area for Sonja's luxury apartment. Everywhere was bustling with tourists and visitors to the popular city which distracted her, dodging people walking off the pavement to the sea wall on the other side. Suddenly she saw the correct side street and swung sharply left and then immediate right, cutting across the path of a gesticulating cyclist, but that couldn't be helped to avoid the oncoming long stream of traffic. She quickly tapped in Sonja's code, the barrier raised and she drove her red Range Rover into the empty space next to Sonja's white Lexus.

Walking to the front entrance, she stopped to gaze at the long line of palm trees and lush greenery, a plethora of red, yellow and blue flowers planted between, listening to the waves crashing over the beach. The tide was high. This was a lovely spot to live and she could understand why Sonja and Johann, her joint CEOs, were very happy there. But Lauren felt an immediate sharp twinge reminder of Mila. She wished Sonja hadn't bought Mila's luxury apartment, but then it had been offered to Sonja for a song when Mila vanished so the deal made sense. She breathed in deeply and walked to the lift, riding quickly to the duplex penthouse suite on the sixth floor. In the end her love and admiration of Sonja overcame any silly and illogical prejudices. Sonja, along with Annabella were the two younger sisters she always wanted but never had; a quite different closeness and intimacy than ever with Amélie or Charlotte. Over the last five years, Sonja's ability to manage day-to-day Cassini so it ran like clockwork had improved hugely along with her business maturity and international standing.

Sonja opened the door and immediately gave Lauren a hug. "Thanks for picking me up, it will give us a good chance to discuss this military proposal. Johann has taken Časlav to my father's apartment who will be looking after him for a few days. He loves his grandfather who takes him out all over town and is even teaching him to play the piano. I can't thank you enough Lauren for creating that highly unusual near-family relocation fund. I know of course we had the income, but your passionate proposal of the benefits and that we should all take a reduction in dividends to create the fund had no dissenters and you've been proven right. When Mila found my father locked away in a Belgrade asylum, getting him out here and properly treated was a godsend. Now he is normal, admittedly his former concert pianist days are over, but he enjoys life hugely again. And of course since my mother died, I had no family close."

"It all made sense to me at the time and still does. You have to think long-term and invest in your staff and keep them onboard, hey even you! Actually it's worked well for Eva too. Bringing her mother here swung the deal. She looks after Paul and Robert in the holidays, and I am much happier Eva is my PA again. Feels just like old times, with Helena down the corridor too. Of course Seb finally has the stable and happy family life he too craved for. They love their new villa in Cannes ... actually I never knew Mila had found your father?"

Sonja looked away quietly and smiled. "You know why you never knew don't you. And I've always understood. Let's face it, you and I know the pain over Mila more than anyone in this world."

"I think ... what I want to say is a long time has elapsed to get over it, and ... well I'll never truly get over it ... but ..."

"I know. Neither of us ever will ..."

"But maybe now ... keeping up the pretence of trying to erase Mila permanently from my life history needs to end. I've had a long discussion for the first time with Charlotte, learned a lot of things, and ... I can't forgive her but maybe I need to try and understand better. You probably think I've been ridiculous these last six years."

"No Lauren, I certainly don't. It took me a very long time to understand why Mila took up with, of all people, Charlotte's father. It was like she had some perverted desire to recreate you in herself and then hurt you irreparably for some incomprehensible reason ... but after a while, and I've kept in touch, not a lot but enough, I learned the truth. They met quite randomly apparently, when Henri-Gaston was leaving after visiting Charlotte in hospital to see her and his new grandson ... and Mila was waiting outside. He first thought Mila was you ... Charlotte incidentally has no idea of any of this. They went off for a drink and something clicked which neither expected nor sought. Up to that point he had been obsessed with finding you again, all those years he had never got over you and him being separated. But with Mila he suddenly and unexpectedly found love again and so did she ... and Adrijana just came along as a consequence.

"Adrijana? What a lovely name. That's what she's called her daughter? She must be around six now."

"Yes, it's a Bosnian name of course. Anyway, Henri-Gaston knows nothing about her past. Mila resolutely has refused to tell him and he's accepted her as she is now, he's never been concerned. He knows nothing of her love for you and me, and never will, certainly not from her. He understands only that she was your temporary CEO and once did security operations. Apparently there was some incident one night in Marseille when they were eating in a restaurant, and she took out a group of Russian mafia causing trouble, handing them to the police, so he couldn't have failed to understand that essential aspect of Mila!"

"An incident? When was that?"

"Very early on in their relationship I think, I'm not sure. Mila never elaborated, just mentioned it in passing. Why?"

"Nothing really, I just wondered."

But Lauren was suddenly pondering hard; something had oddly clicked and was beginning to self-analyse in her sharp subconscious. She needed to reflect later, on her own.

"Lauren, I think you should at least know that Mila was completely devastated over the huge impact that night you all met up. And so was Henri-Gaston. But they've simply and slowly got on with their lives, as we all do. As expected with Mila, she's made a success of the change but I believe a deep sadness hangs over the pair of them. And of course Henri-Gaston has been ostracised by Charlotte, and only the persistence of Kat and Lexi, to keep in touch with their grandfather, has kept some semblance of communication going."

Lauren went quiet and reflected. As ever, the philosophy graduate Sonja finds the threads of clarity and logical sense at the end of the journey and interprets them exactly as needed. Always the sisterly opposite end to Annabella, who cures and heals away the pain when the crisis takes place. "Sonja, as always you bring back some emotional reality into my jumbled mess of a brain. Thank you so much. I need to reflect on everything, slowly and measured. I had no idea how Mila felt but to be truthful my feelings were so shattered and frozen until now, I had no capacity or the will to see anyone else's perspective, least of all hers."

"I know, but I always believed at some point in time the ice might begin to thaw. Take your time Lauren, don't rush yourself. I understand from Charlotte that Kat and Lexi want to visit their grandfather."

"Yes, and I've encouraged that too. I agree—one step at a time, I'm still very fragile about Mila and him, but at least I can talk about it for the first time. That's a big step. Anyway, we'd better get on ... we have a meeting with Nimi when we get to the office."

"Nimi? Right, you'd better explain on the way down."

Driving the ten kilometres steadily out to the Cyclops Fusion Centre, Lauren provided the final pieces to Sonja of the military jigsaw puzzle.

She wanted a new commercial division to be formalised as a subsidiary of the reorganised Cassini, with its own Head who would be given a status of Associate Director in Cassini and would become Managing Director of the subsidiary. The Head would have a budget to recruit a team of ten business managers and an administrator, with a demanding income target to be set and ratified by the Executive Board. The Managing Director would report to Sonja. There would be an additional percentage of booked sales commission incentives for the Managing Director and further down the line for the business team. Lauren especially wanted to cut the blurred lines with Juliette who was beginning to treat the military activity as part of her burgeoning research empire and was, in Lauren's view, the wrong person to oversee full commercialisation. Nor did she want Juliette diverted from the crucial fusion research programme at this important stage. Finally, she wanted Nimi to be given the new job and promotion. Nimi had decidedly proven her worth over the last five years and was turning out as talented as her older sister Bhavika, Juliette's research deputy.

Sonja began to reflect deeply when Lauren veered sharply onto a side road and began a narrow ascent through the picturesque Provence mountains and green valleys.

"This is a short cut I discovered a few weeks ago. Isn't this area absolutely beautiful and peaceful? Just look at those rose fields, apparently they go into my favourite Chanel perfume," Lauren chuntered as she expertly swung the agile Range Rover over a bridge and through some small streams flowing across the road.

Sonja smiled. It was her favourite perfume too. She loved the sophisticated city life where she lived but Lauren's love and enthusiasm for this part of rural France was infectious. Without doubt the enormous work they had both put in to ensure a smooth transition from Brussels to relocate outside Cannes was becoming worthwhile. It made Sonja seriously wonder how long Lauren wanted to continue the high pressure world stage of running her global business and whether at some stage in the future she would sell up and embrace a retired, rural idyllic lifestyle for good.

"Do you ever think of selling up Cassini and living the good life in this type of environment?" Sonja asked.

Lauren looked over thoughtfully. "There have been numerous occasions over the last six years during a few dark days. Yes. But I still get such a big buzz out of the research and the team around me, and most importantly I want to crack the commercialised fusion challenge. That remains my biggest goal, and then maybe I could slowly fade out with my Zimmer frame!"

"Remember what they all say about fusion, same as the hair and the tortoise parable. You should get there but in reality never will. You may be in your nineties by then and still pushing that constantly descending boulder up the hill!"

Lauren laughed. "I'd better raise Juliette's Luddite allowance and get more work out of her. Anyway, tell me what you think of my proposed subsidiary, which I've decided I want to call 'Mughal' and appointing Nimi to run it all?"

Sonja proceeded instantly with a long and detailed SWOT and 4Ps critique she had already mapped out in her head as they journeyed, and then went on to the projected income and expenditure based on some of Nimi's latest research.

Lauren's mind however had drifted elsewhere as they rejoined the main road for the last ten kilometres. Perhaps it had been the stunning views, triggering a wave of desired contentment. Professor Jackson Smythe, her Engineering Director had come into her thoughts. She had personally made the appointment only two months ago to focus solely on the hard, practical challenges facing her fusion reactor. She smiled at the somewhat unconventional job interview. Taking an evening break as usual between sessions at the bar in the Hole in the Wall, with Helena and the guys in her jazz band, she had just finished her usual set and was ready for a long iced vodka cocktail, with rainbow coloured layers in the tall glass, each aperitif, slightly less dense than the one below. She had researched the specific ingredients, calculating the slight but critical differing liquid densities and advised the barman how to make it.

Buying the expiring lease on a whim had been a gamble, the decaying building requiring extensive renovation and modernisation. But gradually the Hole in the Wall attendances had grown over the last three years to heaving levels, especially weekends, and she was quite proud of being the only nuclear company Chairman in the universe who owned a jazz club. She was chatting aimlessly to Jean-Claude, the young and talented double bass player, when a gentle tap on the shoulder made her turn sharply on her stool. She looked up to see the smiling face of a guy in his early fifties, thick head of curly grey hair and titanium rimmed glasses, slim but broad, in tight fitting jeans and wearing an expensive casual check shirt of the type Philippe used to wear in his better days.

"Nikki, I adored that long Cleo Lane number you finished on, you have a very sexy and sultry voice, if I may say so," he said in a clear and refined English accent, looking her over. "I've just paid for that unusual cocktail and ordered one for myself. It exhibits a beautiful differential fluid density, a little like the layers of hot gas surrounding a Tokomak cathode? Perhaps you should call your cocktail invention a Plasma Sling?"

She smiled, immediately sizing up an unusual and attractive admirer for a change. She was the subject of many such boring and tedious advances after she sang ... the downside of going onstage. So she had manufactured herself a series of well rehearsed corny rejection lines at the ready, which included her music pseudonym, Nikki McLean. She was so relationship numb, male or female, that despite Philippe's constant philandering, she had no desire whatsoever to fall into a sordid tit for tat response. And either Giselle or Marie, her personal security minders, were always inconspicuously around, although unusually this night wasn't one of them. She must not get careless and always remember who she was. But something about this man made her look closely. It hadn't happened to her in a very long time, but that stir she first felt when she met her previous husband and even Luis all those years before, fluttered briefly down her insides and made her realise that maybe indulging in a good fuck, which Amélie had constantly urged her to get on with, hadn't been completely irradiated from her emotional system. But instantly her normal distancing response mode kicked in, although she had to admit, this guy had a unique chat line. Who was he? He certainly had some inkling of advanced physics, which she hadn't met before in the club or anywhere else socially for that matter.

Most people had begun returning for the final set including Helena and the band. Lauren was done for that evening, so she remained seated and the man drew up a second stool and sat next to her as his identical rainbow cocktail was put carefully onto the wet bar. He slapped a fifty euro note down and insisted on the surprised and grateful barman keeping the change, who immediately wiped up all the mess and slops meticulously. She crossed her legs and tugged at her short cotton dress, mindful that her tanned thighs were not quite as slim as they used to be, although that certainly didn't stop Dr Plasma from glancing down and back, which amused her.

"You tip generously," she murmured watching his reaction.

"There's only me to spend my hard earned cash on so I can afford to be generous, and without tips those guys behind the bar couldn't afford to eat in this area."

She smiled. "Thank you for the drink. I do love singing Cleo Lane; it suits my blues voice which has always been more precise in a contralto pitch."

"I agree," he replied. "Does that reflect your mood or your philosophy? It's not often you see Schrödinger's equation and the Heisenberg Principle alongside the chicken tikka on the specials board."

"Sometimes I get inspired after I sing; I forgot to rub it off. So who are you? You obviously have more than a passing smattering of nuclear physics."

"So do you Nikki. My name is Jackson Smythe, Professor Smythe. Having escaped the academic tedium of a Cambridge University fellowship, I've spent the last twenty years working around the world, advising governments and companies on forefront nuclear engineering. The more dangerous and problematic, the more I get called in."

She racked her brains hard. All the freelance names one should know in her business were listed in her photographic memory, even the most obscure. But this guy didn't compute. Either, he was a ducker and diver or he worked like Aunt Letty very much under the radar, probably the latter. Suddenly she felt a pang of nostalgia. She wished Mila was there, weighing up and checking instantly ... the first time in many years she had felt that desire return. Yes, a thaw must be happening inside her brain as Amélie insisted would eventually happen. Dr Plasma had at least achieved that tiny bit of good. But more worrying he obviously knew her background, which she had assiduously hidden in this establishment, apart from the careless musings on the chalkboard which meant nothing to 99.999% of the clientele, having taken a cue from the former whizz guitarist Jock McIntosh, aka Edward Jones, her gynaecologist and Helena's errant partner. Thank goodness Marie was picking her up shortly.

"So Professor Smythe, what brings you here to the thriving metropolis of the Côte d'Azur? And especially to this club? A random probability night out or are you in search of some new nuclear adventures?"

"I don't do random, Nikki. But I am bored with Iran. Word on the street is that you're working on a project which may benefit from my hands-on engineering expertise. I have something which may interest you." He thrust his hand into his back-pocket and pulled out a few folded sheets and put them onto the table.

She looked momentarily perplexed; she could see it was an academic paper of some sort.

"I must go, here's my card," he said and held the small card up with two fingers, Chinese style, another intriguing statement.

She took it off him. There was only his name and a mobile number embossed in blue letters on a pale, primrose background. No email, no address, no job title, nothing.

"Do you not have a base, Professor Smythe?"

"No, I live in hotels. Please call me Jack. I prefer that my friends all call me Jack."

"You have friends? But I'm afraid I'm not one of them."

He grinned, gazed fleetingly into her blue eyes again, which made her wince unerringly inside, finished his cocktail and raised himself from the stool. "After you read that, you may be." Then he walked irritatingly off, no handshake, not even a peck on the cheek, which might have been nice.

Her gaze followed his purposeful stride out the door then she unfolded the paper. Helena was now well into her stride onstage, the audience mesmerised as always with her mellifluous playing, blowing her tenor saxophone Charlie Parker style for all she was worth as her guitarist accompanied her in alternating Wes Montgomery riffs, except he had nowhere near the talent of good old Jock Mc. It will be good to see Edward back.

Gazing mindlessly over what was indeed an academic paper by the mysterious Professor Jackson Smythe and published by some esoteric South African science setup, her fast eye scan caught a series of improbably revealing and difficult fusion reaction equations. But it was the title which made her shuffle upright on her stool and wriggle under the bar spotlights. *Towards realisable working fusion reactions.* She read through the first paragraphs, with Helena's slow playing pleasantly filtering through her ears, and immediately rummaged around inside her handbag, in the end with sheer frustration, tipping the whole contents of accumulated detritus onto the bar. She grabbed the mirror and reapplied a smidgen of mascara and bright red lipstick, then picked up her only pen and a small, but very powerful programmable calculator. Grabbing a pile of bar coasters, she began to work, paragraph by paragraph, now totally absorbed. This was a paper at the level of understanding of very few people in the business, including herself, certainly Juliette and Ernesto plus Bhavika, but few others. Scribbling away on a large square of blank coasters, much to the amusement of the barman, she covered the cardboard with a mass of mathematics, typed in and mulled over results into her calculator and continued furiously. Her Jackson Smythe admirer had formulated a radical reactor design to contain the hot plasma, inside something which was neither a standard tokomak nor a stellerator design, but something else which he called a pleidic configuration, made from some variant of graphene, adulterated with sulphur atoms. She hadn't come across the odd material which seemed to possess massive magnetic field capabilities, far above what the Cassini Fusion Centre was achieving. She was pleased and reassured to see that Juliette and Bhavika's new stellerator design was getting close to a predicted magnetic field strength, but this pleidic sphere, in which the plasma was retained in the form of a tiny sun, had much greater retention to prevent the leakage of gas onto the tungsten coated surface. This was a very neat and original engineering solution, totally unlike anything she had seen ...

"Goodness Lauren, I know I get accused of writing in some strange places but this mode takes some beating."

Lauren turned startled from her deep concentration to be met by a beaming smile. Marie was standing there, car keys in hand, with Helena next to her holding a saxophone case.

"We're long used to it, Marie," Helena chirped, putting on her jacket. "I have to replace her white board every month because the surface becomes unwriteable. See you tomorrow Lauren, the new company pension scheme quote I recommended has come in. I think you'll like it. I'm off, must take home the babysitter."

Lauren nodded and hastily gathered her dozen coasters shoving them into her handbag with the rest of her junk. "Oh Helena, before you go. I don't normally ask this but can you possibly get in tomorrow at 7.30am?"

Helena reflected then realised her mother was coming to take out her young son for the day. "Yes, no problem. Don't worry—mum's coming early for Charlie. See you then."

Lauren smiled. "Thanks. Just hang on a second Marie; I must make a quick call."

"Okay, I'll just bring the car to the front, spaces are now cleared."

Lauren dialled and the phone was immediately answered.

"When do you want me to start Nikki?"

"When can you start?"

"Tomorrow."

"What are your consultancy rates, Professor Smythe? I need to have some idea what you're going to cost me?"

"The money isn't important; I just want the challenge of working on the most important project on the planet." He hesitated. "And also to work with you. Pay me what you think I'm worth, as a daily rate and in US dollars please."

As he spoke she checked her diary and had an hour free first thing, she would now extend it to two hours. "Eight am sharp please. Do you know where I am? You'd better tell the gate my real name."

"Of course, Professor Hind. I'll see you then. Thank you. Goodbye, it has been a very pleasant evening bumping into you."

"Goodbye Professor Smythe."

This was the most unusual job interview she had ever conducted. How did he even know she had been thinking about hiring a new Engineering Director? This guy was an amazing find. Hiring on gut instinct was her natural forte, but even on that measure this experience had been extreme. But she would need Helena to do an instant and deep check on everything about Dr Plasma, before proceeding with anything firmer. Once bitten twice shy. Philippe, she reflected again in a grimace ... in all ways.

"So my summary conclusion Lauren is that this is an excellent proposal. I endorse appointing Nimi and will be happy to line manage her. I'll get Helena to quickly draw up a full job description and contract, so when we interview her this morning, we can confidently offer the ... Lauren? Are you okay?"

Lauren suddenly jerked her mind back to Sonja. They continued cruising smoothly, not far to go. "Sorry, I was just distracted for a second by that garden centre, I must buy some new clematis for the front ... yes, I'm glad you approve of everything. Great. Now tell me. What do you think of Jackson Smythe?"

Sonja looked across with a wry expression. Lauren's tone was enough to make her guess that an answer might require more than her usual pinpoint accurate rendition of his work competence and business potential. She and Lauren knew each other in a number of very personal ways and being reminded of those past and deeply shared experiences had already triggered a few alarm bells. It was obvious to everyone close to Lauren that she had a more than usual spring in her step these days.

"In the short time he's been with us, Jackson has been an invaluable contribution towards unblocking the engineering challenges in the fusion prototyping workshop. He's an amazing academic with a sharp innovative mind. Anyone who receives Juliette's admiration and allows them to make jokes at her expense, especially male, must be special. A commendable hire, I must say."

There was a muted silence, neither saying a word. Sonja continued carefully. "But I know that's not what you want me to say is it. Yes, he's very handsome and quite compelling, but you know who he reminds you of, and so do I, we both do. Don't go there Lauren. No mixing of business and pleasure especially in that frame of mind. You'll regret it ... stick to your own rules."

Lauren sighed. The Cassini building could now be seen ahead. She slowed and pulled into a lay-by. "Thanks Sonja. I could only have asked you, and you're absolutely right. I just don't know why I can't have what you've found with Johann, I'm always fated to be cursed."

"Listen, it's not all roses," Sonja replied quietly. "Some days I could wring his neck at home and at work and he still won't do the cooking unless I drag him to the stove. You're doing fine Lauren, the triplets are fantastic and they love their mother to bits. I agree, none of us could have foreseen how Philippe has turned out, but that's not your fault. Something will come along, believe me, and you'll know when you're ready."

"Amélie always knew Philippe would end in tears and I ignored her. But I really appreciate what you've said. Now, let's head for the fray, we've got a revolution to finish off!"

They laughed and Lauren roared off. Soon they swept around the tree-lined private driveway past the newly created lake and fountain towards the inner security gate when Lauren immediately noticed all was not right. People were running around with panic on their faces. As she stopped, Matthew Mayer site security chief ran out to greet them, his usual implacably calm self clearly shaken. She wound the window down. The unmistakeable, continuous wail of the emergency siren was exploding into her ears.

"Boss, you can't go any further with your vehicle. There's been a serious incident. Both of you need to stay this side."

"What sort of incident, what's going on?" she shouted, jumping out of the car with Sonja who had gone white-faced now by her side.

"It's the fusion testing shop. There's been some sort of explosion, only just happened a few minutes ago. Half the roof has blown off. Helena has instituted a code three, three, five, the highest security lockdown. We're instructed not to allow anyone in outside and my guys are closing off the main entrance on the road now. Giselle is down at the shop with the site security team and medics to get people out. We don't know what caused it, whether an accident or deliberate. We need to evacuate the main building immediately. There are not many people in yet fortunately, but the night shift is still around."

Lauren went into her well-rehearsed nuclear emergency mode. She glanced at Sonja's face and knew immediately this situation was not one Sonja would be able to handle, it needed experienced old hands. "Sonja, you go and join Helena, round up Eva and then the senior administrators. Your evacuation protocol needs to be put into action. Everyone should know the drill and where to go. Matthew will help you."

Sonja immediately looked relieved. She could certainly lead this procedure, she had written it. "Okay, I'm off—I'll first grab the whistles, megaphones and clipboards from reception." She ran off immediately into the entrance.

Lauren turned to Matthew. "Go and help her please, all this is new for Sonja. But I'm going straight down to the testing shop. Nuclear emergencies are my area of expertise Matthew, don't worry. I know exactly what must be done. It's certainly not the first time. Is there anyone else there besides Giselle?"

"Yes, Professor Smythe is already inside and directing specialist operations. People have got protective suits on as required."

She smiled. Thank God Jackson Smythe was always in early. She opened the boot of her Range Rover, threw in her five inch Ferragamo heels and pulled out a pair of pink Asics trainers, lacing them up quickly. "Very helpful—provide me an update once everyone is evacuated please."

Matthew waved Hans, his deputy, to accompany Lauren down to the fusion workshop at the back of the site. They began running towards the incident. Plumes of smoke could now be seen drifting skywards and the two onsite fire engines screeched around the corner and roared past them down the internal road. Three things bothered her: casualties, radiation leakage and being unable to contain the incident internally, as failure would trigger all kinds of undesirable outside intrusions and consequences.

She would have to make the final decision on that latter status and quickly.

As they arrived outside the building, she immediately pulled out her pocket Geiger counter. Nothing was clicking except background, a huge reassurance, although the really deadly materials inside were encased in five metre blocks of concrete and could withstand a nuclear explosion. She grabbed an advanced white Demron radiation suit from the external emergency cabinet. She wanted the most durable, not being sure what she would find inside. With no further thought, she hung up her Gucci black jacket on the railing and quickly undid and took off her blouse before unzipping and carefully stepping out of her matching suit trousers. Hans standing at the door gorped momentarily, his eyes on stalks. It was not often you saw the boss naked in her undies. She effortlessly pulled on the Demron along with a pair of the special boots, being concerned most about stray neutron radiation and needed to be sure. She shouted back to Hans to find the special portable neutron and gamma ray detector in the next building. Giselle suddenly ran out with three or four security guys, all in special fire resistant protective suits.

"Lauren there is no way you're going in there. We're getting the fire under control now, thank goodness. The head technician thinks the blast was caused by an electrical fault in the preparation room. Some idiot contractor, not following protocols, had left an acetylene-oxygen welding set inside overnight. That blew up, which is why the roof section caved in. Fortunately the thick walls in there contained much of the blast. Thank Christ none of the night technicians were injured, they were on a break and are all out."

Hans ran over with the bright purple detector. This instrument had cost a lot of money, now it needed to be put to use and only she could work it properly.

"I've got to go in there Giselle and check for stray radiation, something may have cracked." Lauren shouted, anxiously. "That factor determines whether we need to bring in outside emergency and I must decide." There was one other person with the expertise to know. But where was he? "Giselle, where's Professor Smythe?"

"Lord above he's still in there, looking for Juliette. He's a brave man, Lauren, and got the guys organised in a flash. I must get back in."

"Juliette? What the hell is she doing in there this time of day? Fuck it all."

They looked into the smoking doorway as a figure in a blue suit ran out. It was Jackson Smythe. He ran straight to Giselle and Lauren.

"I've found her—she's trapped at the far end. Fortunately she was shielded from the main blast. She was covered in some yellow powder, it looked like clay insulator residues, but I wasn't prepared to take any chances so I cut off all her clothes, admittedly under protest, and got her inside a spare suit best as I could. She's trapped; her arm is pinned by a concrete girder which fell down on top of her; probably broken. I gave her a shot of morphine painkiller. She was very lucky and doesn't seem to have sustained any other injuries."

Suddenly he lunged forward towards one of the technicians holding a portable angle grinder. "Here, give me that, perfect, I'm going back in."

"And I'm going in with you Jackson." She grabbed the special detector off Hans. "Giselle, check the rest of the building for damage and that everyone else is safe. Sonja and Helena should have evacuated the main building. Your men over there have confirmed all the fire is out. Nobody else is to follow us until I've confirmed we are radiation safe."

Jackson Smythe grinned at Lauren. "Let's go boss."

They ran inside together as Giselle switched on the additional emergency lights and made their way slowly through the smouldering mess towards what was left of the preparation room.

"Good news is that the new trial stellerator is all safe and intact, the concrete blocks protecting it took the hit," Jackson began. "We were lucky Lauren. With your approval I would like to take charge of the vetting of contractors in here. I think Juliette's original list needs some drastic cleansing ... I have a very effective protocol devised for that ... this isn't the first time I've seen this sort of thing happen through careless outsourcing.

"Me neither ... approved. Whoever did this I will personally string them up by the bollocks along with their company. I'm sure Juliette wasn't purposely neglectful, she is very thorough."

Jackson laughed loudly. "I can well imagine, I wouldn't want to be on the receiving end."

She looked and thought, some aspects of being on the receiving end could be rather pleasant ... then she thought of Sonja and immediately put her mind to action. "I can see Juliette over there propped up in her suit. I'll just put the scanner on." She adjusted the dials, so far so good. "Nothing out of the ordinary, Jackson, only expected background levels.

"Excellent. Juliette I must say is an amazing researcher. I have a lot of respect for her—she has a fine mind and a great b..." He stopped abruptly as Lauren shot a sharp glance over. "Err ... capabilities."

Juliette smiled vaguely through her helmet seeing Lauren, but then grimaced as Jackson marched up carrying the heavy angle grinder over his shoulder. She looked decidedly woozy; the shot of morphine had kicked in. Otherwise she seemed fine. A radiation bag with the remains of her clothes inside and special decontamination cloths he had used to wipe her body clean were sealed up on the floor next to her. Her left forearm and hand were clearly jammed under the concrete pillar, the suit arm pulled up and specially taped by Jackson, securely before the elbow. A dark bruise was visible on her forehead. A pinkish-yellow dust lay everywhere.

"Don't worry Juliette, this isn't for your arm," he said with a smirk. "I'll cut the concrete each side and pull the piece away then we can get you out. Once Lauren has confirmed no radiation leakage, the stretcher will be brought in. The fire's all out, everything is under control and there are no other injuries. I'll just stand over there and prime up this grinder and put in the right cutter."

As he walked behind the pillar, Juliette beckoned Lauren closer to whisper, slurring. "I'm stark fucking naked down here but in no pain now. He's a fast mover is our Jack ... mmm ... rather nice though ... I'm sorry, I shouldn't have been here. Oh shit Lauren I do feel faint."

She began lolling forward. Lauren propped up her head, smiling playfully at the thought of Juliette protesting vehemently at having her best Prada trouser suit and the rest sliced to ribbons by Jack who obviously had, unsurprisingly, enjoyed the procedure. Then she felt a pang of ... sheer green-eyed jealousy ... which she knew was completely idiotic and totally inappropriate ... she again oriented her mind instantly to the job, but by then Juliette had passed out.

"Fuck, Jackson, Juliette has just fainted."

"She'll be okay, the shot has knocked her out. Prop her against that wall, she won't fall. Right I'm ready."

He pulled the cord and the petrol engine sprang into life and he began to cut away at the heavy concrete, a loud screeching filling the room, white dust flying everywhere. The first cut was straightforward but on the second he met a rod of reinforced steel. He cut all around it then quickly changed the cutter to tackle the metal. Lauren's detector began to bleep, at an increasingly rapid rate.

"Holy shit, something has suddenly escaped, Jackson," she screamed. "There's an increasing reading of neutrons and a worrying rise in gamma radiation. At this rate in a few minutes this area will be lethal."

He stopped and they both checked their protective suit internal readings which were still in the safe green zone but dangerously increasing. They walked into the next section, the pre-reaction area to prime the new stellerator.

"Over there Lauren, liquid sodium. The radioactive coolant is leaking from a split in the tank. It must be that. You have to patch it whilst I cut the last girder which will be dangerous; sparks are going to fly everywhere. He pulled a colour chart from his pocket. And my chemical detector is picking up acetone, God knows where from."

"Patch it? What the fuck with? This will take hours—it's a major procedure as you well know and needs robots. There simply isn't time ..." she shrieked loudly, frustrated with his sudden idiocy. She watched his face, being well versed over too many long years with engineers obfuscating and bull-shitting. This was simply not possible by any stretch of the imagination, and she would therefore need to declare a major emergency, something she was dreading having to call. Either Jackson was concentrating on some ridiculously impossible solution ... or was trying to avoid revealing something he didn't want to.

Suddenly he ran to the doorway and retrieved something from his tool bag, a strange, shiny metallic device, looking like a mini orbital sander she used when she made furniture.

"What's that?"

"Okay, press this onto the tank just below the split, and push the red button. It will start-up, is self powered, and will automatically grip the metallic surface and self guide itself slowly up that tear and weld it together. Stand back. Given the size of the tear it will take about thirty seconds. When it stops, press the yellow button, the magnetic grip will release and you can lift it away. Go Lauren, there's no time to lose."

"Are the batteries charged?"

"It's not battery powered."

"Pardon?" What on earth is this thing, I've seen nothing like it? Anyway it can't grip magnetically, that container is a high corrosion resistant alloy of rhodium and platinum!"

"No you won't have seen this tool. Believe me, it will weld as I've said, using high ultrasonic frequencies, far above normal. Just go Lauren, please."

She snatched the device off him angrily and analysed it for a moment. The casing was an incredibly light alloy whatever it was made of, obviously some aluminium hybrid. Jackson dashed back to Juliette and fired up the angle grinder for the last tricky cut as a huge screeching of hard metal echoed around the building with bright yellow and red sparks flashing erratically about like a firework display.

The tear was around two feet long and small beads of highly radioactive sodium were slowly oozing from it. She placed the device underneath the tear and sceptically pushed in the red button. An unfamiliar humming immediately began and she felt the thing shudder gently from her grip and stick like a limpet to the surface. Incredulous, she stood back. Some kind of directional eye sensor was glowing a faint green, obviously a laser light had emitted and the front end rotated into position. The body levitated an inch or so from the surface then began to move slowly upwards over the split as the frequency of the sound rose quickly, shooting past her auditory ability into an ultra-high spectrum, whilst simultaneously she perceived a peculiar bluish-yellow glow emanate from underneath directly onto the metal surface. Mesmerised, Lauren watched the device ride slowly over the split, sealing the gap completely in its wake. She checked her watch. It took thirty-two seconds and stopped. The leak had halted and the surface looked brand new. What on earth had she witnessed? This was a physical phenomenon which defied all her known knowledge of advanced physics. She realised the angle grinding had also stopped and Jackson was shouting for her to get back in. She grabbed at the device but it remained glued to the tank like a limpet, and pushed the yellow button, when with a faint hiss she felt the grip release and pulled it away, running back to Jackson and Juliette.

"Bloody hell, Jackson, what are you doing?"

She stared wide-eyed. He had finally moved the concrete away, pulled Juliette's suit fully over her arm and hand and had her, still passed out, over his shoulder like a fireman.

"Only sensible way to get her out, I'm glad she's slim and sylph-like. Look, the gamma and neutron readings are going down. That tiny spillage can be easily cleaned up. You've done a great job Lauren, well done. Let's go. Can you carry my bag please? I promise, I will explain my device to you but I can't yet."

She took the mini-welder and placed it carefully back in his bag, zipping it up tight. One glance in his face was enough. He had been distinctly uncomfortable revealing that amazing gadget. They rushed out through the smoking corridor. It was clear that Professor Jackson Smythe was a bit of a secret inventor as well as a nuclear whizz. But undoubtedly, whatever his secrets, he had been the hero of the hour and saved Juliette's life. His prompt coordination and skilled knowledge had been the key factor for the incident to be brought quickly under internal control for which she was very grateful. She would conduct her own internal inquiry and flay backsides responsible, but despite the setback to the programme, Jackson had saved her serious professional embarrassment and a huge amount of money. Getting the workshop back to normal should only take a few months.

Outside, Lauren wished she had taken a picture of Giselle and Eva's faces as she and Jackson emerged into the welcome sunlight with Juliette slung ignominiously over his shoulder. Strong security hands placed her gently onto a waiting stretcher. Dr Moyshe Isaacstein, Lauren's old friend and nuclear medical specialist was there with Dr Eleanor White, the Cassini in-house doctor. Helena had called him from his retirement villa outside Cannes.

Juliette had also come to. They carefully took off her helmet and she woozily thanked Jackson and Lauren profusely with a big smile, before lapsing into another doze. Lauren did a final check. No radiation whatsoever on Juliette's suit. She quickly grabbed her clothes still hanging on the railing and ran into the next building. Taking off her own protective suit, she fluffed up her hair and emerged after a tactical dab of red lipstick to loud applause, her attire back to immaculate as Giselle brought her Ferragamo shoes over.

"Don't remove her suit here please," Lauren barked to the security. "Eva, can you ensure Juliette is taken into the new medical centre. Eleanor will check her over in there. You'll need to help her get the suit off, usual routine, but just the two of you."

Eva quickly realised why. "Where are her clothes?" she whispered to Lauren.

"In this incinerator bag. Tell her I'll pay directly for all replacements in Luddite, even the Versace. That will cheer her up better than anything." Lauren smiled. "Jackson cut them all off as a safety precaution. Oh, and can you ask Juliette discretely why she was in there?"

Eva looked wide-eyed, then grinned. "Crikey. Okay, I'll sort her out."

Moyshe, having had a quick look at Juliette's arm and wrist, came over. "It's about time you used those expensive medical facilities, Lauren. I was most impressed when Eleanor showed me around last week. You instituted all my recommendations in my last assessment report. Nobody ever does that."

"When it comes to health matters and proper facilities in Cassini, there are no short-cuts as far as I'm concerned. Profits take second place to safety. I've seen too many appalling nuclear sites and accidents. What's the damage to Juliette?"

"You remain a breath of fresh air in this sector. A likely fracture across the lower ulna and a few bruises, but she was a very lucky lady. Eleanor will be able to put a light cast on it after X-rays and patch her up, no need for hospitals. Just file a yellow health and safety standard construction accident report to the authorities. You don't want their nuclear bods sniffing about. Your new Engineer, Smythe, who got her out? Intense chap but seems to have a remarkable intellect. He said that a couple of bricks under the pillar, when it fell, had prevented her arm and hand being fully crushed which would have been hugely nasty. That reddish-yellow dust was old plaster. A half filled bag apparently fell on her from a scaffold tower when the explosion took place, but Smythe was right to exercise caution."

Lauren looked around. Where was Jackson? He had sneaked away and vanished somewhere. Why? He never seemed to be the shy retiring type. Perhaps he's a man who doesn't like fuss.

Moyshe continued. "I'd check your contractors in there, are they French?"

"No, an outfit Ernesto had recommended to Juliette from Italy. I'll have their guts for garters."

Moyshe laughed loudly. "Haven't heard that English expression for a long time, I'm sure you will. How's Philippe? I saw him a while back in Nice fronting the election campaign and giving a speech. He's done well politically, but tell him from me he needs to watch his diet."

Lauren grimaced. "I'm well aware of that, Moyshe. Actually, sadly, we've been separated for some time, but we remain amicable and he continually dotes on the girls of course so I'm not complaining."

"Sorry to hear that Lauren but happens to the best of us, me included. Give him my regards. Plenty more fish in the sea however. Anyway, must go, village bridge club to get to." He winked, his eyes twinkling mischievously as ever. "Some very rich English widows in this Provence neck of the woods, you know."

Sonja and Helena appeared as Moyshe walked off to his car. The evacuation had gone smoothly and everyone was back at their desks. Panic over. The technicians and Giselle were already in the building to sort out the extent of the damage and start getting things back into operation.

Lauren smiled warmly at both of them. "Thanks for enacting the emergency procedure properly. Well at least we've tested it for real this time. The fact that Seb was off-site in India with Bhavika was also a useful stress test. I think Giselle was excellent in her handling of the crisis."

"Yes, I agree absolutely," Sonja replied hoarsely, fluffing up her hair. "All went exactly to plan, except my megaphone had a flat battery so I had to shout and I hate shouting."

"Unlike someone who shall remain nameless—she would have been in her element today, bossing everyone around."

They grinned knowingly.

Lauren handed Sonja a bottle of water and turned to Helena. "Jackson was superb in there. He's a true hero of the hour, saving Juliette like that. I would like to organise a little lunchtime ceremony for all staff and thank him formally with a small gift. Also we can use the occasion to reassure everyone that it's business as usual. We were lucky today. I've asked Jackson to oversee our contractors."

"A good idea, Lauren, I'll get it sorted right away, we can use the new training auditorium. Do both of you still want to interview Nimi? Obviously that schedule is already running late?"

Sonja interjected, her throat having cleared. "I'm still fine for a couple of hours Lauren."

"Yes, me too. The quicker we move this plan onwards the better, no reason why not? Can you bring Nimi over to my office in say ... mmm ... about half an hour?" Helena nodded and headed off briskly to find Nimi as Lauren continued with Sonja.

"In fact I've been thinking even more radical about the notion of Mughal being the first of a series of genuine start-up companies within Cassini, benefitting from umbrella support but operating independently with a true entrepreneurial ethos. I want to encourage more innovation. We have excellent staff here and they need incentivising and motivating. This sector is notoriously slow to copy modern practices which the successful high tech companies have been doing for some time."

Sonia's eyes lit up. "Yes, definitely. Johann and I were only recently discussing a similar thought and they could be satellites alongside our other international research bases like Pune with Bhavika."

"Mmm ... I reckon Jackson Smythe would have views on that as a successful freelancer, he goes where innovation is needed the most. Where on earth as he got to?" Lauren replied in a frustrated tone.

"Actually, I bumped into him on the way out through the gate."

"On the way out?"

"He asked me to apologise profusely but some personal issue had to be urgently sorted. He was heading for his hotel but promised he would be back by lunchtime and would work overtime to make up."

"Was he lugging a hefty red bag by any chance?"

"He was actually, why? What was in it?"

"Something I suspect he wanted to ensure was well out of sight. All fine Sonja, he'll tell me himself shortly, he promised. I'll keep him to it."

Sonja pondered. It was becoming increasingly obvious that Professor Jackson Smythe was occupying an increasing amount of Lauren's inner thoughts, rightly or wrongly. Helena however had found only high praise and excellent reference feedback from previous contracts as well as the University of Cambridge, so his professional credentials and capabilities were clear. There had been no security or other issues waving red flags either. But Sonja was still far more concerned about Lauren's fragile emotions ... she and Lauren were too alike for her not to be. "Right, shall we head quickly for your office and correlate our questions? And I could really do with a coffee."

"Yes, me too, I'm desperate after all that kerfuffle. As this is your first crisis management experience, did I ever tell you about mine? The time when I nearly blew the roof off the old research building? ... Around that period, Amélie and I were beginning to ... ..."

Chapter Eleven

Three times she had emptied her suitcase onto the bed and started again. She threw open her wardrobe for the final time in exasperation and began fishing out a new selection of jeans, tops, a couple of summer dresses and one classy evening dress, then grabbed a second long dress because Annabella was insisting on treating them to a meal in Luigi's new Michelin starred restaurant he had recently opened in his hotel. Fortunately, Angelina and her ex-husband were on holiday in the Maldives with their three children, one less potential issue to manage. In fact she was quite certain Annabella had carefully organised their visit to conveniently coincide with that particular timing.

As Johann had now returned from Russia with a contract for two new advanced reactors, Lauren insisted that he take sole charge to allow Sonja to take a well earned break. She could pass on any administrative priorities to Helena and accompany her and Charlotte, bringing Časlav who would be able to keep Arthur company. Sonja was pleased and quite excited when she heard that Annabella had also invited their old friend from the former carefree Rome days, Kristina. Still single, but Kristina was well settled working and living in London with her two children, fifteen year old Eliska and Enrico, now nine, both growing up quickly. Eliska had become an enthusiastic science student and was keen to meet Lauren again. Lauren thought briefly about Luis' children and that strange day, eight years back, she unwittingly met them all in Catania. That was the day any lingering romantic notion she had of a life with Luis died instantly forever. Of course, the fact Eliska and Enrico were also Annabella's half sister and brother would remain her strict secret. Sonja was also keen to see Luigi and the hotel again and catch up with her old colleague Greta, now Luigi's manager. A reunion of old times, they would all enjoy, the one difference now being a tribe of unruly kids had arrived on the scene, running amok together. Annabella, thinking ahead as usual, was marshalling her two live-in nannies to the task in hand on arrival, so at least that welcome intervention would give them all flexibility to enjoy their break in Palermo and relax. She would give Jesse a well-deserved holiday to visit her parents back in the UK.

Just as Lauren had carefully packed her favourite Guia La Bruna lingerie, the door burst open.

"Momie, Momie, you really must come and see what Arthur's doing with Geri?" Magda shouted, with Eve alongside. They viewed Lauren's half packed suitcase with clear disdain.

"Honestly, Momie," Eva began solemnly. "You should be like us. We finished our packing *ages* ago; it really stresses you out doesn't it."

Lauren looked up and smiled at the serious faces of her small daughters, thinking that in five years time they will probably be just as bad. "Okay, I'm nearly done. So what is Arthur doing?"

"He's playing the piano for the first time," Eve continued. "He says he's worked out how to hit the notes in the right order, after listening to Giles's CDs. And Geri is playing the clarinet alongside him. It's weird music Momie, I don't like it much but Arthur says it's called jazz. They are very good. Come on you must listen." Eve grabbed Lauren's hand and began to pull her excitedly to the door.

"Alright I'm coming, oh gosh, typical," noticing her phone was vibrating on the bedside table, as Eve continued dragging her to the doorway. "Magda, can you answer that call please and take a message ... and remember, speak properly like I told you."

"Hello, this is Professor Lauren Hind's telephone, how may I help you?" Magda began in her poshest voice.

Lauren was by then in the music room and stared in astonishment at Arthur and Geri improvising together. She instantly recognised the Dave Brubeck signature tune, Take Five, as she listened wide-eyed as first one then the other switched to a lead, Geri, blowing her clarinet with amazing precision, whilst Arthur jangled his fingers over the keys like a pro. Neither of them was reading music. She realised instantly that both had incredibly gifted musical ears, Arthur could be another potential Jamie

Cullen with the same natural aptitude. He was an incredible child, having inherited a great dollop of the Hind genes. She had to video this for Charlotte who never believed Arthur had demonstrated any musical aptitude, although Lauren had disagreed because as a small baby he had shown clear signs, dancing and moving rhythmically from a very early age to sounds.

Magda suddenly rushed in, her hand held tightly over the phone. "Momie, there's a man on the other end," she whispered. "And although I said I would take a message, he insisted he wanted to speak to you. His name is Jackson Smythe."

"Fine, give me the phone. Eve, can you find my other smartphone, I want you to video these two playing please. Hello Jackson, sorry there's a bit of pandemonium here; my girls are practising in the music room."

"Sorry Lauren, I've clearly caught you at an inconvenient time, it can wait until you return from, I believe, some well earned holiday?"

"No, no Jackson, that's fine, you can call me anytime. I've just finished packing; we're off to see friends in Sicily. What did you want to tell me?"

"Actually I didn't know you had children."

"Seven year old identical triplets, Jackson and they are all very musical like their mother, so we have great all-girl times playing together in the evenings." She heard a faint sigh down the phone and grinned to herself.

"Gosh, that's wonderful. I have five daughters, but they're all well grown up. My ex-wife and I separated many years ago. I just wanted to tell you, I've managed to fire the fusion reactor which is up and running again already. We're only on half power presently but the output is getting back to normal. I thought you would like to know."

"Marvellous!" Lauren danced up and down, as the girls and Arthur looked at her solemnly. "Carry on playing please. Eve, for heaven's sake, will you start videoing. Sorry Jackson. That's fantastic progress, I assumed it would be months off. Thank you for telling me, yes I very much appreciate you calling. But surely you're not in work today are you? It is a Saturday." She began thinking. That was the very first time, apart from the fact she guessed he genuinely had no permanent ties, he had indicated anything about his private life ... at least he liked children ... that could be useful. Then her other subconscious brain side perked up to immediately to question why that information was useful?

"No, I'm at my lock-up in Nice. I've rented a unit to experiment with my new infra-red telescope I've made. I'm a bit of an astronomy freak, always have been."

"Really? Me too. So do you have any innovative theories then about the origins of the universe?" she bantered back, feeling a little flirtatious again.

"Actually yes. I have a number of theories about the interrelationship between dark energy and fusion energy, I'm writing a new paper. I'd love you to come down here sometime so I can show you my electronic observatory."

Dark energy? She gathered her thoughts for a moment, her brain instantly whirring into mathematical gear. That revelation was already setting off thoughts into some new blue-sky research.

"Maybe ... when I can find the time, Jackson."

"Great. Actually I do have one thing to do today. I've promised Juliette I would drive her into Cannes, to a shop with the peculiar name of Luddite. Not sure why, but she said it's important. Her cast has another four weeks to go before I cut it off with a circular saw."

Lauren giggled. "Yes, Luddite is definitely very important. Tell her not to spend too much and to check out the new Guia La Bruna range just in." She suddenly felt that green goblin leering, resting on her shoulder again and metaphorically brushed it off instantly, but still wishing she was with him instead at Luddite, something her former husband used to regularly do which they enjoyed together. Philippe of course rarely had ever gone shopping with her.

Magda sidled up to her and looked at her watch. "Momie, we have to go soon," she whispered loudly. "Are we picking up Papa on the way?"

"No Magda, Papa can't come this weekend. Sorry Jackson, I have to go. Thanks for calling and the great news. We'll catch up when I get back?"

"Okay, enjoy your break."

He rang off as she smiled, pleased he had phoned. She felt suddenly felt very elated and was looking forward to seeing Annabella. "Momie, why isn't Papa coming, yet again? Who is that man?" Magda replied, her eyes screwed up.

Lauren gazed at her daughter and rubbed her head affectionately. Magda was the most astute of the three and they were all so bright and far too attuned to subtleties and nuances for their ages. She had to be cautious. But one day they might find their mother has another man in her life and she would have to think through very carefully how she approached that sensitive issue as they all adored Philippe.

"Papa is a very important man and has to suddenly work on his mayoral duties this weekend, darling, he's very sorry. But next weekend he's promised to take you all, and Arthur, to the new water-plume and fair in Cannes. The man on the phone is one of my senior managers in Cassini. He had to tell me something, a bit of good news after the big fire last month."

Magda perked up at the thought of the giant water-slide. "Hey everyone, Papa can't come today but he is going to take us to the new water park next week. Eve have you finished your video? Momie, look out of the window. Charlotte and Aunt Sonja are arriving with Časlav. Is he coming too? That's great. Look Sushi, your friend Časlav is here, you can talk maths all day together now!"

The girls smirked as they ran to fetch their cases. Lauren raised her eyebrows at Marie standing by the door.

"I'll just let them in," Marie said.

"I'm glad you're coming with us Marie, especially as Giles also ducked out last minute along with Philippe. Men! Are you sure you don't want to go with Jesse to see your parents?"

Marie laughed. "Actually Lauren, although I love my parents dearly, this trip sounds like a whole lot more fun and I've never been to Sicily. So yes. I'm glad Giles has to continue with his trellis work and spraying in the vineyard!"

"The door was open so we just walked in," Charlotte announced giving Lauren a quick hug. Sonja introduced herself to Marie and they instantly began chatting, both women very similar in temperament. Giles drew up outside in his pickup truck.

"Okay everyone put your cases in the pickup." Lauren began, now back in her usual organisational mode. "We can all walk down to the harbour and boat jetty. Fusion Queen is moored in the yard, ready to go. First stop will be Bizerte in Tunisia and then we will cut across to Palermo. We'll be at Aunt Annabella's by Monday."

"But Grandma?" Arthur piped up. "Why are we going to Tunisia?"

"Forgotten already Arthur?"

"Yes," Geri squealed. "Conveniently," and proceeded to nudge him.

"Because Aunt Annabella and Uncle Luigi have friends in Bizerte who breed lovely Arabian horses. Remember, one reason for this trip is to buy you and the girls one each. And if we see any we like they can be shipped here."

Arthur grimaced. He had put that to the back of his brain and genuinely forgotten, a rarity for him. Fortunately, Časlav came to the rescue and pulled out his iPad mini.

"Arthur, come and play this new mathematical game I've downloaded called PiBall." That was enough for Arthur to forget his irrational torment, until Magda piped up.

"I think Časlav means Piebald, Arthur," at which the three girls erupted in laughter.

Charlotte shook her head to Marie and Sonja.

"That's quite enough teasing for one day ... cases please, now!" Lauren ordered as they scurried off to the pickup.

Giles, muscles rippling from his recent weight lifting sessions, also wandered in, looking extremely tanned, as of course did Marie. "I'm really sorry Lauren, I have to finish off the trellis work in the new area and spray it fully, and I have my first course exam on Monday at the University of Nice Sophia Antipolis in vineyard management, so I must revise."

"But think of the company you'll be missing Giles, four gorgeous women on a boat, all to yourself for seven days. What more could a man want?" Charlotte teased, doing up Arthur's jacket. "He works far too hard, always outdoors, but then I'm really glad. He's been mixing some beautiful new wine in the distillery!"

Giles blushed. Lauren caught him glance surreptitiously at Marie who also had slightly reddened. He had once looked at her that way ... years back. She realised another likely reason they were both so brown but decided instantly to let it pass. Besides, she pondered. Who was she to judge anyone especially Giles? Charlotte's attitude to Giles had always been one of realism right from the beginning. He was still hugely attractive, sexy and he and Charlotte adored one another but she certainly wasn't intending getting pregnant by him, that much she had already confided and had obviously factored in some flexibility in their relationship. Maybe that included her too, although there had been no signs that way. Interestingly that was one area of personal judgement where she and Charlotte differed. Then she thought of Annabella, Mila and Rosie ... and latterly Bhavika, still single, ravishing and ... mmm ... decidedly engaging, when she was last over in India at the Pune research centre. Perhaps she and her daughter were not so unlike, except Lauren had restricted her non-committal discretionary desires to women, which wasn't Charlotte's thing ... Where men were concerned, Lauren needed much more than just sex, a factor not always easy to define as Jackson flashed across her mind ... and she genuinely thought, four husbands later, she'd finally found it with Philippe. How sorely disappointed she felt.

"They're on the plane by now?"

Lauren suddenly came out of her thoughts to see Giles driving off to the quay. She shut and locked the door and they all began trouping down to the harbour, Arthur and Časlav running off down the lane with the girls trying to catch up.

"Sorry Charlotte, who's on the plane?"

"Gosh Lauren where is your brain? I hope your navigation skills are a bit sharper when we set sail! I think I'd better have the wheel."

Sonja looked aghast for a second as Marie whispered 'joke' and they then continued walking on together chatting happily.

"Lexi and Kat," Charlotte blurted.

"Gosh, I'd completely forgotten about the twins, sometimes it's hard to come to terms with just how grown up and independent they've become."

"At long last they've gone to New York to see their grandfather. He's even deferred an imminent art tour of South America for them, he's taking no chances. Henri-Gaston is as excited as they are."

Lauren smiled. "Good. Presumably they'll see Mila too."

"Apparently not. She's away somewhere else."

"Mmm ... Wow just look at our boat Charlotte," Lauren cried, pointing at the large vessel sat at the quay edge. "Haven't the fitters done us proud? All shipshape and fitted out, fuelled and ready to go. I've already plotted the entire route; the charts and everything are inside. We can just set sail immediately."

"Great, yes, gosh, I must say, Fusion Queen looks totally gorgeous. You know I do still get a pang of ..."

"I know ... so do I. But I'm sure if DG is looking down, he'd also be proud and happy for you and Arthur and Giles too."

Charlotte laughed. "Guess you're right. Anyway he definitely wouldn't be down there looking up, he would have quickly bribed his way out of shovelling bodies into the flames."

Lauren threw her head back, giggled, and linked arms. "Honestly Charlotte, sometimes I wonder about your humour. Anyway, you may as well take the first leg; I've already had a sail around the coast. She handles beautifully."

Luigi began pouring out a glass each of his best red Chianti whilst Greta beckoned the head chef to bring their special seafood salads, freshly prepared. They had arrived a few hours earlier than expected in Palermo, a fresh south westerly wind having given the Fusion Queen a little more momentum, with Lauren skilfully skippering to maximise the advantage.

"Thank goodness we've got rid of the children for a while," Charlotte sighed, relaxing in a luxury seat. "If Arthur asks Auntie Sonja one more question I'm sure she'll strangle him."

Sonja laughed and patted Charlotte's hand. "I really don't mind, he's a very intelligent, sweet child, don't worry. I have a lot of patience and I'm glad he diverted Časlav from being seasick, he did go quite green initially when we left the Tunisian coast!"

"Yes, the going was a bit rough there," Lauren interjected. "But from the squeals outside, they all seem fully recovered. Annabella, I must say, Francesca and Lia are excellent nannies."

"You know me," Annabella replied with her sultry smile specially reserved for Lauren. "Like Sonja I too am very patient to ensure I have only the best, and with the demands of my sister they have to be, how you say it, top notch? Your triplets are angels in comparison."

"Looks like they're having fun in the children's play area. That should keep them quiet till bedtime," Marie added, clinking glasses with Sonja as they all toasted each other. "I see Lia is bringing out a giant picnic."

"So tell me, Lauren, what happened to Arthur when you met with Hamid and Maryam in Bizerte?" Luigi asked as they started tucking into their salads and warm pita bread.

Charlotte giggled. "Gosh Luigi, it was classic Arthur. You know he is still frightened of horses, and keeps well away from the stables, despite lessons, but the triplets keep teasing him so he's been trying to man up a bit of late. Anyway Maryam brings out this beautiful young and saddled up black gelding to show us and then she shoves a riding hat onto Arthur, who was attempting to be inconspicuous, hiding behind everyone, and she insists he takes a short ride with her immediately. His face was a picture, especially when the horse muzzled him, as if to say come on, make my day."

Everyone laughed loudly.

"The girls were in stitches," Lauren continued. "Especially when Maryam said 'now you must ride, like a man,' and lifted him onto the saddle before he had time to blink, and in a moment the horse was off like a rocket in a cloud of dust towards the sand dunes, with Maryam behind on her horse. Five minutes later they came around the other side, Arthur beaming madly, now in full control and an obvious instant symbiosis established, in some mysterious way behind that sand dune, between man and beast!"

Charlotte took up the rest of the tale. "The triplets stood in disbelief as Arthur confidently trotted up to them and dismounted. Then he turns to Lauren and says 'Grandma, can I call him Herbie please after my favourite jazz pianist?' He means Herbie Hancock; I have a large CD collection. The girls had already chosen their horses, all mares, so Lauren is now the owner of four new horses, and Arthur hasn't stopped talking about how much he likes riding!"

Annabella was still laughing. "What a great story Charlotte. Luigi will talk to Hamid soon and arrange for them to be shipped to Nice; he will take care of all paperwork. Hamid supplies many horses to the rich along the whole south coast of France."

Later, with everyone relaxed, fed and comfortable, Greta insisted on taking Sonja and Marie around the hotel to show them the impressive restoration and new rooms and especially the additional kitchen, with Marie fascinated to learn about Sonja's former master chef expertise, another area they both had in common. Luigi went off to play with all the children and Lauren and Annabella had a long catch up, including the latest Aid Evocative work in India, which Annabella, as CEO, had now set up. Lauren gazed enviously around the red upholstered lounge, looking a sophisticated million miles from the old and tired facade she had experienced when last there.

"This place looks so wonderful, Annabella. Your investment is certainly paying off, everywhere is busier and the clientele look much more upmarket."

"Yes, I spend five million euros. I tell Luigi it is from my old consulting work and he believes me, and that we get it back in three years because upmarket clients will come and pay much more. That he wouldn't believe ... but now he bites lips because money is rolling in for him and Greta is performing an excellent job as overall manager. He has been much happier getting his hotel back and is a good excuse to keep away from Angelina, who is very moody presently, menopause of course. But the children are fine and your ex-husband remains happy and adoring of her as ever ... sorry Lauren, usually I think wiser. It is, I am sure, Luigi's strong red wine!"

Lauren laughed. "Don't worry, I have long gotten over him with Angelina, and when I ran away here and met them together as a family, they do amazingly seem the perfect couple ... I was never right for him, I'm far too ...

"No," Annabella insisted vehemently. "You are perfect for me and even more ravishing than ever. I do love your shorter blonde hair, it suits you so well."

Lauren kissed her cheek. "Thank you, that's made my day. When is Kristina coming?"

"Gosh I nearly forget." Annabella peered at her watch. "She sent me a text. She arrived ten minutes ago at the airport so will be here in twenty. Now I can see your face, but don't feel anxious. Eliska is with her, but Enrico has stayed in London with Kristina's parents who live near to her. He dislikes Italy intensely and avoids this place as much as possible. Much water has passed under bridges since the death of their father, Luis. You may be surprised when you see Kristina again. She has long recovered from the death of Luis who is no longer in her thoughts and has moved on with her life dramatically. Now fluent in English since living in London, but Kristina is a very bright former languages graduate of the University of Prague. After a year she was offered an administrative job in the Czech Embassy. Now she is the official Ambassador for the UK and on speaking terms with the Czech President. Kristina was always ambitious, but the same as my sister, that ambition fell away like scales of a dead fish when she came under the overbearing and obsessive spell of Luis. Men like him, Lauren, you are best well away from as are all women, and he was my father, but I feel no different."

Lauren felt an inner chill. She had never been sure she ever truly got over Luis.

Suddenly Annabella pointed to the revolving door. "Gosh here they are already, walking to reception. Eliska is quite unlike her brother. She is very keen to talk to you Lauren and seek your advice. Kristina will want to meet Sonja and Greta straight away, so I'll take them all to the coffee bar for a gossip. Luigi will take all the children, Charlotte, Marie and the nannies back to our house and get them sorted for this evening. We have plenty of room now that Angelina is away, she is happy with that. I suggest you take Eliska for a walk around the lake. For the next few days I have arranged some trips around the island including a walk up Mount Etna which will be fun, and of course a visit to my little island in the bay for relaxing and lovely beach ... the children will love it and I've built some more facilities. Hey and maybe you and I do some surfing again? I understand Marie is also a keen surfer?"

Lauren smiled. "Surfing would be fantastic, but I'm way out of condition. As usual Annabella you are super-organised, I envy you. My goodness is that Kristina and Eliska coming in here? I see what you mean."

She stared at mother and daughter approaching. No way would she have recognised either of them. Kristina was actually quite petite, still very pretty, but she now had short curly blonde hair and walked with a commanding presence. Her expensive business suit and demeanour expressed her elevated status to a tee, her green eyes flashing as she took in everything in her sight. Alongside her, Eliska, equally unrecognisable, had become a tall and confident young woman, her long tresses of black, shiny hair and flawless olive skin an unmistakable homage to Luis her father, who she obviously took after strongly. But most uncanny was the startling resemblance to Annabella, her half sister. Eliska was equally as beautiful, the same features, brown intense eyes and curvy figure. Surely Kristina and anyone else who saw them together must have worked out the hidden secret that Luis and Annabella were blood related. Maybe Annabella no longer cared. Lauren wasn't going there; the secret she knew, shared after a passionate exchange with Annabella, would always stay that way. If others judged then that would be up to them.

"Lauren, I can read your mind as always. Kristina knows. I told her in confidence some years back. She is fine, we are closer than ever."

"Eliska?"

"Not yet, but one day?"

"Fine."

Kristina walked over briskly, her hand outstretched, directly to Lauren. "Hello, it's a pleasure to meet you again."

Lauren was unexpectedly startled. Her English accent and mannerisms were flawless and very upper class. Kristina would have felt at home amongst Rufus and his aristocratic family.

They shook hands warmly as Kristina continued. "I would like to take this opportunity to thank you for your support alongside Mila and Annabella when Luis died. Moving to London got us all back on her feet and changed my life, as you may know. Thank you so much Lauren, I really appreciated it."

Lauren wasn't sure how to respond. Kristina was so sure of herself and clinical ... long gone was the shy, quiet and retiring woman she had met all those years previously. "I was pleased to help; it was a very difficult time," she replied carefully.

That was obviously sufficiently succinct and apposite for the moment, Lauren realised, seeing Kristina's eyes flash and a tiny smile follow. Kristina understood a lot more that was clear. Lauren breathed easier. Thank goodness for those hard won tactful negotiating skills, honed sharp over the years of running Cassini. "I understand from Annabella that you have done outstandingly well in the Czech diplomatic services, congratulations, Kristina."

"Thank you. And I understand from Mila that you are a colossus within the global nuclear sector and now own the Cassini Power company outright. That too is a formidable achievement for which congratulations must be reciprocated warmly. Annabella, I must tell you later about Mila's breathtaking parties which have become the de rigueur place to be for everyone who is anyone in cultural New York and now of course Washington. Sorry Lauren, I was being rude forgetting. May I introduce you to my daughter Eliska, I think you met previously. She has her heart set on becoming a budding scientist; she takes after her father of course."

Lauren felt her inner clock miss a few beats hearing the New York party revelation. Kristina had obviously not only kept in touch with Mila since the great escape but had even been over there hobnobbing with the great and good; all the intellectuals, politicos and creatives that Mila seemed to be cultivating with a messianic fervour. What else did Kristina know?

She held out her hand to Eliska. "Lovely to meet you again. You've certainly grown up into a beautiful and by the sound of it a clever young woman."

Eliska blushed. She liked compliments especially from someone as prestigious as Lauren whose scientific and career progress she had secretly followed as a role model for women in science. "Thank you," she replied quietly. "Mama is correct, my passion is physics and mathematics, exactly the same as you Lauren," her English accent and diction delivered with the same unnerving English flawlessness as her mother.

Annabella interjected, taking Kristina's arm. "We're going to join Sonja and Greta in the coffee bar. Now I know Eliska you wanted to ask Lauren some advice, so we'll leave you both to chat ... we'll see you later." With that Annabella whisked Kristina away through the door.

Lauren turned to Eliska, smiled and looked her over. To all intents and purposes she looked like any other normal young teenage girl, stunningly pretty but expensively dressed with designer skinny jeans and tee-shirt and they were definitely Louboutin trainers, which Lauren had never seen before. Without a doubt even Lexi, the other teenage super-fashion nowadays in the family, would be envious. But there was something about Eliska's intensity behind those dark brown eyes, the stare said it all. She was sharp and mature. Eliska had an agenda.

"So what advice would you like, Eliska?"

"I'm starting a PhD at Cambridge University this autumn. Initially it was going to be in mathematical physics but I've been offered a special scholarship to consider joining an elite team, sponsored by a US tech company instead, to develop a radical new approach in artificial intelligence. I'd like to know what you think about AI. But bringing forward the day of the singularity worries me."

Lauren immediately pulled herself up in her chair. "Eliska, remind me, how old are you?"

"I'll be sixteen next week. I started mathematics at Cambridge in Trinity College when I was thirteen and have just graduated. It was tough being so much younger than everyone else but I managed my MA in the end."

"And how was the end?"

"Err ... Senior Wrangler, just, by three marks, it was close but I made it."

"Heavens, Eliska that is an incredible achievement. Congratulations. You know, I followed a similar pathway in France but ... well ... I wasn't able to start until I was older, that was tough too."

"Yes I know, you had a baby didn't you. I don't intend to interrupt my studies that way; I have had a coil fitted and definitely discourage relationship commitments. I'm far too busy but I enjoy sex as you did. I only mix with the postgraduates, and some of the staff, they're far more mature and intellectually interesting." Eliska sighed, a reluctant acceptance of having to walk before she can run. "I have to be challenged by an older man, most of them sadly run a mile when they realise my age."

"They won't always do that," Lauren replied softly with a smile.

Lauren stared for a moment as her fast brain oriented into the situation in front of her and adjusted. She realised Eliska was exceptional and very different from normal, and certainly exhibited autistic savant characteristics. Socially and in communication she appeared to be neither shy, withdrawn nor awkward, but definitely very precocious. More worrying was how she knew about Charlotte ... or maybe she doesn't know the baby was actually Charlotte. Lauren reflected. Subtle care with nuances of discussion would be required. She was very used to that but never with someone so young. "How about a walk around the lake? I could do with a bit of fresh air, I'm sure you could too."

"Yes, good idea, I'll just buy a can of lemonade from the bar, I'm very thirsty actually."

Lauren waved the barman over, raised up her own can and handed him a ten euro note. "No need, he'll bring you one and another for me as we go out. Keep the change please."

Outside, the air was quite still and very pleasantly warm. Lauren gazed over the beautiful lake. A feeling of regretful nostalgia crept over her, thinking first of her former husband, then Luis and latterly Philippe. All three in swift succession had walked around this lake with her once, holding hands, whispering sweet-nothings and promising the emotional earth and love forever. None of it was to pass. The two newly installed fountains gushed pleasantly at the far end, large koi and fan-tailed goldfish darting in and out of the ripples. The path and surrounding gardens had all been redesigned and planted with a colourful exuberance of red, yellow and purple flowers interspersed with exotic tropical shrubs, with little waterways and bridges crisscrossing the green and well watered expanse. Without doubt, Luigi and Greta had done a wonderful design job outside as well as inside. Right at the far end she spotted some bench seats and they slowly walked on in that direction.

"What is the singularity, Eliska?"

"It's the day when artificial intelligence in robots becomes self sustaining and exceeds that of human beings. That will be, in my opinion, the start of the fast extermination of mankind ... the singularity is far more significant than the effects of climate change because it will happen much sooner."

They stopped immediately. Lauren stared out over the lake deep in concentration, silent and immersed inside her mind into her secret scientific world, the outside totally walled off, a trait she was capable of doing whenever something fundamentally game changing hit her. Eliska watched, fascinated and in awe. Lauren was exactly as powerfully minded as she had been told at Cambridge and subsequently researched, including Lauren's whole batch of nuclear fusion papers over the years, much of which she already understood. This was the perfect moment. Eliska took off her small pink rucksack and fished inside for a sheaf of mathematical papers.

Lauren remained oblivious still in deep concentration, when she suddenly uttered. "And when is that date predicted?"

"A number of the established top artificial intelligence designers and researchers estimate a time around twenty forty-five."

"And what do you predict?" Lauren replied fast as a bullet, her face serious, her eyes searing deep into Eliska's, frightening her. Even at Cambridge she had not met anyone so intense.

"Twenty twenty-five."

"Why?" Lauren barked.

"Because at that point robots will understand how to use perpetual fusion energy to power and then replicate their own non-biological neuron cells, which will be vastly superior in speed, complexity handling and robustness than the human brain. Would you like to look at my paper I've written, which extends some of the ideas from your latest fusion publication on achieving lower temperature reactions? Sorry it's a bit scrawled, I was in a hurry. I was so keen to see you directly Lauren, because I showed my supervisor at Cambridge last week and he didn't have a clue what I had done. I hope you might be able to understand it."

Lauren immediately turned down the intensity dial of her own thoughts. Eliska was only just sixteen years old. She wasn't with Juliette and Bhavika who were used to this way of intense, fast draw, and deep throat theoretising, batting viciously, no holds barred, from one to the other, a process which occasionally bordered on wild and maniacal sociopathic shouting, but they were all used to it. At such sessions Eva and Helena kept well away from her office. Then afterwards they would all go out and have a nice meal, wind down, talk about men and buy clothes together. She took the paper from Eliska's hands, beckoned towards the benches and began to read in total silence: *On the mathematical feasibility of managed micro-fusion reactions simulating neurone transmissions.*

Eliska sat rigid on the other seat, her heart pounding, staring back. Lauren pulled out her high-powered solar calculator from her bag and began tapping furiously into it, smiled, ruminated and carried on for the next five minutes.

Finally she raised her head slowly. "I'm going to answer your first question immediately. Yes, you must take that decision and research artificial intelligence at Cambridge. You have an aptitude and an insight I have never seen in anyone so young for a very long time. Your paper is an interesting and original approach. I see you've constructed some novel quantum dynamical mathematics to enable you to solve the low temperature fusion conditions I proposed in my last paper. That is good, Eliska, very good, and I think I understand your unique new toolkit, which is a major way forward. However you've made some fundamental mistakes, so the final conclusion is a thousand degrees higher. Some way to go yet before reaching room temperature, I'm afraid. Also you need to acquire the strict discipline of practical research methodologies and correct presentation. That will take necessary time and practice. So view your PhD as a vital apprenticeship to get all the fundamentals and framework for a lifetime's future work right ... then I believe you have an excellent academic career ahead of you."

Eliska beamed, she was so pleased. Her gut instinct was correct. Only her meeting with Lauren directly would provide the feedback she desperately needed. "Thank you so much, I'm so excited. Yes I will opt for that programme. But I will need to be interviewed first by this US tech company before they release the scholarship and ..."

Lauren interrupted. "I have a proposal Eliska. Cassini will sponsor you instead and I'll double your scholarship, but I'll want you to research your artificial intelligence in a particular direction, complimenting the university focus but providing me with some new answers to our work too. I will speak personally with your Head of Department or the Vice Chancellor if necessary."

Eliska thought for a moment then beamed again. "Yes please, that would be an even greater, fantastic opportunity."

"Of course it would if I have anything to do with it," Lauren replied laughing.

"Aunt Annabella also suggested that you may be interested in having an intern over the summer at your Cyclops Centre. I have two months free after I come back from holiday with my mother."

"Well, as ever, your Aunt Annabella is way ahead of me. I was just going to suggest the same, if your mother is happy with the proposal. It would be good for you to get some early hands on experience and see how an industrial research operation functions."

"Thank you Lauren, that is so wonderful, I'm sure she will be." Without any hesitation she gave Lauren a big hug and a kiss on the cheek. "My father would have been so happy too."

Lauren felt that chill again, a mixed chill, cold from an irrational unknown fear and hot from that old Luis desire which never went away. "Your father, Eliska?"

"You loved him very much didn't you."

Lauren went immediately quiet and reflected carefully.

"What makes you think that?"

"I still remember the way you looked at him when I met you that day at the museum. You were very sad, probably because you suddenly discovered we were a family, but I knew even then, although I was only seven, but it is still like yesterday. My photographic memory I'm afraid, a bit of a curse sometimes."

"Tell me about it Eliska, I understand exactly. Yes, I was very fond of your father."

Eliska smiled. "He loved you too. He told me, but he also loved me and my mother, and he said he had to make a very difficult choice which would make you terribly unhappy and he was so sorry, but that he had already decided he would stay with us and be a happy family. But of course, soon afterwards he died in that building accident in Albania. I still miss him terribly, we were very close. My mother used to become annoyed that my father and I always talked and did things together, but Enrico takes after her and they get on very well so that sort of made up for it. My father was very good at mathematics too, that's who I take after academically."

"Yes, I can see that. Did your father also tell you I had a baby when I was your age?"

Eliska blushed. "Yes, he did and that it was adopted, but had to stay a secret. Lauren there's something else I want to confide in which my mother doesn't know. It's about my Aunt."

Lauren stared again and then realised. Eliska knew what was obvious to anyone with her analysing brain. "I know too. How did you find out?"

"I always wondered, even when I was a child. We are so alike. Last year I sneaked into her bedroom when we were on a visit and collected hair from her brush. Back at Cambridge, I asked my best friend, Sew Jong Chen, she's Singaporean and brilliant doing biological sciences, to test it in their DNA lab against mine. It was a perfect match so I concluded we were sisters. Annabella has always been close and looked after me and Enrico, we never wanted for anything when we first moved to

212

London. We had no money after my father died. Eventually of course my mother developed her diplomatic career. Now life is so different it is unrecognisable, but I still wish my father could have seen her success too."

Lauren patted her hand. "I think Luis would have been very proud of your mother and you. I'm going to suggest Eliska that you confide in both Annabella and your mother about what you know. I am sure neither will be angry, and will understand and be fine with it. Trust me, okay?"

"I will, I promise, thank you; I'll find a suitable moment."

"Well, I think it's time to return to the hotel and you will want to freshen up I guess. We are staying at Annabella's house for the duration of our trip. Now, the baby you know all about you will meet very shortly, my daughter Charlotte who is in fact American and with us today. We eventually discovered each other some years back. She lives near me and she has children of her own, twins a little older than you, and her young son Arthur is here too, with my seven year old triplets, Magda, Geri and Eve."

Eliska's eyes widened. "Really? Wow? And you have triplets? How fabulous, my goodness, I had no idea."

Lauren smiled relieved. Obviously there were fortunately a lot of things Eliska, despite her giant brain, didn't know. Walking back, Lauren was formulating a radical set of ideas, following yet another game changing walk around the lake. Artificial intelligence would become a brand new area of research linked to the existing Cassini robotics team. Immediately on returning she would discuss this urgently with Juliette and both go through this original paper. She had deliberately understated the importance to Eliska of what she had just read. The rudimentary paper was not only outstanding but quite revolutionary, showcasing an extraordinary mathematical capability and insight into the deepest workings of quantum energy concepts. What Eliska had outlined could easily herald the same leap forward in artificial intelligence as Alan Turing had done for computing with his early calculating and code papers during the 1930s. Eliska had unknowingly joined a small handful of fusion pioneers who had the ability to understand and take this area of work forward, except her vision was uniquely innovative. But it was obvious that Eliska would need careful and sustained nurturing. Her past emotional issues and over-rapid transition from child to adult in every way could send her amazing brain into all kinds of unhelpful rabbit holes. Luis had returned from the dead but not in any way she would ever have imagined. It was almost as if he had purposely bided his time and engineered their unexpected meeting of minds. She smirked. Eliska reminded her so much of those enjoyable times having Svet around at that age after she returned from Russia, equally mature, confident and capable on the outside but terribly vulnerable and fragile inside. The fact Eliska was Luis's daughter and Annabella's half-sister gave a special impetus and a satisfactory meaning to wanting to personally oversee Eliska's next phase of development.

Lauren thought about her life twenty years ahead. She had found the answer for the first time to a niggling and personal conundrum which surfaced every so often when Helena suggested they sit down and work out a Cassini succession plan model. Helena was right. And Eliska, with suitable nurturing and development would be her natural successor; all the indicators were uncannily present. Luis really had never left her. She looked momentarily at her phone. A text had come in from Jackson Smythe.

Back on full power, all shipshape. Enjoy your holiday and relax. I certainly would be if I was there. Regards Jackson

She beamed and felt distinctly warm inside. She wished he was there. She now decided who would be supervising Eliska on her internships, that man needed a challenge. For the next few days she looked forward to some relaxing fun on Annabella's island.

Packing away the surf boards with Annabella, her phone began to ring. One day of the holiday remained sadly, although tomorrow they would have a final slap-up meal, on her, at Luigi's hotel which she eagerly anticipated.

"Sorry Annabella, please excuse me. I did put a block on work calls, but Eva must have decided this was important," she said placing the last surfboard carefully on the rack.

"Hey you're the boss! I will just make us a very nice coffee."

Lauren glowered at the phone, she didn't recognise the number or where it was from.

"Professor Lauren Hind speaking," she said tersely.

"Hello Lauren, sorry to disturb you, it's Ernesto."

"Ernesto? Why how lovely to hear from you, It's been a long time, I hope you're keeping well. Is there a problem with our partnership?"

"I'll get straight to the point, Lauren, you know me. Naomi has died."

"Naomi? Oh my God, not Aunt Letty, surely not, she's been so well?"

"I'm afraid so. She hadn't returned from her morning walk apparently then her dog suddenly appeared at her boyfriend's apartment, distressed, urging him to follow. They found her on the beach, sat staring at the waves. A fatal stroke, no warnings, died in an instant the way she would have wished. The funeral is tomorrow. I thought you would want to go."

"Where is it?"

"Tel Aviv."

Lauren felt a deep wave of sadness wash over her. Aunt Letty had been such a constant bastion of support for her and for their Israeli work. This was dreadful news; she had to get there, but how?

"Can you email me where and when and I will be there."

"I hope so because the Israeli Prime Minister has promised to turn up too if you do, he wants an urgent chat."

"I'll be there, don't worry," she replied. "Thanks for letting me know, bye Ernesto."

Immediately she put her phone back in her pocket, a text pinged in, followed by a more detailed email with an attached map. At least the venue wasn't too far from the airport. She went to find Charlotte, Annabella and Sonja. Luigi had taken all the kids with Marie down to the beach for the rest of the day. A cold cup of coffee, matched the look on her face as she sat down, pondering.

"We can see that it's not good news Lauren, but you've got the best problem solvers in Sicily sat in front of you," Charlotte began with a pragmatic grin.

Lauren smiled. "Thanks guys."

"And me too Lauren."

She turned at the sound of an unexpected voice to see Angelina walk in commandingly, carrying a giant fresh cup of hot cappuccino with lots of chocolate sprinkled on top, made especially for her.

Lauren was startled for a second. Her mouth dropped. She almost didn't recognise Angelina, not since they met seven years ago when she ran off from the world into the arms of Annabella on that fateful Henri-Gaston evening. Then Angelina had grown reassuringly spaghetti fat, contented and frumpy, surrounded by babies, exactly like a typical Sicilian momma, guarding her brood. Now, holding her coffee was a tall, sleek and elegant woman in a short Versace cotton summer dress, with tanned thighs to die for, her long hair jet black and wavy. This was the Angelina she first met all those years back, lover of Luis, formidable, frighteningly threatening and seductive, when of course her former husband fell instantly into Angelina's sticky web like the proverbial fly.

"Angelina, what a ... pleasure to see you again. You look ... err ..."

"Stunning is the word Lauren, I think you search for," Annabella replied with a broad smile.

Angelina laughed, as she put the cappuccino carefully down on the table. "I decided to get back into shape once my twins were off the breast. Especially after we launched my art gallery, which has truly taken off. I get clients from all over the world, not only for my work but a wide range of Italian new post-impressionism that I promote. With Lia and Francesca looking after the children I've become a career woman again just like you, liberating isn't it," she replied, tossing her thick hair back. "Before you ask Lauren, he's gone down to the beach with my tribe. We reckoned Luigi needed reinforcements with all that lot!"

Lauren breathed in, one less problem to bother her, noting the 'my' rather than 'our'. "You look very well Angelina, congratulations on the gallery success."

"So now you've got four formidable businesswomen to solve your problems, double the last time. Tell us all Lauren," Angelina whispered loudly, to smiles from everyone else, accompanied by her smirk of the old irony look, just like when she had tellingly warned off Luis. But Lauren had decided she would not be intimidated by the new warrior Angelina.

She had come too far in her life for psychological warfare right then, besides, she had just conquered the heart of Luis' daughter, which will kill Angelina's pig when she finds out. She quickly outlined her sorrow and the urgent dilemma of needing to attend a very important and politically sensitive funeral in Tel Aviv the next day.

"Getting you to Tel Aviv will be simple," Angelina replied in an instant. "Luigi's brother Franco now has a charter helicopter business for ... let us say, Sicilian VIPs. Annabella and I will take care of that for you Lauren ... Franco has a slate he needs to urgently clear, so is not a problem. Next however is getting everyone back safely to Nice" In a second she whipped out her phone and was babbling endlessly in Italian in the Angelina formidable way. A deal was immediately concluded. "You will be picked up in one hour."

"No problem with the Fusion Queen either. I can skipper us back." Charlotte quipped. "Marie can read charts and maps with her former training and although she isn't certificated she can back us up ... she's already mentioned that when we were out yesterday."

"And I will take care of the children, so, I think you'd better get packing Lauren!" Sonja added. "That was all pretty easy, wasn't it?"

"I have some perfect clothes for such an occasion," Annabella concluded. "We can still wear each other's things, just like we did ten years ago, can't we, and neither of us have changed a centimetre," she added, with a special smile, only Lauren appreciated, thinking instantly of their designer underwear swaps. "Come with me now to my bedroom. Let's get you, how do you say it, ahh ... sorted out."

Angelina glanced at her sister with a mild glare; she always hated to be reminded of Annabella's deep affection for Lauren ...

Chapter Twelve

Walking briskly to reception to order a taxi for the following day, Lauren looked contentedly through the large glass windows of the indoor swimming pool to wave to Magda, Geri and Eve, splashing about in the warm water with Lia. It was an instant decision but Lauren desperately wanted the girls with her, not only because she had little enough time with them on their own outside of holidays, but because it was good for them to experience a funeral and begin to understand what death as well as life meant. Besides, they all became very excited about wanting to fly in a helicopter with Momie. Also it would be much easier for Sonja taking the yacht back. Arthur of course, deciding in his own individualistic way that there was a symbiosis between helicopters and horses, was far more circumspect and went off to play with Časlav hoping that any proposition would go away for him.

But Annabella insisted it was sensible for Lia to go with them. Lia was Luigi's cousin and knew Tel Aviv well having spent five years there as nanny to an affluent Jewish family. Once done with Aunt Letty's funeral, Lauren and the girls would fly back directly to Nice. Lia was arranging to stay on with friends for a holiday break.

Apart from the taxi, Lauren booked everyone into the opulently themed restaurant for an early evening meal. The triplets had already been warned to be on their best behaviour. The five stars exclusive Gideon Heights Hotel was the epitome of wealthy client luxury, but she decided to hang the expense having seen the enticing advert in the airport. Lia had already contacted one of her old friends who was arranging for some long, black and pretty children's dresses and matching shoes and socks to be brought to the hotel shortly to choose and buy. At least they would all be dressed appropriately and exactly the same size. Lauren liked Lia. Her English was excellent, with that same pleasant Italian lilt as Annabella, and she was as superbly organised as Jesse with the children.

Sat in the lounge, she waded through her phone contacts and went to press the only number she had of him but was irritatingly interrupted with an unrecognised incoming call which threw her thoughts momentarily.

"Hello?"

"Hi Lauren. I just wanted to tell you first. It was quiet and understated as you probably guessed it would be, but we've finally got married."

Lauren sat up sharply. "Svet? My God, how wonderful! My warmest congratulations, I'm so pleased for you both, yes it was about time, but does your father know?"

"No, I'll call him later, if I can get hold of him. But he gets so tedious these days, all I hear about on the phone is dreary politics and deals, the same old Papa only worse. The only people present were Nadine and Roland who acted as witnesses, and then we went for a nice meal together. Sergei and I just felt it was right now to do it. But we don't want kids yet. I really must finish my astrobiology doctorate and I'm so pleased with Amélie as my research mentor, she is fabulously bright."

Lauren bristled slightly; fabulously bright was way too over the top for her best friend. "Innovative and cunning are the descriptors you really mean Svet," she replied as Svet laughed loudly, understanding the joke completely.

"Sergei is spending most of his time on Alzheimer's research in the new research centre he's built here. He's onto a new drug which can break down those platelets in the brain that clog up data transmission in working neurones. We're very happy now I must say, it's sort of nice to be settled and legal."

"I knew your relationship would work out and remain special, Svet, the day I saw you together in Murmansk. I wish the same could be said of …"

"None of it is your fault Lauren, sadly it's deep within Papa's DNA I'm sure. He can't help himself, commitment and women don't seem to link up in his brain. Fortunately I take after my mother."

"Yes, but on a positive note at least he's remained a good father with the girls. Anyway, what exactly is the fabulous Amélie supervising you on?"

"That's another reason I called. I'm working on how high energy plasma could be the trigger of life-forms in other planetary systems and how to recognise the possible signs. Actually, what I wanted to tell you is something quite odd has been happening in my laboratory. I've been tracking something really peculiar. Where are you? Sounds like you're in a bar?"

"I am, sort of ... I'm in Tel Aviv with the girls, staying in a hotel. I have a funeral of an old and dear friend and colleague to attend here tomorrow, Dr Naomi Leibstein; I think I mentioned her a few times?"

Svet's immediate recall kicked in. "Yes, a distinguished nuclear specialist. She helped you out with business in Israel didn't she?"

"She did and a lot more. Sadly Naomi died of a sudden stroke. After the funeral I intend to head straight back to Nice. It has cut short my intended break sailing around the coast on my new yacht so I'll inevitably be drawn back to my office again, with some crisis or other."

"Do you have some holiday time left then?"

"Yes, twelve days still pencilled out, why?"

"Why don't you come here? We've just bought a five bedroomed colonial house in the best part of town. You'll love it. Amélie is in Boston too still. She keeps fretting constantly about wanting to see you. My father can keep an eye on the triplets, although you still have Marie don't you?"

"Yes and her sister Jesse, our nanny, will be back now. The household is highly organised, it simply has to be. Your father is so busy and erratic you never know where he's going to be, although I'm sure he would do his bit if he's around. That's a great idea actually, Svet, I'd really love to see your place. Proposition sold. I'll text Eva to book me on a flight to Boston the day after tomorrow and confirm it to you. Anyway you said about something peculiar?"

Svet went quiet. "I know you're not one to laugh, but my ET tracker has been picking up pulses from a particular direction of the Milky Way. I think they're coded; in fact I'm absolutely sure of it. I haven't told Amélie yet, but I'd like you both, being superbrain mathematicians, to take an objective listen."

"ET Tracker?"

"Just my pet name, remember you promised not to laugh. It's a sophisticated desk-top infra-red receiver, but hugely powerful, based on some recent research work elsewhere here in Harvard. Sergei put some more money into my budget to increase the range. I use it for seeking out data from exoplanets. This pulse stream was an unexpected bonus."

"You remember when pulsars were discovered years back and people thought the next War of the Worlds was being enacted?" Lauren replied with a laugh. "But as I know well, scientific outliers can provide the appropriate antidote to rigid expectancy, so I always keep my mind open to anything, especially if it makes mathematical sense. Sounds like fun. I wonder if they're green."

"What's green?"

"ET of course!" Lauren giggled back. "Sorry, only joking."

"Okay, forgiven this time. Anyway I'll let you go; you must have lots to do. Where are the girls?"

Lauren looked at her watch. "Right now they should be down at the beach, with Lia, Annabella's nanny. The hotel has a private frontage which is nice and secure. We came here by helicopter would you believe from Palermo— I'll tell you when I get to Boston. Without nannies I would be completely dead in the water."

Svet laughed. "I can believe it, the life you lead. Bye Lauren, see you soon, I'm really pleased you can come."

"Me too, bye Svet."

Ordering a fresh pineapple cocktail in a long glass but with just a slight dash of vodka, Lauren peered over her task list. She still had to phone Ernesto, although there were a few hours to go before dinner. Then a silly urge came over her unexpectedly and she pressed on another number instead, which connected immediately.

"Hello Jack. Now, as your boss I'm entitled to recommend you take an immediate holiday break, especially as you always work far too hard. I don't want you keeling over on the job," she chirped. She suddenly wished she had phrased that a little differently, but no matter.

There was a silence at the other end? Then a quiet voice answered. "Lauren? Is that you?"

"Of course it's me. Exactly how many bosses do you have, Professor Smythe? Is this a bad time?"

He coughed. "Err ... no ... fine ... I'm just peering through my infra-red telescope."

"Infra-red is definitely a fashionable colour at the moment."

"Pardon?"

"Never mind. I have a proposal for you. Day after tomorrow, how would you like to clear your diary and take a nice week's break? I'm going to Boston to have some fun with my step-daughter and Amélie, my best friend. We are all rabid intellectual physicists and raving beauties, so what more delectable company could a man like you want?"

"You mean you're inviting me to come with you?" he replied slowly in a monotone.

She felt herself going hot and flushed with stupid mixed up reasons. This was becoming hard work, not what she wanted or expected.

"Yes, all separate bedrooms so you won't have to worry."

She bit her lip again. She was never very good at come-on lines which didn't sound faintly ridiculous. There was a wave of silence.

"That's very thoughtful Lauren, but I don't think it's a ... err ... it's not possible I'm afraid. I've promised my two youngest daughters and ... mmm ...my mother-in-law that I would take them all canoeing ... err ... in Wales."

Mother-in-law? She now decided that the ground opening up and swallowing her would definitely be the best way forward. What on earth had come over her? He must think she was some sort of sex-mad corporate cougar on the prowl. No, hang on. She was younger than him. Impulsive business decisions always seemed to work well normally ... why were men such a disaster zone?

"Oh well, it was just a quick thought. I'm glad you're up to full speed. Got to go, have a funeral to get to. Bye Jackson."

"Oh ... okay, take care ... err, see you when you're back."

She clicked off and swigged the rest of her cocktail and ice down in one go and ordered another with double the vodka. He probably thought, she pondered holding the empty glass, that she'd had an afternoon's worth of these. Time to end the madness and she tapped Ernesto's number.

"Have you decided to go then?" immediately rang in her ears. Ernesto was never one for small talk.

"I'm actually in Tel Aviv, Ernesto. I'm staying at the Gideon Heights Hotel. What time and precisely where is the ceremony? In fact what should I be doing when I get there? I've never attended a Jewish funeral?"

"Hang on."

"Hello Lauren, it's Ephraim here, Naomi's ... err old friend. Thank you so much for coming all the way out to Tel Aviv. I've organised everything for her, so there should be nothing to worry about. Naomi only had her sister in Brussels and a couple of grandchildren. They are all flying in overnight and will be the family mourners with me. Naomi only died yesterday morning, but we bury people very quickly."

"Yesterday? Heavens. Ephraim, how nice to speak to you, I am so sorry about Naomi, she spoke a lot about you actually, all the time."

"Did she?" His very elderly and wavering voice sounded much cheerier. "The ceremony will be at the Amichai Kibbutz, just outside of town. About twenty minutes by taxi. Naomi wasn't religious, she had rejected God a long time ago, but she was very proud of her ancestry. She was, you know, one of the young assistants to Ben-Gurion who directly facilitated the setting up of the state of Israel in 1948 when she was only eighteen. It will be secular burial, no traditional hevra kadishma rites, but with a modicum of words, some music and a few prayers which she would have been happy with, plus a nice Star of David inscribed gravestone. Simply listen Lauren and reflect on her life and the good she did for everyone who had the privilege of knowing her. I know she upset a number of politicians but others loved her work and commitment. The Prime Minister will attend in person and has asked to speak to you at the end."

"Thank you Ephraim. Naomi once said to me that when she died she looked forward to some of her atoms eventually reaching the giant red star Betelgeuse. We sat one evening over coffee and calculated what the likely time period would be before the star explodes and collapses into a tiny brown dwarf and then a black hole. She should just about make it."

Ephraim chortled loudly, in between long wheezes and quiet coughs. "Forgive me Lauren, my chest is not as it used to be, but that is so Naomi. I will think about that too. One thing we will all do each is to toss a spade of soil onto her casket in the ground to speed her on her way to Orion. I look forward to seeing you tomorrow. I understand your three little girls will be with you, Naomi will like that. Bye Lauren."

"Bye Ephraim."

"Momie who was that on your mobile?" Geri asked all three suddenly standing beside her, with Lia behind.

"His name is Ephraim, an old friend of Naomi who died. Now I want to tell you all about tomorrow and why we are going to her funeral."

"Momie our dresses are here in our room. We've chosen the best ones with Lia but we want you to come and look please," Magda cried, tugging at her sleeve.

"Okay Magda, just wait a minute," Lauren replied. "Thank you so much Lia for all your help and looking after this lot, you deserve some time off. I understand you have old friends to see whilst you're here. It's no problem at all now, I can take care of them," Lauren said, putting a hundred Euro note in her hand. "Have a nice holiday and we look forward to seeing you when we visit Annabella next time."

"Me too, Lauren. It has been a real pleasure meeting you and your children. They are lovely actually and so well behaved and talkative. Angelina's children are much more of a handful. I hope tomorrow goes okay and have a safe journey back home."

Lauren looked at the trio of innocent faces, like butter wouldn't melt in their mouths and grinned, especially regarding Angelina, as they all waved Lia off.

"Actually," Eve began. "The lady on the beach said we should visit the zoo. It has lots of wild animals and is the biggest in this region."

"What lady was that?" Lauren asked.

Magda stood up. "She was nice and spoke English but had a very funny accent. We played football with her son though, he was called Vas. That was fun, but he didn't say anything, I don't think he understood English or French properly."

"Vas?"

"Vasily, that was his full name. He had red hair, very curly not straight like ours," Geri added.

They all nodded sombrely.

"Yes," Eve continued. "And the lady even asked whether Geri still liked gorillas, she seemed to know we were all born in a jungle."

Lauren suddenly raised her head from her phone. A raft of weird things rattled through her brain.

"Lots of people know that because photos of you three just born in the jungle that Papa took were published in magazines all around the world. But Eve, what did the lady look like and how old do you think Vas was?"

"She was tall, Momie, as tall as you, very slim with short red hair too. Vas was around our age, in fact I asked him in English, and he made a sign in the air of six, so he must have understood something. When Lia came back with ice creams they both left."

"Mmm ... six? ... Okay. Now, let's look at your dresses, and as I'm paying for them I have the final decision."

They groaned and trotted up the stairs to their room followed by Lauren, who thought hard for a moment about the mystery beach lady. She felt an air of concern but then bafflement, before she suddenly remembered in a trajectory of thought about a strange conversation concerning vasectomies with Philippe. Surely it was simply not possible? That was decidedly something she would put right to the back of her mind. Coincidences can play the strangest of tricks on rational logic, especially if you concentrate too hard.

Headed by a small group of family mourners, an amazing entourage of people had turned up at the funeral. Some were decidedly academics, but many others were former journalist colleagues, the majority very old themselves. The ceremony was short and succinct, led by a Rabbi suggested directly by the Prime Minister who understood and respected Naomi's secular wishes. But they did sing a few musical passages, although Lauren of course struggled because the words were in Hebrew. The triplets, their long hair tied back in pretty ponytails, stood quietly beside her on their best behaviour, wearing their beautiful identical dresses and looking so alike only Lauren could tell the difference. They attracted a lot of attention and admiring well-wishers. The girls knew they couldn't talk until the ceremony was finished, but were all quietly taking in everything around them assiduously, both to ask their mother loads of questions later when they would be allowed, and to boast to Arthur when they arrived home. Once Naomi's' casket had been taken to the chosen burial plot under a lovely olive tree, the girls, wide-eyed, watched as it was slowly lowered on long ropes into the ground. Lauren took her turn to dig a large spadeful of earth from a heap next to the grave and the four each threw a portion on top. A funeral aspect they would likely never experience in France or the UK.

Once concluded, Lauren spoke quietly with the Prime Minister for a few minutes and an aide was instructed to liaise on diary dates when Lauren could have a more extended visit. Unsurprisingly, he wanted to talk about Iran as soon as possible. After a brief chat with Ephraim and Naomi's family, the large crowd began to disperse. She gazed around the large burial area, which was beautifully secluded and quiet but a little overgrown with olive trees everywhere and other shrubs and flowers, the graves irregularly positioned as narrow gravel paths intertwined between them. Immediately she remembered what the area was like. Exactly the same as the Garden of Gethsemane, which was one of the last places she had visited with Naomi a few years before, and a place, despite the religious connotations, Naomi had loved.

Suddenly, some distance further out of the immediate vicinity, behind where the crowds were thinning out, she spotted a lone woman, standing quietly in black. She was tall and slim and wearing a prim hat with a thin veil over her face. Standing next to her was a little girl dressed identically but without the hat, with long, blonde hair. They were quite alone. It was when Lauren stared at the little girl, whose features were totally unmistakable, that she felt a sharp jolt as if a ghost had passed straight through her body.

Magda was also staring at them. "Momie, who is that lady over there?" she whispered to Lauren. "I think she's staring at us, I'm sure of it, although I can't see her face under that net thing on her head."

Lauren took Magda and Geri's hand, with Eve standing in front of them. They all gazed at the mysterious woman in black. Lauren didn't reply, but she knew precisely who it was. Her mind was in turmoil but then she decided. Both prodigal daughters had returned to Israel at the same time.

"Girls, I want you to meet a very old and very dear friend," she said slowly and deliberately. "Her name is Mila and she was also in the jungle when you were born, but we haven't seen each other for a long time."

"Is that her daughter, Momie?" Eve whispered. "She looks about our age."

"Yes, it is." She drew in a large intake of breath and they began to walk over slowly. Mila remained motionless, continuing to hold her daughter's hand.

As Lauren walked closer, Mila threw back the thin veil and tears began rolling down both cheeks, her eyes fixed firmly on Lauren. No words needed to be spoken between them. Years had passed by, but in a moment Naomi's death and funeral had finally brought them together, after so much intense trauma and emotional paralysis. Lauren walked up and hugged Mila hard, who reciprocated, both sobbing quietly with the release of such long entrenched emotions. It was the only way they could let their feelings pass out.

Geri, as usual, sizing up the moment and taking charge on behalf of the three, held out her hand to Mila's daughter. "Hello, my name's Geri and this is my sister Magda and my other sister Eve. We're seven. It looks like your Momie and my Momie are making friends again. What's your name?"

The little girl smiled, relieved as she hadn't been sure what was going on. "My name is Adrijana and I'm nearly seven. Gee, you three are so alike, how does anyone tell the difference?" she replied in a confident New York accent. "There's an adventure playground just outside. Would you like to come and play with me, I'm bored here now. Mom, can I go to the playground please with Geri, Magda and Eve?"

Lauren and Mila drew apart and both looked down at their respective children whose combined best behaviours were clearly feeling an evident strain, but then funerals were not fun places for kids.

"There's a nice coffee bar next to the playground. We can watch them from there. Fancy a cappuccino?" Mila said, breaking the ice.

"I'm absolutely dying. I didn't really want to go on to Ephraim's apartment with the girls. We've had enough to be honest, and not being Jewish as well makes it harder to fit in."

"I agree me neither, and I am Jewish. They'll understand, don't worry. Everyone I spoke to, including the Prime Minister, was really pleased and impressed that you came especially with the children. The present administration had a high regard for Naomi and her past work."

They began to walk out of the gardens into a community area where the girls, having been warned to be careful, started playing on the swings, slide and the witch's hat.

Lauren and Mila ordered their drinks and a large cake each. Like old times, except of course it wasn't and a chasm of days, years, and life changes had elapsed. Where did either of them start? They stirred at their cappuccinos in silence. Finally Lauren plunged in first; she had to get it off her chest.

"I never thought I would forgive you Mila. The hurt was so deep I simply couldn't comprehend the pain, but last year, slowly, I found myself sensibly coming to terms with the reality of the life you've carved out, as I heard more about you, especially of course from Kat and Lexi. And it was then, like a thawing of ice, I realised how much I missed you ... I had no idea you would turn up today."

"No, but I did, which is the main reason I came, hoping that I would see you in the crowd but not expecting anything else. I couldn't stand this separation any longer either. I have felt so abominable since that awful night when Henri and I turned up unannounced and you realised in a microsecond what had been happening. To extinguish the unrelenting pain, I decided to totally change my life and sold a bunch of my security company shares to Emmylou and the girls who took over the running. Then, day after day, I simply immersed myself lock stock and barrel into the centre of the fashion and art scene in New York and looking after Adrijana. Henri is very independent and so absorbed, obsessive basically in his work and we have a housekeeper. I became the social icon, organiser and facilitator for both of us and still am. That wasn't that difficult, the whole socialite thing seemed to come naturally and it's been huge fun. You know me, especially where fashion is concerned, I don't need much prompting."

Lauren laughed. "Yes, I became aware, admittedly of late that you were gathering a cult following amongst the US glitterati echelons, after rather barbed comments from Amélie, who still retains a weakness for devouring the gossip mags."

Mila roared loudly. She certainly hadn't curbed that characteristic, which Lauren always loved. "Amélie? How is the old witch, still mixing toxic nuclear brews up in the wastelands of the UK?"

"Not quite, she's a Countess now. She'd go down well with your socialites."

"You betcha, a bit of UK aristocrat always provides good entertainment, an American fascination quelled by no one. Anyway, I've missed you dreadfully, every single day. I can't tell you how wonderful it is to be here together. I know we have a lot to catch up on, but I just wanted to say before anything else—I never intended whatsoever to fall in love with Henri, it genuinely just happened. And to be fair, he's a good man and generous hearted."

"Now I realise that, but I couldn't understand, not for a very long time. It was a serious shock. I actually ran away that night to Annabella, never intending to return, but did so in the end after a month. I shall never forget the unremitting care and attention, and of course the not so subtle rehabilitation which Annabella and Luigi provided. Nothing was ever too much trouble and I was seriously plenty at the time."

"I really never knew, but I'm not in the least surprised and glad. Like me, Annabella deep inside never stopped loving you either, but she has a doctorate in understanding and caring that neither you nor I would ever match."

"Adrijana is stunningly like you, it's amazing, same hair, eyes and stellar beauty and very confident for her age. I assume she does have some of her father in her though," Lauren said, watching her pushing Magda on the swings.

"Yes, but only his nose although she's stubborn like him too, but has lots of attitude like me. Don't laugh but since age three Adrijana has been doing regular martial arts at weekends. She totally loves it, principally karate including shotokan, shito-ryu and muteki; she'll be a black belt by ten. I spend a lot of time with her; I've loved being a mom again. Adrijana's been a true gift and changed my life."

"Yes, and the triplets with me too, something we've shared but never knew. I'm so pleased for you, honestly I am, I knew having a family again was something you always dreamed about," Lauren replied, patting her hand gently.

Mila gripped it tightly. "He knows nothing about you and knows nothing about me or our past lives either. I've always insisted and he accepted it right from the start."

Lauren looked into Mila's amber eyes. She was still the same Mila, but a deep sadness lay evident there. Mila had suffered inside exactly the same. Lauren had already firmly decided. They would not be going back to the cold war again, ever, such a fruitless and diminishing state of affairs.

"Why don't you both come back to Nice for a couple of days? We have so much to catch up on and the girls seem to have all made friends already."

"I'd love to but I have to return to New York today." Mila peered at her watch. "About now, Henri will be seeing Kat and Lexi off on their return flight home and he's then going on a six week art and promotional tour of South America in a couple of days with his entourage of female assistants who perpetually pamper and cosset him. I don't do that. Being apart for chunks of time is necessary for us. You could come to my place in New York whilst he's away?"

Lauren pondered. She needed to think carefully about that and put the final demons to rest first but the concept seemed a great idea, and Gaz wouldn't be there. "Actually, I have planned to go to Boston and visit Svet for a week, also in a couple of days. I still have some holiday left, so when I'm there I'll give you a ring and we can fix a visit up then?"

"Excellent, but bring your best frocks because I shall take you to some of the glitziest parties you would never believe possible. Although, I suppose you might just still fit into some of my Prada glad-rags."

"What do you mean *might*? Plenty of room to spare these days," Lauren chuntered back, smiling. "Anyway, I'm into other trendy couture designers these days, you won't have heard of across the pond. Iris van Herpen is a real favourite."

"Who? Okay maybe I have been holed up in NYC too long. We do definitely have a lot to catch up on. Listen I've got a flight to catch, it appears, sadly, our time is up. I'll just dial a taxi."

They looked down to see four blonde haired, tired faces staring up quietly. "Mom? Magda, Geri, Eve and I have done absolutely everything ten times in that playground now. We've all had enough," Adrijana pleaded. "Can we get a drink please and sit down?"

Lauren waved over the cafe manager and ordered four lemonades. "Of course, sit on that table. Then we are all going to the airport together to catch our flights home, our cases will have been taxied there by now and if we have time we'll all have a meal first."

Mila nodded. She cast a long glance at Lauren. They both knew that Naomi's final throw of the dice bringing them together, would have no going back. However, the moves to recover their former friendship would have to be taken gently and carefully, one small step at a time.

Chapter Thirteen

Another day, another airport. Walking from the fast-track arrival gate of Terminal E inside Logan International Airport, despite the modernity and orderly bustle of services, Lauren wondered seriously whether her lifestyle needed to change. Maybe she should even sell up Cassini, reap the cash and move on to pastures new. Admittedly, her roving ambassador and research guru role as owner-chairman had put serious pressure onto happily married, husband and wife joint CEOs Johann and Sonja to deliver results especially Johann responsible for sales. They had jointly and separately proved more than capable of continuing excellent profit growth alongside effective company management. But there were days, like this one, when being away from the children gave her periods of ponder time on her personal life and goals rather than hassling with the never-ending daily business challenge. Was it time? Retirement? She definitely didn't want that, but maybe she should start something radically new and exciting? Certainly there would be no shortage of buyers for her privately owned nuclear power company and she would become considerably wealthy with the cash as majority shareholder. But then she bristled at the thought of having to share the proceeds with husband Philippe ... On the other hand his stubborn Russian independent character may be immune to marital equality and enforceable legalities. Perhaps it was time to start a divorce conversation. She would shortly be hitting the big five-zero and in ten years time the triplets would be like Kat and Lexi now, feisty, gorgeous, potentially successful and wanting to fly their wings off into independent adulthood. Would she still want to carry on with doing what she's doing then?

Undoubtedly two factors gnawed at her subconscious. Her twin jealousies of daughter Charlotte and how she has found happiness with her youthful athletic vineyard lover Giles. And now Mila, widely followed fashionista and über-socialite of New York. Both women had changed their lives totally in a short space of time, especially Mila.

She needed a new man like Charlotte and Mila and thought once more of the suitability of Jackson Smythe. She felt her emotions grumble uneasily at her recent base ineptitude of leading him on. Stupid, stupid, stupid ... now lost for good. In her usual scientific compartmentalising manner she put him instantly into the outer reaches of her mind. Trundling onwards and gazing nonchalantly at the endless meet and greet placards and taxi touts, a wild waving at the end of the long barrier caught her attention.

"Hey, Lauren, this way, we've got you covered."

What a stupid phrase, but she smiled to see Svet with a decidedly American accent, jumping up and down behind a short railing, her mane of thick red hair even more prominent as she stood tall as ever in big pointy heels, expensive skinny jeans and tight crop top. But who were those other two women walking towards her and dressed similar, certainly with the skinny jeans? She immediately recognised the unmistakable short and coppery, spiky mop. Oh my God, it was Amélie and ... no, it really couldn't be but it was. Charlotte was walking alongside her? She certainly wasn't expecting that surprise. What on earth was Charlotte doing here and who was looking after Arthur? She was glad she had rushed into the arrival toilets and put on her red lipstick, green mascara and new Jean Iverson black skinny jeans and Mila looking cage boots. Against her snow white blouse, all of her looked stunning and cool country-singer chic, especially as she had been growing out her short bob for some time and had it subtly waved and highlights put in before departing.

"Svet, how lovely to see you and you look stunning as always. It seems ages since I saw you last but you haven't changed at all. Marriage is definitely good for you, I can see that."

Svet grinned and lunged at her with an accompanying giant hug. "It is ages Lauren, like almost two years! You look amazing too. Say, that long wavy style really suits you."

"Yes, I have to reluctantly agree ..." a familiar voice sounded out from behind the advertising board. "The only thing missing is her gee-tar and backing group. Is this really the chairman of a global nuclear giant or has she boarded the wrong plane intended for Nashville? And who makes JI Jeans? I want ten pair please."

Lauren immediately hugged her spiky-haired best friend. "Oh Amélie, you never change and I love you for it. Gosh, it is so good to see you again. *Mon Dieu*, it's been nearly twelve months. I think I've been in a time warp or something, the months have flown by lately, I've been so busy."

"It's age sadly or you spend far too much time gazing at the accumulating oodles of nuclear cash," Amélie replied, also imparting a giant bear-hug. "But we old birds aren't doing so badly are we? Now before you ask, I invited this not so old bird beside me. It's about time we three got shut of the little buggers and male hangers-on and had some hilarious nights out on the town again, don't you think? The original Murmansk invaders have just been reborn."

Charlotte and Lauren hugged and laughed.

"I certainly never expected to see you here, what a fantastic surprise too," Lauren uttered, bewildered.

"I'm staying at Amélie's beautiful flat, just a few blocks from Svet. I came immediately after we arrived back from Palermo. I really needed more holiday as well. Giles is fine back home, Kat and Lexi are back with him and Jesse and Marie have happily taken Arthur into your guest room, so as Amélie says we're all fancy free for a change to hit the big city!"

Svet suddenly looked at her watch. "Can I suggest we all head to my new house? If we hurry, we can say hi to Sergei first. He has to go out shortly, his first meeting as newly elected deputy chairman of the Boston Chamber of Commerce. Apparently there's some big medical and IT networking event on that he's organised, so he's somewhat nervous everything will go okay. The great and good of all persuasions are turning up."

"Gosh Svet, that's really positive for Sergei. I'm sure the evening will go well, he has an innate knack for getting things done and understanding people," Lauren replied, pushing her trolley again as they set off to find Svet's parked pickup truck.

"Yes, he's worked really hard locally to become a key part of the business fraternity. They love him, he's a natural networker and a big supporter of business start-ups and his English has improved beyond belief with special lessons. He's lost the former Russian accent, sounds quite American now."

"Like you, Svet," Charlotte commented, her Dallas twang more noticeable again, despite her long sojourn in France, probably because she was back on US soil. "You've both settled in really well."

Svet grinned. She had never been happier at long last, although she still wished her father was not so awkward. They reached her giant, new white Isuzu, and Svet put her parking ticket into the machine. "Good, a minute to spare on the free time. That's also why I was in a hurry. Jump in everyone, plenty of room in the back for your case, Lauren. We're only fifteen minutes away, if the traffic isn't too heavy."

She started the big petrol engine which roared into life, shoved Izzy into drive and they shot off through the barrier and out onto the open road. "Now, tonight, I have a treat in store for everyone, all on me, seeing as there is a universal desire to be painting the town red. So once we've freshened up and had a quick look around, as I know you'll want to do, then we'll hit the road again, out towards the coast."

Amélie, sat in the back with Charlotte, leaned over Lauren's shoulder. "That sounds distinctly intriguing, Svet? So are you going to tell us more?"

"No, definitely not. You'll just have to patiently wait Amélie," Svet chirped back, in a jovial mood now with some fun female company again.

"Anticipation was never one of my best friend's virtues," Lauren added with a sigh. "You'd think as she got older and wiser, she would savour life's little treats with some patience."

Charlotte laughed loudly, understanding Amélie now as well as Lauren. They too had become such good friends.

But in no time at all as the traffic hadn't reached peak clogging up time, swinging into a very upmarket area with new individualised houses and large front lawns, the Isuzu pulled up outside a large residence totally different from the rest. Bigger grounds were surrounding it, bordered by large mature trees. A pretty white, pointy railing enclosed the whole property. They tumbled out of the pickup and Lauren and Amélie stared in amazement at the unique design. The wide wooden gate was fully open, leading to a large red brick-weave drive where a black Lexus was standing in front. In America, old was anything before 1850 but this property was built some time before that again, positively ancient. But Charlotte, a connoisseur of old American, knew exactly what she was looking at.

"My oh my, Svet," she began, realising that the moment she set foot back in home territory her instinctive mode of speech seemed to return all by itself. "Darn, that sure is some hell of an original colonial home. Your place looks very Georgian to me. Down in the Deep South we love these houses, not many left this age and so well preserved, although in Texas they're heavily Spanish influenced. The house looks more like you'd see, very occasionally, in the likes of Georgia or Memphis, but the shuttering is different, panelled rather than louvered, presumably to kill the wind and snow here rather than the sun."

Svet laughed. "Spot on Charlotte, I'm impressed. In fact all the land these other homes are built on belonged to the family McGill owners of this house for generations, right back to when it was first built in 1769. They only sold out in the 1970s."

Lauren, always a lover of anything Georgian, immediately noted the strict symmetrical shape of the exterior, the three rectangular upper windows each side balanced by exactly the same below, and the middle upper window lying exactly in the middle over a beautiful pillared porchway. A V-roof and a marble inscription on the front finished off the whole structure. The interior was, she thought, likely symmetrically constructed too with a central staircase. She counted twelve panes of glass per sash and looked at the simple side gabled roof with three additional dormers jutting forward and a chimney stack each end. Lots of bedrooms in there.

"What a fabulous house, Svet. I admire your taste."

"Lauren, everything I know I've learned from you, especially this Georgian architecture. I never forgot," Svet replied smiling, pleased that Lauren was suitably impressed. Her father had no idea she and Sergei had bought this place. In fact she hadn't yet told Philippe they had even gotten married. He was never interested in property as long as he had a bed to sleep in, big enough for … but she moved on, sick and tired of thinking about his lifetime of infidelities. "Unusually the exterior is brick and mortar rather than wood clapboard, which has been regularly maintained over the years. The house has six bedrooms, each with their own bathroom, plus four reception rooms and a huge kitchen-diner. We're really pleased with it. Hey, look who's coming to greet us."

They glanced over to the side and saw Sergei bounding around the corner with a large grin. He was formally dressed up in a very smart grey suit, polished expensive black shoes and a white shirt and tie, obviously about to leave. He strode to the gate and gave first Lauren and then Charlotte and Amélie a large hug each and a big kiss for Svet … They still looked at each other with exactly the same love and passion as when Lauren first set eyes on him in Murmansk. She had forgotten how tall Sergei was, about the same height as Giles but slimmer. His hair was fashionably styled and his dark beard trimmed tightly.

"Hey folks it's really great to see you all, especially you Lauren. You look terrific, it has been far too long." he said in a distinctive Boston accent. "Now we're settled here hopefully you'll come more often, plenty of room to stay including the children. Hope the girls are keeping well and Philippe too?"

"We will definitely Sergei, everyone is fine. Philippe sends his regards."

"Super. Sorry but I have to get going to my business event, but I'll see you all anyway in the next few days. You must come and see my new Alzheimer Centre, powered totally by renewable energy, wind, solar and ground heat source."

"Impressive. Wow, love to," Amélie responded. "But Sergei, I have to insist that Lauren and I will really have to get you your very own nuclear power plant. Even more sustainable and will still run when the sun doesn't shine and the wind is still."

They all laughed at the intended and understood irony. Sergei waved goodbye, jumped into his car and shot off towards the city. Following a quick coffee and a short but breathtaking tour around the house, whose interior and furnishings were even more luxurious than Lauren and Amélie would have believed, including the indoor swimming pool extension at the rear, they were soon ready, using a bathroom each, to be back on the road.

Walking down the drive behind Svet and Charlotte who were admiring the unusual monkey puzzle trees in the corner of the garden, Amélie turned to Lauren and whispered. "Doesn't it bother you?"

"Doesn't what bother me?"

"That all this gorgeously high living has been bequeathed from the ill-gotten gains of a certain man that you or I could have been indulging ourselves with instead?"

Lauren stopped for a moment and grimaced. The thought of Vaag hadn't flashed across her brain for many a long while. But in an instant she had rationalised him away as quickly as Amélie had dredged him up. "No, actually it doesn't. Firstly, because Sergei is a marvellous and kind man, unlike his erstwhile nefarious brother, and is doing a power of good using most of that money on his personal commitment to solving some of the most intractable world health problems. And secondly, because Svet deserves a good life of her own, she's worked hard for it. Heaven knows she had a difficult childhood with her father, and he hasn't exactly measured up since. In the end you make your own chances in this world however that may be accomplished, and reap the rewards accordingly. Nobody is going to do it for you. You and I know that better than most."

Amélie grinned and linked her arm as they walked to Svet's Isuzu. "I'm glad you said that. I agree entirely. Anyway how is Mila then?"

Lauren glared back mildly. "You know don't you. How do you know I've seen her?"

"Because the New York dynamo phoned me and told me. She was so happy you've made up and wants me to come to one of her way-out parties too when I'm over here."

Lauren laughed. "I might have known, nothing remains discretely secret when either of you are around."

"Absolutely not. Anyway I'm really pleased for you. It's taken ten years off those frowns already and at our stage in life every little helps, especially if we're painting the town red later!"

"Ha, ha, I think I've got way past those old licentious, and bawdy anything goes nights we used to have in Paris, twenty five years ago. At the stroke of twelve I'll want my cocoa and be off to bed."

"Yes, but whose bed, Lauren?" Amélie whispered, a naughty leer passing across her lips.

"Get in the car and behave!"

After about ten minutes, the city long left behind, they found themselves driving through a vast but low lying woodland area, the smell of sea air wafting hazily through the window. Through the clumps and gaps in the trees they could see they were driving almost parallel to the seashore about half a mile to the left. Suddenly right ahead of them, high in the fading blue sky, Lauren spotted a series of very sharp, strange lights surrounded by purple and yellow halos, moving slowly eastwards out to sea.

"Bloody hell, what on earth are those?" she shouted, pointing up to the top of the large windscreen. "The iodide twenty K spectrum range doesn't compute and I'm sure they're pulsating."

Amélie and Charlotte leaned forward to see, as Svet glanced in her mirror quickly and then pulled over into a dusty lay-by. They all got out of the car and stared upwards. They could now see six distinct tiny lights, moving slowly across the sky, out to sea.

"Probably some kind of covert military activity I assume," Amélie proclaimed, looking at Charlotte who was pondering hard.

"Those lights are flashing to a definite pattern, watch the sequence from right to left," Charlotte announced excitedly. She grabbed open her handbag and pulled out a notebook, making scribbles, dots and dashes, but it was all over in a trice, as the festoon of pin-prick colours disappeared over the horizon, way out over the Atlantic Ocean.

Lauren looked at Svet who had been noticeably silent, deep in thought. Svet looked up. "I'm sure Amélie is correct. We do get a lot of new aircraft testing here, there's a base about thirty miles away."

Charlotte stuffed her notepad back into her bag and breathed in hard, closing her eyes. "Doggone, isn't this area lovely and peaceful? Four super-brains out together for the first time in six years and no kids, absolute bliss."

They all giggled and walked back to the car.

"This isn't the right time, Lauren. Tomorrow, when we visit my laboratory," Svet whispered to her outside whilst Charlotte and Amélie rearranged themselves inside. Lauren had already realised and nodded. Obviously Svet hadn't yet mentioned to the others that they would all be doing a little mathematical group work, putting their heads together over Svet's clandestine research results on her infra-red pulses. Anyway, this evening they were simply out to enjoy themselves, brainwork could wait.

The long and wide sweeping driveway curled and wound around the blur of thick trees, finally opening out to reveal another wide porchway facade of white pilaster columns fronting a large colonial country house. Dusk was beginning to hover and the car park was already well packed with an array of expensive looking SUVs and pickup trucks. They found a reserved place at the front, Svet parking next to a large, black Lincoln limousine. Lots of people of all ages were wandering in and out, mainly couples but also a few groups of men and women obviously out to enjoy themselves on a Friday night office party or birthday celebration. They appeared to be outside some upmarket club or restaurant. Instinctively Lauren and Amélie carefully perused the dress styles of the women walking in, including their ages. Many were wearing smart and certainly expensive casual jeans and tops, similar to what they all had on, so relief all round, but they trusted Svet who had insisted they were dressed fine before setting off. Mixed in with the jeans were numerous variants of summery cotton dresses and a few very tight, leather, short skirts displaying tanned, beefy thighs.

"Wow, this sure ain't a cowgirl area but some of those girls would fit inside a bullhorn corral really well," Charlotte remarked, also gazing analytically. They smirked agreeably.

"Let's go then girls. Welcome to the Sargasso Serenade," Svet began, as they opened their doors. "Hey, the owners are coming out to greet you."

Lauren stared hard and couldn't believe her eyes. It surely wasn't possible but the confident, striding and tall figure, with a wild mane of curly, black hair was unmistakeable in the glare of the entrance lights, followed behind by a much older man with silvery, swept-back hair in a small ponytail.

Lauren rushed over to greet her with a hug. "Nadine. I can't believe it's you. It has been absolutely ages. I don't think I've seen you since Murmansk? You look absolutely lovely in that long dress. Are you really the owner of this palace?"

"Sure am, or should I say, you betcha," Nadine replied laughing, grabbing the hand of her companion and pulling him forward. "May I introduce you to my husband Roland, we jointly own the club. We decided to get married last week, I'm afraid the Svet effect is catching on!"

"I told you it would be a nice surprise," Svet shouted, grinning wildly to Lauren, who was being kissed on each cheek, French style by the urbane Roland. Lauren then remembered instantly. He was a high flying English computer professor in Harvard, who had dated Nadine for years, in fact ever since Svet moved to the US. But buying a place this size indicated he was likely developing some innovative commercial software on the side or had a large inheritance.

Nadine then moved on to greet Amélie and Charlotte warmly as Roland led Lauren inside. They were met by a cavernous interior of a main dance floor, the evening being a country dance special, already well in progress with the lights dimmed. Coloured arcs of light flashed around the room accompanied with a live band fronted by a curvy blonde female singer. This would be followed up by a disco later. Winding corridors led off towards themed restaurants and bars around the periphery, some quiet and select, well away from the din and the action. Upstairs were around twenty select bedrooms which revellers could book and stay over in if they wished.

Nadine and Roland explained how they had decided almost on a whim, having come across the house one Sunday out walking, to invest and turn the place back into the social hub it had once been in the 1940s, during the war years. Sadly, the colonial mansion had become run down and was closed for years. Lauren was correct. Roland was a visiting Harvard academic who also ran his own successful software company based on intelligent data mining with a unique analysis function he had invented. He and Nadine had fallen in love with the house immediately and had done up their own large apartment at the back, next to three sumptuous original libraries. So the club was also their home. The original house used to belong to a scientist, a relative and descendent of the great Benjamin Franklin, one of the founders of the US, and had for a long time in the 1900s been a place of frenetic scientific learning and discovery. Much of the work was focussed on early electromagnetism and electro-technology experiments. Whilst Svet went to talk to some friends, Lauren, Amélie and Charlotte wandered around with Nadine and Roland, mesmerised, perusing some of the books and examining the original experimental equipment which they had set up in cases inside the library as a form of homage to the illustrious scientific past. What a wonderful place to live in. Lauren felt a pang of envy.

"Anyway," Nadine began. "I'm going to join you guys tonight for some fun. Roland has a card game and a bottle of whisky set up in the house, he's an avid poker player."

"I like to live dangerously Lauren," Roland added with a smile, as Svet rejoined them. "But don't worry; I know exactly when the odds are against me. I practice secretly with my robot, programmed by a special piece of software I wrote. To be honest Alicia is already slightly better than me, but who wants to admit artificial intelligence is ahead of us poor humans? Least of all in poker!"

"He would like to add 'especially as Alicia is a female robot,' but he knows I'll slice him in two with my little silver stars if he even dares!" Nadine said in a low voice and mild glare at her husband.

Everyone roared laughing; from past experiences they could well believe it. As Roland ambled off to his card game, Amélie immediately piped up. "Lauren, I don't know about everyone else but I think you, me and Charlotte need to work off some of Svet's monster apple cake and get down and dirty on the dance floor. Shall we show these Americans how ex-Parisian hipsters can really swing?"

Lauren felt like fun too, and it had been far too long since she had been on a dance floor, never Philippe's thing, but then what was? "Honestly Amélie, sometimes I wonder about you, but yes, why not."

Charlotte nodded. "Hey you two, this is country music playing, not your 1980s David Bowie punk rock."

"Cheeky."

Nadine cut in as they started to head back to the central club area. "Svet and I will join you shortly. If you want anything to eat later, just head over to any of the restaurants and give the waiter the first six digits of pi ... all food is on the house, Roland and I insist."

Lauren laughed. "I admire your unique promotional code, Nadine. I hope we can remember that later after a few drinks—I'm glad it isn't Planck's constant!"

Charlotte and Amélie giggled loudly, an old joke only the three of them shared. As they headed for the dance floor, they passed the country band suddenly making a beeline break for the bar. The disco cut back in with 1970s soul music. Lauren smirked ... it had been a long time since she listened to Gladys Knight and the Pips. A lot of locals had arrived and the three pushed themselves onto the middle of the crowded floor and began letting go, coloured lights pulsating through an array of colours, the deep base of the tall speakers thudding away behind them. As the music moved on through the Isley Brothers and the Temptations, Lauren gyrated through all her past moves. She had always been an excellent dancer, a musical natural from a child, which Amélie knew and hated, but Charlotte was very surprised how fluid she was as Lauren garnered increasing attention from people around, male and female who were taking particular notice. Lauren closed her eyes and let her mind fade away into a pleasant oblivion, whilst thoughts of previous male lovers who could dance properly flowed in a reel clip through her brain, Philippe of course decidedly not one of them.

Suddenly she felt a light tap on her shoulder from behind and a deep male voice whispered in her ear. "You're quite a mover, who would have guessed? Would you like to dance with me?"

It startled her for a moment. She opened her eyes and turned to see a total impossibility, it was her subconscious desires playing tricks. But it definitely wasn't a trick. She smiled stupidly, amazed and flustered to see the grinning face of Professor Jackson Smythe alongside, and Amélie of course taking everything in quietly, her face in neutral. Charlotte however had already met and chatted to Jackson Smythe numerous times inside Cassini and gave him a little wave and a big smile.

"Jack?" she blurted. "What on earth are you doing here?"

"I changed my mind. So are you going to dance or not?"

"Okay, hope you haven't got two left feet?" she replied, still stunned but inside pleased as hell, especially watching Amélie's face.

"You may be surprised. That's the second time you called me Jack. Perhaps we're becoming friends after all?" he whispered nonchalantly, as she smiled flirtatiously.

Charlotte caught Amélie's attention, who was still desperately trying to work out who on earth this guy, who obviously knew Lauren, was and the dynamic. However Charlotte, as ever quite relaxed, had suspected for some time, from the nods, winks and dropped conversations that Lauren quite fancied Professor Smythe. Charlotte nodded towards the bar for her and Amélie to retire for a drink and leave them to it.

Finding a couple of spare bar stools, Charlotte ordered a couple of desperately needed Singapore Slings, explaining to Amélie the composition of the long, cool gin cocktail made from cointreau and fresh lime juice. They looked back onto the dance floor, watching Lauren and Jackson moving like pros, synchronised perfectly with each other, like they were a glove fit. Amélie stared mesmerised and annoyed, partly jealous and partly irritated that she had no idea who this flirtatious Jack person was. Certainly he was a very attractive man, physically fit and a little older than her, but not only could he dance amazingly well but he never took his adoring eyes off Lauren. She gazed in astonishment at Lauren's gooey-eyed expression of overt reciprocation and only one small glass of wine had passed her lips! They had joked about Paris earlier to Charlotte and Svet but that was literally the last time Amélie had ever seen Lauren so engrossed with a male, like they had time-travelled back twenty five years.

"Okay, I'll put you out of your misery," Charlotte murmured with a smirk, sipping at her deep red cocktail as Amélie, still glaring, rattled the ice in hers. "Cheers. An interesting evening isn't it?"

"Certainly for some," Amélie replied sharply. "That guy is going to fuck Lauren rotten that's for sure. Gosh, I'm sorry Charlotte. I always forget Lauren is your mother, how inappropriate."

Charlotte laughed. "And why shouldn't my mother have a little fun? She's been stubbornly miserable inside herself for far too long, diverting her unhappy emotions into work and the kids. Anyway, his name is Jackson Smythe. He's a professor of nuclear engineering and heads up the practical side of Lauren's fusion centre brilliantly. She appointed him some time back to fill a gap in the team. He's a great guy, a very nice man, I've met him a number of times and the Cassini staff love him. I think Lauren has grown a bit of a soft spot for him."

"That's an understatement if ever there was. You mean he's an employee at Cassini? That is really bonkers given her position, something I never did or would do."

"He's actually a Director, reports only to her although Lauren insists he's not strictly an employee as he's on a rolling consultancy contract. Like, I recall, you were one time?"

Amélie grimaced again. "That distinction is academic. Anyway, I'm not sure I like the look of Mr Smythe. He reminds me too much of Lauren's previous husband and Luis all rolled into one."

"Who is Luis?" Charlotte replied gulping down her cocktail. "I like these. Want another? Hey, there's Svet and Nadine coming our way."

"I'll explain Luis later, Charlotte. Yes please, and then I fancy something to eat. Those two look rather serious. Gosh what is all that commotion on the dance floor? Oh my God, look."

Svet and Nadine pulled up some stools as Charlotte ordered another four Singapore Slings and handed over a twenty dollar bill, at least it was a lot cheaper than in Singapore. They stared silently at the crowd which had gone quite still when the clapping restarted and a long line of people parted down the middle to make a wide space. The disc jockey, after a word from Jack, had put on one of Lauren's one-time favourites from the film Grease onto the turntable, and she had whispered to Jack whether he had the stamina to be John Travolta to her Olivia Newton-John. She had done that sequence many times before, with someone very special nearly thirty years ago at University, but her razor memory recalled the moves perfectly in an instant. At the same time she mischievously wanted to test Jack out. Just how good a dancer was he?

He nodded immediately with a wide smile, and they were off, dancing the classic sequence to perfection together with no prompting, amid a chorus of claps and shrieks of encouragement from the audience everywhere. The finale came. She felt a wave of trepidation but also complete confidence in Jack as he mouthed 'ready' and she flew to him leaping up into the air as he caught her firmly in his strong arms and whirled her about his shoulders. She was even now with Juliette, well almost. The clapping went demonic, even around the bars. Nobody at the club had ever seen such a performance.

Jack gently put her down, holding her close as she looked into his eyes silently. He whispered in her ear. "They expect us to finish it like the film," and bent forward and kissed her gently on the lips. Lauren felt a surge of electric shock pleasure flow right through her body and responded; all over in five seconds, but long enough for her to know. She wanted him badly.

"Shall we go for a nice quiet meal now Lauren and a chat?" he said, "I'm getting a bit old for this!"

"You are brilliant Jack. Yes, a lovely thought. I noticed a Japanese restaurant at the far end. Can you remember pi to six decimal places by any chance?" She threw her blonde, wavy hair back coquettishly.

He stared perplexed. "Pardon? Yes, I suppose so ... of course." Lauren was the most unexpected but exciting and desirable woman he had ever known, in all these years he had ... but then he stopped. Was he actually falling in love with her?

"Good, then come on," she whispered, took his hand firmly and they walked off in the other direction towards the restaurant, three of her original companions watching intrigued, whilst Amélie still fumed.

But it was immediately obvious that Svet and Nadine were very relaxed and nonchalant about Lauren's behaviour, even more so than Charlotte, so Amélie inwardly decided to let it lie, despite her doubts about Nuclear Black Jack Travolta, and put her mild envy to the back of her mind. Anyway, Charlotte was right. Philippe as she had always predicted, was a real emotional loser, and they were here to have fun and relax. Lauren was a big girl and deserved to do exactly what she wanted. It was obvious Professor Smythe was a man pressing the right buttons for a change.

Amélie turned to Svet and Nadine. "You two look a little glum for a girl's night out? Want another drink?"

Svet looked up, and then smiled. "Sorry Amélie, it's the lights. They've been bothering us."

Amélie stared up at the fittings, puzzled. "They all look fine to me. Very contemporary I must admit but in line with the rest of the renovations?"

Charlotte giggled. "I think Svet and Nadine mean what we saw outside before we arrived." She turned to Svet. "Have you been conferring about something? I have to admit, I was going to come back to my notes when I went to bed."

Amélie blushed. She wasn't normally so dense, no more Singapore Slings. "Well?" she began. "Although the fifth superbrain is unexpectedly otherwise engaged, four of us should crack the puzzle. Spit out your theories Svet, so we can tear them apart."

Sitting close together on their table, Lauren and Jack held hands as they watched their suki yaki, consisting of thinly sliced beef, vegetables, tofu and exotic noodles, prepared by a personal chef in a special sauce, then cooked in a hot-pot at their table.

Soon, both hungry after their super-dance extravaganza, they were wolfing down large portions of the exquisite meal, accompanied by a bottle of Lauren's favourite Merlot red wine.

"So, tell me, not only why did you come but how did you know I was here then, Jack Mysteryman?" she began, feeling both content and excited inside, with him next to her.

"I simply wanted to be with you, I'll tell you later how I found you, but it wasn't so difficult."

"Mmm ... okay, for now. That's nice actually. So, time to reveal more about your opaque past, Jack, now we're friends. You can start with your wife and five daughters."

"Err ... ex wife. She remarried many years ago, after a long affair, to a heart specialist, but I suppose it was mine that felt broken. Although to be honest I deserved it. I neglected her and the family, always out of the country on contracts and exploration. She never really understood my scientific wanderlust."

"Exploration?"

He blushed slightly. "Sorry—wrong terminology. I meant new technology challenges."

"Like your odd welding device robot for example? I've been trying to work out how that operates, and after much scribbled mathematics and deep thought, my conclusion is you are able to generate high frequency electromagnetic heat waves, well outside of the normal existing operating ranges. Nobody else can do that yet, as far as I am aware Jack, let alone robotically controlled. So?"

"So what?"

"How come you know then?"

He stopped eating and held her hand again. "Good inventive intuition, exactly as you have. My daughters are still close however and I have adorable grandchildren."

"Where are they all? Back in the UK?"

"Partly. Do you really want to be friends now?"

She realised he was not going to be forthcoming but she didn't care; she loved him exactly as he was. Fun, sexy and a little enigmatic, a good combination for her as she always liked challenge and radical, especially wrapped up together in a man. Then she stopped in her mind. What had she said to herself? *She loved him exactly as he was?* Oh God, she had admitted it ... falling ... and it felt really good again and different. "As they say in the dating ads ... and maybe more," she whispered, sipping her wine slowly.

He smiled and they continued eating silently, glancing at each other contentedly.

"You really fancy a burger and fries, Amélie?" Charlotte queried as they looked up at the bar menu.

"Actually, this isn't just any old burger and fries but a special recipe sauce, made from prime steak like you've never tasted, lovely cheese and a generous serving of home grown salad," Nadine responded.

"You betcha," Amélie and Svet replied in unison.

Nadine waved to the barman to lay a quiet table near the large window where they could look over a small illuminated pond and laid out garden. They ordered some beers, with a non-alcoholic one for Amélie who was now feeling too light-headed and woozy with all the gin, especially as she would have to talk some sense into Lauren later, after of course quizzing her on all the gory details.

Svet had decided after talking earlier to Nadine to describe her wider research aims in more detail. Especially after this evening. Although Amélie now supervised her specific work on plasmas, and Lauren had some idea she wanted to extend her knowledge of astrobiology, nobody but Nadine and Sergei knew what she was really doing. As their huge plates of burger and accompaniments were brought to the table, Svet began. "This is going to be a bit of confession time Amélie, because it's time you knew what I'm really researching, not just plasmas. And now I have a genuine problem and need all your collective mathematical brains please, including Lauren's."

Amélie smiled. "I had guessed Svet that your plasma work was a routeway to something bigger. I'm too long in the tooth in this research game. I just wanted you to tell me when you felt the moment was right."

"And tonight is right. The lights have brought everything to a head."

Svet then digressed slowly and methodically through her extended research. She had been concentrating her work for the last two years, all focussed on the four large moons of Jupiter: Io, Europa, Ganymede and Callisto. She soon answered the most obvious question, why, talking volubly about primordial soup, volcanoes, the huge electrical and magnetic field effects and potential plasma charges from Jupiter ... and then moved onto her theories of alternative life forms, not silicon based as most people usually thought about distinct from earthly carbon, but based on sulphur. She expounded her hypothesis that such life forms could not only theoretically exist but would potentially 'live' off pure chemical energy.

"That's fascinating Svet and I can see fully why you're researching plasmas, but what has that all got to do with the lights we saw earlier?" Charlotte responded, listening intensely and trying to put the threads together as Lauren being a keen astronomer would be doing if she was sat listening.

Svet drew in a deep breath. "Because something else in the course of this work arose a few weeks ago, some recorded results following my pointing of a special infrared receiver towards Jupiter. Roland and Nadine have built the kit specially for me. I've picked up a series of strange and unexpected pulses, all at the far end of the infrared spectrum, a little like the random ones that pulsar stars emit but with a big difference. They're not random. They follow a definite mathematical series of patterns. I believe they're some sort of code, but working it out is really complex and I need help. That's also why I wanted you all to come and see everything in my laboratory tomorrow. But I have some examples here."

Rooting around in her bag, Svet withdrew a number of sheets of paper, overwritten with a set of complicated mathematics, integrals and probability equations related to coding methodologies. "I feel like Alan Turing must have experienced in Bletchley Park during the Second World War after picking up the Enigma coding, knowing it was significant but struggling desperately to find the right approach. Nadine, Roland and I have been burning some midnight oil, but something is fundamentally missing in our approach. But look at the pattern structures."

Charlotte grabbed the papers and laid them out in front of Amélie. Both began to concentrate hard on the mathematical sequence of patterns of artificially converted digits from the data, with Svet and Nadine alongside.

Amélie suddenly jumped up out of her seat, as they stared alarmed at her manic expression. "Jesus fucking Christ, it's just struck me. You're working in binary Svet; of course you would, following your natural computing instincts. But you need to change your equations and work in another number system, maintaining invariance. If my gut instinct is correct these mathematical patterns are pulsing in base four, it's a quaternary numerical system you need to use."

She sat down, red in the face. Maybe the gin had had the opposite effect on her brain this time. Charlotte meanwhile placed her notes on the table of the short series of light pulses she had noted, drawing up the data into a square table. She then converted the calculations into base four and they studied and compared Charlotte's pattern with a few of Svet's. They were remarkably similar, like matching samples of DNA in a forensic trial.

"Bloody hell," Charlotte cried. "My instincts were right too; those lights *were* flashing in a coded sequence. But what does this mean? The US military in the skies above us with matched pulsations from Jupiter? Doesn't make sense."

Amélie and Svet began excitedly discussing quaternary systems in data transmission and even their use in old American Indian languages. Nadine suddenly pulled up both her hands in the air to get everyone quiet. "Hey guys, let's stop for a moment. All this might make sense if we discount the US military instead."

Amélie, Charlotte and Svet stopped talking instantly. They stared in silence at Nadine, who was her usual calm, assured and determined self.

"You must be joking Nadine," Amélie began slowly. "Surely you don't mean ... like UFOs? Extraterrestrials and little green men? That is taking lateral thinking too far. ET and cold fusion have exactly the same origins ... fucking bollocks."

Nadine remained implacable. "I simply suggest we keep an open mind, as genuine scientists Amélie."

Svet interjected. "Remember, I am researching non-carbon life forms so I think Nadine has a valid point. Whatever these pulses are and whatever is causing the lights, they are linked in some way. That's all we know. More work needs to be done."

Amélie drank up the remains of her beer and drew a long breath. "Actually, Nadine and Svet, I agree one thing and we mustn't discount any lateral thinking. Sometimes I get a bit animated. If Lauren was fucking well here, she would have some definite views from her super-brain, instead of shagging Neutron Jack. Sorry guys, I didn't mean that either. I just worry about her that's all, after all our time together."

Svet looked across. "Actually I hope she is shagging Jack. My father has been a real bastard to her over these last seven years. She deserves some genuine love and respect now."

"Hear hear, here's to Lauren," Charlotte added, smiling, as they clinked glasses and finished off their drinks.

"Actually," Nadine began. "The music stops about now, eleven pm, we have a by-law strictly enforced and the club closes at twelve. Let's find Lauren if she's still in the restaurant and all go for a walk on the beach. The sea air is lovely out the back ..."

Chatting quietly over coffee, their lovely meal finished and cleared away, they looked wistfully at the beautiful, lit up gardens outside, when Lauren suddenly turned to Jack. A cunning plan had naughtily filtered through her mind. "This house has a truly amazing history of scientific discovery in electromagnetic physics during the nineteen hundreds. There is a lovely library at the back, full of equipment Nadine has set up and original books. Fancy a look? I know Nadine won't mind at all."

He looked up and smiled warmly. She knew he wouldn't be able to resist. "Yes please, a bonus for the evening."

"In that case, recite pi please to six figures to the waiter here and I'll leave a tip."

He looked again puzzled, but recited anyway, "err ... 3.141592653 ..."

"Okay, you don't have to show off; you've accomplished our free meal from Nadine and Roland."

"What a lovely idea. So where's this library?"

"Follow me."

She took his hand and they walked off through some winding corridors into a back area with a clear sign saying private. Ignoring that, she continued down another corridor to the far end, noting one corridor led to Nadine's private quarters but remembering the other went to a series of doors, which were of course the libraries she had seen earlier. She quietly opened the end door and they walked in. The evening light was drawing in fast so she switched on the table lamps and drew the long purple velvet curtains across the deep Georgian windows. Jack was already pressed against a particular glass case, peering in avidly.

"Good heavens Lauren. This is very similar to the same equipment used by Rudolf Hertz in 1888 to measure electromagnetic radio waves and provide experimental proof for the first time for Maxwell's Theory. But this lot is dated 1885, John Steibler. This experimenter may have predated Hertz but never published the results. Wow."

But Lauren was pressed against him, her arm around his waist. He smiled and looked into her eyes.

"Never mind about Maxwell's equations," she whispered in her most sultry voice. "I need a friend like a hole in the head right now. I want your love and your body wrapped around all my heart instead. What do you think?"

His eyes widened ... she never failed to amaze. "Where?"

"Right here, on that cloth covered table, now," she uttered determinedly, deftly lifting up his shirt out of his jeans and undoing the buttons. Excitedly he began to undo the buttons on her blouse at the same time as she pushed backwards onto the flat table. In a moment she had his shirt off over his head and uplifted arms and threw it over Maxwell's case, as he kicked off his shoes. She turned instantly to the task of unzipping his jeans and pulling them down, watching with fascination as his large erection popped into the air. In one wriggled motion, socks and boxer shorts together were tossed over the floor. This was the fastest male *dishabillé* she had ever done. At long last Jackson Smythe was gorgeously stark naked and she had to have him there and then, driven by a wild desire, unlike anything she had experienced for far too long.

Without any hesitation she kicked off her shoes, impatiently tore open her own blouse, unclipped her bra and threw them both on top of his shirt. Climbing alongside him, his face stunned with amazement and equal desire for her, she drew up her legs, unzipped her jeans and removed them and her underwear in an instant, wriggling strenuously out of them provocatively. He gazed all over at her compelling, tanned nakedness and light brown nipples. They turned on their sides and kissed passionately, his hands everywhere, over her breasts, her bottom, finally fondling her wet labia. She drew in a sharp breath and gave out a gentle moan as three fingers pushed inside, rubbing her expertly to perfection, a feeling of intense pleasure she had not experienced with any man for years. She gripped his erection and gently bit his bottom lip in a passionate loud cry, feeling herself coming instantly, the need so long for his touch, forcing the reaction from her body like hot magma pouring out of an erupting volcano.

Pushing him gently on his back, she climbed on top. "Oh God, Jack, I've wanted you to do that for so long, the thought has been driving me crazy," she cried, as he ran his fingers through her wavy hair and kissed her again tenderly.

"I love your new hairstyle," he whispered. "I've wanted you more than any woman, more strongly than I would have ever thought possible. I've fallen in love with you Lauren, I'm crazy for you. I can't understand it, these feelings shouldn't compute ..." He stopped when she pushed his legs further apart.

"Good, because I love you Jack and I never, ever believed I would ever say that to a man again but I do, a passion which fills me with fire. I want to fuck you slow and steady, until we both scream. I don't care who hears. Okay? Does that compute?"

"Every fucking zero, one, two and three digits," he screamed, wriggling the tip of his erection against the sopping lips of her opening.

She pushed hard and entered him in one gurgling sound, shouting with the invasive sensation. They began to move together, in and out as he found her rhythm and pushed and pulled in time, feeling their groins meet, as she rode the whole length of him on every stroke, crying with the wave of orgasms searing through her insides. She saw Jack begin to shake. He too was coming far quicker than normal but so was she and for the fifth time.

He concentrated his gaze unwavering and steadfast at her. She stared back mesmerised into his eyes. They had transformed into an unusual elliptical shape, the pupils having dilated enormously, with a yellow luminance inside the corneas. Her mind was blowing crazy, she felt exactly like when she had smoked great spliffs of marijuana at university, immersed into massive waves of rolling fantasies, scenes and lust intertwining and transported into cloudy visions, hearing Jack, his muddied voice, far away, echoing in a whisper in the background.

"I know you want to fulfil all these fantasies. Let your mind go completely and do it, I'll help you, Lauren, it drives me insane anticipating your need and desires together. This will feel like nothing you have ever experienced ..."

She heard no more, completely lost, mechanically thrusting harder and harder, when masses of naked bodies appeared all around her. She was sprawled and exposed, her legs splayed open on a giant circular bed with lush white sheets, her head lying on deep, soft pillows, a Bach prelude playing softly in the background. They were all around her, fondling every part of her body and inserting themselves into every orifice. She was submitting completely, screaming and crying to their insatiable demands. Luis, smiling in the only way he could alongside her former husband and Vaag, rubbed themselves against her breasts, masturbating in unison furiously over her naked body. Other past lovers were behind, and women appeared too. Mila, holding a huge purple dildo, was pushing Vaag and Luis away and climbing on top of her, with Rosie and Annabella pulling her arms up and forcing her legs further apart, as Luis clambered behind Mila and began to fuck her rearwards at the same time as Mila inserted the dildo and began to pull and push on it furiously. Philippe appeared next with Olga, both naked and grinning alongside Luis, her huge mane of red hair wafting into her face, sucking his cock and fondling her hair. The crazy, erotic scenes flashed by faster, the noise and heat became louder and she felt her whole body rise high into the air with a depth of pleasurable intensity that was so unreal she couldn't stop and screamed out as loud as her lungs would let her once her final orgasm began to reach a massive crescendo.

She looked down, the visions were fading away and Jack was back, alone, holding her tight, and equally shaking from top to bottom. He was letting her scream and create unbridled mayhem, unlike other men she had slept with who became uncomfortable when she went wild and out of control, as he too shouted incessantly. They finally came, miraculously at the same time. She gripped his head viciously as wave after intense wave overpowered her body and senses, then she clawed madly at his shoulders, creating instant deep scratches, which began to bleed. The waves of pleasure seemed to go on for minute after minute, as if time had become dilated. This was an experience she would never have believed possible in her wildest moments. What on earth was this man capable of? She had made love to him like a crazy woman. The purest ever rippling sensations gradually waned and she flopped silently on top of him, drained completely, as he stroked her hair gently and whispered in her ear how much he loved her.

"I've not known any woman like you Lauren, never, not since I first arrived and met ..." he whispered, his voice croaky and hoarse with shouting. But he stopped. Anyway she didn't care about his past affairs, discretions or indiscretions. Such women were irrelevant. She would be the centre of all his dreams and desires. How far her hopes had become driven and focussed in such a short time.

"Good job there are hefty, solid walls and a thick, old American oak door in here," he mumbled, breathing heavily, his face a bright cherry red. Lauren wasn't faring any better. "But," he continued, "Maybe it would be wise to now put our clothes back on and take a walk."

"Agreed Professor Smythe, you have my permission this one time," she replied with a smirk. They pulled themselves off the table and began to dress quickly, Lauren dabbing his brow and cheeks and then his shoulder scratches, which didn't look as bad as she first thought, with some moistened, cold tissues from a packet she had kept on the flight. Brushing her blonde hair back to some semblance of normality, Lauren pulled out a tiny mirror and reapplied her bright red lipstick, smudged badly in the melee. She wiped smears off Jack's cheek and neck, then realised, looking at the time on the huge ticking mahogany grandfather clock in the corner that she needed to find the others. To simply depart without as much as a by-your-leave, as she did had been a little antisocial. But, she thought, it was very nice to be an emotional renegade again. She had definitely become quite boring of late, even Amélie would agree. Although Amélie was not going to be told one micro-word of her incredible sex with Jack, she would simply have to guess and imagine instead. Lauren smiled.

"What was the name of that woman who was almost as amazing as me?" she uttered, putting some powder and mascara back on.

"Err ... Ada," he replied quietly with a cough. "Just got to nip upstairs and find something, Lauren. I assume you'll return to your friends?"

"Ada? That's a quaint name," she mumbled, still staring into her mirror. "Jack? What room are you in?" anticipating that a repeat later in a luxurious bed and a long sleepy snuggle would end the evening very nicely. She would get a taxi back to Svet's, even if it was in the early morning.

No reply. She turned, but he had already quietly disappeared out the door. She smoothed down her jeans, ruffled her blouse and dabbed her face, still a tad redder than desirable and decided to head for the loo quickly after first carefully rearranging the cloth on the table. But something odd suddenly struck her. She realised she wasn't feeling wet, or beginning to drip as expected. He had certainly come and violently with a passion unseen, but hadn't actually ejaculated anything. She thought, maybe he'd had some treatment or perhaps a past illness? They needed to talk more and she needed to dig further and deeper into his past. He was probably much more willing after that session of shared passion, to also reveal his past, and she was always a good listener as well as a master wheedle-outer of male secrets. Nor did it matter, not with that fiery libido. But she wanted to know much more about the whole Jackson Smythe, she cared about his well-being dreadfully already ...

There was still no sign of Jack anywhere. He didn't return to the library, she went to reception and found his room number but no answer there and he hadn't checked out either. She looked around the bars and restaurants. No sign of him anywhere. He'd simply vanished into thin air, how was that possible? She felt herself feeling increasingly upset and stupidly angry. Vanishing just when she wanted him seemed to be a bad habit of his. Walking back to the main club area, she was feeling increasingly frantic and dismayed. She noticed that many people were gathering their coats and departing. The Sargasso must be closing, but where were the others? Then around the next corner she was confronted by a loud gaggle of tall women, talking intensely and fronted by a slim, Afro-Chinese beauty with the unmistakable mass of curly black hair.

"Lauren, at last, we wondered where on earth you'd got to? We saw you having dinner with Jack in the restaurant and decided to leave you both to it," Charlotte cried out, grinning broadly.

Lauren looked at Amélie. She was being the silent Ms Inscrutable again. She knew that face of old, which radiated intense disapproval, but she didn't care one tiny jot. "Sorry folks, Jack and I had a nice walk through your library Nadine and a long chat. He was hugely impressed with the equipment, I got a forensic equation by equation analysis of James Clerk Maxwell for most of the time," she quipped, trying hard to hide her disappointment of not finding him.

"That's cool," Nadine replied. "Where is he? The club is closing now but we've decided to have a walk by the shore. The night is lovely and warm outside. Perhaps Jack would like to come with us?"

Lauren's face dropped. "I don't know to be honest. He's gone off somewhere and he's not in his room either, I checked." She glanced for a second at Amélie, whose eyes had narrowed, still taking in and analysing every nuance in her annoying way.

"He's probably just getting some fresh air too," Charlotte responded, putting her at ease. "Anyway, we want to talk to you about Svet's amazingly original research mystery which we have been poring over assiduously in the bar. We desperately need your opinions, always guaranteed to be mathematically prescient and practically controversial."

Svet appeared a little embarrassed by Charlotte's eulogy, but smiled and nodded.

Lauren raised a half smile back. "Okay, sounds good." But all she really wanted was Jack by her side again. They began to walk towards the exit. Charlotte, Svet and Nadine were ahead and continuing their intense discussions together as Amélie deliberately held behind with Lauren.

"Well, I hope you've got that out of your system," she began haughtily. "You look like you've been at it all night; you and I go too far back, Lauren. You need to dab your cheeks a bit more."

"You don't have to be jealous Amélie. Why are you so angry? Jack is ..."

"Listen," Amélie interrupted sharply. "I'm just looking out for you. I care deeply about my best friend and I simply don't like him. Call it instinct, whatever you want. I don't care what you call it. He's Luis, ex husbands and Vaag all rolled into one as far as I'm concerned."

"He's sexy, adorable and a good, kind man and yes, I fucked him rotten, it was out of this world. Satisfied now? I just wish he was here holding my hand again."

"Jesus Christ Lauren, just take some deep breaths and slow it down will you. I've never seen you like this. Fuck it all, of course I'm happy for you and pleased. I just wish it was with someone else."

"I love him Amélie, I really must go and find him, where the fuck has he gone off to?" Lauren replied, her face red again with emotion and tears welling up in her eyes. Svet, Charlotte and Nadine were now outside. She began to turn to go back.

Amélie grabbed her arm hard and held her firmly. "No Lauren. Now stop, get a grip," she whispered loudly into Lauren's face. "I can see you're upset, but he's probably out there getting some air after you probably nearly finished him off in that library knowing you, the emotional state you're in. Jack sees a calm, beautiful sophisticated and intelligent woman in you. He's that kind of man, or you wouldn't have fallen for him this way. He doesn't want to meet up with a weeping hysteric who can't get her act together. Do you hear me?"

Lauren drew a few deep breaths and stood still and silent for half a minute, rationalising her emotions back to some normality. This was not her, she repeated over and over in her head. Falling madly in love was one thing but becoming out of control was not acceptable and Amélie was absolutely right.

She put her arms around Amélie and hugged her tight. "Thank you, as ever, keeping me on track when I get like this. But Jack's not a baddie, he's a good man. I know the Hind man-curse will undoubtedly be back, as ever, but I have some hopes. I feel as passionate about Jack as I ever did about Luis."

Amélie smiled. "Okay, I know. Let's agree to say no more, for now. I think you do owe Svet some listening time though. Your step-daughter has outstanding research capabilities and has assembled some unusual data which has more than a passing interest for a super-brain mathematician like you. Of course I've put her on a core pathway but you need to provide the icing and decoration."

Lauren laughed, feeling her red face returning to normal in the cool draft of the breeze blowing through the door. "Bit of a mixed metaphor there, but yes, fine, absolutely. I'm still brain functioning, despite the booze. Who else can recite all of Maxwell's electromagnetic field equations, even three dimensional, whilst being shagged?"

Amélie giggled. Lauren as usual, always had to be different. "Certainly not me, horizontal or otherwise," she retorted laughing and linked her arm into Lauren's. "Come on."

The others outside breathed a sigh of collective relief ... They patiently were waiting, assuming that Amélie had been quickly drawing out all the salacious gossip of what had actually gone on between Lauren and Jack, and by their expressions that was true. They would find out more later.

Walking along the winding and newly made path between the conifer woods and the wide beach, lit up by a series of well placed, LED antique lampposts which Nadine had personally ordered, the cool sea breeze was a welcome relief from the heat of the day. A nearly full moon peeked through the haze, the thick clouds having dispersed earlier in the evening. Svet talked through her findings again about the infrared pulses and they discussed the best ways of a potential decoding alongside Amélie's revelation on the group match to a quaternary number system of four digits. Lauren took out her calculator and started to independently solve some unconsidered data transmission equations using first binary and then quaternary digits, using the numbers zero, one, two and three. She smiled and showed the results, which displayed another close match with the patterns Charlotte had ascertained roughly from the earlier viewings of the military display. There was no doubt now there was a connection.

But Lauren had something further to add, which she was familiar with, from work done in Nimi's new, blue-sky military division of Cassini. "There is a mathematical connection," she began, "between the quaternary number system and the building blocks of genetic DNA, which seem to follow an ordering and pattern formation based on that system rather than an expected binary sequencing. I think we've proven beyond doubt that the earlier lights and the infrared pulses share such sequencing, so why not continue to think latterly? What if we are seeing a coded reference to our own human DNA? What I'm trying to say is could this be a message ... forget military for a moment or any rational explanation ... simply that we are being told that our DNA is being monitored and understood ... perhaps the US government is attempting a more technological update, to keep the pot boiling but suitable for this century. Remember what happened in 1948?"

Everyone looked back puzzled. "No, brainbox," Amélie replied waspishly. This was like the last Lauren puzzle time back in the pickup at Murmansk when they all had to try and remember the 1908 Siberian meteor explosion. "Want to put us out of our misery? Oh shit." Her eyes blazed. Her fast brain had been chewing over their earlier discussion without Lauren. "The Roswell UFO mystery. Spaceships crashing and dead aliens found. There are still plenty of conspiracy theories about despite the so called incident now being solved as a weather balloon incident. Gosh Lauren, your mind really does traverse odd paths, but keep up the genius bit; I see what you're getting at. We might need it later when ... gosh what's that weird noise?"

They all stopped and listened. A faint, but high frequency humming could be heard out to sea, but they could see nothing whatsoever. Suddenly they were all bathed out of the sky in a greenish-yellow circular hue, as if a number of large theatre spotlights had converged on them.

Herded protectively by Nadine, they huddled together, the light from above blinding and the humming growing louder.

"What the fuck is all this about?" Nadine cried out, instinctively pulling out the knife she always carried inside her jeans, but the light had reduced in intensity and the glow felt peculiarly warm and relaxing. Their senses were being inescapably numbed, as if they were inside a sauna or undergoing a relaxing massage. They all began to feel pleasantly woozy.

"Fuck!" Nadine looked up, followed by the others as a large circular spinning object high in the sky came into immediate view, the obvious source of the light beam. It was distinctly disc shaped, a highly polished metallic hue and must have been about a hundred and fifty feet across. Flying saucers were the subject of fantasy, wishful thinking and deluded rantings but their imaginations were not running riot. One was up there in full technological glory.

Lauren looked at her watch. It was just turned midnight when out of the trees a person suddenly strode forward, dressed from head to foot in a bright white suit ... but with a pale purple emanation surrounding him, an ethereal aura around a foot wide. He stopped and smiled. It was difficult through the haze of the light they were bathed in for any of the five to see clearly who or what it was. Lauren squinted hard when she realised, and lurched forward with a cry.

But Amélie swung around instantly and grabbed her arm, aided by Nadine. "No Lauren, no, no, you can't. Jack's a fucking alien!"

Chapter Fourteen

The last thing Lauren remembered was Nadine grabbing hold of them and screaming 'we must all keep together.' Then she felt herself rising slowly upwards, the sensation like flying inside a dream with your arms outstretched wide. She passed through a corridor of weird green light, but her mind went blank and she passed out. However this was certainly no dream. She was awake, lying tightly held by some invisible force inside a body-hugging transparent plastic tube. All she could manage was to turn her head ... and to her left she could see Amélie and Svet, equally encapsulated and terrified, their heads also turned staring back. But she couldn't speak, her mouth simply wouldn't open. She turned to the right to see Charlotte faring the same and Nadine at the end equally immobilised, whose eyes were ablaze with a palpable fury and frustration, turning her head furiously from side to side.

Lauren concentrated hard. Her head was still fuzzy but her memory was returning fast. They must be inside that hovering spinning disc ... holy fuck ... the only dominant theme churning through her mind were those bizarre stories surfacing occasionally in the press of crazy people claiming they were abducted into spaceships and fucked by aliens ... then she felt her mind begin to lull dreamily, like the sound at the end of a record as the music slowly diminishes away, a feeling almost like going asleep, but more likely to be how death feels and this was it.

Lauren came to again—now her eyes had opened wide and she was sitting fully alert alongside the others, except they were all totally naked, which itself was an immediate shock. They remained sat silent in a circle on some kind of an unsophisticated and dull crimson-red rubbery couch watching each other, but strangely she felt no ability or even compulsion to move. This was like being subjected to an ultimate and helplessly facile submission, both mentally and physically. Even Nadine looked resigned to her fate whatever that was going to be. There were no sounds and their voices simply didn't function either, but her mind remained undaunted. She began a rapid process of mental stimulation, racing through a checklist of recent memories, mathematical formulae, reactor equations, the villa where she lived, the children, Philippe, everything was still as clear as ever, then her heart sank ... as she thought of Jack.

But now he was there, standing in front of them. How he appeared she couldn't work out, he simply was, wearing what looked like some form of radiation suit but it was formed tightly onto his body like a dark grey skin, reminding her of Annabella's wet suit she went surfing in except it was more subtly shaped. She stared stupidly at his groin. Five luscious and desirable women sat naked, but no sign of that rampant erection earlier. Jesus, how on earth could she be thinking of sex now ... but she still desired him ... ET or not. He smiled and they turned their heads and gazed mournfully, feeling completely worn out. Pointing to a rack of similar radiation suits, he indicated silently that they would have to put one on, but nobody could get up, their muscles had seemingly frozen up, or maybe they were thawing out or something equally bizarre. She tried to speak to Amélie next to her, but nothing emerged. Amélie mouthed back 'no sound means no atmosphere' and looked equally puzzled as did Charlotte, Svet and Nadine because their vocal chords were moving and they appeared to be breathing something. There was science going on here which she didn't understand.

She looked again at Jack and mouthed 'tell me what is happening' but he awkwardly ignored her and instead continued to stare for some reason at Charlotte, who shuffled about quite embarrassed, covering herself as best as she could. But Jack maintained a puzzled expression which irritated Lauren highly. Why she felt jealous, heaven knows in these circumstances, although she understood his expression well enough by then and it was decidedly not lascivious lust drawing his gaze, justifiable though it would be with her daughter. Then she noticed that Charlotte's caesarean scar had mysteriously vanished. Her skin was smooth and homogeneously tanned, exactly as existed before baby Arthur-George. Very strange.

Amélie, who was now mouthing something to Svet and Nadine, was sitting at such an angle she couldn't see Amélie's appendix scar properly, although how Jack knew about Charlotte's section in the first place irritated her again. Sitting naked and struck dumb amongst your friends, daughter and step-daughter was an odd, even bizarre experience. She never realised Amélie had large pink nipples and Svet small brown ones in contrast to her now large light brown ones, although they used to be a dark pink before the children. Nadine of course she always knew had a beautiful oriental body from every perspective you looked at her.

Returning to Jack, they followed his action of busily examining the rack of suits and simultaneously touching a large screen with what looked like a map and various digital controls. He hadn't leered at her but had surreptitiously given her another dazzling smile with that look in his eye again, like when she first met him at the jazz club. Her mind veered again to the ridiculous to match the mood of the situation she was in, contemplating if she wasn't dead already there might at least be some hope of a repeat of their earlier night, before she ended up dead anyway.

After a further analysis of the screen data, he suddenly waved to them to each put on a suit. Their muscles had finally defrosted, whatever that signified, and they were able to stand up silently. Thank God they could move again. Quickly they stepped inside the tight suits which cleverly moulded themselves comfortably together to each individual body, quite sexy in fact, and they aligned their heads inside the small helmets which automatically gripped the suit tightly like a magnetic zip, providing a perfect seal. But what sort of polymer were they made of? Certainly the fabric was not like anything fashionable she had come across, or even amongst the well known radiation suits she was familiar with. Her suit felt beautifully satin smooth and very light in weight, but then Lauren felt much lighter anyway. Wherever they were standing, gravity was definitely reduced. Jack pointed to his watch and drew the figure ten in the air and pointed to the giant couch again. Nadine led the way, they had to sit down and wait—for ten minutes?

Lauren noticed her watch lying on a small rocky, lava-like table and grabbed it. She immediately realised they were inside an equivalent of a very sophisticated decompression suit. She mouthed it to the others who nodded in recognition. Jack smiled warmly, acknowledging her correct hypothesis whilst maintaining his concerned gaze with her this time, a much clearer look of relief fanning across his face. Whatever critical phase they had been going through must have been successful. And whatever Jack understood about love, he still seemed to display it for her big time. That boosted her confidence immeasurably, because wherever they were and whatever was in store, Jack seemed to have reverted to his old and confident self again. Amélie, quick off the mark, observed it too and gave a knowing nod back to Lauren.

Assuming they were still on the spacecraft, Lauren looked at her watch and worked out from the time that had elapsed since they 'defrosted' that around thirty-five minutes had gone by from the moment when they were teleported aboard to when she came to stark naked. Her mind went immediately into calculating gear. She needed to think very laterally, this was her forte, only radical concepts could prevail. Running over and over in her mind, the same question kept bubbling up. What was significant about that time period? Discarding any notion of reality, she began calculating in her head using the speed of light—almost two hundred thousand miles per second—times forty three minutes—times sixty seconds per minute equals an awful lot of miles, but being an astronomy nerd the answer was significant. It equated to roughly the distance of Jupiter from Earth.

She looked up again at the perfectly symmetrical and high domed, spherical ceiling, which was semi-transparent. There was what appeared to be a dark, black liquid above them—oh my God. She could see life forms, like weird fish, swimming around but with bloated, pink radiant bodies, spiky all over, and with light emitting yellow eyes. Was that actually liquid water? With its strange and almost surreal properties, water was one of the most highly incompressible and pervasive liquids, whether on Earth or anywhere else in the universe. The inky blackness and the deep thickness of the wall which she could see through the glass, if it was glass but likely some other unknown material, probably indicated they were at the bottom of some extremely deep ocean, and whatever that roofing material was it had a huge strength to resist the immense pressure. Then she began thinking more laterally.

Why were they here? What did they know? What did they have in common? Apart from being females, they were highly intelligent, forefront in their fields even Svet and Nadine already ... oh shit. Her synthesising brain began to pull the strands of the last few nights, the focus on Svet's research. They were somewhere that simply wasn't possible. Absolutely no way was it possible. They couldn't travel at the speed of light. Einstein wouldn't let them whether they were on Earth or circling around Alpha Centauri. They had mass, the time elapsed would be infinitesimal and their sizes would be zero, plus the energy required would have smashed their puny bodily atoms to pieces before they got near wherever they were.

Fuck ... there was only one way to have achieved the impossible, and that would be via some technology totally unknown and conceivable. They really had been abducted by aliens into a highly advanced environment, perhaps many millions of years ahead ... Given the thirteen billion year age of the universe that was perfectly feasible in theory. Look at the progress of human-kind over the last hundred years let alone the next million. She stared at Jack again, and from his look back he knew, even probably expected that she would be going through a rapid mental in-depth sequencing and analysis of where, how and why. Oh Jack, I wish we could speak again. You have an awful lot of damned explaining to do.

She turned to Amélie, just as gifted mathematically, who now conveyed that characteristic intense stare—she was working her own conclusions and getting it fast. Charlotte was also staring at the ceiling, probably working out the engineering implications of why her breathing was reducing and what sort of material could possibly withstand that pressure and prevent the water bursting inside. Svet looked frightened, but Lauren knew that inevitably she too would be working through some logical hypothesis. She was a brilliant researcher after all and Lauren was confident she would be coming to the same daunting and inconceivable conclusion as her and Amélie. Nadine had already concluded in her inimitable Nadine way. She had exactly the same expression as in Murmansk when she took off Dmitri's head with a Samurai sword. Never frightened, it was obvious to

Lauren that Nadine was already postulating how to escape, her survival and training instincts coming to the fore.

Jack was watching each one carefully. His research and final selection had taken many years, but this time he believed he had chosen well. However one thing had happened which wasn't supposed to ... he had fallen in love. How? It was physically impossible. He still couldn't keep his eyes off her. Lauren turned away from Jack, directly back to Svet and mouthed 'Europa?'

Svet nodded her face glum and tense. She knew there was no other logical explanation; there had been too many leading coincidences. And there was no way, despite Nadine's likely ingenuities, they could ever escape. They were like apes in a zoo, to be studied and gorped at, maybe provide entertainment, but from now on reliant on their masters as the world around them was too advanced to understand.

Lauren sensed and understood Svet's mind process and obvious fear, but was taking the situation a step further. If ever there was a time when she had to remain analytical, sharp and muster together every ounce of intellect, scientific, mathematical, emotional, whatever then now was it. She returned determinedly to her initial hypothesis. Why them? Was it because they excelled in their own scientific fields and had garnered one common interest when they gathered together for a girl's weekend away? ... The fascination to solve Svet's coded impulses? The five of them must have been nearer to working out the truth than they realised ... but 'they' in here, whoever 'they' and Jack are, knew. How? Some sort of telepathy? She, Amélie, Charlotte, Svet and Nadine were all specifically needed here for some purpose. And Jack may be an alien but undoubtedly he was the best fuck by far that she had ever indulged in, male or female ... and stupidly she still felt she loved him, an unaccountable complication. She was sure, catching his gaze, the same feelings for her applied to him as much now as before. She immediately concluded that their shared emotion could be a useful future bargaining tool in some way which she retained, unlike the others.

Jack motioned to them to remove their helmets but keep their skin-tight suits on. Of course he wore no helmet, he must be already acclimatised.

He pointed to the throat in the suit, which was slightly darker, like a gill covering, obviously significant, at least for them. Nadine was the first, helmet off in a trice. Lauren suddenly had a flash of unease. Jack probably didn't know about her special physical capabilities only her intellectual ones ... Nadine had already published two well received and ground breaking papers in artificial intelligence and computer controlled robotics, jointly with Roland. So why wasn't he here? And why all women? She suddenly thought of Eliska, Luis's prodigy daughter, another potential candidate for the Europa day trip, but Jack hadn't met her yet, just as well, which was likely why she wasn't here. So perhaps telepathy wasn't the answer, perhaps he just had highly formidable data collection and analysis skills.

They quickly followed Nadine's lead, helmets off but they were breathing only about once a minute, in short breaths, very puzzling. Jack observed them continuing to acclimatise. He tapped his watch and a round table, very wooden and earth-like, with what appeared to be plastic bottles of water standing on it, arose quietly from the floor surrounded by matching chairs. The lighting, definitely, Lauren thought, was a type of advanced light emitting diode seemingly coated over the entire white walls like paint. The light levels uniformly increased and the whole room became bathed in a very credible and pleasant representation of sunlight. Only the black water and the eerie fishes swimming above outside the protective dome gave the game away that they were not enjoying a sunny morning at home on the veranda.

Suddenly Jack spoke and they could hear him for the very first time. He immediately confirmed they were adjusting to a different atmosphere, which was pure nitrogen at normal Earth atmospheric pressure.

Lauren spoke first. Relieved, she felt the vibrating sensation in her throat and heard her own voice. "Why? Jack? Why are we on a moon of Jupiter? How did we get here? And who the fuck are you?"

He smiled uneasily back to Lauren. She could see he was terribly uncomfortable and conflicted, but that was too bad. The deed was done. They were here and he owed them an explanation at least, and he owed her a lot more besides.

Politely, he asked them to sit around the table and began. "I realise that you will all have a myriad of questions but what I propose is this. I will talk first, and speak in your scientific terminologies and in your language. But, we are not alone here. You will meet others very shortly. But please, this is very important. Take a bottle of water each and drink all of it now please, then I'll start. You must not under any circumstances get dehydrated."

They drank down the water and sat quietly. Lauren was immediately concerned that Nadine might do something with or to Jack, but when she looked across Nadine shook her head a couple of times. Nadine had already sensibly concluded that now was not the time. She needed to assess the situation and learn much more like all of them.

Jack turned initially to Lauren. "I'm so sorry that we couldn't bring you here any other way, but we had to act fast in the final hour. I realised how quickly all of you were nearing the truth of what was happening outside."

"You mean the pulses, the lights and Svet's research, Jack?" Charlotte responded.

"Yes,"

"You knew, but you weren't with us? How come?" Svet chipped in, now decidedly curious.

"Because we were bugged Jack, weren't we," Nadine interrupted. "What did you use? Was it Lauren?"

"Yes?" Jack blushed. Whatever he was he had very human characteristics and flaws.

Lauren suddenly remembered. When they were making love his eyes turned odd. He must have been pulling information from her mind and transmitting it as they both climaxed. The heightened emotions must have increased her brain activity sufficient for him to telepathically read it. His dick was an antenna. She felt instantly cheap and used. Her face dropped and he looked alarmed, turned to her and held her hand.

"No, Lauren. I meant every word then, truly."

Amélie immediately realised that a very intimate betrayal of some kind had unwillingly happened. Jack also had a duty to perform to his superiors. She drew the dialogue to a halt. "Listen everyone. Let's give Jack the chance and space he requires to tell us and summarise what he needs to do. We all must realise that whatever we are experiencing and are part of is, by any stretch of the imagination, absolutely unique, and knowing us there will be a great barrage of way too many questions. Scientifically, we're hugely privileged. No more questions for now. Okay?"

Lauren withdrew her hand.

They all nodded.

Jack looked instantly relieved. "Thank you Amélie. Okay here goes. Yes, amazing, but you have all come to a correct deduction. You are indeed on a colony of Europa, a colony of an advanced civilisation. I am the chief envoy to Earth—sorry I sound like I've just come off the Starship Enterprise."

"That's fine Jack," Lauren interjected with a renewed grin. "As long as there are no Star Wars intended any time soon?"

"No, at least not in the next one thousand years," he replied, "and then we'll all be too old to care."

Somehow injecting a little humour into the situation relieved the tension somewhat, everyone laughed for the first time—instinctively they were rational scientists anyway. They had to make the best of what was going on as they weren't going anywhere fast so what was the use of getting worked up. Jack continued.

"Above you there are around one hundred kilometres of liquid water and an icy thick crust like Antarctica, on top. You guessed all that correctly from the information published through the series of Pioneer, Voyager and other Jupiter flyby missions, which caused huge scientific debates when the analysis sent back provoked ideas of potential life on Europa, but your data was insufficient for more precision. However what you may not know is that more missions from NASA and the European Space Agency to Jupiter and Europa specifically, are planned in 2016 and 2022. Not long to go to investigate the perceived life conundrum further. This is why we decided to act."

"We?" Lauren interjected. "Sorry, I'll shut up and listen."

"I'll get to that in a minute," Jack replied softly. "I know you have a mountain of questions but I'll try and stick to essentials because time is limited. You are presently inside one of a series of bubble colonies, all interconnected, lying on the hard crust mantle. The material covering the room and the roof is a form of transparent plastic, related to graphene, but even stronger to keep the huge pressure from imploding on us. The main colony however is on Io, inside the active crust, an evolved life form but not as you would know it. Although now I have to say, Svet has had the remarkable foresight and prescience to begin researching on this. On Io they gradually adapted and evolved over billions of years, to now be structurally based on sulphur, hydrogen and silicon, not carbon, oxygen and nitrogen. They exist through utilising pure chemical energy, augmented by Jupiter's huge electromagnetic field.

Svet's eyes widened. How close she was already getting to the truth … then she drew breath and muttered 'holy fuck,' as she realised. That was why she was here … to be first tapped of all earthly information and then eliminated. Somehow Jack read some aspect of her thoughts; he looked directly at her and shook his head gently.

"Now I can clarify. You also are all keeping alive through chemical and electromagnetic energy provided directly by your suits into your skin and bodies. You won't need to eat, or create waste, or breathe … oxygen is unnecessary and not around. But you do need to replenish water, lost by evaporation through mouths and heads, and you will sleep as normal to refresh your brain cells. This bubble dome has an artificial gravity, almost like Earth but slightly less, so you will feel lighter. The gravity manipulation uses a process of matter accretion, like the creation of a dwarf star, similar to Lauren's discoveries of energy fusion on a small scale relative to what happens on the sun but the process technology is far, far more advanced. Your internal digestive, lung and waste organs will go into a safe hibernation, in fact as will everything internally connected to energy conversion from food, but eventually the organs atrophy through lack of use and they would die. The process takes about a year before it starts. Me, and others like me, have been genetically remodelled as earth clones, but we can exist dually in both Europa and Earth environments."

"Jack, I've just got to ask one quick question," Lauren suddenly uttered. "What was the name of that woman again, the other one?"

Everyone stared bemused at Lauren. What a strange question now? And why? But Jack knew instantly. This was personal and Lauren was incredibly smart and deductive, never forgetting a micro-comment.

"Ada,"

"So how old are you Jack?"

"I think you already know, Lauren, don't you."

"I would say around two hundred years, give or take ten or twenty and taking account of the foibles of an older man pursuing a younger woman, but sadly for not very long?"

"Correct." Shit, he thought, he'd better get a move on.

Even Amélie looked puzzled, but Nadine had got it instantly, this was her area of expertise. "Lovelace?" she said slowly with a wide and knowing smile.

Jack nodded reluctantly.

Lauren felt a strange wave of silly and inappropriate exhilaration, like a lift to her spirits always her problem at the wrong time, but she was at least in somewhat exalted historic company in Jack's eyes. She knew too his wife and five daughters were a little white lie diversion.

Jack continued. "I know what you all want to ask and I'm coming to that too. But I think it's time for a coffee break. Just relax and think what you want; a cappuccino, a tea, large piece of carrot cake, anything, and your suit will simulate and create the experience in your mind as part of the energy provision process. The action takes a little getting used to but you'll get there. Amélie you won't overeat and put on weight don't worry, the action also is programmed to make you feel full and satisfied so is self-limiting. Have a quick chat. I'm just going to fetch Hermione. She will help with a quick history presentation."

They looked over at a grimacing Amélie, constantly complaining of watching her diet as she was becoming menopausal, and laughed heartily. And there were females. Lauren of course asked instantly, her eyes narrowed.

"Hermione?"

"Hermione is a robot."

Nadine immediately perked up. "A female robot?"

"I thought, Nadine, you would be fascinated, but I'm afraid she is nothing like the robots you have developed so far. Although I must admit, you and your husband have recently made a huge leap forward in your understanding of artificial intelligence. We've had the benefit of a much greater time period to refine that branch of programming and mathematics, admittedly in a different type of language, and match up the engineering."

He pressed his watch again and a door at the end slid across and a tall and very blond woman walked in, hips swaying and wearing a tight crop top and skinny jeans. They gaped incredulous. She looked for the entire world like a Mila cloned twin; even her amber eyes flashed the same determined way.

"Hello everyone, I'm Hermione. Jackson has asked me to assemble and present a short history of where we come from and how we got here. I'll just call in a screen ... I'm afraid it will only be a simple three dimensional hologram."

But the cloning hadn't been perfect. The voice was very English, in fact very old fashioned aristocrat. She sounded to Amélie and Lauren exactly like Rufus's half sister, Cordelia. Hermione pulled a light wand device from her jeans pocket and a quiet and motorised large white screen rolled inside from wherever she came. Amélie couldn't contain her laughter any longer; the irony was just too much. They all understood and joined in, except Jack who appeared perplexed.

"Mmm ... I made Hermione some time ago, remotely, from Cassini, beamed the instructions through on infrared phone. Sorry Lauren, I took a series of photos of you and your ... err ... friend. I thought you would like the concept. Have I got something wrong? Is her name Mila?"

Lauren, choking with laughter on her imaginary cappuccino, caught her breath. Jack, despite his advanced alien brain, was far from perfect. "Making Mila 2 is a wonderful thought, Jack. She looks perfect, we love it, but I'm afraid she's Serbian and certainly doesn't speak 1950's BBC English!"

274

He realised and smiled stupidly. Of course, he had a visual only. Hermione however was undeterred, focussed solely on the task in hand and certainly not diverted by unnecessary gossip, again very unlike Mila. Lauren reflected; her memory on warp-3 recall. Where had Jack got the photos from? This was old Mila, pre the Henri-Gaston catastrophe, even the hair was the same. He had been stalking them for some time ... oh shit ... that hesitation in his voice ...?

Suddenly, Lauren was distracted back to the presentation. The whole screen expanded to fit the full length and width of the room and became a perfect three dimensional landscape of a very green, luscious area. They were immediately sitting alongside a wide running river, small trees stood nearby, but an array of interconnected, silvery dome structures and tall, black buildings were prominent in the distance. A very red and jagged mountain stood behind and the sun was visible but much smaller and paler, way into the distance. They appeared to be standing somewhere at dusk. The quiet trickle of water and some birds in the background could be heard.

"This is like our presentation equivalent of PowerPoint, I've not had time to develop anything more sophisticated," Jack murmured apologetically.

They stared, silent and open-mouthed quite incredulous, wishing their own PowerPoint was a tenth as lively. This was a helmetless virtual reality experience on a massively sophisticated scale. But where was this place Hermione had taken them to?

"Welcome to Mars, but an extraordinarily long time back," Jack announced nonchalantly. "Hermione, would you like to take over the rest of the story please?"

Hermione began. It was like watching Mila's ghost. Lauren was feeling quite disorientated with the likeness, the pose, the eyes, the body. She wished Mila was genuinely here. Shit, she thought, Jack the Stalking Sleuth must have taken a lot of photos but now she suddenly realised when that was. Her brain had synthesised the necessary data from the gaze and manner in which Hermione had looked her all over. But Hermione was good, for a robot brilliant. Her voice was clear and precise, like she knew exactly, despite her peculiar vocal affectations, how the audience of five female and eager super-brain scientists wished to receive and process their slug of information ...

"The ancient civilisation, Arrhya, is two billion years older than the first single cell, amoebic life on Earth and originally manifested on Mars, when the planet had an oxygen, nitrogen and carbon dioxide atmosphere, lots of water and a temperature similar to Earth now. Mars was hospitable then for carbon based life to develop. However Jupiter was gradually changing orbit and at one critical point destroyed a planet the size of Uranus between it and Mars, leading to the formation of the asteroids. Some of the small asteroids had unstable orbits, and despite efforts to alter the trajectory, one eventually hit Mars direct. Arrhyan life was at a comparable stage to Earth presently, but more scientifically and technologically advanced. Life forms had evolved very similar to humans but were taller. The effect on Mars was catastrophic, similar to the wiping out of the dinosaurs on Earth but worse, causing the atmosphere to dissipate into space and water to evaporate. The two Mars moons, Deimos and Phobos were formed out of the impact and eventually were selectively colonised, using the most advanced Arrhyan technology known at that time, to escape the increasingly rapid devastation on the main planet. Earth then was still a giant volcano, a pre-primordial life soup, hot with noxious gases, and uninhabitable for their form of life, despite being a logical escape route."

"There was no future or hope on Phobos and Deimos and all life left on Mars had virtually died out. The surviving colony decided that Io and Europa, which had already been studied as you are doing now, held out the best hope and was reasonably accessible. The Arrhyans had long mastered nuclear fusion, a holy grail to assist potential survival and the remaining moon colonists could manufacture oxygen and hydrogen from the rich carboniferous rock, but were living on shrinking water supplies dangerously transported from the diminishing ice caps on Mars. The moons of course orbit closely. We reasoned that the huge electromagnetic plasma energy from Jupiter, water on Europa, sulphur and volcanic hydrocarbons on Io could be utilised to reform a new civilisation and continue life. And that is what we did, in Earth time around three billion years ago."

"Ultimately, over all those billions of years we evolved. Arrhya on Io would be unrecognisable to you. We look like great blobs of living liquid sulphur, encased underground in atmospheres of hydrogen sulphide, cyanogen and sulphur dioxide, perpetuating indefinitely through pure chemical energy, fed via plasmas from Jupiter, a huge and inexhaustible supply of energy in the Solar system. Jupiter is essentially our sun. There is no need for eating, drinking, or sex, the concept is alien."

Amélie and Lauren burst out laughing. Jack stared incongruously and Hermione looked blank and serious. Obviously she was not programmed for irony and Lauren, now was fully cognisant that Jack displayed some mild alien version of Aspergers Syndrome, probably they all did, which more rationally explained his occasional miscommunication and anti-social behaviour.

"Sorry Hermione, do please continue," Amélie uttered calmly. "Earthlings can be very strange too, every now and then," but giggled again before stifling herself further.

Nadine whispered something in Svet's ear which Charlotte caught and the three watched Hermione carefully. Already, Nadine was analysing weaknesses in the modelling. Hermione was absorbing and trying to reprogramme and compute Amélie's response, and then she smiled. Something had finally locked inside her brain, whatever that was composed of, electronic or biological or maybe a mix.

"All we do on Io is to think using vast communication networks of silicon; we interconnect like a giant computer. Long before that evolutionary stage we had created intelligent robots to do work and make things. This colony was created by robots like me, but far more advanced than anything on Earth, with artificial intelligence greater than humans. You will be wondering how you got here? Already you have worked out that the journey is impossible in the time taken?"

She paused, waiting for some response and after hearing a yes from Lauren, continued. "Inside the light tubes, using an advanced matter dissection technique, everyone was deconstructed into photons and then reconstructed back on arrival, to allow travel at the speed of light. Effectively you became light beams, wrapped in a guided infrared casing which prevents dissipation into space. A computerised and safe technology, now well over a million years old. We have travelled all around the Milky Way, from star to star, to re-colonise but nothing has yet been found for Arrhyans like the Jupiter-Io, planet moon system. But we on Europa are a different prospect. We genetically engineered ourselves to monitor Earth and look like you, and we fear that you are now evolving at a pace that would become a threat in the near future. In the last ten years, think of your progress and what you know, especially the composition and structure of the key Jovian moons allied with the suspicion that there may be life-forms here. In a hundred years time you will be here trying to colonise. Europa Arrhyans age slowly, as you have now deduced. I cannot share with you how many of us are on your planet but it is tiny in number."

Hermione suddenly pulled out what looked like a pistol from her bag and began to peruse it carefully, holding a silencer in her other hand. Lauren gazed in alarm at Hermione's puzzlement and her brain lurched into gear once more. Something about Mila's habit of occasionally shooting up boardroom meetings for excitement, probably after harmless conversations between Jack and Juliette who were now close Cassini Director colleagues and friends, had obviously been transmitted during her construction but got lost in translation.

Lauren called out as calmly as possible. "Hermione, can I suggest you give me that device for the moment please. Amélie and Nadine will show you later how to use it if you like."

Hermione's amber eyes narrowed and flashed clear irritation, so that at least Lauren realised she had assumed right. But then Hermione looked down at Jack who nodded for her to comply. She reluctantly handed the gun and silencer to Lauren, as Amélie leaned over to peer at the make.

"A Beretta, Lauren, a perfect copy, probably some kind of highly advanced 3-D printing," she whispered. "Except— look at the safety catch. It's been welded shut!"

Jack immediately caught the drift and sighed. "I need to work on importing characteristics. I thought this would amuse you Lauren."

She smiled back. "Not, darling, if it went off inadvertently and Hermione shot a hole through the roof."

He grinned, chastened again.

Amélie glanced momentarily at Lauren who ignored her and remained implacable. What was the 'darling' bit about? Did Lauren still mean it? Shit. Or was it a Vaag type ploy to keep Jack onside, because it was becoming abundantly clear to her own sharp and observational insight that he wasn't supposed to fall in love with Lauren.

Nadine meanwhile continued to take in the strengths and weaknesses of the unfolding and incredible Arrhyan saga being openly laid out for them. But one key question still remained. She glanced at Hermione, who reciprocated with more than a smile; a decidedly flirtatious Mila leer. That was enough of a hint, one reason they may be here.

Jack suddenly halted Hermione's presentation and asked her to leave. As she strode out through the sliding door, he gathered them together into a tight circle. "I need to leave you for a while and confer with my colleagues. It is time for dinner. Think what you want and it will feature again in your mind. Lauren, can you come with me for a minute?"

Charlotte stepped forward, sensing that she needed to also play a sweetly reasonable line. "Jack, that presentation was hugely illuminating, thank you, but there is one key question that Hermione didn't cover. Why are ...?"

He became decidedly uncomfortable. "I can't answer that right now, I'm sorry but I can't," he replied brusquely in a monotone.

Amélie interrupted fiercely, as always demanding and never accepting. "You mean now or never?"

But he ignored her and took Lauren's hand. She stood up quietly. Whatever he wanted she had to make the most of it. The sliding door opened again and he led Lauren through it. It closed immediately. She was now separated from the others, but this room, like where they were, was very minimalistic. No furniture, the walls pure white and lit up, not even a table merely another wide rubber couch. She also realised her sense of smell wasn't functioning either.

They sat down and immediately he held her tightly and then kissed her gently. She was caught in an immense dilemma. She wanted to respond, his feelings for her clearly hadn't diminished that was obvious, and neither had her emotional desire for him. But she had key questions. Her inner scientist was overwhelming and she must ask them now she had the chance whilst they were alone. Suddenly, she smelt his aftershave, like when they were in Nadine's club. She closed her eyes and continued kissing him passionately, that was easy. She still wanted him as badly as ever. But around the room everything had suddenly changed. She opened her eyes again and the hard rubbery couch had become her huge, old and comfortable four poster bed in her Chelsea apartment in London and they were lying underneath soft and exquisite silk sheets and their heads resting on fluffy white pillows. Jack was kissing her neck and fondling her ... shit she was totally naked and so was he, his hard and hot erection pressed against her.

"Fuck, Jack, where the hell are we?"

"Inside our minds. This is a Europa version of true virtual reality, where your thoughts, desires and dreams are created on demand. I'm locked into and following your thoughts, because this is what you want and this place must have a special meaning because you have recreated it with me."

She realised in an instant. She had subconsciously homed in on some of the best times of her life in bed, the best sex and the closest communication with a lover she had formerly indulged with. Her former husband was now Jack. But as he kissed and fondled her, that wild intensity they shared in Nadine's Sargasso Club returned with an earthly jolt. She was incapable of resisting the pull, or him, as once again they repeated a long bout of wild and passionate lovemaking, both screaming and shouting again for all they could.

Coming eventually down, she snuggled into him, copious sweat pouring off both of them. "I can't really say the Earth moved for me anymore Jack, but that was just as amazing as before. You definitely made Europa move!" she purred, twizzling his curly chest hair.

He laughed ... her humour was always something that had attracted him, something he needed to understand and learn better.

She continued. Now was the moment. If ever he was vulnerable this was it. "So why am I here Jack? Are you going to finally tell me? You know I'm well practised in keeping secrets. Also, for how long are we being kept prisoners? We are going to be missed by our families and partners and especially our children."

"I know, I really understand all that Lauren, but I'm not allowed to tell you. On Io the Arrhyans have forbidden the knowledge."

She raised herself up, wrapping a sheet around her naked body.

"You mean you can't tell me a simple answer to a question? Just like you're not supposed to fall in love with me either are you. But you have, and love is like that Jack, there's no going back. We have to confide and share with each other. I'm afraid you're adapting. Are you worried you've gone over to the other side?"

"Yes to all of those things. Fuck it Lauren, I'm the most senior on this Europa colony, so I'm taking the decision."

"You mean you're like the King of Europa?" she said feigning wide-eyed innocence, to make him laugh again. Humour was obviously the key to modifying his pre-programmed genetic behaviour set.

He laughed again, a big genuine roar and reached for her to hold close in his arms again. "So," he began. "Why are you here? Because this colony wants to move to Earth and intermix before you find out who we are ... a little akin to the gradual interbreeding between the Neanderthals and the early Humanoids. On Earth, for the tiny number like me who spend time there, we artificially eat, drink, breathe like you, but only recently have we evolved one truly pleasurable function ... and I'm now deemed the expert." He smiled and fingered through her hair. "Only you know what that is."

She pondered, synthesising more generally what he had said. "You mean, the lack of what I think are normal pleasures, like being surrounded by nice furniture, clothes, cars, a big house, your children, pets, holidays, you don't actually have those things in reality, because you don't need them physically ... you experience your life in your mind only and conjure up what you need. Like now, lying in bed?"

"Yes, certainly here on Europa. But on Earth, me and the few like me have begun to experience a cross-over. Whether it's because I spend most of my time there or whether there is a subtle mutation happening ... at the moment we don't know. My feeling for you, this love attribute is new and genuine. I've studied it for too long not to be certain. That part of Earth ... combined with Europan sex ... is dynamite.

"I agree with the dynamite ... but love? ... except for Ada of course," she retorted sharply.

"No, no Lauren, no. Ada was far too early. Our attraction was incredible but pure intellect, nothing physical. She stood out as a unique harbinger of what was to come in the next hundred years. She genuinely understood the fundamentals of modern computing but was surrounded by disbelievers and sadly succumbed to and was torn by the rigid cultural and societal norms of the time and tragically a lack of medical knowledge, dying far too young."

"Jesus Chris Jack, this is so ... out of this world!"

They both laughed again. "You betcha. Now where have I got that from?"

"Svet and Nadine ... it's a family joke."

"Even jokes are beginning to compute; slowly ... you've had an amazing effect on me Lauren?"

"I wish they all said that ... so, spill the beans, the grand master plan, Jack? Us and Earth. You've got this far, out with it." She snuggled her head onto his chest, her hand around his renewed erection, amazing what her mind could achieve. He can now forget Ada forever.

"The plan is pretty simple. As you so clearly can perceive, we're not evolved sufficiently. Since my last recent report, my team wants to know more and quickly, and experience and test their reactions out here. And time is running out. In return we want to start to share some key technological knowledge—particularly in nuclear fusion, plasma energy generation, robotic computing intelligence and alternative life forms. The five of you are highly adept and at the forefront of knowledge in those fields. You will then be in a position to seed the next stages of rapid development and prepare for our coming. Exciting isn't it?"

Exciting wasn't exactly how she was reacting inside. She needed to get back to the others, although she suspected that between them, they had already worked out a good part of this plan. But something else needled her. "You keep saying time is running out. But it's not solely because of the threat of Earth finding out about the existence of Arrhyans on Io and Europa. This is a small colony of revolutionaries, Jack, isn't it? You want to experience the real thing, the pure delight of physical pleasures. You're all sick of living in your brains and you want to combine what we have and what you have and become super-humans. But not everyone agrees?"

"Shit Lauren, why are you always two steps ahead of where I think you should be. Yes, it's time for our band here to head off onto the road, as you would say. I'm sorry but your mind is drifting and the normal, soulless environment of our landing base will return—it's time to return to the others. You all need to sleep and recharge. Close your eyes and think of Amélie. This mind selection needs some getting used to but you will master it fully eventually."

"Before that, I need to know."

"I really do love you Lauren. You're the most important thing in my life now."

"I believe you Jack. But are you a robot or a manifestation in my brain of a sickly yellow, sulphurous blob?"

"Neither ... Europan Arrhyans are a genetically refined direct descendent, a specific evolution of the original settlers from Phobos and Deimos all those billions of years ago. We looked like you and still do, but we lost too much over time through technological DNA interference. Robots like Hermione are the link, the worker drones, operating between Europa and Io. We have always up to now been able by continuing to genetically reprogramme ourselves, to stay ahead of the artificial intelligence of our own robots. That's why they've never taken over."

She contemplated for a few seconds, then closed her eyes, thought of each of her companions and opened them again. She and Jack were back, sitting apart on that dull, red rubbery couch.

"Let's go."

She got up as he took her hand, the door slid open and they strode in to the identical bare room where Amélie, Svet, Charlotte and Nadine were absorbed in intense discussion, huddled around their own rubbery red couch ... shit Jack and his team badly needed a good injection of earthly design and creativity.

He called out. "I'm going to leave you all to relax. Can I suggest you sleep in the next hour or so? Lauren will tell you how. Then in the morning I shall join you for breakfast and we'll begin experiments in the laboratory."

Amélie's face, on seeing Lauren and her radiating blooming complexion, was a picture. She mouthed 'experiments?' to Lauren who sat down quietly, everyone now staring at her, trying hard to summarise some semblance of all she had discerned. Jack was gone in an instant, they never noticed how or where.

"Before you start Amélie, yes it was worth every minute and not just because of the information that I need to tell you."

They laughed out loud, even Nadine realised and joined in the humorous aspect, as Lauren continued.

"Now, I want to try something. I reckon it's time we went out for a celebratory drink. Can you close your eyes and concentrate hard on Nadine's beautiful Atlantis bar-restaurant then open them in about ten seconds ..."

The old jukebox was playing Buddy Holly's Peggy Sue in the background, the lights were romantically subdued and a warm buzz of voices in the background sounded above a clinking of glasses and cutlery. They were sat around a lovely table, near the large Georgian window and gazing out at a beautiful Japanese water garden outside. The clock on the wall showed six-thirty.

"Holy fuck, how did you do that? We're back home. Bloody hell, but where's Nadine?"

"Right behind you Amélie."

They turned to see a smiling Nadine holding a tray of five wine glasses and a bottle of her best, cold Californian Sauvignon.

Svet opened the packets of nuts and nibbles and put them into the two plates. "Except we're not home are we Lauren. I'm sure I never bought this summer dress, but I like it."

"Me neither but I like mine too," Charlotte said, "All the people serving behind the bar are women."

"That's because you would like that to be the case. I wanted us to wear nice cotton dresses for a change. Nadine you look lovely."

"Yeah, I've kinda never got into this wear but I must admit it does really suit me. Roland loves the black jeans look normally; I think he'd be surprised. So, where are we? I know it's not quite my bar, but close."

"Sadly we're still on Europa but in a virtual reality we've just created in our heads. Just one example of the Europa advanced technology which Jack shared with me in bed. Now you can understand why all the rooms are so bare and dull. You create what you want, when you want it in your mind, although I assume there must be some sort of control, otherwise you would become equivalent to drug addicts, feasting on brain pleasure."

"Wow, this is amazing. So has Jack got any nice friends, Lauren?" Amélie chirped, "Whatever you're getting I think I fancy some too, it's taking years off you, you look terrific."

"I'll get to that. Grab some peanuts and listen … I understand now why we are here."

"And how we get out?" Nadine queried, pouring a generous slug of wine into each glass …

They listened, fascinated, to all Lauren had managed to wheedle out of Jack and as expected a babble of questions and discussion ensued. Not ending up on giant fucking machines was unanimously agreed, although Amélie could be definitely swayed towards alternative methodologies if there were more aliens around like Jack. Svet was horrified. But they all agreed they faced a massive dilemma. They wanted to acquire the Europan technology and scientific knowledge but they also needed to escape. But how? And how long had they got as they would eventually be missed at home?

"But, don't forget," Charlotte reminded them. "We are all supposed to be on a girls-only retreat and away from the families for some peace and quiet ... nobody was expecting to be contacted unless there was a problem. Certainly Giles wasn't. He was looking forward to working the vineyard from dawn till dusk and catching up."

"Yeh, same with the Earl of Rufus, he's too busy down at the House of Lords to even notice. And Lauren, we have our backs covered too with the kids with nannies."

"And that includes Arthur of course," Lauren added," because he's with the triplets and Marie. What about Roland and Sergei?"

"Sergei was flying to London for ten days after that Chamber event to meet with Edward Jones ... Did you know they've jointly set up a London research centre for stem cell development work on Alzheimer's and birth defects? I said we'd be busy. He was cool, like speak to you when I get back."

"Gosh, Svet I had no idea," Lauren replied. "The beginning and the end of a life cycle type research, that's terrific. Medicine? An area of science Jack and I didn't discuss."

"Because they don't need it," Svet added. "They've moved on from primitive health care millions of years ago and probably just gene reprogramme themselves out of disease, maybe even death. Mind you, Jack may be aging slowly but he does age, even a star burns up into a brown dwarf and then a black hole eventually. They haven't cracked eternal life yet."

"Mmm ... true," Charlotte began. "So we have at least a week then before being missed."

Lauren pointed out that travelling on a light beam as it were, then they were creating a time dilation effect. Everyone will have aged slightly but not them when they return, only noticeable if they had gone off to Sirius or somewhere more exotic.

Nadine suddenly interrupted. "Roland may be a problem, he's expecting me back. I wonder how interactive this VR is because I've got my phone in my pocket."

The others rooted around in their bags and found their phones too, although Amélie's had changed from an iPhone to a Blackberry, same now as Lauren. She glared mischievously over as Lauren looked innocently back.

Nadine continued. "Look, I've got a signal. I'm going to text Roland and tell him we've all gone on a whim to my friend Hillary Deates's mountain retreat for some scientific reflection and girl talk. Back whenever, don't worry. He's so absorbed in his robotic control work at Harvard, he even has a bed there, he won't be bothered. He becomes totally shut off from normality in those periods. Okay—send—wow it's gone. Shit, he's just replied. Cool — have a great day, Rasputin is mowing the lawn."

"Who's Rasputin?"

"His new toy," Nadine replied. "Roland is programming in a new language which facilitates self decision. Good, that's him covered. Now all I need to do is find out how those glass tubes are programmed to assemble and disassemble us. I think I understand the Arrhyan social hierarchy however and ..."

"Sorry to interrupt," Charlotte said. "But do you guys think we're being monitored inside this virtual reality?"

"Who knows? Not much we can do anyway," Amélie replied. "So let's continue the blue-sky erudition. Somehow I doubt it. Jack is a bit of an old-fashioned English gentleman, Lauren. He's retained some odd sense of 19th century decorum and formalities, probably after shagging all those aristocratic society women ... fuck; I'm really sorry, totally thoughtless again as usual."

"Don't worry, I think you're right. And I don't care about his past because I know a little more about Jack ... I'm not telling you everything ..."

"Spoilsport," Charlotte jested. "Go on Nadine, you look like you've come to some profound conclusions."

"Svet and I talked it through earlier. Certainly there's only one way back, disassemble into photons and reassemble and so far we definitely need Jack for that so Lauren does need to keep him on board by all means fair or foul."

"I don't think there's much evidence of foul, is there darling?" Amélie quipped to roars of laughter as they swigged their wine down and ordered another bottle.

Nadine continued. "Arrhyans may have evolved to become sentient beings, but over the millions or billions of years, that evolution has created two distinct life forms—Europa and Io variants. Through choice or environment, Jack and his fraternity are like us on steroids. We recognise them, they look like us and maybe he's right. A future intermix where we go up ten notches in scientific and technological capabilities may be the only way our Earth future is secured ... We all know the hazards coming in the next few hundred years, global warming, energy crises, even water wars and potential nuclear oblivion when some terrorist group presses a red button. The other guys, sitting in sulphur swamps thinking great thoughts inside a blazing hot volcano really are alien. We have no idea or desire to be like that. And obviously neither does Jack. In-between we have the robots.

Svet continued. "Mmm ...the robots, assuming there exist many more like Hermione, are obviously autonomous and scarily intelligent, at face value subservient and under control, a bit like enlightened slaves in ancient times. They look like us but they're not, and nor are they Arrhyans. But they act as some sort of vital communications bridge of understanding between Io and Europa, keeping peace and harmony. The three-way intermix is obviously complex."

Lauren interjected. "Okay listen up. Nadine and Svet, I agree, brilliant conclusions. Because I too sensed that Jack is in more of a hurry than he's wanted to let on. Something is going on. Maybe on Io they are unhappy, possibly jealous if they have feelings that way, with Jack and his team making giant strides with project Earth. He did say the sulphur brigade have had them searching the Milky Way for another planet for millions of years and found nothing suitable yet. The Io folk can only exert their authority through robots."

"Or maybe," Svet began slowly, "the robots are improving their own artificial intelligence faster that the Europans can genetically reengineer themselves. Perhaps Jack and his colony colleagues are experiencing a sort of Moore's Law slowdown and are predicting a critical juncture is imminent. Their own singularity. But with potentially devastating and destructive results because of the overall distribution of far greater technology and intelligence everywhere. The robots would be no threat to Arrhyans on Io; who wants to become a hot molten sulphur blob? But they could be a real threat to Jack and friends on Europa."

Nadine came back into the lead. "Okay, I think we have a plan. This is what I suggest we do. Tomorrow we meet the others, and we need to do what we need to do to glean more information. The more we contribute the more they share. The robots may be useful to us in the end; they also probably know how to programme those ionisation tubes. I'll concentrate on any robots that turn up, this is my forte."

Svet's face fell. "I'm not doing that. I love Sergei."

Lauren turned to her and held her hand. "Nor do you have to Svet. Jack has promised to share scientific and technology knowhow. You and I can do that, and we need your expertise."

Svet smiled. "Thanks."

Lauren turned to Charlotte. "How do you feel Charlotte?"

Charlotte looked up, her mind had returned to first Murmansk and then DG's yacht. She was prepared to do anything then, this situation was no different. "No dilemmas, I have a completely open mind. I agree Nadine's plan is a good strategy. I'm feeling quite tired. I think probably we do all need to genuinely sleep. We need to return to base. What do we do Lauren?"

"We close our eyes and concentrate on each other back at base, but if we also concentrate on where we would like to individually sleep, in a nice clean bed, then in theory we should arrive there. I can't see any other way. There's literally nothing in the base room except that uncomfortable rubbery couch. Programme your thoughts to wake up at seven am. Over and out Professor Amélie Spock"

They laughed and drank up the last dregs of wine, Lauren nibbled down some nuts then they closed their eyes and thought hard ...

... Lauren felt very happy, snuggled against the quietly sleeping naked body of Jack, back in their four poster bed. He murmured and groaned as she put her arms around him, feeling his warm skin, and then went immediately to sleep.

Chapter Fifteen

Jack, confident and impressed that they could already manage the essentials of the advanced virtual reality world, was reformulating his tactics. He had indeed monitored them during their evening drink at Nadine's bar, but refrained from joining their celebration. As expected, their analysis and synthesis of their situation was excellent. He needed his collective captives to feel free to discuss, criticise, feel fearful, dislike him and what he had done, indeed everything, because the building up of total trust between him, his team and them was critical. But for now that information would remain only with him as leader. Time was indeed running out but nowhere near as quickly as Nadine had insisted, although he had to admit, her strategic and tactical skills of environment, conflict and warfare surprised him. He knew she was a highly innovative computer software designer, analyst and robotics expert, which was why she was brought to Europa. But this protective and aggressive survival aspect of Nadine's skill set had eluded him and would urgently need investigation. Moreover, somehow she was creating a barrier to his penetrating her thoughts as easily as the others, although except for Lauren, that too was becoming fuzzier. Perhaps independence of thought was an unknown side-effect of transportation from Earth. Lauren, through their established emotional bond, still remained strong and robust for indirect intercommunication. This group of women, his personal selection to transport in, were the first ever so everyone had to crucially monitor and learn. It was time to reveal the centrality of virtual life for everything done and existing on Europa.

Lauren had revived from a deep sleep and looked around. The sensation wasn't like normal waking up, more an instant coming into and out of a dream midway through, but with a pleasant sensation emanating throughout her body. Amélie and Charlotte were sitting primly next to her.

They were all dressed in smart and classy skirted business suits, with matching blouses and five inch heeled shoes but no tights. Amélie looked gorgeous in aquamarine blue, Charlotte adorable in pale crème and Lauren stunning in crimson red. Looking around, the environment was almost a replica of the Cassini restaurant area, except the colour scheme was different and the entrance and exit the other way around. It was definitely breakfast time, as a faint smell of hot cooked bacon wafted into their nostrils. Some security staff and changing shift workers were around but none had faces she could recognise.

"Christ Lauren, we're back in your canteen," Amélie uttered, gazing around in amazement. "Jack has obviously created this setting for us based on his memories, some of which are not quite right. You never cooked bacon, eggs and sausage did you?"

"No, he's English remember!" Lauren replied smirking.

"We can also see what Jack's favourite attire is. He must get excited seeing us all in formal business wear, but I like his taste," Charlotte said with a giggle. "He's managed to match things extraordinarily well. He's an observant man isn't he Lauren? I'm sure this is Versace."

"It is," Amélie replied, "in fact we're all wearing Versace but I must confess, for a bloke you really can't knock the effort. And our shoes are Lauren's trademark Manolo Blahnics; I do adore these spiky heels. Here comes Jack with Svet."

Charlotte turned and got up to greet Jack and Svet walking towards them from the far food counter. Svet was dressed in a lovely fitted Prada trouser suit, similar to what Eva wore in the office. Eva had clearly been his inspiration for that style. Jack was smartly dressed as ever, but in a dark brown Armani business suit and open necked blue shirt.

"Shit Amélie, I've got no underwear on," Lauren suddenly hissed, uncrossing her legs and pulling her short skirt further down.

"Looks like Jack's got a fascinating day planned for you. Have any time for serious scientific discourse will we?" Amélie replied, grinning. "I must say for someone not quite of this world he has rather familiar earthly male fantasies. Override him Lauren, concentrate hard and pick a compromise. Agent Provocateur will work best."

"Good God, it's happened, like Nadine's text," Lauren replied, wriggling into a more comfortable position. They looked up at Jack who had handed Charlotte a tray of coffees, whilst he and Svet returned to pick up their breakfast, freshly cooked. He turned back surreptitiously and smirked slyly at Lauren.

"He's testing you out, the little bastard," Amélie muttered quietly. "Give him no quarter, he should have to work harder for his favours—you can out-concentrate the best of them."

"I think we're okay for now," Lauren replied with a nudge under the table. "But where's Nadine?"

"Good morning, hope you both slept well," Jack began cheerily as the food and drink trays were carefully laid out, with lots of choice for everyone.

"Where's Nadine, Jack?" Lauren said quietly.

He didn't react for a moment. A distinct look of discomfort had radiated fleetingly across his expression. They immediately heard a familiar clicking and clacking of heels from behind, and all turned to see Nadine, dressed in her trademark all black smart wear but clad in chic skinny silk trousers and a matching embroidered jacket, cheerfully strolling down from the entrance. From where or how was anybody's guess. Jack certainly was not quite his happy earlier self, but Lauren watched as he took a deep breath and walked up to Nadine and gave her a brief, friendly hug.

She sat down next to Lauren. "Sorry I'm late everyone, I didn't wake up on time ... didn't quite programme my alarm correctly."

Lauren thought otherwise, but what had Nadine been up to?

Amélie immediately turned to Jack and gently touched his hand, which he oddly withdrew immediately like she had the plague. More food for thought. "Before we tuck into this wonderful breakfast, courtesy of Cassini ..." she began ...

"Gosh I really hadn't realised where we were until Charlotte told me," Svet suddenly interjected, "Sorry Amélie."

Lauren smiled at her ... For the first time Svet was looking her old self. This bizarre experience had been harder on her than anyone else, especially as she was clearly missing Sergei dreadfully.

"So I was wondering, Jack," Amélie continued. "Your virtual reality infrastructure here is quite amazing. I can genuinely appreciate that this technology is millions of years in advance and it shows, but ... well ... what is real and what is imaginary? How do we know whether we're in a dream or not, like right now?"

"You don't. Because there is no distinction any more on Europa. We have evolved our technology to create what we want or need through our minds, which reduces or eliminates unnecessary infrastructure, overcrowding and energy use. Massive memory databanks, accessible by all Europans but not robots, and going back millions of years, provide an infinitesimal repository of scenarios at all kinds of stages and developments. Remember, our colony is on a moon, smaller than Earth, and whilst it has water, the rest of the moon is not exactly a hospitable environment to explore, mine, or manufacture stuff on. So we have learned, over many millions of years, to imagine what is required and effectively 3-D print the need into reality. So you're not experiencing virtual reality as on Earth. This is the real thing; this is our reality, our Europa world. That is why your landing area is so sparse, same as inside the rest of the interconnected spheres. The base is the staging point, a no-man's land or the dead-zone chamber between coming from the exterior solar system and entering our civilisation. And you are the first non-robots, I suppose aliens in our terms, to cross over that threshold from beyond Jupiter. But I understand the whole thing will be a strange concept for you to grasp."

"No Jack, we're actually cool with this concept already," Nadine unexpectedly said, in the middle of everyone hungrily wolfing their array of yoghurts, fruit, croissants and even bacon, sausage and egg for Charlotte and himself. "The advantages are obvious."

He looked at Nadine, with a fleeting glance then made a polite smile. Of course he knew that fact very well. He had underestimated their adaptabilities and capabilities so far, especially her. But an interesting test was about to happen.

"I'm glad to see everyone enjoying the Cassini food, I have breakfast every day here, I love it," Jack continued.

"Now I know why you're always in so early," Lauren murmured, giving him a knowing smile, to distract him from Nadine who was clearly giving discomfort. Jack reciprocated. He loved her, he was never supposed to. Arrhyan love hadn't existed for three billion years and it wasn't possible but he did, and that factor was now a critical reason for hurrying the project along. He would have preferred instead to have had only Lauren here to himself and on her own for many years first, but that was not to be.

A clattering noise rang through the cafeteria as a trolley was knocked over when a side-door, which Lauren was unfamiliar with, opened wide and a group of four confident looking people strode out, three men and two women attired in smart business dress like themselves.

Jack leaned across the table. "I'm now going to introduce you to my senior management team."

They all stared, doing a fast and inevitable weighing up of Jack's associates, the first Europans they had encountered. From the entrance another small group appeared, led by Hermione. They were mainly women like her but a few men as well. They turned and stared hard at this second group, the only difference being their dress; they were all clad in casual wear, admittedly very smart, expensive jeans and polo-neck tee-shirts.

"And ... my team of robot technicians."

Lauren began a swift analysis. Apart from the dress code, obviously crudely differentiated by Jack, she could now see why. Any difference in outward appearance between robots and Europans was negligible, certainly to the human eye, but of course yesterday Hermione's appearance as a Mila look-alike had already clearly planted that concept.

"Jack, darling?" she whispered. "How will we know who is a robot and who isn't?"

"Simple," he replied, elated with his top team ensemble so far. "And of course a key question. Robots do all the physical work. We Europans think and instruct but in a subtle spirit of genuinely cooperative team work, not master-slave stuff like on Earth. They also only appear in our realities where and when we want them to for specific tasks. They can't call themselves up independently and they have limited access to the master knowledgepedia. But they do all have a full range of the same potential emotions and feelings as we do and you do and are self-aware. They're not cold, hard slabs of clever polymers, so will be included."

Lauren glanced fleetingly to Amélie and Charlotte who were pondering the same question as her. Included in what? Nadine was once again deadpan as both groups approached. Lauren sensed a smidgen of apprehension sweep across Svet's face once more, but she was determined to keep her promise the previous night to avert any suggestion of anything compromising and unsavoury.

They were all immediately introduced with no fuss, exactly as if everyone was attending a key business meeting to negotiate deals or solve problems. There was a genuine warmth and radiance of friendliness emanating from all of Jack's companions, real and robotic. He had briefed, programmed or taught them well about likely expectations and probable comfort levels of meeting up, as the first fact Jack made clear was apart from him, nobody in this group had been to Earth.

However, as before, not all of Jack's planning and preparation made the sort of sense he assumed it should. Especially their names. The two women were introduced as Persephone and Juno and the three men chattily shook hands with each of them in turn—being Apollo, Hercules and Romulus.

It was all Lauren and Amélie could do to contain themselves and remain serious. Charlotte and Svet looked puzzled, trying to work out why, but Nadine was distracted as she was the first to be introduced immediately to the six robots by Hermione, and their names were Jimmy, Charlie, Pete, Ellie, Sue and Barbarella.

Lauren really did wonder how on earth Jack could have chosen such odd Roman and Greek mythology names for the Europans. They all understood the significance of plain and simple names for the robots, another clearly forced differentiator, like the dress code, for their benefit. But when she forced her brain to match her knowledge of mythologies to the characteristic appearances of Jack's management team, she could see a sort of relational link. He really had tried to characterise his colleagues in some understandable way, perhaps as a crude proxy for marketing their attributes. She glanced at Amélie, predictably chatting up Apollo already, patently having immediately decided that his intellectual skills and physical attributes were worth exploring further if necessity forced deed.

After about ten minutes of general and pleasant ice-breaker chat, it became clear to Lauren that Jack's team had expertise areas not dissimilar to their own, aided by relevant robots. Apollo was a fusion expert, but so was Jack so she needn't worry on that score if Amélie was wading in fast. Interestingly, some anonymous restaurant assistants brought over a few more cloth covered round tables, certainly none like she had in the real Cassini, and Jack encouraged them to informally split up and mix and chat science and technology. He didn't suggest who should mix with whom, it just happened almost naturally. Perhaps, Lauren thought, his associates had his mind perceiving abilities too or they had been secretly briefed somehow. The buzz of discussions and relationship building was becoming quite frenetic and engaged.

Jack suddenly clapped everyone to attention. "I think we are making an excellent start already to interplanetary scientific understanding. Now ... err ... we are looking for volunteers for our first key experiment. The purpose of which is to improve our Arrhyan underdeveloped senses of ... err ... culture and tactility, which as Lauren and colleagues know has been engineered out long ago. If our civilisations are to integrate fully in the future, we need ... more physical empathy, which Lauren and I have discussed extensively and ..."

She blinked and stared at Jack, clearly out of his comfort zone and talking gibberish even for him. "I think he means choose your dance partners ladies," she quipped.

Charlotte giggled loudly and Amélie put her hand over Apollo's large mitt. The Europans and robots looked blank, despite their inherent super-mega brains. A deficiency of subtle relational communications on this moon was a key problem, also engineered out millions of years past in the interests of pure practical thinking efficiency. Jack, clearly experiencing the emotion of deep embarrassment so something had been working between Lauren and him, concentrated hard and transferred the rest of the instructions into her mind, but she decided to amend a few parts seeing Amélie almost licking her lips.

She continued on his behalf. It was time for some objective scientific leadership. "You all have an hour to go into a specially equipped and furnished pod, where you take off your clothes and have sex. Invisible infrared monitors will measure an array of reactions and then you'll have time to jointly reflect and write up notes on how you feel on available iPads. *Really? She thought. But Jack mentally confirmed that was a technology bridge he had dreamt up.* This will be repeated over the next four days and provide a body of scientific results to then be fed into the Europan knowledgepedia database. In between, we will work together in the Europan laboratories and workshops on selected technology and science experiments to augment our joint knowledge bases."

Amélie suddenly mouthed to Lauren. 'A high-tech Johnson and Masters experiment? What an opportunity!'

Lauren had to look away and maintain a serious composure. The Europans and robots were smiling, at long last the tasks had computed. Her legendary communication skills even worked orbiting Jupiter, thank goodness.

Amélie was adamant, she would volunteer with both Apollo and Hercules together—Lauren grinned, it must have been the notion of four days worth. Amélie's prodigious sexual appetite had certainly not waned with either age or apparently location. She was going to definitely maximise the opportunity to find out what Lauren had got all excited about with Jack, and lie back and think of Earth, as well as use her well-honed pillow talk skills to tease out their secret plans.

To everyone's surprise, Charlotte volunteered with the gorgeous and statuesque Juno and Persephone ... she had decided this was a chance to experience and understand her mother's bisexuality full-on and what she too may have been missing, but most importantly they were engineers like her, so strengths and weaknesses of the unknown infrastructure they were contained within could be ascertained, including what the robots could or couldn't do and how things were made. All would be useful knowledge.

Nadine immediately fancied the grey haired robot called Jimmy ... much older than the other males but with an air of culture and sophistication, her weakness of course, as ever. All in the name of acquiring more key escape and confrontation knowledge.

Svet had by then walked up to Jack alongside the small and skinny Romulus with the intense stare. "We would like to join you and Lauren to start the technology and science sharing and set the parameters for everyone in the labs and workshops. Romulus is an expert on carbon life forms and viruses and is keen to work with me."

Jack looked at Lauren and nodded. "That would be perfect Svet, yes please. I'm glad you've chosen Romulus, he has an incredible bank of acquired knowledge of turning research into practice," he replied immediately.

Lauren breathed easily. Jack either had worked out or knew, but no argument over Svet was going to be necessary. Everyone was a winner ... so far.

At the end of day one, the two groups virtually assembled themselves in their own environments to discuss findings and results, in true serious scientific style. Lauren discovered they could all write papers onto their iPads though sheer thought; no screen tapping necessary ... the increase in speed was mindboggling. Svet and Romulus had instantly become friends and were intensively collaborating on a whole array of radical ideas. He was Sergei all over bar the size difference and without the hindrance of any sexual attraction either way, so finally Svet could let go and immerse herself in the most intense of academic pleasures. When Romulus volunteered to show Svet his personal laboratory for a few hours, so she could get an idea of what forefront areas of work he was doing and relay how experimental work was conducted, Svet leapt at the chance.

Equally Jack and Lauren leapt at their chance ... for some of their own style of catch-up in a spare pod, which both instantly decked out again with their favourite four poster bed replete with soothing music, wine and Barbarella, his personal robot for added zest. Jack was feeling experimentally frisky. Each day he wanted to absorb new experiences together with Lauren ... and now for the first time, so did she. What would Mila have thought? ... She pondered after recovering from the intense throes of a giant threesome … the first time she had thought of Mila, but then realised the limits of conjuring up fantasy scenarios. Only if Mila was here on Europa could she create her alongside. This was a safeguard relating to people. She wondered whether Jack knew how to override that or whether he had any idea of her personal wider predilections, probably now after Barbarella he realised fully, but had become so excited with it all, it didn't seem to matter.

But Jack also needed to know that she was not the norm with her likes either … getting carried away all together with Barbarella in bed was one thing, but careful scientific extrapolation of findings still had to be applied. She realised at that moment that she was accepting the terms of his project and grand plan … the merging of Europa and Earth could only have long-term benefits for mankind and womankind. But what were the downsides? There hadn't been any enumerated in their terms of reference within this collaboration … because of course Jack had one overriding objective; no downsides, only conquer and integrate … She needed to think hard about that strategy and his forceful single mindedness quietly to herself and then follow up with the others.

She was also learning for the first time how to blank him out for short periods, when she decided and wanted to … She could tell he was mildly dismayed about how quickly she had learned that skill without being shown. But Jack had to understand and never forget … she had always been a very resourceful woman and used her gift of high intellect to the full, including ensuring her independence, wherever she was.

Day two end and Lauren and the four had retired together again for the evening in their favourite setting, Nadine's Atlantis bar, which gave them a boost of reassurance somehow, that going home was still a viable option. Seeing Amélie, grinning permanently like a trio of Cheshire cats, needed no further explanation of what was or was not being enjoyed during her 'experiments' with Apollo and Hercules together and individually. Everything imaginable, which in Amélie's case was a vast, voracious database, had been indulged in to the greatest of excess that only Amélie knew how. Lauren realised why poor Rufus spent so much time down in the UK House of Lords. It wasn't the politics. The parliamentary building was a necessary island of physical recovery. Poor Hercules too, by the end of the day, also looked a pale imitation of his mythical self, but still remained game for a day three. They spent a good serious hour, sharing and pulling together their scientific and technological acquired knowledge and could only dream about the processes of experimentation and engineering they saw. There was a huge resource of rare earths available, used for an array of different and powerful semi-conductors and energy management electronics, including massive battery storage, in ways not yet discovered on Earth, utilising germanium, dysprosium and yttrium, in conjunction with sulphur. These and other elements had been mined regularly from Callisto, another large Jupiter moon orbiting further out, an interesting indicator of the future benefits of space exploration for resources.

Engaging with fusion and plasma engineering was to the Europans like conducting Boyle's law or working an Archimedean Screw, basic and simple O-level physics. Of mind boggling perception was how the robots worked assiduously on daily tasks and how much they knew and could quickly self-learn. Pete, a technician robot, was a specialist mathematician and happily showed Lauren how they solved a space-time general relativity equation. He immediately calculated and ran off pi to fifty decimal places in an instant to ensure the accuracy of measurement of light deflection around a spherical red giant to the nearest millimetre—in fact Antares was used as a demonstrator.

Hello? Lauren thought. Am I actually dreaming here? This technological experience was so out of this world ... but of course they were exactly that. After a couple of detailed and methodical explanations, the robots displayed unending patience with her and Amélie, both feeling like first year students again. Between them they had just about mastered the basics of their completely new and novel mathematical methodology. Once again they were using a number system to base four. But overall, Lauren's assessment was that she and Amélie were as mathematically good as the robots on conceptualisation, but only just, and nowhere near as quick calculating. But once onto discussions of nuclear fusion with Apollo, they were lost completely from the start, and had to resort to slow, tedious first steps and try and translate the Europa slick methodologies into what felt now like clunky Earth partial differential equations. They were incredibly behind in knowledge in comparison, but had to start somewhere, and these guys had a billion years head start. Lauren was desperately storing everything she could into her photographic memory, for use if and when she ever returned to her Cyclops Fusion Centre. Jack stayed out of all the discussions but always returned later at the end of their lab sessions.

As they sat around their favourite window table, Nadine walked back from the bar with a large plate of chicken wings and a tray of mixed salad. "I've also ordered some garlic bread," she said, carefully balancing the heavy tray. "This is a weird experience because although the surroundings are very familiar, nobody in here I know, including the staff, and they serve food I would never have dreamed of, including this little lot. Although I must admit these chicken pieces done in mustard sauce are a favourite. A manifestation, they agreed, of Jack's own observations and likely food likes."

"Mmm ... looks great," Charlotte replied whilst Lauren handed round plates. "Is Svet bringing some beers instead of wine for a change?"

"Yes," Amélie replied. "She's just coming although by the look on her face they are also not what she expected."

Svet set down a tray of glasses and opened bottles of a very pale beer. "They only had something called Cumbrian Lynx White Beer? Actually I had a sip and it tastes very good, but it's not American that's for sure."

"It's an English real ale speciality from up north," Lauren cut in, holding the bottle up to the light. "Wow this is strong though—my ex-husband and I used to drink bottles of it cycling around the English Lake District."

"Which ex-husband was that, Lauren?" Amélie chipped in to giggles from everyone. "Sorry I'm being my usual bitchy self. Still one is definitely acquiring an unusual insight into Jack's peccadilloes."

"Talking about polyamory and men mounting up, I hope Hercules and Apollo still have their wits about them tomorrow for our special session on large energy storage. They look like they may require an extra jolt of plasma themselves."

Everyone roared laughing and Amélie glowered. "Okay, Professor Comedienne—touché. Anyway, the way I look at it is because we are living in our virtual minds, this experience isn't really cheating on your earthly partners is it—more like imaginary masturbation, so make the most of your rhapsody of moon."

"Bloody hell Amélie, you have novel ways to justify your endeavours, all in the name of science of course," Charlotte replied, laughing and patting Lauren gently on her back, who was choking with mirth on her mouthful of chicken wing. "But yes, I suppose that's one way of putting it!"

Lauren sipped her beer and waited until her throat was clear. But she had something else to bring up, which had been ruminating since they were in her canteen. "Nadine, can I ask you something? Where were you on our first night?"

Nadine went quiet. They stared at her, the silence suddenly embarrassing. She had hoped to covertly glean more information, but probably now she needed to come clean. "Just wait a moment Lauren. I need to concentrate first on something, okay … that's better."

"Vaag?"

"No, Dmitri. How did you know?"

Amélie, Svet and Charlotte were completely mystified.

Lauren suddenly rubbed her temple. "Because I worked it out accidentally and can do the same. Fuck, would you believe, my little bastard is trying to outwit us, and is trying to go through me to you right now."

"Outwit him Lauren, you can do it, try again."

"Done it … he knows too, at least about me, and he's quite miffed but that's too bad. He can't have his own way all of the time, only when I want him to."

Amélie cut in, her patience already run out. "If you're talking about both men and aliens, we agree wholeheartedly. Now would you two like to share your fascinating secrets?"

"We're putting a temporary block on Jack's ability to do a little mindreading and poke about inside our v-world," Lauren replied. "What happens, I think, is it messes with his subconscious emotions and fuzzes up the transmission of data, like a mobile signal blocker. Jack's quite an emotional guy although he struggles to openly admit it. Who's your blocker again Nadine?"

"Dmitri."

"Come on spit it out, fun time over," Amélie resounded, becoming quite irritated. "We need a slice of that too ... ahh ... I think I get it now. You have a good set of choices of course, Lauren ... but let me see ... although why you've obviously been thinking of him when Jack's around defies the imagination. Are we Luis by any chance?"

"Yes!" Lauren replied with a glare.

Amélie smiled at Charlotte and Svet. "Baddies, you may have 'engaged' with. Obviously Jack and probably all of them don't like or understand the concept, another Europan weakness to be clocked and stored. Vaag here I come." She concentrated hard and smiled. "Unintended consequences. Hercules, sadly, will have a droop coming on."

Charlotte did the same. "Janos and I'm glad the fucker's dead. Mmm, see what you mean Amélie, like having a headache relieved except you haven't got a headache."

Lauren gaped at her daughter, amazed. "You mean that bastard Belarusian terrorist did something before Giles and Marie got to you?"

"Yes, I fucked him; I had to, when he separated me from the others. Then he laughed and said too bad, he'd already planted the bomb ... which killed DG."

"Dead? How do you know?"

Charlotte hesitated. "I will tell you Lauren, I promise, but not now. When we're back home."

Lauren hugged her. "Fine, I'm so sorry." But then she looked at Svet who was blank for a moment, before she too concentrated and let out a sigh of relief. "Svet, you can't have anybody ... surely ...?"

"Yes I do, Ivan."

"Ivan?" Lauren replied puzzled. She only knew one Ivan, Irena's father who had fleetingly at the last minute stood in as Philippe's best man at their wedding.

"Yes him Lauren, Ivan Luchenserkov. When I was a child, around ten, he used to babysit at the flat in Brussels occasionally when my father had things to attend. He threatened bad things if I told my father what he did. I was scared, and then one day he never returned to the flat. The first time I saw him again was at your wedding. I never told my father. Luchenserkov was his best friend ... and the time has long passed now. Anyway he has terminal cancer of the pancreas. Good riddance."

They all remained contemplative for half a minute. Amélie broke the silence. "Well, we've certainly chosen a few good blockers. So, back to where we were, now in our alien-free zone and I'm going to order another round of those white beers, they are rather good." She waved down the barman and Lauren picked up the cue as they all returned to the job in hand.

"Sorry Nadine, you were going to say?"

Nadine fell silent as she began to carefully assemble her thoughts in as concise and logical summary as she could. They didn't have long before Jack might eavesdrop in. "I slept with Hermione."

Another silence, not really disbelief but certainly surprise, especially Svet. "Gosh, Nadine, I had no idea you fancied ..."

Nadine patted her best friend's hand. "No, I don't, well I have done, but I don't now, all in the past, so it wasn't hard. A couple of things suddenly came to me that first day connected with the Mila lookalike appearance. I quickly realised Hermione fancied me quite intensely ... because her brain was programmed in automatically when she was cloned from the Mila 'impression.' Robots here think autonomously. Hermione had absorbed some of Mila's sexuality which became clear immediately we received the presentation. But as we all know, the Europan Arrhyans have long lost the use of emotional communication, irony etc so I figured the robots would likely be the same. I knew Mila used to fancy me, we'd laugh and joke about it in Mila's way, but Mila is far too sophisticated to let her fanny rule her head."

305

Lauren winced inside momentarily, but let it go, life was always complicated anyway.

Nadine continued. "Mila wanted me from the start as a friend and a protégé, which of course I became. All the time I was working out how Hermione must likely be constructed and programmed. So I reckoned there could be a chance Hermione also possessed in her circuitry, Mila's strong bond of friendship and trust even if she didn't know how to manipulate it. She could be a sort of innocent to be plied. I know that sound callous but needs must here. Combined with her obvious desire for sex, there was a powerful and sudden opportunity to wheedle out information from her, but I knew the pillow talk might have to be subtle and careful. At the same time I had randomly concentrated on Dmitri and that brutal experience in his cell in Murmansk. Dmitri only liked anal. An off-chance thought, I suppose, I was trying to remember the steps I took to survive for use here. Then I immediately felt my head clear and when Jack looked at me for a moment, puzzled and then irritated at breakfast I knew. He had some monitor on my thoughts and I had disrupted it. To be honest Lauren, it was only watching him with you that made me work out that I had blocked him off ... it lasted about an hour. We have half an hour left."

"So, did your plan succeed?" Charlotte asked.

"Yes, surprisingly easy. I knew Mila was passionate, but not that passionate, and Hermione was amazing so I had to respond with the same enthusiasm, that wasn't actually hard either then I got her to talk."

"Well?" Amélie growled, her impatience rising fast.

Lauren glanced at the floor momentarily. Mila's passion wasn't something she expected to be reminded of either.

Nadine carried on. "In a nutshell, Jack hasn't been wholly open—not about why he is in a hurry to get us 'primed' up to spearhead the Europan coming. Hermione was very worried. It appears that the original Arrhyans on Io, the thinking liquid sulphur, are very unhappy with Jack's grand Europa exit to Earth. Remember H. G. Wells, the War of the Worlds? ... How did it end?"

"The humble microbe," Lauren answered, with a fond smile. He had been her favourite childhood author. "Despite the advanced technologies of

306

the squid-like Martians, stomping around in their huge tripod machines and laser blasting everyone, they succumbed in the end to a little, harmless cold bug and died dramatically at their posts."

"Correct," Nadine replied. "And it appears that Jack's sulphur counterparts have retained one rather Earth-like characteristic amongst all that perpetual thinking. Absolute power and the need to exercise it at all costs. Because for hundreds of billions of years, Io has been the dominant colony, using robots to do their bidding and keep their hegemony in shape. The Europa colony was only ever allowed to develop as it did, retaining both their Earth-like appearance and advanced technology capabilities and ability to move around, solely as a means of finding the next suitable Io for the sulphuric Arrhyans to escape to. That has been the sole Europa objective for millions of years and as you may know, so far, that odd combination of star, planet and moon in the shape of the sun, Jupiter and Io has not materialised, after millions of Europa Arrhyan voyages all over the Milky Way, many still ongoing. The Io metabolism, for want of a better word, is very acutely chemically balanced, a plethora of conditions must be exactly right."

"But why do they want to escape Io?" Lauren interjected, her mind trying to recapture all the small things Jack had said to her.

"Because Io is beginning to change, volcanic activity has been gradually increasing lately especially in the last few decades. You may be aware, even on Earth we have also noticed the phenomenon, analysing ongoing comparison photos of Io and Jupiter flybys since the first orbital took place. The Io Arrhyans have had to import more plasma energy from Jupiter to balance it off, which in itself as you'll appreciate Amélie is highly dangerous ... but at some point, they fear they can't hold the tide back and our liquid sulphur blobs ... well ... become vaporised or turned into some other undesirable chemical. They die. So they need to retain their power over Jack and his comrades to keep focussed on the sole objective of space exploration."

Nadine interrupted her thoughts, reflecting deeply. "Jack however, has now for the very first time in Arrhyan history been riding roughshod over that old and time honoured arrangement—call him a revolutionary or better still a renegade. There is a group of about a hundred plus an equivalent number of allied robots that's all on Europa residing within eight interconnected spheres, including our base, which happens to be the largest and most sophisticated. Jack, as we know is the leader. They all want out ... wave goodbye to their Io bondage and leave them to their sulphurous fate ... off to Earth ... and very soon with the five of us as their advance guard, and certainly well before we discover in the near future with more advanced probes about life on Europa and Io and get wiped out easily in some process of retribution, like lambs to the slaughter. Hermione has been made the robot leader. Jack's taken some inspiration from you Lauren, choosing Mila as a role model. How he knows is anybody's guess."

Lauren came in again, her mind reeling with all of this. "He's undoubtedly researched well Nadine. Jack has never hidden the fact that he's always travelling, a rolling stone gathering no moss and all that ..."

"Until you appeared and have had a profound effect on him and now their plans." Nadine replied instantly. "However, Hermione divulged something else disturbing. She and the other robots discovered an Io spy, one of the robots inside Jack's cell, now let's say, disassembled. You can't really say killed. She had been feeding back secret information to Io ... sorry I forgot to add, Hermione also learned that the Io Arrhyans have been establishing their own covert robot colony on what we call Adrastea for some time."

Lauren's eyes narrowed. "Jesus. One of the tiny moons discovered by Voyager 2 in 1979, the first planetary satellite to be pictured by a spacecraft rather than a telescope. Adrastea orbits very close to Jupiter, nearer than Io, but is more like a giant piece of irregular rock, only about twelve miles in diameter, far too small for gravity to have formed it into a sphere. Jupiter has a faint ring around it like Saturn, only first seen by probes and it's thought Adrastea is linked in some way to the ring formation. The moon must be quite hidden, like being in a fog, from a Europa view perspective and it orbits extremely fast."

"Correct. Jack doesn't know about activity on Adrastea. His robots have kept back that information until they've established, without any doubt, the purpose of such a colony. Normally all robots are made here, under overall Io control. To me it's pretty obvious. Io is amassing a covert strike force to invade Europa and put down Jack's adventures. Moreover what will our presence now do, assuming they know on Io, through their former spy, we are here too?"

Charlotte had already concluded the obvious. "It will rapidly accelerate the Io robot invasion. My God, Nadine, this situation has become very complex and we're in the middle of it and highly vulnerable. What do we do? We can't even escape."

Lauren suddenly burst out, her emotions overcoming her normal rationality, large tears running down her cheeks. "I have to tell Jack, I can't let him be killed. I love him."

Amélie put her arm around Lauren immediately, as Svet took her hand. "No, Lauren, shush and listen, please. Let's hear Nadine out, she's obviously given this much intense thought. It's the nearest thing we've got yet to trying to escape. Can Hermione and her robots help us to escape Nadine?"

Lauren forced herself to calm down. Charlotte had already ordered her a large gin and tonic which she swigged down instantly. "I'm sorry. Of course, please Nadine, I'm on board. Shit, I wish Mila was here too."

Nadine drew breath and her thoughts together again. "Okay. I agree with Charlotte. I suspect that the Io Arrhyans know we're being primed up to facilitate Jack's master plan and will decide a preemptive strike very soon, before we and Jack and his conspirators get a chance to return to Earth. We don't have much time. Tonight I've agreed to return to meet Hermione and Jimmy. They really haven't a clue about warfare, fighting, defence and attack strategy, any of that. None of them have experienced it first-hand so they're not programmed, because Europa lost the necessity for war billions of years ago. I'm going to look at the weapons they're now assembling and try and advise them. Amélie, I know you can use a gun, but I suspect we're talking about sophisticated laser or plasma vaporisers. I need all your expertise with me too. All the so called protection of the colony has been assigned and programmed to female robots under Hermione, who form the majority on the eight life-spheres. A number in storage hibernation are being brought out and back to life, to double the defence force if the Io robots do attack.

"You mean like fucking Amazons fighting each other? Bloody hell. Okay, I'm in," Amélie responded. "I'll try not to faint, sorry an in-joke Nadine and not very funny. We really have to get on with this. But what do we do with Jack now and the other Europans?"

"Our fighting robots will need support, with back up intelligence, communications and technology. Svet and Charlotte, by now Hermione will have advised Juno, Persephone and Romulus as well as Apollo and Hercules. They and others will be able to do that. The concept of fighting and destruction is equally undeveloped. You need to help them focus their minds, on being the engineers, intelligence and logistics behind the scenes as it were as best as possible. That group, with their male technician robots which Jimmy will lead, meet in the Cassini cafeteria again first thing tomorrow. We still all need to sleep, they don't."

"Why is Jack being left out?" Lauren demanded, still desperately unhappy with what seemed to be unfolding.

"Because they all know he's madly in love with you, Lauren. And Hermione is worried that his judgement and thinking will not be up to dealing with fighting. He's become almost human, the first Arrhyan to mutate back two billion years into a level of emotional consciousness which disappeared and became extinct. I think Hermione's right. So we need to leave Jack to you tonight. He needs to know what's likely to be going down, and will only accept it if you persuade him."

Lauren pondered. She nodded. The logic made sense. "But we still don't know how to get off this damned moon."

Nadine smiled. "The reason I was late at Cassini was because I met Hermione at our base—I persuaded her to show me how the transportation tubes are programmed. I've memorised it. Only Jack and a few robots know including Barbarella—he keeps the master code of fifteen digits, of course in base four. She said she thought it was based on an important constant which applies to the whole universe. I'll leave you to ponder that, we can confer tomorrow."

Lauren looked at Amélie and then Charlotte. "I think we know that ... but fifteen digits? Then into base four?"

Charlotte pondered. "The base four is easy ... Pete will do the fifteen digits immediately. Svet and I will check later."

"Planck?" Svet whispered, eyeing Lauren.

"Yes, I'm certain."

Nadine interjected again. "Just had a final thought Lauren. This is a long shot but when you said I wish we had Mila here, me too. What if we could turn Hermione into the complete Mila, add the Special Forces and martial arts? That would shorten the odds in favour of Jack if there is a sudden attack. You need to ask him Lauren, could we do that? ... I mean call her in without bringing her here? We can't call her into our reality scenes because she isn't on Europa, but maybe Jack knows how to get around that barrier? I've just tried my phone, it won't dial ... even though I could text Roland last night, and I can't do that now either, obviously there are intermittent flaws, like dodgy Wifi."

Lauren reflected. "Yes, I'll try. But I don't see how it can be done. Look how far we are. It takes around thirty minutes for electromagnetic wave travel to Earth ... you couldn't conduct a synchronous communication, only send signals. We can't override the fundamental physics."

Nadine sighed. "Of course, I guess you're right. Anyway, we're done now. Drink your beer and then let's concentrate on our respective destinations ..."

Chapter Sixteen

Lauren snuggled in closer to Jack again. She felt his warm bare body breathing slowly and quietly and ached for his touch. Why, when after all this time, she was finding genuine love again, did all this bizarre complication have to be going on? She wanted him badly on so many levels. She began to reflect much more deeply on the revelations during the evening and the experiences since landing. If they couldn't leave together, neither could she desert Jack on his own here. She had to be with him, whatever the consequences. Perhaps she should bring the triplets to Europa, dive in and create a whole new family concept with Jack; after all she didn't need money, her villa, or any earthly goods whatsoever. They could virtually magic up everything together, pure thought, whatever they desired. She even knew now how to ensure her independent, monitor-free space whenever she wanted it. Europa could become the true family good life she still craved. Fuck Philippe, why should he even be considered, the way he had treated her. But, thinking rationally again of the triplets, who she was already missing badly, she immediately realised there was something absent in this virtual reality world, so focussed had they all been on science and technology. Music, art, opera, culture and creativity? Where was it? Yes, she had heard some 1960's music and a little jazz from an old jukebox and seen some banal paintings hanging on the wall of Nadine's lounge, but they were not her choice. They were Jack's memories and his tastes, maybe culled from other alien additions to the so called Europa knowledgepedia database. This world either never had or was now incapable of its own cultural creativity ... the right brain had been lost aeons ago in time, shrivelled into a peanut and rejected, rightly or wrongly, as a superfluous and inconsequential thinking activity alongside science. Was she comfortable with that? She wriggled uneasily, huddled Jack tighter and looked at her watch. It was almost ten thirty pm; he wouldn't have been asleep long. She moved her hand down his chest and stomach and around his warm manhood and felt everything gently, all on standby, squishy and flaccid. But it wasn't long before life began to stir, rising and hardening with her deft touch as he began to come to and groaned, unsure of what was happening. Turning around to face her, side by side, he half opened his eyes, smiled and kissed her warmly as she pulled him closer.

"I've missed you terribly tonight, I assumed you were with the others again but I really don't know what to do with myself when you're not here. I love you Lauren."

"I know, and I love you too Jack. I need you, now."

She gripped his large erection and positioned it against her body and pushed herself partly into him gently. He closed his eyes and she grasped him under his arms and around his shoulders as he began to move gently in and out, a tease feel but she already began to experience a deepening intensity inside. It didn't take long for a great gush of pleasure to engulf her, knowing she could howl, scream and wail as much as she liked, because they were in their own private and secure world, created to suit only them. She turned him upwards slowly without losing their intimate connection so she was in her favourite position, on her back and her legs up and over his shoulders. He stopped for a moment to align himself, then they kissed passionately and he began once more, fervently increasing in speed and pressure until she was overwhelmed by a massive orgasmic miasma, both climaxing at the same time.

She suddenly felt an unexpected reaction, that familiar sensation from pumping and release. Jack was actually ejaculating. Somehow his body had been relearning the ancient ways and the biology readjusting. He screamed for all eternity with the increased pleasure and sensation, never before experienced. His climax seemed to go on forever, making up for lost time, she was overflowing all over the sheets as he excitedly rubbed whatever it was all around her bare bottom. He finally collapsed gently on top of her, his breathing shallow and she could feel his heart beating very rapidly. Jack had experienced his first complete earthly orgasm with her, the full package and likely the first Arrhyan true fuck for a billion years.

She knew it was a seminal moment, an orgasm to be captured and remembered by both forever. Shrinking fast he gently withdrew and they held each other closely, coming down from the high slowly like a pair of virginal adolescent lovers experiencing their very first sexual sensation each.

"Jack, that was unique, sensational, total and complete."

"I know, at long last. I've been working on this possibility so hard in my mind and the barriers have finally flipped open. I'm certain only because I genuinely love you. Finally, I'm acclimatising, learning and physiologically adapting to be a true Earth colonist. It can work Lauren for us, I just know it."

She leant over him and kissed him gently. "I know, I really love you but I need to tell you something, very, very important."

They sat up quietly, and he slowly poured out a glass of cold lemonade each from a large jug on the table at the side. "I'm listening."

She knew this would be one of the trickiest and most delicate discussions she had ever faced, and she needed to draw on all her experience and her powers of persuasion and facilitation. But ultimately Jack was like her, a scientist. He would receive best what she had to say via a clear, concise logical explanation and proposition. And if she got it wrong he would become a spurned lover, unforgiving, unrelenting and full of hate and she could become the victim of a genuine crime of passion, Europa style.

She went into the facts from the start by steadily outlining everything that Nadine, Amélie, Charlotte, Svet and herself had now analysed and knew for certain. He said nothing whilst she continued, taking the information sequences in quietly and intensely. He asked no questions and she talked for over half an hour and then finally Jack went quiet into a very deep thought. She saw his eyes change again; they were wide open, the pupils dilated massively and that strange pale green luminescence was emerging, exactly like the first time they had made love in Nadine's colonial library. This, she decided, must be a process called up by Arrhyans under times of extreme necessity, decision making or stress. She said nothing as he pondered, totally inside his own mind, staring at the ceiling and making no bodily movement except very, very slow breathing, minute after minute. His hand was gripped relentlessly inside hers.

Gradually his eyes returned to normal, he turned and looked into her worried face. "Lauren, this changes everything. From all kinds of small things I've now assembled as leader, into a large picture of events unfolding that make sense. You five Earth women are remarkable, way beyond what any of us here would have believed, especially the abilities of Nadine. I realise now she is different, almost living a dual alter-ego, which I had not researched. In one respect it was careless and stupid of me, because if I had she would not be here. But my error, fortuitously, may actually be the most important and critical outcome we all face here to survive. Of course I knew how the Io Arrhyans would ultimately feel and believe— that I betrayed them by leaving to colonise Earth, an old Martian dream to make a legend come alive, never enacted before. And I gambled that the time to make the break was now, for all the developing Earth reasons we've discussed and because the Io colonists were in a weakening position with their moon degenerating. I had passionately believed warfare, fighting and our Europa colony wipe-out was an impossible concept for any of us to enact, especially Io. Those destructive ideas had been eliminated many, many millions of years ago from Arrhyan civilisation. But of course all this time, inside their amorphous, liquid networks, they secretly retained those old defects way back from early Mars. Indeed, the reason why our existence as Europans was acceptable for over a billion years, to find them a new world, was because it was built on the notion of a deep and genetically implanted trust and respect for each other. But I should have used my Earth experience, thought laterally and worked out that their jealously, the retaining of absolute power, maintaining ultimate and perpetual control had never been given up. I and my team have been extremely and damagingly naive. They must have kept their intent quietly stored; hibernated deep in their own knowledge base which we can't access as our life forms are so different—there is no commonality to begin. Our agreement to support each other has been a giant con trick, always one-sided for their benefit only. I'm the first one to challenge the unwritten code."

She hugged him hard, he was releasing all his fears and frustration, and she could see it was killing him inside to have to be so frank.

"Yet," Jack continued, "You five, in the space of a mere three days, have unravelled the billion year old enigma. To you the whole plot is clear and unambiguous. Lauren, for all our immense science and technology prowess, our massively learned analytical thoughts and unique virtual worlds, we Europans dangerously totally lack what you on Earth still take for granted to survive. Guile, suspicion and mistrust. That is our ultimate evolutionary weakness; our own goodness has become a rope to hang us with. Finding a so called spy in the camp and learning of the Io plotting must have been hugely upsetting to the robots and my senior colleagues, but why didn't they come to me immediately?"

"Because they were unable to assess what was happening until Nadine took time and slowly made sense of it for them. And they realised that you were seriously distracted ... grappling with a vital new learning of what true love and its emotional implications for Europa Arrhyans actually could mean ... which was why me and only me needed to tell you. Hey, and you've been rightly distracted I would add!" She smiled and he kissed her again passionately.

"Absolutely," he murmured and grinned ...

She now knew, he was back to his earthly side and out of alien mode thank goodness, and the hardest presentation she had delivered seemed to have worked. But what do they do now?

"You say our robots have been making weapons?" Jack whispered. "What are they and how did they know what to do or even know what weapons are?"

"Because Hermione has been guiding everyone. You made her Jack, based on your knowledge of my friend Mila. What you didn't know is that certain aspects of Mila's background must have imported and become mixed in with Hermione's own technology knowledge."

"What aspects? There are none. After I photographed her with you and then researched her it was all very clear. Mila is a sophisticated, clever and highly attractive socialite, living in New York. I understood immediately why you found her ..." He stopped.

Lauren's eyes narrowed. Now she needed to hear the answer about that conundrum which she already suspected. And straight from his lips. "Where and when did you photograph us, Jack?"

He thought, and decided. No more secrets from Lauren, not now. "I ... err ... took a series of pictures one day near Nice, when you and Mila were out riding ... and ..."

"We were shagging, Jack. Out with reality please."

"Yes. It was then I became aware that you were ..."

"I'm complex Jack, and I'm bisexual, which you very well knew when we had a tryst with Barbarella the other night."

"Yes, and it makes no difference to me Lauren, I love you, complex and beautiful. It's all of you and that's what always attracted me before you even remarried."

"You've been stalking me all that time? Bloody hell?"

"From the day you published that revolutionary paper on cold fusion ... It made me jump off my chair, after all those years, looking for the best talent. I knew you had a brilliant mind unlike any other. What I hadn't reckoned on was the rest of you ... and I fell in love ... initially I had to google what that meant, it was such a strange feeling."

She roared laughing and hugged him hard. "You are indeed a daft alien. I assume you googled Mila too."

She watched him blush shyly, another first for Jack on Europa. This earthly metamorphosis was developing very nicely. "Okay Jack, you need to help me do something impossible. You've been impressed with Nadine ... but Nadine and a myriad of others like her have all been trained ... by Mila. She is actually a highly formidable special operative, martial arts and weapons expert from Israel. I need to contact her, but not bring her here, I'm not suggesting that. Her value will be to advise and assist Nadine and that could be done by merging in Mila's full range of skills by proxy. Can I contact her and do the impossible physics as I know it? A synchronous communication link of Mila's formidable warfare capability into Hermione's formidable technology body, with Nadine continuing to overall assist and advise the robots on the ground. I need to speak to Mila properly, but at thirty nine minutes of light speed away, I can't. How advanced is your most forefront technology?"

"My goodness, Lauren, your idea is brilliant," he replied. Then he fell silent, his face creasing with more thoughts. "It may be possible but is very dangerous. We would have to make use of original and very complex work which Apollo has been leading on over the last two years. But we haven't literally done any test, and not on this scale. We would need to marshal together his best robots."

"Do it Jack. Explain to me, the principles at least."

"A number of years back your science community got into an uproar when a paper was published demonstrating that Einstein's fundamental principle of constancy of the speed of light could be violated in certain conditions. It led to a raft of controversy, stances were taken worldwide and papers since written in refutation, a position now accepted."

"Yes, I followed it myself. That paper was nonsense, plenty of theoretical holes and incorrect experimental results were found. I too was a staunch sceptic from the beginning and remain so."

"I'm afraid Apollo's work has shown definitively that in certain circumstances the speed of light can be exceeded, in fact by many times. But it requires the creation of an unusual pair of black holes, and a special spiral wormhole vortex in between. Energy drawn into the first black hole will accelerate where there are no longer normal applicable physics conditions, directly into the second black hole. But if the velocity reached is sufficient, and we calculate around one thousand times the speed of light, the energy wave moves through an unstable barrier—you call it a Cauchy horizon—and leaks out. By creating a directional lens to capture and manage that leakage, this electromagnetic wave will continue at such a rate out into normal space. Apollo has shown that the wave should be reflected back to source by feeding it through a simple amplifier circuit—simple in our terms, very complex in yours but a highly capable electronic engineer would be needed to make it work with precision.

"I understand. The experience would be amazing to see. Could this amplifier effect be simulated in an iPhone by building a special app?"

"My word Lauren that is a novel concept. I don't know but Apollo and Hercules have a team of expert robots which certainly could build one, the process would be elementary for them if they had the specification of the application infrastructure."

"A naive question, but I suppose Europa has long moved on from using emails to transmit file data? Thought communication power has replaced it?"

"Correct, but an email address could be resurrected from the knowledgepedia database, we'd need to go back at least half a billion years. I can see where you're going to with all this Lauren, but we have one major problem. The light accelerator has never been built. It would be an enormous feat to do it. Creating a black hole is hugely dangerous. Get it wrong and it would grow and suck in the whole environment around it. Compare it to building a nuclear reactor. Insufficient control and the chain reaction becomes unstoppable—the environment turns into a nuclear bomb and blows sky-high. Black holes are many orders of magnitude worse. Europa, even the whole Jovian system could collapse into itself and disappear."

Jack sat up and levered himself out of bed, throwing a towel around his waist. "Lauren, you really need to sleep. Remember I don't need to but I must have a shower...then I'm going to ..."

He was interrupted by a message bleep on his tablet and peered at the three dimensional screen after tapping in a long code. His forehead furrowed into a series of deep lines as he concentrated hard on the message, silently transmitted on a thought channel only to him.

She knew instantly it was something extremely serious. "Jack, what's happened?" she whispered, fearful immediately of the others working away inside their allotted virtual realities.

"It's Hermione. She's with her top team, Nadine and Amélie, testing out the new laser guided plasma weapons. It appears the prototypes are working well and Nadine has already mastered the most powerful one, which instantly vaporises the most resiliently built of robots ... we have never had such lethal armaments since the forced evacuation two billion years ago to Deimos and Phobos, when desperate fighting broke out. Only a few hundred made it off Mars, my ancestors. That's the good news if you can call it that. The bad news is Barbarella has vanished. Hermione and her apparently fought hard but Barbarella, wounded by Amélie, escaped in a chamber to the surface and then a robot craft waiting for Adrastea. They couldn't prevent the lift-off in time. Barbarella became desperately jealous, Lauren, apparently of you and me. Robots rarely demonstrate such emotions and she was trying now to break into your reality world with me to attempt to re-enter and destroy us, but fortunately my security shield held. I can't believe it. She ... was my personal support for so long ... very capable and loyal ... but she knows all my inner thoughts and plans ... Fuck it Lauren, she's gone over to Io and will tell them everything. The situation is changing very fast ... I must go and call everyone together, now, especially Apollo's team and our best robot engineers and bring them all into our high technology workshops. We are going to build your black hole tonight Lauren, use all our ingenuity that we can muster ... You're right. We do urgently need Mila onboard. We have to stay ahead of Io's tactics that is our only advantage. Although I suspect they've been training up their robots for some time and been attempting to source information using spies, because Earth-type lethal warfare information for them will be second-hand. Only Europa Arrhyans can travel to Earth, certainly not robots on their own. Tomorrow, you and your team must meet at seven again with all of us ... in our workshop, which will be transformed into a recognisable reality fusion laboratory in our familiar Cassini setting. Nadine and Amélie must rest and sleep too Lauren, tell them urgently please."

Before she could say yes he had quickly yanked on his jeans and tee-shirt and shot out of the door ...

Chapter Seventeen

Breakfast was a dashed cup of coffee and a rushed ham croissant back in the Cassini canteen. Nadine had brought in a small bag of Hermione's laser weapons now being mass constructed in the empty warehouse next door, to show Lauren and Jack, before departing again to assist further. Charlotte and Svet had already gone across to help on the virtual production line.

Grabbing some fruit as she was still hungry, Lauren, followed by Jack, walked out of the back entrance and both strode quickly towards the building housing Jack's fusion reactor. Everywhere was freshly painted and rebuilt after the explosion. Again, lots of people walked past going to their jobs. Security waved them as usual through the barriers but nobody was the slightest bit familiar, and of course Juliette and her team didn't figure anywhere. She realised why when they opened the workshop door. There was no fusion reactor. Inside, Apollo and Hercules with Amélie were pouring over a huge data and specification sheet on the computer bench. She looked in disbelief at the shiny machine standing in the middle of the room, rising from floor to ceiling. A plethora of large brown insulators were connected by thick copper cables to a huge transformer which in turn was linked with bulky aluminium conduits on poles through the wall, and connected directly to the pylon and electricity grid outside. A large amount of power was going to be utilised.

Amélie spotted Lauren and Jack and waved them over enthusiastically. Apollo was beaming alongside her ... as Lauren inwardly smiled to herself, this time an obvious admiration for her brains not just her body for a change. Jack, after a hushed word with Apollo, went off and joined Nadine and Hermione to see the weapons and get a briefing on how they worked.

"I've suggested that we create a hybrid reality to fire this quark compressor up?" Amélie burbled away immediately, clearly back to her practical element once more.

"A quark compressor?"

"Yes, Lauren, get your grey matter into gear. In simple terms those two spherical chambers mounted on these three huge legs set into a metre of concrete will enclose the potential black holes, isolated from any matter by a huge magnetic field, same principle as we've been playing with inside fusion stellerators. The attached array of finned cylinders will be cooled to a billionth of a degree above absolute zero to maximise the speed and flow of incoming particles. In simple terms, inside the chamber quarks are pounded into a compressed state by bursts of ultra-heavy plasma until the resulting matter, unlike anything you and I are familiar with, becomes so great it envelops itself into a black hole. As for my hybrid? We've used some Earth resources. They needed a tungsten-niobium alloy and you have that on site at Cassini in storage, they don't. But the outside electricity grid isn't quite what it seems as the power will come direct from electromagnetic energy linked to Jupiter. No way could anything on Earth provide such a huge source of intense energy. I've concluded an Earth-Europa business deal. Neat isn't it."

"Jesus, Amélie, only you could dream that one up ..."

Apollo had sidled up to her and put his arm around her waist affectionately. "Amélie is wonderful, we simply don't think like that here."

"Later, Apollo," she purred back, and kissed his cheek before barking instructions. "Switch on time in ten minutes Lauren, optimum position of the Jupiter red spot which sources the power, countdown from now."

Lauren gaped. Amélie was still an incredible technologist, and forced her own brain back into familiar high pressure practical work mode. She had been holidaying for far too long. "All this was built last night?"

"Yes, I helped." She downed another cup of coffee. I've only had three hours sleep. "But ... well ... we will witness a real first ... an advanced technology test."

"A test?"

"Yes. Assuming it works, you link with Mila in real time and Apollo receives a science commendation. If it doesn't then you, me and everyone else here will spend the rest of our days rotating in a ring around Jupiter in fundamental particle mode and one moon less. If this lot goes up, it will make a five hundred kiloton nuclear explosion sound like a firework cracker. And before you start sighing, we have no other choice. Our defending robots, if there is an attack, are vastly outnumbered by Io, and they have a cache of weapons too on that little moon where Barbarella escaped to, although I took her arm off with this, but sadly she can get it repaired. Nadine and I have shown Hermione some tweaks to increase the laser power of ours, but we absolutely need Hermione to become the full Serbian Wonder Woman. Your pillow talk thoughts to Jack were brilliant."

"Jesus Christ Amélie, you're like one of them already ... and how do you know it was pillow talk?"

"Your cheeks are still cherry red." They both laughed, breaking the tension. "We have two minutes, Lauren. Can you dial Mila directly on your mobile phone? I need to bluetooth link you now into the master console."

They walked over to a desk covered in screens and monitors with Hercules peering into a tangled mass of tiny wires, holding a device like a laser soldering iron, as he patched together some sort of intricate connecting cable.

"Hercules is very good with his hands," Amélie purred, as Lauren glanced again with a wry grin.

Hercules nodded and Lauren put her phone onto bluetooth. Amélie turned a couple of dials and a few ecstatic shouts later indicated they were linked. Lauren pondered. She hadn't used that number for so long, not since the Congo triplet birthing adventure, but her earthly thoughts were immediately disturbed as she felt Jack take her arm.

"Apollo is ready. Switch-on time. I love you Lauren, I always will, even if we end up a swirling mass of quarks and hadrons together."

She kissed his lips passionately, spying Amélie over his shoulder doing the same thing with Apollo. It was only then she realised the similarities of

Apollo's build and beard to Rufus. Nadine and Svet were standing on the other side with Hermione and Romulus alongside Hermione's advance guard of robot warriors, all armed and bristling to the teeth with weaponry. Nadine had really got into her stride. Charlotte, dressed in her element in a pair of tightly fitting Cassini engineer overalls, was still tightening the final connections to the outside power line with Juno and Persephone, but a thumbs up to Jack indicated they were ready to go.

Jack turned to Lauren. "I'll tell you when you can make that call." He took her hand and they both walked slowly to the master switch and checking his watch, without any further ado, he threw it across.

A loud bang and a continued crackle sounded loud from outside. She looked in complete amazement to see a huge lightning arc flashing continuously out of the clouds onto the thick spike on top of the specially built pylon, initiating the massive power surge necessary to kick-start the particle compression and provide the giant magnetic holding fields. The machinery feeding into the two large spheres began to hum louder as they shook in their rubberised holdings tied into the thick legs. Amélie and Apollo began to slowly turn dials in coordination and the frequency of the humming slowly increased until it was beyond their hearing and the laser pumps, in clusters near the bottom, suddenly shone a deep red. Amélie checked the chart print-outs, conferred with Apollo and he pressed a green and a yellow button. The spectrum of the lasers changed through from red to yellow, green then blue and violet before disappearing altogether into x-ray and gamma frequencies, although how they were all shielded from stray, lethal rays was a total mystery to Lauren. She looked over and Nadine was excitedly conferring with Hermione and adjusting dials on the weapons, something had inspired her.

The crackling had now stopped. There was merely a continuous lightning type stream of energy pouring down; in fact the whole room was getting quieter. Was this, Lauren reflected, the prelude to their own imminent 'big bang'? She thought immediately of the triplets, laughing and playing on the beach, her beautiful little girls, Magdalene, Eveline and Geraldine and tightened her grip on Jack's hand, waiting for instant vaporisation ...

All she heard was a whooping chorus of cheers and clapping from Apollo, Hercules and Amélie and Jack's voice shouting. "It's worked! We have incredibly created the very first black holes on Europa. Lauren, you must phone Mila now. Go into the soundproof booth near the door. Hercules will patch you into the wormhole. The signal will then be carried to Mila on our special infra-red channel that Charlotte helped to build."

She ran inside the booth, quietly shut the door and looked outside. Hercules was giving her another thumbs up at the console. She was almost praying that the special number still existed. After all, Mila was out of her security work and had been for years—this was a real long shot. She tapped over the application icon, which somebody had humorously named Sargasso and then dialled the number. There was a click and the number rang ... and continued to ring. Shit, Mila always used to answer that immediately. She let it ring on and on ... maybe?

"I absolutely knew one day you would ring this number, but not when I was sat on the loo. Okay Lauren, you're obviously in serious trouble, you know the drill. Explain carefully starting with where you are."

"Europa, Mila."

"Pardon? Where the fuck is that? I thought I knew most places, but that one beats me, I must be out of touch. It sounds like an airport."

"No, it's a moon."

There was silence for a few seconds. "Sorry Lauren, but I have to seriously ask. Not indulging in those Singapore Slings again are we? Now let's start once more, only slowly and coherently please."

"Mila, what I'm going to say is going to really test your sanity, but do you trust me? As much as you ever did? Because I'm going to need you to remain calm and very, very focussed. And deeper explanations will have to come later."

"It's supposed to be me saying that to you. Yes, of course, you know I do, and I still love you as much as ever too, I never stopped. Now, let's get on with it. Are you in immediate danger? Because wherever you are I need to get a move on and organised to reach you. I'm at home in horrible sweat pants perusing the latest Prada catalogue, Adrijana is at school and the great artist is away again in South America with his muse, fuck him."

"I'm with Amélie, Charlotte, Svet and Nadine, now outside this ... err ... telephone box."

"I know, supposedly at your girl's only retreat and having a great holiday. I hope to see you all in New York when you've finished."

"So do we, but we're not at the retreat, Mila, and we have a major problem. Okay, here goes, it's a long story ... Europa is one of the four large moons of Jupiter. We're three hundred and sixty five million miles away with an advanced alien colony called Arrhyans ... and Star Wars is about to break out big time between Europa and Io, another major moon orbiting nearby. Nadine and Hermione need your help urgently. You can't get here but you can direct and advise through my link, from your computer screen. We and the Arrhyans live inside virtual reality worlds which we create with our minds ... Right now I'm calling you from a Cassini workshop, which we created to connect to you in real-time."

There was a long pause and a silence. "I learned a long time ago, never to be surprised by you Lauren," Mila eventually said slowly. "And, you never let me down. So I'm going to first take a deep breath and accept all that you've said exactly at face value, unbelievable though it is. Who is Hermione?"

"She's a female robot and leader of the Europa warriors, our side. All warfare will be between female robots. The Io blobs can only assert their dominance through robots; and they have been training their own army up, on another moon."

"Io blobs?"

"The Arrhyan life form on Io. Essentially, huge masses of yellow interconnected and thinking liquid sulphur, who live deep underground. The Europans look like us, a genetic cousin to the blobs, both two billion years older than us so technologically far in advance, or we wouldn't be here."

"Abducted?"

"Yes."

"Okay, got it, so essentially, the horrible Io and nice Europa folk are going to slug it out using robots and I assume nobody is using standard military hardware?"

Lauren laughed. "No. This is where Nadine comes in ... she's developed their weaponry. Call them laser vaporisers."

"X-ray vaporisers now, I had a brainwave," a voice called out beside her. "Retuned to a frequency which will atomise their secret metal alloy shields and then vaporise them. Hermione sent out an advance party to spy on the other icy side of Adrastea. Their forces are amassing now ..." suddenly her watch flashed alternate blue and green. "Fuck, they're setting off. We've got to move."

"I heard that. Is Nadine with you there? I need to speak to her."

"Yes, I'm going to put you on in a second. There is a bit more. Hermione is more than any old robot. She's built as an exact clone of you, Mila ... don't ask ... with many of your attributes but not all, as well as her own, super technology abilities like the rest of them. But warfare hasn't happened here for billions of years. It's a concept long died out. They are relearning it, all of them, in a hurry. Hermione now needs, with your link, to become all of you, by directing her thoughts and actions. One more thing ... Jack is with me, he's the Europan leader."

There was a further pause. "You mean Professor Jackson Smythe, your Cassini Engineering Director?"

"Yes."

"Are you shagging aliens?"

"Yes?"

"And is it as good as they say on YouTube?"

"Better."

Mila roared laughing, her raucous deep belly cackle down the phone, which even Nadine could hear and smiled. "I might have known. So essentially I need to get to my sixty inch high definition 3D screen and gaming console in the drawing room that I've been using to play and teach computer games with Adrijana? You link me up, my avatar is Hermione, and then Nadine and I blast the sulphur blob robots to kingdom come. Got that. Err ... one key question. How the fuck do you lot get back here?"

"Yes, except she and Amélie will be there in the flesh so to speak. Jack, Charlotte, Svet and I will oversee the whole thing from our headquarters which we need to create. We have a plan to return home. I'm going to put you onto Nadine now. Good luck Mila."

"Amélie? A robot warrior? Bloody hell. I hope she's got something better in her belt than the equivalent of that ancient luger. Bit of a change for the Countess. Hey you take care because you have a party to celebrate at when you get back."

Lauren handed her phone to Nadine and left to confer with Jack. Her calculation, from what Hermione had said about the slow robot ion propulsion ship was they had about twenty hours before the first landing force arrives at Europa.

"Hey Nadine," Mila called out. "Sounds like old times. You've been your usual busy self?"

"Absolutely, although I must admit this assignment is somewhat unusual."

Mila roared laughing again. "You can say that again! I understand the plan. I'll leave the obvious myriad of why, when and how background questions till later and we stick to the task. Now, outline your strategy, and when is this lot going to kick off."

Nadine talked through what she had advised Hermione and her elite robot warriors, the weaponry and how it will work and the peculiar fighting environment where advanced technology will be used but that the fighters have no experience and little understanding of what they are doing. Mila tweaked some of the tactics and thinking but overall it was excellent—then again Nadine had always been her best student.

"I've also got a batch of laser guided and self propelled silver stars," Nadine added. "Built them last night, wow they are awesome."

"Great. Now Lauren talked about living within a created virtual reality world ... so will the warfare also be conducted the same way?"

"Yes, these are thought worlds, a little like in the film Inception, except these worlds on Europa are not dreams, they are real. You live and die in them. We have a strategic advantage with this ... because Jack and his colleagues can create the environment, and so now can the five of us. So when they land, we can create the setting where they land on. Lauren and I already learned how, although we're not as good as them yet. I suspect the sulphur blobs can do the same. The robots are so realistic you can't tell them from us and Jack and his Europa Arrhyans. They do all the fighting, but I intend to join in with Amélie and assist on the ground, like Special Forces. I've already taught Hermione and an elite group of her best ten robots. They learn extraordinarily quickly but they can't create the environments, only live and now fight in them.

"Right. That's good. Let's select an environment that you and I know how to fight in very well. Remember your first assignment, at the very beginning?"

"Chechnya? You mean like Grozny? Urban warfare, street by street? Mmm … yes I like that. Lauren said we have around twenty hours before their robots land. I can easily train up Hermione, her special forces and a squadron in that time. I have a virtual training ground prepared already."

"Agreed. Tomorrow is Saturday. Adrijana will be home … she's going to join me at playing a great game as far as she's concerned, and she'll watch Amélie's back. She is only six but really hot at computer games, very fast, beats me often. I'll watch your back as well as me, I mean Hermione. We need to match our console guns with your weapons. Can you do that?"

"No problem, email me your specification. Apollo has confirmed your real time link, which has been an incredible feat of science to create overnight. He thinks the transmission can be maintained for enough time, at least three days. It depends how long we can stay aligned to the Jupiter red spot. Hercules will do it tonight. Use Nadine at Arrhyan dot com. I'll call you when you need to switch on."

Mila chuckled. "You must be joking. Who the fuck are Apollo and Hercules? Do they look the part?"

Nadine laughed. "Absolutely. They're cool guys, the best of the Arrhyan technologists … and Amélie's lovers."

Mila roared until she coughed. "I'll give the old Countess her due. She doesn't waste time grabbing some fun wherever she lands! Right, I think we're ready to go. This warfare will be conducted at two levels. The robots and you on the battlefield, and Lauren, Jack and the Europa generals who need to counter the blob attempts at reconfiguring the virtual world."

"Yes, spot on, Mila. I need to find out how Jack and Lauren will try and avert any Io counter-thinking. At least you and I are far more adept on warfare and weapons tactics, but they will all learn very fast."

"So we don't want three days worth. We need a few hours and get the job surgically done and completed. If the Europans lose then what happens?"

"This Arrhyan colony exists inside reinforced spherical pods on the bottom of a hundred kilometre deep ocean. They will implode and vanish, and the five of us with it. Europa dies."

"And if you win and the blobs lose?"

"We come home?"

"Is that all?"

"No, but I'm thinking about that, one thing at a time."

"I understand, agreed," Mila replied, extremely anxious inside about all of them, but maintaining her routine and second nature discipline and confidence in Nadine's calm and measured capabilities. But no doubt this would be by far the riskiest and scariest assignment both of them had attempted. "I'm going to spend the night googling Jupiter and making some discreet enquiries about the latest clandestine US military developments on autonomous lethal weapons. They are robots which fight and make decisions on who dies unaided by humans. Crude, obviously, in comparison to your robots, but becoming very advanced here and will ultimately change the face of warfare. There may, I hope, be useful tactics to glean."

"Excellent. I bet Rosie would be very jealous if she knew what sort of fire-fight she's missing."

"I don't necessarily think so right now."

"How do you mean, Mila?"

"Nothing, we'll talk when you get back ... and I say *when* not *if*."

"Absolutely, contact you tomorrow, over and out."

Jack paced silently up and down the room in Lauren's office, now the designated war room. Early morning again and one of the robots entered with two cappuccinos and bowls of muesli, no sign of course of Eva— the clear limitations of the Europa reality system. "So explain again," he said to Lauren, wolfing down her muesli, yoghurt and fruit. "What is this urban warfare about and where was Nadine training Hermione?" He peered at his watch screen. "What—in Aleppo?"

"Yes, because the whole place resembles a Mad Max scenario, perfect for the tactics Nadine will show them. Mila reckons this sort of training normally takes three months but Nadine's done it with Hermione's team of crack defenders in five hours. Impressive speed of learning."

"That's because Hermione is special ..." He went quiet, which of course Lauren picked up instantly.

"Like Barbarella you mean, Jack?"

He looked back from nervously staring out of the window at her narrowed eyes. "No, of course not, I mean ... she adapts extremely quickly, faster than any robot we have created."

"Good. Now, how do you intend countering Io's attempts to thought-alter the reality settings, change the scene and gain tactical advantage?"

"Do you really think they would do that? I don't even think Io Arrhyans are capable of thinking such treachery."

It was then she realised, exactly how badly naive and unsure Jack was on Europa. On Earth, he seemed to act far more decisively; every step was confidently taken forward in a crisis, like when he dealt singlehandedly with Juliette becoming trapped in the fusion laboratory. Yet his love for her appeared unwavering, strong and he certainly listened better.

Watching his tortured expression, she suddenly wanted to hold him again, but not in her office and there was too much now to do. Time was indeed becoming critical and her support to him seemingly vital and crucial. The Europans had to maintain supremacy by every means possible. Thank heavens at least Mila was involved in a key role, even if in some disembodied spirit, giving her a renewed confidence of old. Odd too that Nadine had earlier mentioned Rosie. They had kept in touch by email since the triplets were born but contact was so sporadic. Rosie seemed constantly to be busy with China intelligence work and clandestine assignments and she hadn't seen her for two years and even then Rosie seemed distracted. She also wished Rosie was here.

"Jack, you talked about security shields blocking Barbarella's intrusive thinking. I know she's a robot, but could that process also be used to block any Io Arrhyan thoughts, ensuring our reality scene remains intact? And can you come and eat your breakfast please."

Jack stopped pacing and his face lit up for the first time all morning. "Great idea, I'll pass that onto Pete and the team of code experts right away. The shield relies on the embedding of a complicated mathematical algorithm to scramble thought waves into meaningless gibberish. Perhaps we can encrypt that procedure even more strongly. I've asked Juno to bring all the monitors we need into here as our headquarters, which will be re-sited and protected inside the fortified Presidential Palace in the centre of Grozny, as Nadine suggested. What's that sound?"

Lauren stopped downloading Hercules's special software to ensure Mila's console was patched into the network link. A wailing frequency, alternating between high and low had begun, increasing in intensity. Jack opened the window and it was unmistakable ... exactly the same as a World War Two air raid siren going off.

"Holy shit Lauren," Jack shouted. "They are twenty minutes away, that warning begins the countdown. They must have managed to speed up their ship to surprise us. We have to get Mila in, phone her. What time is it in New York?"

"Five thirty am, I'm trying." Thumping the phone screen buttons, she watched beads of sweat pouring down from his forehead, and he was shaking. Jack was terrified. His usual Earth confidence hadn't translated whatsoever into Europa emergency situations, particularly when the concept was almost incomprehensible to him, all out war. Her call was answered almost immediately.

"Good job I'm up already, still the early riser. For whatever reason, I assume things are happening aren't they?"

"Yes, we have nineteen minutes to the first landing assault." Svet and Charlotte had run in and she waved them to the console, pointing to the screen. Svet immediately understood and restarted the software.

"Patch me in now," Mila shouted. "Adrijana, get here immediately please, no you don't have to change out of your pyjamas, nobody is going to see you. Jacquita will bring your orange juice and our breakfast; we play, fire and eat at the same time. Right, sorry Lauren. We're ready to go but I can't get a fucking picture, only sound."

Lauren walked over to her console and peered over Svet's shoulder as Charlotte, quickly perusing Persephone's instructions, began connecting the many output cables into the reality mixer. "Fuck it Jack, the entry permission needs a twenty digit password," she shouted, her mind pouring over possibilities. "Jack, will you answer me?" She turned and saw him sat near the window, his head in his hands sobbing quietly.

"I can't cope with this anymore Lauren, I can do so many things, but I just don't know what to do in this situation. I'm fucking useless as a leader, I don't want us to die, Lauren, I love you ..."

"Mila, hang on, I've a problem here. Svet and Charlotte have just got you working except for this fucking password."

"I know, I heard. Listen, is it mathematical? If so, at least you're in with a chance. You'll have to take charge of HQ Lauren, immediately. Chairman and CEO mode is necessary now, alongside Svet and Charlotte. Sorry, but in this situation Jack will become a liability. Leave him where he is. Try and muster in his deputy Europans."

Watching the dynamic carefully, Charlotte had analysed the situation, immediately thinking of DG and what he would have done. She ran out to fetch Juno and Persephone. Apollo and Hercules and their teams were tied up with the technicals maintaining the essential plasma power and reality links to Jupiter. If Io cut that off they would all be finished.

Lauren ran to Jack. Sitting on her haunches, she put her arms around him tenderly. "No Jack," she whispered. "Listen to me; you're the only true leader Europa has ever had in a billion years. You're fantastic, and the progress made is down solely to you. Europa Arrhyans can finally find their true destiny. But leave this warfare part to us, just sit quietly for now. But I need you to think one more time. The password Jack, is it mathematical?"

He stared aimlessly out of the window then muttered. "The code is 'e' but you actually need the number to fifty decimal places, the highest encryption possible was put on automatically. I have no idea, my mind is dead."

"e? The natural logarithm?"

He nodded vacantly.

She ran back to the console and Svet looked up. "We're ready? Give me the password."

"We need 'e' to fifty decimal places. Shit, think Svet." Lauren tipped out her handbag over the floor, grabbing her usual power calculator, but which was only able to compute to ten decimal places.

Svet concentrated hard, drawing on her deep memory reserves of her undergraduate pure mathematics first year classes, which she had long moved on from. She began writing down a number of algebraic series to generate the number and switched the console to Pete's mathematical screen mode and began coding a programme in Ruby. "Pick the best series, Lauren."

Lauren ran over the choices and added a few more she recalled. "Programme this one, Svet. It's an old Gauss series from the eighteen hundreds, but very fast converging in an iterative calculation."

Svet maniacally pounded the keys like a dervish, ordered the information and finally pressed the enter key. Whatever the processor was, it was a billion times faster than any Earth supercomputer but the screen simply stuttered, flickered and outputted gibberish, before Lauren suddenly realised. "They use the quaternary system for calculations. Put a conversion to base ten in at the end."

Svet rattled over the keyboard again and 2.7182818 … filled up the screen instantly, to exactly fifty places. "Eureka!" Svet screamed as Lauren hugged her tightly. She copied and pasted the huge number carefully into the password box and bingo. Mila's smiling face lit up from her New York webcam, followed by a hearty wave and a 'hi everyone' from Adrijana.

Svet, Lauren and Charlotte studied the fifteen 3D screens set up by Persephone, exact matching banks of security monitors all moving from one scene to the next and showing rotating key positions around a war-torn scenario of Grozny, exactly as Nadine had ordered but devoid of people, animals, in fact any signs of life.

Persephone and Juno entered and immediately began calibrating and ordering the new visual screen information. Juno, the most senior Arrhyan below Jack and effectively his unsaid deputy, glanced across the room at him. He was lying flat out on the couch, his eyes closed.

"He's not well, Juno," Lauren whispered. "We'll have to run things. All of us here. We've got Mila linked now too."

"That's not possible, Europans don't get ill," Juno replied perplexed. "Sickness was genetically programmed out of our systems millions of years ago. I don't understand."

"I think Jack's exposure to Earth has made his system acquire some characteristics," Lauren replied tactfully. "Managing HQ will definitely be down to us."

"Men!" Juno growled exasperated, causing Charlotte and Svet to smirk.

"Right, we're cooking on gas down here," Mila shouted, twiddling the sound. "Patch me to Nadine and Hermione ... good ... wow that's some army behind you Nadine," she exclaimed. "I approve wholeheartedly."

Nadine and Hermione stood smiling together alongside twenty of her tall female Special Forces, all dressed in identical metallic coated, super-graphene purple suits and helmets, each armed from top to bottom with an array of laser guns. Mila, using her controller, moved further around to see masses of other blue-suited soldier robots, also armed, sitting in groups of six on open-topped SUVs, floating without wheels, motorised and guided by miniature versions of ion propulsion engines used on inter-moon spacecraft.

What looked like rocket launchers were piled up, except they fired tiny neutron bombs, to impart instant vaporisation of groups of robots or support machinery. Amélie too had been busy, helping to pile in the launchers. Her earthly expert armaments knowledge was not going to waste. She'd spotted plenty of plutonium in storage and the robots were not affected by radioactivity, so under her careful and precise direction, keeping well out of the way, the robots had assembled their warheads with ease.

Mila suddenly shouted out. "Nadine, think. Why have the enemy speeded up? To arrive earlier but I reckon to try and create their own landing area which would give them an immediate first fire advantage. We must override their tactic by setting a reality landing on our terms and disorientate them. Think quickly, we have three minutes. How would you ideally like your landing assault?"

Nadine instantly smirked. "I want the Battle of Culloden in 1746, when the Jacobite uprising of Scottish Highlanders and Stuart Pretenders to the English throne were instantly ambushed and wiped out by the English Redcoats. Two thousand Highlanders died in an hour. Hamish, sorry Dmitri, Hamish was his real name, in his better moods after drink kept me amused in that Murmansk prison with his vast knowledge of Scottish history. I visited the place afterwards with Roland. Flat, open and barren, beautifully exposed, just small shrubs and heather to hide in. They won't know where they are ... We surround their expected landing with this battalion here, take out as many as we can, then retreat into Grozny and continue face to face urban warfare, also on my terms."

Lauren listened and watched on the monitor. "Nadine, concentrate hard, create the scene exactly as you know how, Persephone has you linked. Do it now."

Charlotte turned some dials, and a new picture flashed onto the screen, of a barren, purple heather area, dark rugged mountains in the background. Mila reversed the scene and already Hermione and Nadine and her Special Forces were digging themselves into tiers of hidden gun-nests, alongside half a dozen soldier robots, behind the desolate outskirts of burned out and shelled buildings. Amélie could be seen at the boundary, alongside trucks filled with bomb launchers and more robots.

Mila zoomed in on Amélie looking at her watch screen. "I see you haven't fainted yet?"

Amélie grinned. "They must be desperate digging you out of retirement. Shouldn't you be at a party or something?"

Mila guffawed. "Old soldiers never die. You need to have snipers on the roof, preferably with some of those suitcase nukes on steroids, you've designed."

Amélie twiddled her watch again and Mila found herself on the main road in. "Look up Mila."

On each strategic vantage point were two robots, lying flat on their stomachs pointing down with launchers.

"Excellent, I'm impressed. My daughter Adrijana is a super-hot shot with a ray gun. I've taught her. She's your back up. You'll meet her shortly."

"I'm actually enjoying this. Well, let's face it, what else is there to do? I hope you admire the Versace design of the army suits. We can't have our female robot fighters looking anything but smart. They want a Europa Luddite here when this is all over."

Mila laughed again, and then a blinking on her screen changed her tone. "The first craft has landed. I'm off, good luck Amélie."

"You too, see you at that party."

Mila grimaced. She knew what everyone faced was going to be extraordinarily difficult. In an instant she was alongside Nadine and Hermione, who also had computer tracking watches on, peering at the first Io robots disembarking from a large saucer shaped craft on the ground in the middle of nowhere. They were obviously disorientated as predicted. Nadine's strategy had worked, but the Io robots were rapidly disciplining themselves and forming into fighting groups of twenty, like Roman Legion warriors without the shields, an ancient combat role model gleaned from somewhere. This was Mila's first close up of Hermione, and looking at her made her skin crawl. It was like watching herself in a film. Hermione was an identical twin, done up in that purple suit.

"Mila, concentrate hard on Hermione," Nadine whispered into her watch screen, analysing with concern the numbers of Io robots increasing dramatically, far more than estimated. Their secret moon manufacturing plant had been working overtime. Two more identical craft now landed behind the first one and the same was happening as they began pouring out. There were hundreds of them. Her Europa robot fighters were heavily outnumbered.

Adrijana suddenly split their screen in two, and using her controller, brought up Amélie, now lying with ten others behind a thick barrage of bricks and old concrete blocks at the only entrance into town from the Culloden reality setting outside.

"Mama, I'm tuned in now to my fighter. I'll take care of her whilst you help Aunt Nadine."

"That's Amélie. Adi say hello, she's expecting you."

"Hi Amélie, I'm Adrijana, I'm your back-up. When do we start?"

Amélie looked with amazement into her watch, very disconcerted that her back-up was only six years old, but she was a hugely pretty little girl, exactly like Mila in miniature. But then she instantly rationalised, remembering that for Adrijana, she was playing a computer game and would be fast. "Very soon Adrijana. Hey, my English twin daughters are the same age as you."

"Wow, that's cool. Sure hope to meet them soon when we're done with this turkey shoot."

Amélie smiled. Adrijana's Bronx accent was as far away from Mila's staccato Serbian English as they were from Earth. "I hope so too, Adrijana. You will have a much bigger picture of what's going on so you need to shout to me what to do."

"I know, that'll be a cinch, no bother," Adrijana drawled back in her distinctive twang.

Mila returned to concentrating on Hermione, when a short flash of light across her eyes caused her to blink. Immediately she focussed again, she was lying next to a smiling Nadine, staring directly at the robot legions still assembling. No Hermione, but then she realised being clad in a strange, purple combat suit and a helmet which had no weight whatsoever. She had become Hermione, they had seamlessly merged. Holy hell.

"Mila, welcome to the battlefield," Nadine whispered. "Look at your watch."

Mila saw herself in the screen at the console next to Adrijana.

"At the moment you and Hermione are combined," Nadine continued. "She has just ingested your combat skills and other thoughts pertinent for the moment. They are stored and will be used as required in her next confrontation, so she unforgettably learns at each event. Touch your watch and you return to the console to back you and her up. You need to assess immediately when you need to be on the ground as Hermione and the actions you will take, then when you return she combines you and her together to do it, with you backing her up remotely. She has some of your fighting skills but not sufficient yet. Remember too these guys, on both sides, have no concept of killing each other until now."

"My word Nadine that is so powerful. Me fighting and backing me up simultaneously? How do you know whether I'm me or Hermione?"

"Your bright red lipstick. Hermione hasn't learned about your makeup peccadilloes—yet," Nadine replied with a grin. "But she does sex well so far."

"I won't ask. Shit Nadine, look over at that last craft. They've got World War Two tanks rolling out, but those peculiar barrels?"

"Barbarella the spy. She's undoubtedly been relaying Jack's inner thoughts as we feared to her Io masters. Jack is obviously some kind of military history hobbyist back on Earth. This is going to start weird for us with normal expectations of combat—gradually the scenes will evolve as they all learn."

Mila pulled out her binoculars. "Gosh these glasses are clear?"

"They're X-ray—not visible light or infra-red."

"The troops are all out and assembling into Roman Legion style groups, six with around eighty robot warriors each at the rear and ten smaller ones of around thirty, spreading out in a strategic formation. They're using the tanks like cavalry, ready to go. We're hugely outnumbered," Mila grunted.

"We only have a few launchers out here too. Amélie has most of them, up on the roof and main streets."

"This has to be it. Use the best launchers and destroy the craft, then they have no escape mechanism to return to base. Simultaneously, destroy as many tanks and groups as you can, then pick them off individually in the pandemonium that ensues. They're not expecting you. Only retreat when you have to, back into Grozny for the next phase. Now, Nadine. Go."

Nadine turned and Hermione had loaded her launcher, coordinated with her Special Force commanders and fired. A green ray zapped across the landscape and the first craft vaporised with a bang and a cloud of dust. The Io robots, startled, all turned, the tanks started rolling forward, to be met immediately by a great cross firing of zapping rays, whizzing everywhere. Three tanks disappeared and another craft, but they missed the third one. Standing behind the tanks as a shield, the Io robots returned fire with their own vaporising laser guns. Then the tanks fired shells, which landed around them but didn't explode.

Pandemonium was already resulting as robots became confused on both sides, with smoke and steam creating a great pall of fog over the landscape. After half a minute, Nadine looked around. Hermione was stood up, pumping her laser gun like a maniac, as if she was in a sci-fi film. Nadine pulled her down. "No, Hermione, keep flat, you're a sitting duck doing that." Nadine adjusted her watch screen. Mila was clearly back behind her console.

"I can only take out individual robots with my console, those tanks and craft are impenetrable," Mila shouted, "but Adrijana and I have got a number of them already. We need Amélie to take out that third craft, some robots are heading back into it already, for reinforcements probably."

Nadine switched into Amélie. "How good is your long distance? That third craft has to go using a launcher, the rear unit of eighty are already climbing back in," she shouted loudly, bright green rays whizzing all around, the noise like she imagined an eighteenth century battlefield would have been like, with screaming and shouting as numerous robots were half vaporised and wriggling around on the ground.

"Just watch," Amélie replied, as Nadine spied her through her binoculars from a roof, carefully aiming a large shoulder rocket launcher on her shoulder and then Amélie fired. The third craft disappeared with a huge explosion taking half of the robots clambering in with it.

Mila came back in. "You've lost some commanders, our foot soldiers are running around aimlessly not knowing what to do and the Io robot Special Forces behind the tanks are picking them off, vaporising them. The enemy are learning fast. Shit, some of our guys are just walking forward then keeling over flat on their faces. Apart from vaporising, how else do robots die?"

"Only by their chemical energy being shut down, normally impossible here," Nadine replied.

Amélie returned in through their watch consoles. "I can see those landed shells. There's some sort of smoke and gas quietly emerging from them, I'm certain that is affecting the robots near the shells. Our soldiers are keeling over but not theirs. Hermione, what is the most deadly gas to affect your chemical system?"

"Only ... oh fuck ..." Hermione responded loudly. A bleeper was sounding on her other arm. "It's oxygen in a mixed ozone form, a very rare gas here, but it causes our robot chemical digestion to oxidise up in a hugely accelerated fashion, like aging in a micro-second. We digest ourselves and die instantly. The bastards on Io, they must have come up with and engineered it in beforehand. That's what's happening. We have to retreat into Grozny ... to urban warfare. Now. They must have ozone resistant suits on." Hermione gave the order.

Fighting a rearguard action, her robots rapidly fell back down the main road, melting into their agreed group formations where possible, into the ruined buildings and side streets. One more tank blew apart. Adrijana, in a chance screen position had managed to fire a console ray blast exactly down the barrel, their obvious one non-armoured weak point. Hermione had lost half the Europa robots, but the number lost on the Io side was more than ten times as many. That part of Nadine's strategy had worked. Each side had become about equal in number, but the Io robots still had fifteen tanks providing cover, which rumbled into the main street, guarding their own robots behind. By now Hermione, Nadine and her soldiers had vanished like ghosts into the urban woodwork. Silence suddenly prevailed and the tanks stopped. Obviously they had no idea again of the landscape or where to fire their ozone shells.

Mila adjusted her console screen. Adrijana shouted out immediately. "Mama, we can't shoot the tanks. Amélie has to destroy them from the roof tops. Already the game is getting harder, our opponents are learning fast. This is fun, quite a different challenge."

Mila looked at her daughter. If only Adrijana really knew. Mila barked an order to Amélie to take out the tanks.

In an instant the firing began again from the roof tops as a volley of launchers were aimed directly at the tanks, who responded by firing ozone shells onto the roof tops. But within half a minute, amid the huge explosions and more screaming, robots toppling off roofs and mangled up arms, legs and other bits visible in the main street, the smoke cleared and only two tanks were left, all the rocket launchers had been fired. Amélie took aim. She had lost her robot team around her, all lying immobile and prostrate on the roof to an oxygen shell, but she of course, being human, was immune, just a faint whiff of pungent ozone perceivable but not enough to affect her whatsoever. She saw the Io commanders on the ground point with incredulity, as she stood high, aimed again and the first of the two tanks vanished in a cloud of smoke as the Io fighters all dived everywhere on the ground for cover. Amélie inserted her last nuclear launcher shell, but the mechanism jammed. Immediately a blast of rays zipped past, she felt her stomach hot and dived to the ground. Her suit was smouldering but it had saved her, just a light scorch mark, but not too painful. She had to join Nadine now and Hermione.

The lone tank, unhindered now, began rotating its turret firing more rounds of oxygen shells onto the roofs of buildings. More robot snipers began to topple off.

Nadine turned to Hermione, saw the red lipstick and Mila was off like a rocket. On the way she picked up a canister of something from the store. Heading down the side streets with a small ray gun, using her instinctive combat training to advance corner by corner, she double-handedly picked off five stray Io robots, one by one, all unaware and flustered by Mila's type of attack, speed and agility. Finally, pulling off her laser Kalashnikov from her back, she raced headlong towards her target, the rear of the one remaining tank, still firing deadly oxygen shells. Peppering her advance with a wide burst of spray, she scattered the Io robot rearguard. Six Io Special Forces, coordinating and guarding, saw her and approached, fanning out, but Mila, using all her martial arts and her large trusty knife, aimed at the poor seam weld on their necks, kicked, head butted and disabled one after the other in a flurry of flailing limbs, a trail of decapitated forms, wriggling on the ground like giant maggots. Leaping up the side, she tore open the hatch and threw in the canister, racing off again, ducking and diving into the backstreet dusty shadows, retaliatory laser rays bouncing off the walls. They were too slow. Soon she was alongside Nadine as a huge explosion rocked the main street causing various buildings to collapse. Peering through the smoke, the remains of the tank, still on tracks of tungsten, ran around in ever decreasing circles then stopped. Pandemonium again ensured as the remaining Io robots began to regroup in small units to take on the hand to hand street fighting.

"For an oldie, you sure can still run Mila. That was impressive. Do you like the mood music? Our robots love it," Amélie's distinctive voice crackled over the radio, with the sound of the Dam Busters playing in the background.

"If you got to the gym a bit more, you too could have a body like mine," Mila retorted playfully. "Great tip—that worked a treat. I admit your chemistry is still much better than Lauren's."

Lauren suddenly appeared on their watches. "What chemistry?"

"A little tip from Romulus," Amélie continued. "He surmised that the Io robots had changed their chemical synthesis to resist oxygen, using reservoirs of nitric acid. Sadly somebody forgot that it doesn't mix well with hydrogen sulphide. There was a store of canisters here, they use for making heavy water. Nice one Mila."

Mila smiled. "Okay everyone listen up. Lauren, your information stream has been invaluable. It's down to hand to hand fighting now, street corner by street corner. Their game plan will be to capture and eliminate your headquarters, Lauren and vaporise Jack. We have the advantage for the moment on this. Numbers are even and those fucking tanks are gone, but these guys learn extraordinarily fast. The best of them will be using my combat techniques already. Amélie, can you make your way to headquarters and join Lauren. Nadine and Hermione will be doing the same. Our top commanders will lead the street fighting. I'm just afraid of any stray Io robots that manage to get through the defences. I'm off, need to survey the bigger picture at the console."

Nadine turned to Mila, lipstick was gone, and in place was Hermione, bristling with weapons, her brain already imbued fully with Mila's advanced combat and ready to go, her expression ominous. "We go, Nadine, those Io fuckers, they die, one by one."

Nadine laughed, now that was more like her language. She slapped her new friend on the back and they sprinted into the shadows.

"Mama, was that really you fighting on that tank? It sure was kinda awesome. Can you teach me to do all those moves please?" Adrijana burbled, wide eyed, alongside her mother.

"In good time darling. Now, I know it's difficult in these streets, but do your best please to protect Amélie as she heads back to base."

"On it," Adrijana replied, concentrating hard, both hands gripping the console tightly as she followed Amélie's team through the rubble of wrecked houses and streets. "Got one hiding behind a burned out car ... What's an Io fucker, Mama?"

"Never mind, grown-up talk. You're doing a great job, baby, keep at it. Damn why is this screen flickering? Lauren, we've got a bit of a juddery reception here, is there a problem?"

Mila tuned in her side console into Lauren's office area to see Svet and Charlotte, with Apollo and Hercules, their heads inside a large electronic cabinet the whole length of a wall, pulling and pushing on wires with laser soldering irons.

"We're facing some power discontinuity," Lauren shouted back. "Europa's orbit is nearing the edge of the Jupiter red spot and the Io Arrhyans have been attempting to divert our plasma link back into Io. Apollo has come up with a temporary supplement, via another gas band around the planet pole, we're aligned to presently, but it's much weaker than we need to power both the black holes and our own infrastructure on its own. We've got much less time that we thought."

"On it. Nadine, get the commanders to raid all those H2S canister dumps. Hermione will now have the assault tactic in her brain, you know it well. Use them as grenades and destroy nests of Io robots, hiding in buildings. I'll guide you, I can see three groups ahead already, they're marginally slow and confused still, but you won't have long before they begin to counter the same. Adrijana is following Amélie to join you."

"Mama, I can see the headquarters ahead. Amélie is standing alone near the entrance, but there are four robots approaching in bright green suits, one is pulling a great long tube thing. I can't get them. They've pulled up a transparent screen. My gun is just bouncing off."

Mila stared at the scene. "Hell, four Io Special Forces commanders. They're approaching from the west side, they must have managed to get through our defence lines. I knew the bastards were learning fast. Lauren, can you hear me?"

"Yes, struggling with the power link still. Why?"

"Pull up your outside cameras, west wing, a few degrees south. You have potential intruders. I'm coming back."

Lauren ran to the console, twiddled and saw the four tall green-suited robots, all with long blond hair, their helmets discarded for some reason. "Jack, for fuck's sake wake up will you."

He stirred from the couch, drowsy, and opened his eyes. "Sorry Lauren, I'm so sorry, my brain shut down with the stress. Is it all over now?"

"Never mind that, get here, now," she shouted. "Who are those Io Amazons and what are they dragging towards the entrance? Oh my God and there's Amélie, do something will you?"

Apollo turned around sharply hearing Amélie's name.

Jack's expression dissolved into abject fear. "No, I can't, I don't know how. Oh fuck—I don't believe it. They've recreated the rogue Barbarella clones. They're not all robot, frozen genes from Mars have been used. I would never have believed anyone could do that. They are now part original Arrhyan warriors, invincible, no ... oh no, they've got a portable tube, we're done for."

"Just do something Jack," she screamed.

"They're coming for me, I have to escape," he screamed hysterically, his eyes popping with fear and despair. Suddenly he turned and ran through the end door.

She watched him disappear in disbelief then turned to see Apollo, a large metal bar in his hand, running towards the other exit.

"We lost power a minute ago, but I'll get it back," Hercules shouted over. "Svet, come here quick and hold this germanium power capacitor whilst I solder it ... old technology but it still works. Charlotte, point that directional antenna towards Saturn, use the sky map on the yellow screen and find Titan." They watched Apollo tearing madly out of the door. "He loves Amélie," Hercules whispered. "He said he'd die to protect her."

Lauren stood silently, dismayed. Wasn't Jack supposed to love her? Why had he turned into a futile piece of alien imbecility? Then everything around her suddenly went woozy, the room was spinning like crazy. There was a sweet, sickly smell in the room and she felt her legs buckling beneath her, but somebody had picked her up before she fell. Jack had come back, he was saving her after all. "Jack I love you ..." she muttered before her brain went into oblivion ...

And Mila and Adrijana stared at a blank screen ...

Chapter Eighteen

Svet opened her eyes wide to see Charlotte bending over her, muttering something indiscernible with a deep, echoing voice but smiling and holding a glass of water. Nadine was standing behind, her face drawn with concern. The power was back on. Hercules and his team were behind their consoles, pushing and pulling at buttons and dials. Amélie was sat on the floor, her back against the wall with her knees up to her chin, dishevelled and also recovering from something. Apollo was stroking her hair carefully and handing over a mug of tea. For a moment she couldn't remember where she was ... it must be a dream, then her mind fired up ... no dream ... this was her reality.

At the far end Hermione and a clutch of her commander robots were huddled around a table with Jack, all conferring in a babble of intense noise and pouring over more screens alongside a bunch of large old paper charts. But where was Lauren? Svet took the glass and drank down the welcome cold contents, which revived her system back into gear. She was sat upright, also on the floor and her head hurt. She felt a large bump at the back where she must have hit herself against something. What on earth had happened?

With a helping hand from Charlotte, Svet levered herself up. The screen on the ceiling showed Hermione's soldier robots strolling around their zones in clear jubilation. But Lauren was still nowhere to be seen; perhaps she was in an adjoining room or the toilet. "What happened?" she croaked, her throat still throbbing with a burning sensation and a bad taste inside her mouth.

"That fucking whore Barbarella. I wish I'd got here a minute earlier and I would have cut out her energy pack and jumped on her head myself, but at least we've won for now anyway," Hermione grunted from her table, wiping a knife blade lovingly on the curtains.

Amélie sauntered over to join Charlotte. Their worried expression could not be disguised as she commenced an explanation to Svet. "Four elite Io robots managed to infiltrate our defences around the headquarters and got inside here. The rest of the enemy have finally been eliminated around the Grozny ruins. They lost over five hundred robots, our casualties numbered over sixty so we still lost half our women-power."

"But where's Lauren?"

Tears began to trickle down Charlotte's cheek. "We're not sure. They've taken her. That's what Hermione and Jack are trying to work out now. Amélie, you explain what happened." Charlotte sat down, choked and visibly upset. "It's like Vaag and Murmansk all over again only worse."

"I was outside," Amélie began, "about to enter the compound when I was grabbed from behind by two Io robots. Barbarella strode up, hissed in my face and insisted I was coming with them, once they got hold of Lauren. I tried to shout but then everything went dizzy and I blacked out."

"Same as us," Svet replied. "What did they do?"

"Chloroform," a deep voice cried out from behind the cabinet. Apollo walked over. "The compound does occur naturally on Io in parts, especially in volcanic vents. It doesn't affect us but somebody on Io found out that chloroform acts as an anaesthetic on humans. Fortunately they released a measured dose, enough to knock you out but no damage caused. In the confusion they dragged out Lauren unconscious and shoved her into a pod and then they all vanished. But after decapitating one robot with my iron bar I managed to grab Amélie first over my shoulder and got her inside."

Nadine strode across to Hermione and Jack. "So where is she, Jack? Have you no idea whatsoever? I presume, surely, they've taken her to Io as some sort of hostage."

"No, they can't because the whole environment there is completely inhospitable except for the Io Arrhyans. She may be on the robot moon Adrastea, but I doubt that too because the robots don't have the knowledge to build a Europa type environment compatible with your life-form. I have no idea. This is a disaster."

Nadine was becoming hugely irritated, her body stance had turned aggressive and her face uncompromising. Svet had seen Nadine before like that in Murmansk when Dmitri's head removal and ending followed immediately afterwards. She stepped back and the whole room went quiet apart from the humming of the machinery. Hercules ignored everything, he was still trying to restore power to the black holes and reconnect Mila.

"So far Jack your actions have conveniently been next to useless since this invasion started, especially for Lauren," Nadine growled her tone clearly harsh and threatening. "Thanks independently to Mila and Hermione, we've saved your colony. Have you got another agenda in mind? Something, Jack, you're not telling us? One way to find out." She pulled out a large knife from her belt.

Jack eyes widened in abject fear as he stepped back, stumbling over a large cable. He was now well aware of Nadine's capabilities, never having trusted her from the beginning.

But instantly Hermione stepped inbetween and put up her arms "No Nadine, this is not the way. If Jack says he doesn't know, then he doesn't know. Don't force me to fight you, it's the last thing I want to do but I'll have no choice. I have to protect Jack first and foremost, that's my duty ..."

Nadine stopped. The atmosphere was as tense and electric as anyone could imagine; one could hear a pin drop. She stared deeply into Hermione's eyes, looked across at Jack and immediately realised. Something that should have been obvious from the moment Hermione emerged for their first presentation on day one.

She changed tack; the last thing of any benefit to them all was internal warfare breaking out. That would be the obvious comment which Mila would be barking right then. "You're right Hermione, I'm sorry Jack. Heat of the battle moment. I suggest we all confer together on those charts and try again ... Wait Jack, what's that flashing on your belt?"

Everyone else turned to stare at Jack, whose intricate, fancy belt buckle, a form of violet glass substance, began to emanate a series of coloured flashes, in a sequence which depicted a code was being transmitted. Hermione gasped. "Oh fuck, Jack ... this says Project Torus Sky ... is alive and well."

Jack's strained face whitened even further. Angrily he tore off the belt, threw it across the room and the glass buckle smashed into tiny pieces. Juno, Persephone and now Apollo and the rest of the robot team were quietly puzzled.

Juno, whose body language was clearly hostile to both Jack and Hermione, spoke up first, her tone dismissive and harsh. "Obviously you and your personal robot have an intimate knowledge of this Project Torus Sky. I think the rest of us need to know, fast, and what it has to do with Lauren. Out with it Jack, now."

After a silence Jack resumed, holding his head in his hands again muttering something inaudible. He pulled himself together and slowly began. "Project Torus Sky was a highly secret initiative, conceptualised by Scarletta to form a new base colony populated by a small elite group of Io robots."

"Scarletta? Who or what is Scarletta?" Nadine immediately asked. Charlotte, Svet and Amélie were now standing together with Juno and Persephone. Apollo and Hercules had quietly resumed their engineering work, they were struggling hard with the power still.

"Scarletta is the largest mass of thinking sulphur on Io by far, so by logical definition, is the most powerful brain and has now assumed the role of leader. Scarletta grows continually through being situated next to a massive volcanic vent which spews sulphur dioxide, which he converts to sulphur through harnessing plasma blasting," Juno replied.

"He?" Amélie interjected in disbelief.

Jack continued quietly. "Scarletta has taken a male mantle upon himself, the first Io Arrhyan to do so for billions of years. Thus he has an identity, a more human form to project his will against me. Scarletta and I have opposed each other for many, many years. Project Torus Sky brought the conflict to a head, two hundred years ago."

Amélie turned to Charlotte, Svet and Nadine. "Clearly, the Vaag of Io emerges finally in the grand scheme of things. Interesting isn't it that such base characteristics of earthly human nature, like power, evil and domination have permeated this civilisation too, even with a different life form altogether. Should we be surprised? Absolutely not."

Jack pondered that bit of philosophy and sighed. "That is why we on Europa decided to escape and start again."

"By colonising Earth headlong and fuck the residents you mean?" Amélie retorted, her face reddening.

Jack ignored her. "Torus Sky was intended to build an alternative colony, transport humans down from Earth en masse, millions of them, withdrew their brains and collect together a massive new knowledgebase. Once emptied of all humans, and I mean every man, woman and child, then colonisation to Earth would begin. Europa would take the land masses and Io would invade the ocean depths and rebuild its own colony inside volcanic ocean vents which lead deep inside the mantle of the Earth's crust, an ideal environment to procreate. But Europa and Io Arrhyans need each other to do that successfully. I opposed it, on the grounds that the knowledge base in the early eighteen hundreds was too scientifically naive ...

"Except finally our Earth scientific knowledge and technology is becoming acceptable, at least to you Jack, isn't it. Hence the timing to do a sole Europa runner to Earth now and hence Scarletta's reaction to stop you," Amélie continued, dismayed she had missed the early nuances too late. Her distrust of Jack had been correct.

"So really we, the five of us transported here, are merely disposable pawns in a complex interplay of internecine Arrhyan warfare, plots and ultimately who between Io and Europa has mastery of Earth to save their own skins." Nadine uttered in disdain. "So why do they need Lauren?"

"No Nadine, that isn't why you are here. We are not Io Arrhyians. What Hermione and I said at the beginning is totally correct. I genuinely want a harmonious, peaceful and formidable integration ... Europa and Earth, joined up forces, science and technology with culture, especially now I've discovered the glue to make it work, love. They want Lauren because she is a prize specimen, a highly advanced Earth life form with a formidable intelligence and knowledge of technology. And Barbarella wants personal revenge. They will be sucking her brains out right at this moment to impart the crucial Earth knowledge into their own robots. I have to find her."

"That's so sweet," Amélie intervened sarcastically. "But the truth of the matter is Io doesn't need you any longer Jack. Scarletta and his morass of blobs and robots can undertake the invasion on their own. Correct?"

Jack shuddered, crestfallen.

"Wait a minute," Charlotte shouted, pointing to the screen. "That monitor is flashing in the same sequence as the belt did ... Juno, can you tune it in?"

Chapter Nineteen

Peering tentatively upwards, the sheer scale and breathtaking beauty of the stark and peaceful environment around her was breathtaking. She was lying on a long couch, similar to the one she woke up onto when they originally landed. Her head was pounding and a horrible taste ran around her mouth making her want to spit, but she couldn't move her limbs, only her head. Something was holding her to the couch, but there no straps ... a force field of some kind, likely magnetic.

She gazed upwards and then side to side. She was inside a massive and transparent dome structure, oddly geometric, realising after a moment it was fashioned in the shape of a dodecahedron, made of some kind of glass or clear plastic. A batch of seven screens stood nearby on flexible stalks from out of the white floor, flickering but not showing any picture or emitting a sound. On the other side was an array of complex machinery, humming slightly with thick feeder cables running off insulators sunk directly into the floor. Outside the dome she could see the same cables snaking into the distance on some kind of giant pylons, obviously a power source, probably similar to what they had been using before.

But the most impressive was the staggering view around. The sky was pitch black, stars of various sizes and colours clearly visible in the background but not in any constellation shapes she recognised. But everywhere was eerily lit up by the reflected light from Jupiter, its giant red spot unmistakable, clearly sitting high up and dominant in the sky in front of her like a giant moon, at least ten times bigger in diameter than the Earth's moon. Then unmistakably, as she looked on each side of Jupiter, she saw two smaller circular objects also reflecting light, one more prominent than the other, clearly moons but which ones? One was distinctly dull and yellow in appearance but the other much brighter, very reflective indeed. Very thin wires ran up the sides of the dome, for what reason she could only speculate, perhaps sophisticated antennas.

Outside she could see a dark, reddish ground nearby overlain with chunks of white ice in pockets around a myriad of various sized boulders and rocks. In the reflected light from Jupiter, all around looked like a stunning night scene in the American desert. Sharp and rugged mountains, in all kinds of spectacular reds, browns and yellows, rose up high in the distance, also covered in great crevices of ice but to the left the ground extended flat for some distance with a huge array of craters visible, some deeply inlaid inside other craters. In fact, as she took in as large a panoramic view as she could, magnetically strapped to this awful couch, she realised the dome may well be inside a huge crater itself. But along the flatter ground, a small number of interconnected pipes were sticking up out of the ground. Definitely what looked like steam and liquid water could be seen dripping, then forming small heaps of icy white solid underneath, as whatever it was froze instantly ... more than likely it was gaseous, possibly methane, depending on the cold severity of the outside temperature.

Where on Europa was she? Her mind began calculating hard. Europa had a surface of solid ice; this area was very mixed and rocky. There were two moons visible. Io was covered in sulphur, and so the yellow hued moon was likely to be Io. She remembered that the orbital speed of Io around Jupiter was fast. Using her experimental eye, she noted the gap between each of the two moons and a vertical antenna wire, counted a full minute and perceived a visible small shift. A rough calculation in her head revealed that the yellow moon was travelling exactly twice as fast as the white moon. Her conclusion was immediate. She recalled the tidal facing eccentricities of the largest moons of Jupiter, or should she say three of them. She definitely wasn't on Europa, because she was looking at it and Io. And by the size of their disc in the sky, she estimated their inclinations to the ground, and knowing their diameters, calculated backwards how far she must be from each one ...

"So Lauren, we can see from your expression your formidable brain is nicely active. Guessed where we are?"

She looked to her right and five stunning women had walked in. Immediately she recognised Barbarella. They were all robots. One had wheeled in a trolley with lots of tubes and an array of medical type mechanical drills, cutters and laser knives, on their own flexible drive shafts. They were wearing individualised, brightly coloured suits of a material that looked more like leather. They could have been fashionable molls of Hells Angel bikers, certainly their jackets and trousers looked very nice. She jerked her mind back to reality, this wasn't a fashion show. She had been drugged and abducted. Barbarella's face was the last thing she remembered in Cassini, their headquarters, before blacking out. They had clearly got past Hermione's defences.

The weird dentist's chair however made her feel very nervous. Suddenly she could move and Barbarella indicated for her to join them at what looked like a dining table and six chairs, exactly the same as she had in her own villa. Swinging her legs off the couch, she realised she too was dressed in a similar suit but all black. The trousers even had a zip but which was half way down and she pulled it up fully before walking across to a vacant seat.

"It can only be Ganymede."

"Well done. We're impressed as ever. But what you see on Ganymede, the largest moon in the solar system, is what you get, unlike Europa. You view everything on the surface in its stark, beautiful and unreformed normality. No virtual and artificial worlds here, but of course there aren't any on Earth either. None of us like virtual reality. Isn't the scenery simply wonderful? This moon even has its own magnetic field from which in conjunction with Jupiter we have harnessed our power. Gravity inside the protective dome is the same as Earth, a trivial matter accretion exercise and you may notice you are breathing normally, an Earth like atmosphere minus the rare gases but who misses them? We too need to get used to a breathing process which duels with our chemical energy absorption. Underneath us, deep below the crust, lies a vast ocean bigger than on Europa and providing the oxygen we are all happily ingesting. We're genetically different here, half robot and half Arrhyan, like the original Mars pioneers who fled to Phobos."

Lauren pondered hard, whilst taking in every piece of information analytically, lodging these incredible facts inside her mind. "Yes, Ganymede is quite stunning, I like your outfits."

They all giggled. She hadn't seen robots do that. They were exhibiting very earth-like female characteristics all of a sudden. "Good. Now my apologies Lauren," Barbarella began again, pointing down to her zip. "I could see you noticed. We were asked before you woke up to show you off to our leader, in all your unencumbered naked glory and I know intimately just how beautiful and desirable your body is of course. He wanted to know what Jack was getting uncharacteristically worked up over."

Lauren felt an icy chill, the thought made her go quite cold and sick. "Your leader is a male robot?"

"Ah, I'm afraid another of Jack's secrets he never got round to sharing with you. I mean our Io leader. Like Jack only far more clever. There he is."

Barbarella pointed to a metal cabinet behind the screens, on top of which was a large glass bell-jar. Inside was a writhing yellow liquid mass, a blob of something not dissimilar to a brain but with wires attached. "To be anatomically correct, that is a miniscule piece of our President. He actually covers about fifteen square miles now. He lives near a large volcano on Io, which your astronomers quaintly named Pele after some Hawaiian volcanic Goddess. How bizarre. But there are enough sulphur cells in that jar for him to command and review our work directly here and communicate everything back to himself on Io. That little piece is more powerful than a hundred thousand amalgamated human brains."

"What exactly *is* your work, Barbarella?"

"We're building a new Io colony, Lauren. We have three bases already and around a thousand robots, ready to return."

"Return?"

"To Europa. Of course you won't have heard. The bitch Hermione and your friend ... that harridan Nadine. A minor setback, but I have to give them some credit. We should have overrun your rag-tag army but we were outflanked completely by far superior warfare tactics. But we learn very fast Lauren. And we'll be back, better, stronger and fully disciplined.

Then we move onwards to our next home—your Earth. However, to start with I have a preparatory job."

She beckoned for the dentist chair which was moved forward.

"You're our guinea pig, Lauren. The very first Earth pioneer. I promise it won't hurt; we use marvellous magnetic field local anaesthesia. I'll drill a tiny hole in your skull; we extract your brain wholesale and then drain out all your knowledge into our new databank."

Lauren felt that familiar icy chill run headlong from top to bottom. She slowly stood up looking where to run, anywhere, the whole situation was incomprehensibly hideous. Seeing a door at the far side, she made a break towards it when something ran out and barred her way, barking. A large robotic dog came from nowhere, all shiny and metallic but built crudely, very like the efforts of Bhavika and the robotics team in Cassini.

"Lauren ... meet Buster. He's very much initial work in progress. We don't have animals and pets here but I know from Jack about such things. We stole a swipe of Jack's mind database on you and your pet and Buster came up. Hope he's a good likeness. It's very rude to walk off before I've finished."

Lauren stopped; she had to stay calm and think very hard and clearly, not miss any moment of insight. There had to be some way out of this nightmare. She stared at Barbarella who continued softly.

"I'm sorry but we then, after brain removal, dissect you into individual pieces, all your organs, limbs, everything for minute observation on the lab bench and detailed analysis. The good news is you'll stay alive and scientifically participate, that's a vital part of the experiment and fun. All your pieces will be joined up with rhodium fibre infra-red carriers, but obviously you won't be going anywhere after that. Following your experimentation, we will bring your four colleagues across here for a repeat examination and then we should be primed up with human body knowledge for cloning before a continuing mass withdrawal. Over a period of a few months, using our most advanced tube transportation, all of Earth's population in huge batches will be brought to Ganymede and processed in massive ... err ... I suppose you could call them ... mmm ...slaughter houses? Brains only will be needed by then to become the grand

357

aggregated knowledge database of all humankind on Earth, before we finally arrive to our new home. Ambitious isn't it."

A strange voice suddenly came through the monitor speakers. "Hang on a moment Barbarella. I have decided on a different approach. I think, Lauren, I should explain instead. May I introduce myself? My name is Scarletta."

She looked up at the bubbling yellow sulphur brain, very startled. She recognised with instant dismay the lilting Italian male voice instantly. Was Ganymede actually the final resting place of the departed ghost of Luis? On a faraway cold moon of Jupiter?

"I've chosen to communicate through a familiar sound ... The signal from your mind-map of this tone was very strong, so I assume it is someone you have a strong attachment for. Barbarella can be a little hasty and crude with her surgical enthusiasm, but I assume you get the drift. But I need Jack here first, and as he seems to also have a very strong attachment to you, I will exploit his weakness. Link my monitor to him."

Buster growled to her and like an obedient sheepdog, nuzzled and corralled her into a small annexe, with a layout similar to her office in Cassini, except the chairs and sofa were green and not orange. Information about Cassini, her life, her achievements, her desires perhaps, had been fed back but reception was flawed, distorted, not quite the reality she would have expected of these super-techs. Barbarella had even oddly adopted the very English speaking but sinister mannerisms of Vaag, wherever that had come from. Poor Jack had certainly assembled a very muddled database on her but maybe that was a weakness, down to his conflicting feelings and hers for him. A weakness she could exploit ...

Jack listened downhearted as the monitor screen flickered into life and the familiar digital monotone dirge of Scarletta began to be transmitted. Juno fiddled with the settings and a stunning landscape image of Io appeared, all smoking red, brown and yellow, criss-crossed with symmetrical channels, out of which pools of molten lava and sulphur bubbled up. The sky exhibited a dark haze of patchy green and yellow mist, the sulphur dioxide and chlorine clearly evident, but the unexpected large planetary sphere of Jupiter in the background, a quarter below the horizon, cast sufficient reflected light to view high, craggy black mountains, some with lave flowing out and others receiving layers of white sulphur dioxide ice snow. A huge volcano in the left foreground was actively spewing all kinds of molten magma. Bolts of lightning flashed through the sky, the whole atmosphere alive with high voltage energy. To the wide eyes of Charlotte, Amélie, Svet and Nadine this scene, despite its intense splendour, was about as inhospitable as you could possibly imagine. The huge heating and energy releases caused by Io caught between a constant tidal gravitational pull of the massive Jupiter and its sister large moons orbiting close by, coupled with the colossal plasma effects from circling like a great dynamo constantly through Jupiter's huge magnetosphere, was live and visible as plain as the eye could see.

Jack turned to Amélie and the others, still quietly mesmerised. "Scarletta and the rest live underground, in liquid sulphur form, usually around large volcanic vents." He looked at the screen then shouted up. "We have guests here Scarletta. You'll have to tune your digital transmission code into our reality language."

There was a slight hiss and a voice sounding exactly like Winston Churchill began to sound across the room. Jack of course had been watching a news clip of the 1945 Armistice Day in Nadine's club before they left. He raised his eyebrows but the voice continued.

"I won't beat about the bush, Jack," Scarletta started. "You have a simple choice. We have Lauren, here on Ganymede. You know why of course." He called to Barbarella. "Bring her out."

The screen changed and a view of the inside of the Ganymede base with a small inset of the bell jar, containing a heaving mass of liquid sulphur inside became visible. By now everyone in the Cassini headquarters was huddled together peering at the monitor.

They gasped loudly. Lauren, naked and magnetically strapped onto a metal vertical X-frame over the surgical machine emerged, wheeled out triumphantly by Barbarella herself. Hermione couldn't contain herself. Uttering a deep moan, she paced the room like a panther, holding her knife menacingly and lamenting how much she wanted to be in that room right then and carve Barbarella up into tiny pieces.

Barbarella gleefully started up the machine and unhooked the flexible drive with a laser bone cutter on the end, slowly lifting up Lauren's hair, her eyes wide and petrified, to begin cutting off the top of her skull.

Jack was beside himself and screamed out for Barbarella to stop. "You damned, fucking savage. What have you become? A great and peaceful civilisation brought to the level of this barbarity. I'll swap with Lauren, spare her now. Take me instead, I don't care, just take me. You can have all of me, my entire knowledge the lot, I love her."

Barbarella stopped and looked at the bell jar. She was perceptibly licking her lips, leering directly into Lauren's face. This was the ultimate payback time, the chance for her to dissect Jack instead on the machine and then they would return anyway for Lauren and the rest later, using their new massive robot firepower amassed on Ganymede ...a huge boost to their knowledgepedia at a stroke, and she gets to personally cut his balls off.

"Call it progress, Jack my friend," Scarletta replied. "Your offer is accepted. Stop please Barbarella. Jack, you know how to get here ... you have one hour to prepare yourself. Set your probe to exchange and we'll do the same, in good faith with Lauren. I'm going to run through a list of things for you to bring ... oh, and Barbarella would like Hermione's head on a proverbial plate as well. Now first of course must be the acquisition of the Europa Charter of ..."

But Scarletta's glib dialogue was suddenly cut short. The scene on the monitor began to shake and a deep rumbling could be heard on the speakers. Barbarella and the robots were nervously looking around with increased concern. Some were running to the side machines controlling the energy input. Something on Ganymede was happening but exactly what was unclear. Amélie stared at Lauren, still strapped up but looking remarkably placid, almost as if she knew ... suddenly a door burst open at the back and a four-legged metallic robot hurtled headlong into the room, it's head swivelling rapidly from side to side and laser green eyes pulsating, assessing everything meticulously before taking action.

"What the fuck is that?" Amélie screamed her eyes like saucers, glued to the monitor.

"A robot dog, they must have been experimenting for some reason," Jack shouted, "but what on earth is ..."

"Holy shit," Hermione yelled as they watched in disbelief as the dog, its mouth wide open and metallic teeth gnashing viciously, launched itself into the air towards the camera with a huge growl. The screen juddered, a loud crash boomed out and girders could be seen swinging down. Screaming and shouting began everywhere ... but the screen suddenly flickered off alongside a maddening total silence.

Juno and Apollo began to frantically change monitors, twiddling dials and pulling at an array of switches but the connection remained dead. Hermione pointed to the door of the room containing their own inter-moon probes. "You and I have to get there Jack," she wailed. "We can't leave Lauren."

But he pondered for a few moments. "Just wait, leave it for a few minutes, Hermione. Something about Lauren's expression. I'm sure she was aware of what was happening, maybe even triggered it?"

Amélie and Charlotte nodded. Svet and Nadine had rushed across to Apollo's desk, they needed to urgently try again and link up to Mila.

Lauren had indeed made maximum thinking use of her short time in the annex with Buster before Barbarella and her henchwomen returned to remove her clothes and tie her on that obscene frame. She had pulled all the disparate strands together, rapidly analysing the scenarios of weakness in Jack's distorted communication of her personal mind map. Buster unexpectedly trotted over and lay down at her feet, simulating sleep and that provided her with the key. He had, of course, absorbed some of her own thinking. Buster wasn't solely an earth-like inanimate collection of metal and electronic bits. She had a brainwave. A year ago, she had reluctantly and illegally looked after Naomi's last pit bull for two months when Naomi went in and out of hospital for a series of treatments. That had been her last canine interaction of any significance. Fortunately she and the dog and especially the children all got on amazingly well, the girls and even Arthur adored him, he loved the villa and even she was sad when he was eventually returned back to grateful Aunt Letty. She leaned over. "Muon, what a lovely surprise to see you. I think I need your help."

He immediately stirred, gazed up at her and raised himself, rubbing his metallic front affectionately against her leg and emitting a friendly whine as she stoked his head. He wasn't Buster any more, if ever, but he was definitely Muon.

She gazed at the bank of monitors ... in the annexe they were focussed onto Io and the area surrounding the Ganymede base. But it was that moment she saw it, a huge plasma bolt, directly from the giant red spot had shot across the dividing space between Jupiter and Io. She counted the seconds and it landed on Io, creating a massive, smoking cleft on the ground, and began running along slowly towards the huge Pele volcano, rising up in the sky. Yellow plumes of liquid from the depths shot up out of the crevice, spewing high into the sky under pressure and floating slowly down as a great shower of yellow particles. Liquid sulphur was being thrown into the air and was then solidifying in the cold, like a hailstorm. Her experimental mind synthesised the scenario instantly, exactly as Hercules was speculating. He had said the Io diversion of their plasma energy link could have dangerous and significant consequences if they didn't monitor the current flow precisely. The old Earth paradigm of basic chaos theory had set in, where the flapping of a butterfly's wings could set of a typhoon. That was happening on Io. They were so engrossed next door communicating with Jack that Barbarella and her robots hadn't noticed the looming catastrophe. Effectively the plasma was acting like a knife, cutting Scarletta and his sulphur compatriots around on Io wide open, he was cascading up to the surface in huge amounts. The first flash was followed by another and then more, as the intensity of bombardment increased. A Jovian electromagnetic hurricane of incalculable magnitude was happening before her eyes. She switched to the Ganymede monitors and great flashes of lightning had also started outside. The energy link to Ganymede from Io and Jupiter had resonated and was being replicated, great fissures were opening up and the ground beyond the dome was heaving up and down like an earthquake. How long would it be before the base itself was breached and destroyed? She had to get off. Significant destruction was about to happen.

"Muon, do you understand how to operate a probe back to Europa? Can you rescue me?"

He stared, his eyes mournful, this was definitely a robot dog with a difference. He whined again and nodded his head and looked towards another door at the far end.

"Do you have to go and prepare something?"

He nodded up and down again, with a long moan, walked towards the door and stopped for an instruction. She could hear Barbarella, barking orders to her robot underlings, they were coming back to fetch her, whatever outcome the discussions with Jack had been.

"Go Muon, quickly, get the probe ready then find me immediately."

He ran silently, nudged a plate on the wall and vanished through the sliding door.

At that moment, Barbarella returned, cursing the absence of Buster and vowing to smash up the useless experiment, but she was in a hurry. Two robots grabbed Lauren who struggled desperately as Barbarella instantly relished cutting off Lauren's clothes with her sharp surgical knife ...

Panic was well and truly ensuing in the Ganymede control room. Equipment and apparatus flew everywhere; the whole building had started to shake. The electromagnetic storm had finally become apparent and started to rage. A loud lightning blast visible through the window blew out a main power circuit, cutting in the emergency lighting but severing power to her magnetic locks. She fell down, landing heavily but feet first, as the surgical table also toppled. Barbarella was now wrestling with Muon, his great jaws around her neck, when there was a loud crack and her head lolled back. He had severed her energy pack. He dropped the carcase triumphantly which fell limply onto the floor. She looked around, still naked and saw astonishingly under the bell jar a great red robe and pantaloons lying there, definitely some kind of eighteenth century male aristocratic apparel. Her love of old French historic fashions was never wrong, even on Ganymede. She grabbed the trousers and jumped into them, pulling on a buttoned shirt top and wrapped the robe around herself. The large black wig underneath gave the game away. Scarletta clearly fancied himself as Louis X1V, the Sun King of Io, master of all he surveyed in the solar system. The concept was so bizarre it was unbelievable. She pulled the wig over her head. Then she smelt a familiar bad smell and a loud thudding of pumps began kicking in. Hydrogen sulphide was leaking inside, the dome was cracking and gases mixed with steam from the volcanic eruptions outside were already seeping from the magma, the ground pounded continuously with plasma bursts. The emergency pumps wouldn't hold it for long and all around other panicking robots began to keel over with a thud, their energy packs exploding, exactly as happened on Europa when Hermione threw around the hydrogen sulphide canisters. Muon was standing patiently by her side. Without any ado, she reached up and pushed the bell jar hard off its pedestal, immediately smashing on the floor, the yellow sulphur solidifying with a loud scream.

Jumping onto Muon's back, she clung hard to his neck as he turned. His four legs flew, galloping madly through a series of doors and corridors, deep into the interior of the dome, passing more robot bodies along the way their spines split open with exploded energy packs. Soon they reached a launching area with half a dozen large transparent tubes, ready and open. Diving inside one, Muon nudged a button with his nose. The door shut tightly. Two huge cracks opened and joined together on the outside of the dome above. A massive triangular piece from the apex of their two hundred metre radius dodecahedron, fell out, the whole dome was ready to collapse. Muon sat on his haunches and using extended claws as fingers began pushing a series of buttons then nodded, with a low whine, for Lauren still dressed in her royal regalia to turn a gate valve open.

As she did, everything around them instantly vanished. If this was ion propulsion it was impressive. They were in space, moving at a tremendous speed and she could see the spherical shape of Europa increasing rapidly in size. Soon they entered a thin atmosphere and dropped onto the icy surface, everywhere looking exactly like a more spectacular version of Antarctica at a deep dusk. The probe began to bore through the surface and quickly they descended smoothly through deep black water, those luminous fish, their eyes lit up, swimming past. A few bumps and chamber openings and the craft stopped. They both blinked and looked about quietly—they had arrived inside their original base. Deep concentration was needed as she hung onto Muon, when instantly they found themselves in Eva's office. Muon gave a short growl of satisfaction. She was sure he was smiling, but dogs don't smile— do they? Maybe robot ones.

Walking straight into her large office, red robe billowing and her wig straightened with Muon alongside, the noise abated instantly.

She saw Jack first with his mouth incredulously wide open. Amélie was nearest. "Jesus fucking Christ," was all she could mutter.

"Can you find me a pair of my best jeans and a decent top please ... I really need to get out of this bizarre outfit," she muttered with a scurrilous grin. Then they would all have to act extremely fast ...

Chapter Twenty

Hercules painstakingly pieced together a panoramic three-dimensional storyboard of the unfolding catastrophe on Io. Enough monitor pictures had been saved to provide a dramatic backcloth to the relentless pounding by hot, violent plasmas across the surface always facing Jupiter, where the Arrhyan colonies had been established billions of years ago. Europa Arrhyans had been warning for many long years that the unpredictable and increasing volcanic instability on Io, a moon heavily pushed and pulled by enormous planetary forces from its Jovian parent, could potentially turn into a giant nuclear explosion, exposing the underground life forms to chemical transformation at the surface. A slow death, the equal of the old alchemist workings in reverse— a transmutation of gold back to base metal.

Lauren knew they hadn't got long. Electronic surveillance indicated that the robot colony on Adrastea was already combining with the survivors from Ganymede. Total numbers were still considerable as six bases on the dark, cold side of Ganymede, like Europa and Io, being tidal facing to Jupiter in orbit, had survived. Ganymede was big enough with its own unique and protective magnetosphere, to have not fared so badly on the dark side from the sympathetic plasma blasts flashing between Jupiter, Io and itself.

The robot war was going to be reignited but very quickly, as those sulphur Arrhyans surviving on Io now had little time and nothing to lose. They had to wipe out Europa and then utilise the Europan technology to invade Earth and colonise under the oceans and beneath the crust. All other bets were off. Even Venus would be discarded, the enormous atmospheric pressure, intense heat from the sun and sulphuric acid air was incompatible, even for them.

Lauren carefully and concisely outlined her scientific and logical arguments, backed up by Apollo and Juno, the most trusted of Jack's immediate senior staff. But Jack remained reluctant to accept the conclusions. There was no way he would leave his beloved Europa to be destroyed by Scarletta, they would battle to the end, robot to robot ... he would use all their technological expertise to hold off Io until it imploded and Scarletta and his associates destroyed from the massive increase in volcanic eruptions.

Charlotte, Svet and Hercules emerged, clad in overalls, red in the face and covered from head to toe with black insulating oils from his workbench in the next room. Nadine swiftly followed, holding Lauren's mobile phone.

Hercules was babbling incessantly, caught in the heat of the moment with an amazing breakthrough. "We've managed to restart the wormhole and boost the quantum tunnelling effect using gasified and excited fluorine ions so we can connect with the reduced power from Saturn's moon, Titan. A gem of theoretical genius from Svet, she really is an outstanding scientist, Lauren. You must be proud of her. We don't quite understand why, but it works."

Lauren hugged Svet tightly, she was hugely proud of her.

Nadine cut in. "I've got Mila on the phone, Jack. Charlotte is linking to the ceiling speakers. We can only do audio but that'll do. I've given Mila a rundown of the facts and analysis as Lauren has succinctly explained. You've admired Mila's defensive tactics; now let her give her opinion."

Jack nodded. He had sidled up to Lauren whilst everyone was listening to Hercules, and given her a quiet passionate kiss accompanied by a whispered request for forgiveness for being so useless under attack. She knew what she wanted, but had refrained from saying it; she was so emotionally bound up with him. She still loved him desperately and accepted his warmongering failings without malice, because Jack had exhibited so many other important positive and worthwhile leadership qualities, distinctly human including loyalty. In the end he had been willing to exchange himself for her, no questions asked, which would have been the end for him that much she knew. He did love her. She hoped Mila would objectively draw the same conclusion, when Mila's distinctive loud voice immediately boomed across the room.

"Hello Jack and everyone, great to be back onboard. Lauren, I can't tell you how worried Adrijana and I were when we lost contact. You have had an unbelievable brush and escape from a form of everlasting death which even defied my imagination and I've seen most things horrific in war. I'm going to be succinct, Jack. Here are the stark facts. Europa won the last skirmish, a fantastic achievement by Hermione's robots considering how outnumbered they were. You have one hundred robots and now only two bases on Europa. This one, sitting in the Cassini reality setting and the other interconnected base, headed up by your other deputy Arrhyan, Klinga, with ten others like her. The other six bases have been destroyed in the past twenty four hours by Io sympathisers, using suicide robots."

Jack was shocked, he had no idea. He had switched off through far too much, it was indefensible. He turned sharply to Juno. "Where's Hermione?"

"I'm here, Jack. Klinga also has a proposition for you. Let Mila continue." They all turned and Hermione strode in with an equally athletic Arrhyan female counterpart. This was obviously Klinga.

Mila summarised the Io position. Rapid degradation of the Arrhyan sulphur blobs, especially Scarletta, but a working manufacturing base surviving on Ganymede with over five hundred Io robots training ready, combined with a further next phase batch of six hundred war-ready Io robots on Adrastea.

"I draw only one conclusion ... you have to make a tactical retreat. Enemy robot numbers are overwhelming, even if you choose the same fighting reality, you will lose and they can keep on coming, and they get better each time. And the next invasion must be imminent. The Io Arrhyans are themselves under severe threat of wipe-out. You have no time to make or build up your defences, and so my recommendation is ... shit ... I'm breaking up ... get out of there fast Jack ..."

Silence, despite frantic efforts again by Charlotte and Hercules. They had lost line of sight with Titan. They needed a day at least to rebuild the alignment mechanisms and improve accuracy and they didn't have it.

Jack looked ready to put his head in his hands again, but Lauren took his arm. "There's only one escape plan for you ... back to Earth, to lead the rebuilding of Europa from there, back to Earth with me and Amélie, Charlotte, Svet and Nadine. Take me back, Jack, take us all back."

He stared hard into Lauren's eyes ... the logic was unassailable but what about ...?

"You need our proposition Jack, before you decide." Hermione's voice rang out, so Mila-like now it was indistinguishable. "Mine and Klinga's."

Lauren glared at Hermione. Just at the point when she had perfectly timed her finale and conclusion, when all the dice were at last spun her way, Hermione again had to come in and spoil it. What the fuck was Hermione's agenda?

"We agree with Mila one hundred percent," Klinga began softly. She was tall, blonde, willowy and graceful, a very beautiful individual with a soft and determined voice. Lauren was puzzled, reflected and then she shuddered as she realised, looking more closely. Klinga had adopted a persona. She was not a robot, she was an Arrhyan. Clearly Jack had been trying to do this with all of them, start acclimatisation with Earth mannerisms using people he knew. Klinga's persona was the first and most obvious she had seen ... she was Sonja minus the green eyes; Klinga's were brown.

Klinga continued. "And we agree with Lauren to depart but not just you Jack. You take Hermione your most advanced robot, but also Apollo, Juno, Persephone, Hercules, Romulus and Pete. We have enough transfer tubes. I managed to get the other spares into here from the bases before we lost them. You need your top science and technology team with you Jack if you want the faintest chance to either integrate on Earth or rebuild and return to whatever is left of Europa. I will lead the remaining defence from our one base. We have identified our next reality setting ... it's going to be the 1815 Battle of Waterloo. If we lose I will guarantee there will be nothing left on Europa for the robots to utilise and without our technology they will be useless on Ganymede. Especially as our assessment of Arrhyan survival on Io is virtually zero. The plasma destruction there now is immense and showing no signs of abating. The tipping point has been reached; they can't reverse it, through their own greed and stupidity, trying to corral all the plasma power together. Jupiter as ever will never be defied."

Charlotte suddenly cried out. "We've established the power link again. I can't connect to Mila but have contact with your insiders on Ganymede. They've started, we have only hours. Jack. We really have to go."

"This all sounds irrefutable to me," Amélie added, already factoring in a cunning plan to continue a torrid affair with Apollo at Harvard whilst maintaining her family life with Rufus and the children.

Lauren glanced over, saw the gleam in Amélie's eye and despite her disapproval, she had no choice. This was the only way she returns with Jack ... Hermione would have to be accompanying baggage whether she liked it or not. Winning wars involved compromise. "I agree too. Klinga's proposal makes most logical sense. Klinga you're amazingly brave and insightful, I wish I could have known you better here. Jack— we must get to the transfer tubes now."

He finally and reluctantly agreed. Hugging Klinga warmly and wishing her the best of luck, they gathered their belongings, performed a group concentration and raced out of the room, led by Hermione directly into the old base. Everyone was dressed back into their drab and tight fitting latex suits. Virtual reality was over. Entering the departure area, they began opening the tubes. Amélie chose the tube next to Apollo, as they held hands briefly. Muon ambled up to Lauren, her handbag around his neck. Jack had already programmed the key input data and his master code. Nadine was assisting Hermione with the remaining settings.

"Right, everyone in," Hermione bellowed. "Nadine and I will complete lift-off and follow."

Lauren climbed in and noticed Muon next to her whining softly, his face, even for a metallic robot, showing mournful sadness. He knew she was departing. Without any further thought she yanked his collar and pulled him in, closing the lid fully. The lights began to change colour and fade.

"Right, Nadine, do it now."

Hermione jumped into her tube, but Nadine lingered, the last one remaining, with just enough time to turn two dials a further amount. She flicked the master switch and dived straight into her own tube, slamming the lid shut, as the motors inside whined and their minds faded into dreamy oblivion ...

Lauren opened her eyes to the sound of ducks quacking loudly. She was sat in a pile of muddy green reeds alongside a wide blue lake. The air was fresh and clear and the sky a beautiful blue, a few white clouds slowly scudding by.

A hand gripped her shoulder, making her jump sharply. "Sorry Lauren, I didn't mean to startle you."

She turned to see Charlotte behind her, also soaked to the skin with Svet crawling towards both of them, sporting a giant grin from ear to ear. They were all wearing dirty old jeans and grey fishermen's jumpers, wet and covered in mud from head to toe and it was warm. They were boiling hot.

Svet joined them and they hugged each other hard, despite the horrible smell of stagnant water and rotting vegetation on their clothes. They were back, back on Earth but where they were was anybody's guess. As they stood up, Lauren immediately glared at the figure, twenty or thirty yards away, dressed in a very figure hugging bikini, raising herself up reluctantly from her sunlounger on the mown grass and waving enthusiastically.

"You might have known. Amélie of course had to land in strict Countess style," Lauren muttered, but couldn't keep up her scowl any longer and stomped through the reeds intending to give Amélie a giant hug too, even if it meant spoiling her precious outfit, with Charlotte and Svet staggering behind.

A loud barking caught her attention as some odd looking metallic thing thundered out of the large wooden shack behind Amélie to greet her.

"Oh my goodness," Lauren cried tearfully. "It's Muon. You actually made it all that way. Jesus, what am I going to do with you and explain you away?"

Muon lolloped alongside, his metallic tail wagging clunkily, as the three stomped up to Amélie, who backed off a little, throwing up her hands. Then Nadine emerged from the shack, looking glamorous in dinky shorts and a bikini top, her generous thighs tanned and smooth, holding a large fork in her hand.

"Whoa everyone, you guys don't smell brilliant. I'll happily hug you to bits when you get showers and changed," Amélie hollered, dodging playfully out of the way of Lauren who was trying to catch her.

"Sorry, I'm afraid I was slightly out on the Earth adjustments and the timing, some scenes in my head got a bit muddled but you made it," Nadine said, joining them as they gathered round. "We've returned to my retreat—where we were supposed to be going in the first place remember? And we have until tomorrow before anyone expects us to get in touch."

Svet gasped with relief. "Gosh Nadine, that timing was very tight, but equally we may never have got back at all if it wasn't for Lauren. Never again. If I see any lights in the sky I shall run hard."

Nadine continued. "There are enough spare clothes, bikini sets and accessories to fit everyone. Svet and I, between us already had wardrobes furnished up, the last few times we were here. We like to retreat in style. Four bedrooms in the shed, Svet and I will share."

Lauren laughed ... Nadine was so amazing and mature. She was the real reason they had survived Europa and made it back ... and Mila of course. "What are you cooking? Is there enough food for everyone?" she said, immediately assuming Jack, Apollo and the others, even Hermione unfortunately, were back inside the shack somewhere.

"A barbecue of course, what else when the weather is this good. Been defrosting steaks and burgers."

"And I even picked wild mushrooms in the trees behind," Amélie added cheerfully, but then glanced warily at Nadine who took a deep breath.

"There's only us here, Lauren," Nadine whispered.

Lauren stared hard, her head immediately spinning with a disarray of mixed up thoughts. She felt her stomach drop like a stone, a great wave of sadness and disbelief was washing over her, filling her whole body. "Where's Jack? Where is he Nadine?"

A voice sounded from behind. "We decided to change the plans, Lauren. There really was no alternative."

She turned around in disbelief to see Mila, standing there in the tiniest of a black and yellow spotted bikini, so alluring and desirable, it visibly took her breath away. Mila was the last person she expected here.

"Mila ... oh my ... gosh ... you look fabulous," she stuttered, before the most searing question she had first and foremost took over again. "We? What's happened to them? Jack and Apollo, Juno, Persephone, Hercules?" She omitted robots or one robot specifically.

Nadine intervened. "In agreement with Hermione and Mila, I changed their coordinates just before we took off. Hermione showed me how to do it," Nadine said quietly. "They are travelling onwards to Kepler-995 in the Cygnus constellation. It has uninhabited earth-like exo-planets and a Jupiter system, similar to our own solar system, so they will have a real opportunity to build a series of new and interrelated colonies and a future civilisation of their choosing."

Lauren was stunned. "How far is Kepler-995?"

Nadine hesitated before confirming clearly and unequivocally. "Around twelve hundred light years. But they'll all be fine, and reconstitute perfectly, it's like a long hibernation."

Tears began trickling steadily down Lauren's cheek. She began to sob and turned to Amélie "But what about Apollo? Don't you miss him, don't you fucking care?"

Amélie felt so bad, she could have died on the spot, but there were good reasons to remain resolute ... she too was in on the decision before they left. "Yes, I do, on both counts. I owe my life to Apollo, but it would have been far, far too complicated, Lauren. This is for the best, I'm sure he would agree."

Lauren felt immediate anger building up. A jealous conspiracy led by Amélie had been afoot; she had always hated Jack from the beginning, all designed to prevent her and Jack being together. Her face reddened. She began hard, her tone threatening and very unfriendly. "I had no complications as you well know. I loved Jack, I really, really loved him, and for the first time I was going to find some real happiness, here, together. How could you do this to me, Amélie, to your best friend, after all these years …?"

Muon was trying to get her attention but she had to ignore him and lunged at Amélie.

Mila immediately stepped between and held Lauren firmly in her strong grip. "No, Lauren. This was not Amélie's doing, she remains very much your best friend. I told Nadine to take action. It was my decision."

Lauren shook Mila's grip from her arm and stood aside, breathing heavily. What was she hearing? "You? You decided Jack and I wouldn't be together? You cooked up the plot to send him thousands of light years away so I would never see him again? … But why Mila? Why again do you want to hurt me?"

"Not to hurt you, quite the opposite. Because Jack, the real Jack, is still here, on Earth. Quietly beavering away in the Cyclops Centre with his fusion reactor on your behalf, playing around with his infra-red telescope and I'm sure missing you hugely and looking forward to seeing you soon."

Lauren jerked her head up and pushed her hands through her dirty, wet hair forcing it all back off her face. "Here? Jack is here? But how? He's millions of miles away, a vaporous cloud of photons. I don't understand?"

Mila continued calmly and assuredly. She knew Lauren for far too long … a simple and clear logical explanation was required to be digested instantly by the luscious brain-box, despite the smell, in front of her.

"When I engaged with my doppelgänger, Hermione, what nobody else realised was it worked both ways … as she became more like me, I too absorbed Hermione's thoughts and desires. That's how I knew. Remember, we were all living, communicating and fighting in a virtual reality world … and I discovered that alien Jack was a special genetically engineered Arrhyan, modelled around the real Jack, to become the leader they had desperately needed. He had been stalked too. The others, Apollo, Juno etc were genuine. Some aspects of Jack's DNA transmutation seemed to have got lost in translation, as you probably realised and must have come to a head the moment the crisis hit. But you forgave him all his inadequacies because ... you really do love him. The real Jack isn't perfect either.

"But what about ... well all the ... you know ..."

Amélie cut in, to laughter from Charlotte and Svet. "The out of this world sex, you mean Lauren? You're with friends now, we get it, well I certainly did, not with Jack of course ..."

"You'll probably find, waiting to be discovered under that rather shy exterior, there is still plenty of fire left in the old engine of earthy Jack minus the luminescent, swivelling eyes," Mila added with a grin.

"How do you know about Jack's eyes?" Lauren responded immediately. "And he's not that shy."

"Because orgasmic eyes also turned Hermione on. She loved him Lauren, she was specially built as a unique robot, and she had mixed genes, half robot and half Arrhyan. Hey anyone modelled on me would have to be pretty unique, and he was engineered to love her too ... and did many times, but your appearance tore apart his emotions—he didn't know which way to turn. He badly wanted you but would ultimately have had to choose. That was never the plan intended, but it happened, a love spoke in the wheel again of course but unexpectedly from the blue planet. When Charlotte link-connected me up the second time, that was the opportunity for Hermione, with me in her head, to divulge all to Nadine and suggest her Plan B, her ultimate goal. It would never have worked here Lauren. As Amélie said ... way too many convoluted complications. Think about it, two Jacks, Hermione my double on the loose jealous and vengeful plus, equally importantly, the grand plan for Europa was always to find a virgin planet to colonise ... it was Jack's sole fantasy which Hermione had to promote, to become obsessively focussed on Earth. They'll all be very happy in twelve hundred years time, long after all of us are kicking the daisies. But your real Jack, just as before, is here available and fancy free, to mould exactly as you desire."

Lauren's body language had instantly changed. Her eyes narrowed and a wide smile creased her mouth. All kinds of intriguing possibilities were suddenly zipping around her head at triple the speed of light. "Really?"

She hugged Amélie hard, who breathed a huge sigh of relief. "Sorry, best friend, I was a little hasty wanting to throttle you. Your men instincts right at the beginning were correct."

"As usual of course," Amélie replied tersely.

"But how can I be sure the genuine Professor Jackson Smythe is still here? He has a habit of disappearing at crucial times whenever I want him."

Svet decided ... the subject needed changing, there was important science to be getting on with and she desperately wanted to see Sergei. It was time she had her say. "Romulus and I talked for hours about all the serious genetic doubts they had, out of earshot of Jack's ear, over an intermixed Earth colonisation. We agreed. He also affirmed that even in the short time we were there, the brief knowledge we all acquired on Europa has amazing potential for transferability and to really move forward a number of sectors and areas of scientific work. I think we've been privileged with a great gift to do that, whilst retaining our secret. We really have to do that or we'll be in danger of being locked up."

Mila nodded. "I agree, Svet is completely correct, lots of exciting things to do in the future. Anyway, everyone here bar me is a potential Nobel prize winner ten times over in secret so that shouldn't be difficult."

Mila put her fingers to her nose. "More importantly, some of us desperately need a shower. Nadine and I will have the barbecue going, Amélie is on wine and sun lounger duty, it really is time to relax and gossip Cassini style. At my last house soiree, I became salaciously privy to some interesting tittle-tattle from the President's wife's chief fashion designer. It's amazing how I manage to get women to unburden their innermost desires at the drop of ... well we won't go into that drop ... quite yet ...!"

Everyone giggled. Mila as usual was transforming them back to her usual world view of tendentious normality.

"Lauren, can you do something about your new dog? He's trying to get your attention," Amélie interrupted, pushing Muon away.

Lauren could feel a cold, metallic nose shoving into her rear. "Muon, why are you bringing me my handbag? How on earth are we going to explain you away?"

"That's easy," Nadine said cheerfully. "Part of our retreat was to supposedly look at my latest mindboggling robotic project. I do have secrets from Roland too, and you loved Muon so much you agreed to adopt him."

Muon blinked and let out a quiet whine, still gently shaking her handbag.

"Brilliant," Lauren replied, taking it off him and pulling out her phone which was flashing with sudden received messages. "Oh my God, it's a WhatsApp message from ... Jack." She read it out. "Hope you've had a good break in the Appalachians, a very beautiful area. Reached the target five hundred megawatt yesterday, thought you might like to know. The team misses you, look forward to seeing you when you get back. There's an attachment ... a romantic picture of him standing next to a dial on the fusion reactor in his dirty overalls."

"See ... do I ever lie?" Mila shouted, walking off with Nadine to the barbecue. "There's your proof, satisfied? Will you get in that shower please ... and don't spend too long in there!" she added, a sly Mila grin creasing across her face.

Full Moon —Epilogue

The rest of the day and evening relaxing on the sun loungers, occasional swimming in the outdoor pool and munching their way through Nadine's freezer full of steaks and chicken pieces, expertly cooked of course by Mila, finally allowed Lauren to desperately offload completely and sit quietly and reflect. She no longer needed to be the centre of attention as she had been, relentless and unending over the previous nine days. Most importantly she was relishing the thoughts of returning home and seeing Magdaline, Eveline and Geraldine shortly, returning once more to the blissful comfort of her research work at Cassini and especially of seeing Jack, the real Jack, as Mila had put it. She giggled inside, already making plans to test Mila's hypothesis once and for all. And she had firmly decided. This was decidedly the end of an era and the start of a new one. The possibilities of exploring radical science and technology with her new knowledge could keep her active and busy for years. Forget retirement. And her deep love for Jack had only one inevitable conclusion. It was time for a divorce from Philippe. If it hadn't been for the children she would have done it long ago, in fact probably the moment Olga appeared on the scene, never mind his continuing affair with Gabrielle Legendre and others. She had drifted for far too long down a stale emotional pathway which was not, in reality, her genuine choosing. There was something pleasing in her head about the mathematical notion of fifth time lucky ... and Jack definitely had something innately appealing about him that none of her previous husbands possessed, including Philippe, and she didn't care that she couldn't define it in her usual scientific fashion. Her instincts and feelings were good enough.

Turning Muon around, she found a tiny screwdriver in the pen pocket of her bag and adjusted his sensitive solar panel settings down. He was obviously uncomfortable in the far more intense light in his new surroundings and then lay down at her feet, with a contented moan. He didn't sleep like a real dog but kind of shut down his thinking facility, presumably to maximise an energy charge-up refresh. Whilst his mechanical workings and appearance were relatively simplistic, although far better than the Cassini lab creations, his interior electronics were a complete mystery. She hoped that in due course she could use Muon to self-describe how he worked. Nadine had managed to prise some of that robotic construct information from Hermione. Maybe Nadine could spend some consultancy time at Cassini in her personal research workshop with Svet and help her. That would be lovely.

She watched Mila and Amélie bantering loudly again, one off the other like old times over couture fashions, men and sex, egged on mercilessly by Charlotte and Svet.

Nadine came over and sat quietly next to her.

"I've already phoned Roland. Apart from asking whether we got all our suitcases that he had couriered to the retreat, thank goodness the local postal office had a key to the secure outbuilding, all he was concerned about was getting back to his new programming language he was writing. *Plus ça change, plus c'est la même chose*, as you would say, but that's what I like about him and the freedom and independence he gives me."

"Yes, I understand exactly what you mean, a bit like Jack. But it's clear that Roland adores you."

"Yes, I know ... he's a daft romantic underneath his armfuls of screwdrivers and soldering irons," Nadine replied, smiling. "Actually, may I ask you something? It's about ... err ... Mila's husband, Henri-Gaston. Sorry, I know he's a taboo subject, but I'm worried?"

Lauren patted her hand. "Henri and my emotional baggage is firmly in the past, demons vanquished now Nadine. Mila and I are sort of reconciled, even more so now she's saved all our lives in the past week, once again! But I'm aware that not all is as well as it could be in their relationship. Something about South American muses and artist predilections for the exotic? So what are you specifically worried about?"

"It took a few years, but his old and engrained habits began to resurface ... Sadly Henri-Gaston remains and is now fully returned to his serial womanising ways. You know Mila. She never sets her expectations above what she decides is minimal. Her independence and her secretive special operations and intelligence past have always remained paramount. It was a trade-off I suppose. He never demanded to know her background and she never demanded to know what he got up to, and to be fair he was discrete, albeit prolific. Besides she now has Adrijana to focus on, the centre of her life. She's a gorgeous and intelligent little girl and takes after Mila almost a hundred percent, although she does apparently paint and draw exceptionally well."

"Yes, I know about well engrained old habits," Lauren replied.

Nadine smiled ... the disdain well understood.

Lauren continued. "I met Adrijana with Mila in Israel before we came to Boston. She is lovely, quite precocious for her age and instantly made friends with my triplets which was amazing considering how culturally different they are."

But she hadn't realised that Henri-Gaston and Mila had a sort of open marriage. They obviously lived their lives like English upper class society in the 1920s that her ex-husband used to prattle on about so much, the renewed Bloomsbury set of New York now in 2016. And of course Mila was excellent at creating an extravagant environment of cultural excesses and designer fashion if she wanted, to take the edge off any emotional discomfort ... she had the means, the looks and the natural talent. A perfect setting for Henri-Gaston to exploit his urges, which now Lauren wasn't at all surprised about, especially thinking back objectively to his long past behaviour when she became pregnant with Charlotte at sixteen.

"So what's changed?" Lauren asked.

"Luciana," Nadine replied. "The muse has taken a turn for serious. Sufficiently so, I understand, that he's bought her an apartment for trysts exactly when he wants her, which presently seems to be constantly. Mila is her usual bullish self and shrugs it off as irrelevant, but I'm sure it isn't ... I know instinctively when she's working up for another dramatic change in her life. Already she's immersed herself quietly back into intelligence work ... the old team, including me were recently in South Africa, I'd better not tell you why, and once more flawlessly led by Mila. She's lost none of the old touch and physically is fitter than ever, as you can see. Useful extra money too for Roland and me. Her company has made loads of it over the last five years. Financially she is still totally independent."

They both gazed across the grass in silence to watch Mila effortlessly playing netball with Charlotte, both toned and fit in their bikinis, but Mila looked sumptuous, and her body could easily have passed for a thirty year old.

"So this Luciana? Her name sounds Spanish actually, where does she live?"

"Montevideo."

"What? In Uruguay? I knew Henri was touring in South America but would never have guessed ..."

"That's where they met, I gather a whirlwind romance," Nadine continued, calling up a Google image on her smartphone. "But something you should also be aware of. Luciana is an up and coming hot-shot academic at the University, a mathematician, specialising in quantum mechanics. She's tall, blonde, very fashionable and bilingual in English and made quite a name for herself in the trendy art world for her computer generated pictures based on the motions of sub-atomic particles. And of course she's twenty five."

Lauren stared at the picture.

"Shit," she exclaimed, thrown unexpectedly. She could have been viewing herself twenty five years previously. Luciana would have made an excellent twin sister, the likeness was uncanny.

"To be honest Lauren, I think if Mila hadn't got Adrijana, then 'the muse' would have mysteriously vanished from this world, but her child has fortunately grounded Mila a lot from irrational responses of former times. Also this particular relationship has added complications, as you can well see."

"I really believed Henri-Gaston was done with all that obsessiveness, especially given the distinctive allure of Mila. Why would that idiot want to jeopardise his whole life, for some academic bimbo. He has everything now with Mila, exactly as he always wanted. It makes no rational sense."

"That's men for you," Nadine replied.

Lauren smiled. "Yes indeed. Does Charlotte know?"

"No. I need to tell her quietly before anyone else finds out, especially Amélie."

"Especially!"

"I would more accurately depict Henri not as obsessive but rather possessive—of an ideal he'll never let go of. You."

Lauren thought for a few moments. As ever, Nadine could fire at the target with pin-point precision accuracy. "I'll tell Charlotte, Nadine. It will be far better coming from me. I'll find the best time, I promise. Also I'm sure Mila will have something to say to me too, very soon, when the time is right. It always seems to go that way between us."

"Thanks, I know and I agree ..."

"Agree what Nadine? What are you two in a huddled conspiracy about?" An unmistakable but panting loud voice boomed out. As ever, Mila always had that peculiar knack of creeping up on people unawares.

Lauren responded in an instant. "That we need to spend time analysing how Muon works inside. Nadine is going to come and spend some paid consultancy time helping me at my Cassini robotics laboratory."

Nadine nodded, hoping that Lauren's little white lie would actually happen.

"Excellent," Mila replied happily, waving at the others to come over immediately and join them. Nadine pulled up the giant umbrella in the centre of the outdoor table and went inside to get a tray of cold drinks ...

Lauren sat sipping her organic lemonade, quite stunned at what Mila had just announced; a fait accompli organised quickly and quietly by her own hand and already paid for.

"So? What do you think Lauren?"

"Honestly Mila, it's a fabulous thought. I really appreciate it, as I'm sure we all do. But will we have time to buy the right evening wear? Although of course we've got our suitcases, I did bring some stuff."

"Of course you will and even better than you brought. I have a mobile Luddite-type courier who will bring up an enviable collection of all the top couture brands and in every style you adore, to try on and pay for in the comfort of my luxury pad. No need to rush around like crazy in Manhattan on a Saturday afternoon. Remember this is me you're talking to, queen of the frocks. Nadine and Svet, I know money is tight so I insist any expense goes onto my account."

But Lauren was still amazed that Mila could pull all that off whilst they were battling the robots on Europa. So next day, she wasn't flying off home to Nice. Instead, everyone was being flown business class out to New York, put up at the arty and luxurious James Hotel in Soho Manhattan, to then be whisked by limousine to Mila's massive apartment in the evening for one of her grand parties, with a select invite of the politically great, disgustingly wealthy and exorbitantly fashionable. But it was the 'everyone' that Lauren couldn't believe was possible. Top of the list were her triplets, accompanied by Giles and Marie, together with Arthur, Kat and Lexi. As soon as Mila mentioned Sonja, Lauren knew that this detailed project plan had a master executioner behind it. Without doubt the hand of Sonja, coming with Johann and Časlav as well as Eva also on the list with her two children and Seb was very evident. Sergei and Roland of course were a given. Rufus was coming from Heathrow with Leonora and Caroline. And Helena, with her son and Edward Jones. A jazz trio with a singer to entertain everyone had been booked, including an upright piano, the lifts were strong enough and Helena and Edward were invited to do a few special numbers together. But most amazingly Mila was bringing Annabella, Luigi and her three children plus Eliska. With all the myriad of children, a few extra nannies would be needed to keep order and sooth the inevitable crying eyes, so Annabella was bringing Lia. Juliette was also invited, but unfortunately was on holiday in the Seychelles with her new beau and the children, but wished everyone a great time.

Lauren's mind immediately returned to the lovely surprise party that DG and Charlotte had thrown in their new villa for their wedding night when the same people had been invited ... this was grander and now included the children. But of course at the time Mila had disappeared into the swamps and was uncontactable ... she was obviously intending to make up for it, but would be equally sad that DG wasn't going.

The opulence was way beyond any comprehension by Lauren. She was sitting quietly on a couch having a breather from a feverish networking conversation with a Manhattan industrialist who traded in rare earths, a gem of a find. She casually people-watched, taking in the nuances of social interaction and conversation. She always knew Mila had extravagant tastes, but never in a million years would she have believed the sumptuous surroundings they were sitting amongst. This apartment was painted and furnished in the most expensive and fashionable decor, with portraitures, pictures and artefacts expected of any billionaire socialite in the top echelons of New York society. The invited guests, mingling happily and easily with everyone were relaxed, obviously used to Mila's largesse and the way she personally made each person welcome, their plates filled with all kinds of tasty tit-bits, glasses topped up with champagne, all organised of course by top outside caterers. But the frisson of wealth, ambition and politics was instantly evident in the fabulous evening dresses of the carefully coiffured society women, lavished with oodles of fine jewellery, the fine suits of the men and the conversations. She was used to lavish parties, often having been a guest at some laid on event of a head of state or business partner with whom she was agreeing nuclear deals. But this was quite different. A number of the guests were clearly well known celebrity artists, actors and media personalities from the local area; everyone seemed to know each other, almost like family. Helena and Edward had just finished a select and well received set and were both being feted in a corner by some TV producers, this could be their big music break. Annabella and Luigi were having an intense conversation in Italian with some developers, a possibility of property investment in the US? Charlotte and Giles, with Lexi and Kat, were talking to the Principal of one of New York's prestigious art and sports universities, no doubt considering a possible future placing for her two big grandchildren. Sonja, Svet, Amélie and Nadine were busily discussing the running of the Zenoville fashion house with the female owner and her CEO live-in partner, both exquisitely dressed in their creations, making waves across all the US big cities with shops popping up galore. Other male spouses, led by Sergei, had sneaked off down to a bar nearby which he knew well for a cigar smoke and a beer, but returning later when the main food was being served. It probably wouldn't be long before Luigi hightailed it there too.

The apartment was a huge penthouse duplex with five bedrooms and five stately interconnected reception rooms, of which they were using three for the party. One of course had been done out specially for the children who were running around or playing on computer games, all overseen with watchful eyes by Lia and Mila's nanny, Maybelline, a no-nonsense and middle aged African-American woman with a huge sense of humour. Marie had also sneaked off to the bar with Seb.

Having just fended off one lecherous and rich millionaire night club owner with her usual off-putting tactics, she was glad to simply take a deep breath, watch and relax. But of course, it wouldn't have been necessary. Because the great coup of the evening was that Sonja had persuaded one further addition to the flight retinue after a mild protest that parties were not really his thing. But inside himself he was hugely pleased to have been invited, because he had already said so. And that could only have been for one reason. Jack did look fashionably smart this evening as she watched him, talking intensely with Eva to a NASA executive and his wife. She would join him in a minute after she topped up both their glasses of wine next to her. She was booked into a suite with all mod-cons in the hotel with Marie and the children, but Jack had been tactically placed in the room next door by a grinning Mila. Once everyone was tucked into bed, Lauren planned a little nocturnal visit ... This would be it, no more bunking off for him. It truly was time she fully consummated her relationship with the real Jack, and see whether he could make Europa move under her feet again ...

"Grandma, would you like to see this amazing computer game?" Arthur had emerged from the giant den holding Adrijana's hand. "Adrijana is my new best friend but she's beaten me three times on the run despite me working out the best moves. She's an awesome gamer," he beamed. "She's invited me and the girls for a week here at the end of the summer before school starts. I hope Maman will allow me to go."

"I'm sure Charlotte will, Arthur, and Magda, Eve and Geri can go too once we work out who can accompany you four trouble makers on the flight."

"I promise I'll be good, Grandma. Come on Adi, this time it's my turn to win ..."

As they ran back in ... a voice whispered, "that might not be necessary actually." She turned to see Mila standing there, in her figure hugging crème Prada ball gown holding a large glass of champagne.

"Why not?" Lauren replied.

But Mila ignored her, gently pulling on her arm. "I've just been told there's someone at the door. A special guest ... you might want to meet."

Lauren stood up, motioned to Jack who smiled back and carried on his serious discussion waving his arms about, before she felt herself being led out through the high arched passageways into the dimly lit hallway. But when she saw the smiling person standing there she couldn't believe it, not after all that time.

"Oh my goodness, Rosie? Is it really you? How absolutely wonderful, I've missed you so much. What have you been up to lost in China?"

She rushed forward and gave Rosie a giant hug, her figure warm and lithe as ever inside the beautiful blue evening gown she had on. However, in her initial excitement she had missed one other important addition to the visiting entourage. Glancing over Rosie's shoulder, she immediately caught sight of two little girls with long black pigtails standing shyly in the shadows, and withdrew gently.

"Lauren, I miss you too so much. It give me great pleasure to be back in US and see Mila's grand palace, but you most of all. It has been far too long."

Lauren couldn't help staring at the girls, one looked about five and the other younger, probably three or so. They were of course beautifully dressed, their skin pale like baked porcelain in contrast to Rosie's darker, half Indian and half Chinese mixed heritage. Rosie took each one by the hand and brought them over.

"Can I introduce you to Mei-Zhen and Lien-Hua or in English, beautiful pearl and lotus flower. They are my daughters."

"Daughters?"

"Hello Lauren. It is a great pleasure to meet you," they said formally in unison, obviously their English prepared in advance with a big smile and held out their hands to shake.

Lauren hugged each one warmly. "What gorgeous little girls, Rosie. And they look just like you; their features are so strikingly similar. I don't need to ask what you've been up to now, that's pretty obvious. You have been a dark horse, not a mention on your emails?"

"There is reason actually."

Mila cut in. "I'll take Mei-Zhen and Lien-Hua to meet some new friends. I'll be back shortly and join you. Why don't you both use my sitting room, through that door at the end, where it's nice and quiet? Come on you two, I know you like computer games."

"Yes please Auntie Mila," they said excitedly and went off hand in hand.

Lauren and Rosie sat down around a large coffee table, in Mila's luxury armchairs. A pot of freshly made green tea and three cups had been placed there on a tray. One question was obvious to be asked. Who and where is he? But Lauren also realised from Mila's judicious managing of their encounter again that this had been planned ... Rosie's children clearly knew Mila already.

"Shall I pour, Lauren? Then I not beat about bush, I tell you what you deserve to know and where I have been."

Rosie filled each cup with the refreshing tea and Lauren immediately picked hers up and sipped slowly, blowing breaths over the top, and waited. She could see that whatever Rosie wanted to say was not easy.

"I have been spending the majority of my time over last five years living on border between China and Vietnam, on Chinese side of course. Much work has needed to be done, orders direct from Ministry, and I report to Chief of Staff of Chinese Intelligence. You will be aware of increased tensions between China and Vietnam over disputed islands in South China Sea. China of course is not intending to relinquish control, for strategic and security reasons, in fact strengthening military presence. Not for war, but all part of gently challenging US hegemony in Pacific. We plan to be big geopolitical player in world and I have had much to do, surveillance, monitoring, but also some anti-insurgency curtailment and rooting out of terrorists and spies, usual work, for me and Mila."

"Well it used to be Mila," Lauren replied, putting down her cup and crossing her legs. "But as we can all see, not anymore."

"I get a lot of help from a special man; we work and live together. He is father of my two daughters. I now love children very much. I know you would not believe me say such a thing. Life moves on as mystery doesn't it."

Lauren smiled. She was pleased for Rosie, unexpectedly, but obviously finding love and a proper family life with a man. But she also felt a tinge of jealousy. Her relationship with Rosie had also been special, exciting, and more so because they had always carried on their affairs in abject secrecy, which enhanced the thrill and the chase. She still loved Rosie the way she always had, and it was clear that Rosie still felt the same too. The body language between them couldn't have been more obvious, but Rosie was having real difficulty with her explanation. But it didn't matter. She truly wanted Rosie to find long term happiness and now being a mother too was quite something, which nobody would have predicted.

"And I'm really pleased for you, Rosie, I really am. You look wonderful on motherhood and finding true love. So who is the lucky man? Could he not come with you?"

There was a long pause as Lauren drank the rest of her tea.

"Father and husband is DG, Lauren."

Lauren held her cup in mid-air. She was hearing weird things, perhaps it was an after effect of space travel.

"DG?" She gazed at Rosie blank, totally dumbstruck.

"He not dead, he never dead. DG fled to Vietnam, penniless but resourceful. I was first person he contacted. We always got on well and love grew from there. I helped him, day after day, to rebuild his life again, his whole esteem. I got him both physically and mentally fit, we overcome his heart condition with local Chinese medicines. Now he has new identity. We found he still had a secret bank account which he could access in Macau. Not huge amount of money but between us enough to begin a new life on Chinese border with me and begin working together on regular intelligence and counter-terrorism work. Very handsomely paid by Chinese government. DG had hidden it well but he had developed a deep depression ... all he wanted was to return to his soldier roots, become the man and leader he was forty years ago. All started when he was part of the rescue of you in Congo jungle, but came together into searing climax with heart condition, when he believed his end was near. Blowing of hole in side of yacht catalysed an instant escape plan. Thrown into sea, incredibly he swam and swam to freedom and reached the shore, and then ran, and didn't stop running until he arrived in place he knew best, place of refuge to disappear, Hanoi, where I found him. He is desperately sorry about leaving Charlotte and his son and was angry, year after year with himself, but through meditation and hard work we have reconciled his decision and he now calm, thoughtful and happy. And we become pretty rich. Chinese government also rewarded me for my North Korea work in Murmansk and I receive highest commendation and a medal from President. Then two daughters came along, DG adores them. We have a big house on the border, prestige, security and even a cook and servants, but I call them housekeepers. Migrant workers of course from Vietnam."

Lauren remained dumbstruck. She didn't know what to say. This bombshell would never in a million years have been contemplated. What on earth could be said to Charlotte?

The door opened and Mila came back in, quietly shutting it behind her. She carefully wiped Lauren's tea, which had fallen out of her cup onto the Turkish carpet, with a tissue. "I can see Rosie's announcement has been made. I think we'd better tell Lauren the rest, don't you Rosie?"

"Yes of course. You start Mila."

"The rest? I don't know where to begin with the first," Lauren replied, her mind reeling with all manner of legal, emotional and financial tangles and huge complications.

Mila began. "I've know about Rosie and DG for a long time, before the girls were born. You know she and I have always been close working colleagues and friends for many, many years. We've saved each other's lives too often to remember on countless special operation campaigns."

"But we have never been lovers, Lauren," Rosie cut in.

"No, and never would be."

Lauren gazed from one to the other, her brain seared with idiotic emotional thoughts which made no sense whatsoever. She wished Jack was here. One thing she loved about him was his ability, like her, to think ultra rational and logically about a problem. The only man she had known who turned her on that way. Together, she and Jack were as scientifically matched and shit-hot as Mila and Rosie were in martial arts and killing people. But she was still pleased to hear what Mila had just said.

"You won't recognise DG. He has lost weight, become much leaner, stopped drinking and smoking and eats sensibly. For sixty-eight year old he is now in remarkable shape," Rosie continued. "They call him Fidel in our village. Because of the grey beard and hair, he look like Fidel Castro and is viewed by Vietnamese as big revolutionary, especially after he single handedly destroyed hidden nests of people traffickers, big growing curse in poor parts of Asia and which both governments must stamp out."

Lauren took another deep breath. "You said he has a new identity? And passport?"

"Yes and Chinese surgery?" Rosie replied, cheerily.

"Chinese surgery?"

"Some facial remodelling, make more handsome to go with new identity. But I have something else to tell, something which Mila you too have not heard. It will have consequence. I think you both should sit down and listen please."

It was Mila's turn to stare hard. She thought she knew the whole story and was ready to discuss the most sensible way to inform Charlotte. But of course Rosie as always would have to throw in a new angle, controversy naturally followed her throughout her life. Mila stood up and walked to her drinks cabinet. She brought back three wafer-thin balloon glasses and her best bottle of very old French brandy, an unopened wedding gift from Annabella and Luigi, and carefully set them out on the coffee table. A generous measure of light brown liquid was poured out for each of them. "I have a feeling we're going to need this. Bottoms up Lauren."

They clinked glasses.

A deliciously delicate sear drifted down her throat, as Lauren took a large swig, immediately feeling the benefit of the fortification. Silence prevailed. Mila and Lauren waited for Rosie to continue.

"It is very simple. Our work is almost finished on Chinese border and we have decided we need new challenge. DG wants to come home and I and our daughters want to come with him. Your new business idea, Mila, you contemplate in wake of failing marriage with lothario Henri-Gaston Landry? DG and I will join you in grand partnership of new specialist intelligence business and conquer world ... much opportunity. Bottoms up again everyone?"

Lauren and Mila both gaped, mouths open, staring at Rosie holding up her glass, a wide smile across her face.

"Rosie ... just one small question ... where is home?" Lauren whispered, topping up her and Mila's glass with another large measure.

"In Nice of course. DG now become Denis Groulx, former French citizen and born in lovely city. Groulx means 'hungry wolf,' very apt don't you think?"

But all that Lauren could utter very loudly was ... "fuck!"

"Holy fuck indeed," Mila added in disbelief.

END

This story will be continued in Book Six of the Rhapsody Series - Rhapsody of Deception

About the Author

Roy Baldwin was born in South Lancashire and has lived and worked around the UK in various mathematical and scientific guises as an educationalist, night club owner, civil servant, musician, house conservator and management consultant. His last novel Prism of Purpurine, a contemporary ghost story, was conceived and written in thirty days, during the NaNoWriMo 2014 competition.

Rhapsody of Moon is the fifth book in the Rhapsody Series, which follows the romantic exploits, adventures and challenges of nuclear scientist, Professor Lauren Hind. He is a full time writer, book designer and women's fiction publisher, and regularly commentates on books and indie publishing through twitter.

In between writing and digital publishing, Roy tries to enjoy the fabulous beauty of the Norfolk countryside and seashore where he now lives.

All Rhapsody novels can be bought in eBook and print versions from online bookstores worldwide.

Further information may be obtained from visiting the author's writer site on http://www.creativepubtalk.com where you can subscribe to an email newsletter keeping you in touch with further writer releases and developments.

The author hopes you have enjoyed this book and welcomes any feedback or questions on any aspects of the story, characters or settings. Please support the author by providing a personal review on Amazon, Goodreads, Twitter or any other favourite online book site or social media.

The other six books available for purchase in the Rhapsody Series and Mauveine Series are listed below:

Rhapsody of Restraint (Book 1)
Rhapsody of Power (Book 2)
Rhapsody of Fate (Book 3)
Rhapsody of Succession (Book 4)
Mauveine (Book 1)
Prism of Purpurine (Book 2)

Twitter: http://www.twitter.com/creativepubtalk
LinkedIn: Roy Baldwin—Women's Fiction Author

The next book in the Rhapsody Series, titled Rhapsody of Deception, is being written and planned for release early 2016.

Have you read the other Rhapsody books?

RHAPSODY OF RESTRAINT

Professor Lauren Hind is a scientist who appears to have it all. Global recognition for her nuclear energy work, a doting designer husband who she loves and a mega salary in a large corporate so she can indulge in her joint passions of haute couture and mathematics. After leading a prestigious research conference, she unexpectedly meets up with the mysterious and beguiling Luis who lures her into a culture she had not experienced. Fuelled by drink and intrigue, a train of events takes off and Lauren finds herself desperately buffeted by a seemingly irresolvable kaleidoscope of emotional and confused outcomes, which threaten to violently overturn her well-structured lifestyle and relationship bearings. Trying hard to salvage her way out of the mess she has created and save her marriage, new and interrelated twists and turns throw her into further turmoil, entanglements and more betrayal as she is forced to question everything she has stood for and make fundamental choices. But someone else turns up who has the capability, passion and desire to take from Lauren whatever she wants. Lauren needs to find the will and strength to confront this additional adversity and resolve her own complicated needs – but can she overcome the temptations...?

RHAPSODY OF RESTRAINT is the first book of the Rhapsody series which tells the story of the intriguing scientific and emotional destiny of Lauren Hind. "Where romance and adventure meets nuclear fusion!"

An excerpt from Rhapsody of Restraint ... she sauntered to the table already occupied by around a dozen other Sicilian men, some similar in age to Luis but many others younger. As they surrounded her, she sat down deciding not to take off her jacket immediately but flaunt her new outfit a little longer. They were dressed smartly, like they were all part of a group and were engaged in what appeared to be quite intense discussion on some hot topic or other in Italian.

"May I please ask your name?" He grinned warmly towards her. "We think you are the most interesting and desirable person to have crossed past our table tonight ... well so far anyway! It is nice to meet again in much more pleasant circumstances."

"I'm sorry?" Then she looked again and that minute before of déjà vu was confirmed with a jolt, the colour draining from her cheeks as her mouth dropped. He laughed vigorously at her seeming discomfort.

"Let's say my near decapitated legs in the airport are now fully recovered. Don't worry. I could see you were somewhat preoccupied then. Now tell us about yourself. I hope you're happy that we speak in English. I sense somehow that your Italian is less well developed."

"Gosh ... Yes thank you, please continue in English that's fine. I don't know what to say except to apologise profusely. It was rude and unacceptable of me to react that way when I had just arrived and ..."

He interrupted her gently. "My response back to you was not exactly civil either, so let's call it quits. No harm done and anyway I admire assertiveness in a woman and you certainly appear to have that in spades, as they say!"

Lauren, although embarrassed and somewhat taken aback with his immediate forwardness, nevertheless returned the smile and replied warmly, her composure returning quickly as she surveyed all the inquisitive faces.

"Hello everyone, I'm Lauren. I've been staying in the hotel over the last couple of days with the conference which has now ended. We've been doing some international exchange work in sustainable nuclear energy, networking, new developments all that sort of thing," she said clearly and deliberately.

She could hear herself sounding unnecessarily formal and not really knowing why she was speaking so wooden, when everyone around was being quite casual and laid back. She felt displaced with her thoughts, and especially with Luis who was deceptively and deliberately disarming her normal flow of reaction when meeting new people.

RHAPSODY OF POWER

Nuclear scientist Lauren Hind returns to Brussels to find her company, Cassini Power, riven by upheaval and turmoil and her Director role threatened. Confident in her adaptability and desperately needing a change of direction, she decides to face down her antagonistic Chairman, whilst seeking solace in a splurge of fashionable indulgence in advance of her expected big payoff. Appearances however can be deceptive and out of the blue an unexpected turn of events shakes up her perception and sets her off on a new path towards career possibilities and a world stage she could only previously have dreamed about. But threats and a puzzling technical dilemma shake her out of any cosy feelings of finally being in control of her life because she has to decide where her loyalties lie, and confront once again who she really is and her true feelings. Aspects of her recent past have not quite gone away as she had hoped and expected. A looming catastrophe, with enormous consequences for Europe and the rest of the world reveals the true extent of her capability to deal with serious dangers. To add to her confused feelings and foreboding, her Chairman is at the centre of the murky wheeling and dealing and she is summoned to engage in an adventure which could lead to her death and destruction. She badly needs help and there is only one person to turn to again – who could annihilate her in a moment. Can she let this happen or are the consequences and payback already drawn in the sand? And there is still her Chairman...

RHAPSODY OF POWER is the second book of the Rhapsody series continuing the science adventures and romantic escapades of Professor Lauren Hind

An excerpt from Rhapsody of Power ... Lauren saw immediately that Amélie was massively irritated and annoyed by what had been said in the first five minutes. "Honestly Amélie, I have not got a clue what all this attention is about. Listen, you can bank on me, once we get into the meeting, to step swiftly into the background, I'll back you up at every turn and when the time is correct follow your lead into what Cassini can do on fast plutonium reactors. And then let's sew up whatever deal we can muster; first and foremost to benefit you, remember just like we did in the old days? Anyway you look stunningly immaculate as ever, whilst I look like I've been dragged through a hedge backwards after that damned gust of wind outside. Have you got a decent hair brush?"

The tension in Amélie's face dissipated as she dug into her handbag. "I'm sorry Lauren for snapping. This deal is actually potentially more important to me than maybe I let on. Things have become a bit tricky back at the ranch, you know what I mean?"

Lauren patted her arm affectionately. "Of course, fully understood, you can tell me later. Hey, what are friends for. Now, let's get in there and give them the old one-two sales patter. I just hope my Chairman isn't there, I really do."

They strode out and over to reception where a smiling Valerie whisked them off to the lift and up to the fourth floor. As they stepped out into the executive corridor, an amazing view of the sea and the coast hit their senses, an immediate impact from the unusual design of the building, built like a glass atrium with a steep vertical wall immediately beneath going directly into the sea.

In a few seconds they entered the Board room to be greeted by a sea of male faces stood around the large buffet table, beautifully set out with an array of hot and cold food, salads, vegetables and sandwiches. Amélie immediately took a glass of white wine off the waiter near the entrance, with Lauren in close pursuit of the red, when a deep, clearly very English accented voice, familiar but unfamiliar, spoke out softly from behind.

"Ah ... so you must be Professor Lauren Hind. I have waited quite a long time to meet you." Lauren turned around and her face dropped as she found herself shaking hands — with the UK Prime Minister!

RHAPSODY OF FATE

A fun holiday in Rome beckons for scientist and Cassini CEO Lauren Hind to forget the recent nuclear debacle in Sicily. Looking forward to a new relationship with Philippe, her Chairman, her business and personal life should at last become rosy and settled. One revelation changes everything, discovering her lost adopted daughter, Charlotte and new family. But will this upheaval be a force for good or an uncontrollable disruption in her life?

She needs to find out, confront the demons and reconcile her feelings and admit who she really loves. But unexpectedly, in China, the marital happiness she had sought and won is violently disrupted leading to unwanted challenges and distractions. She is forced to question Amélie, her best friend, who she had always understood and trusted.

Something oddly sinister unfolds leading to a set of destabilising coincidences and finally a kidnapping which even her worst nightmares couldn't have predicted. Never before have her technical skills and bravery been tested so much. Could there be a man even more evil than Luis, capable of lacerating her emotions and loyalties at a stroke? And why does she have to travel to the Arctic to find out? Many may die, the dice is thrown and she must finally make the ultimate decision, one way or the other.

But which way does she turn? And who really loves her enough to pull her away from the deadly consequences?

RHAPSODY OF FATE is the third book of the Rhapsody series, continuing the science adventures and romantic escapades of Professor Lauren Hind

An excerpt from Rhapsody of Fate: They were soon heading out of town and into the surrounding countryside. The wide city beltway had dropped from a major highway down to a series of small rural lanes. Lauren gazed with interest at the great expanse of landscape, a mixture of parched and green rough grass, undulating hills and some meadows, but also randomly interspersed were a number of flat desert-like areas, on which stood interesting large contraptions with long beams, bobbing slowly with a counterweight and some kind of motor. Lauren immediately began working through the physics of turning the fast rotary motion of the motor, through a crank to upwards and downwards slow reciprocated pumping. But what was being pumped? Presumably, she thought, oil, but there were a lot of them and she was under the impression that inland oil reserves in Texas were long depleted.

"I can see you are intrigued Lauren. They're called pump jacks or nodding donkeys. Most of what is coming up is water with a bit of oil, but it remains extractable as does the gas often associated which can power the motor."

"Fascinating," replied Lauren, quietly.

"Okay, I'd better warn you in advance. Lyell's father Doug, who you are going to meet, although everyone, including us, calls him DG, is not only a Senator but the family have been big in the oil business for four generations and made a lot of money. I was just getting going with my engineering company when I met Lyell, but all the family connections and expertise were so useful, which is why I supply specialist parts to the industry. DG was a big help, and when we got married he insisted on buying us the ranch as a wedding present, as all my money had gone into the business. I lived in a small apartment in downtown Dallas. The ranch is a fabulous place.

"Really big Grandma," added Lexi. "And we keep our own cattle as the ranch used to belong to a cowboy. And we have our own nodding donkeys as well."

"Yes, DG insisted we exploit the mineral assets which had never been done, and he got it sorted out. In the US, mineral rights belong to the landowner not the government, like many other countries. Now it provides a useful addition to our overall income."

"But Lyell never wanted to be part of the oil business then like his father?"

"No, he never took to it. He loves the outdoors, and is very physical. He was a bit of a rebel in his youth, which is why he ended up in the army when he left school, but did very well and yes; he was in Special Forces when we met. He is very talented too with computers and software when he can be bothered, and has written some software for me, which has got me a load of new business, but I just wish he stuck at it. But when you see his wood carvings you will see why he doesn't need to."

Lauren nodded, taking in the information, her mind ticking its inexorable way through detailed analysis then synthesis of the data. Charlotte didn't seem to have anything in common with Lyell, but then again, who was she to judge or comment, three time married and soon Philippe the fourth to be added, especially on her own daughter? Everyone has to find their own way in life, even Lexi and Kat. She thought of Svet and wished she was here to enjoy this outing and vowed to bring Svet the next time she and Philippe visited Charlotte, although everything was getting so busy and the original planned arrangements with Svet had gone astray. When indeed would she have the time? Many mothers with a daughter of Charlotte's age would be more carefree in their later middle-age — shit, she was just forty-three and Charlotte was twenty-seven, they were like sisters. Then she reflected on the twins, nine years old. Something wasn't mathematically quite stacking up.

RHAPSODY OF SUCCESSION

Following confirmation, scientist and Cassini Chairman Lauren Hind adjusts to the realities of becoming pregnant with triplets at the age of forty-three. But husband Philippe, struggling to return to normality after the trauma of Murmansk, loses communications on an extended hunting holiday in Siberia. Whilst her news filters out, he remains unaware of Lauren's plight, adding to her frustration and growing alarm with unresolved dilemmas, as she falls back on past affections to try and come to terms and understand.

In the midst of this and grappling with continuing international success, Lauren suddenly finds her daughter, friends and colleagues making their own declarations of pregnancy as a veritable epidemic ensues, with major consequences as daughter Charlotte announces it's time to wed again and step-daughter Svet abruptly ends family ties.

When a mysterious Russian gas engineer, Olga, appears from nowhere into her life, she is reluctantly forced to reassess her foundering marriage and make an array of life changing decisions. An unexpected phone call triggers a journey to the darkest interiors of Central Africa. Why must she go, given her condition? And can anyone confront the murky plot and consequences that await and save her before the nightmare of the last nine months finally knits together for a devastating conclusion?

RHAPSODY OF SUCCESSION is the fourth book of the Rhapsody series, continuing the science adventures and romantic journey of Professor Lauren Hind

An excerpt from Rhapsody of Succession: Rosie had saved her life twice, each time from terrorists both in Beijing and latterly Murmansk with that dazzling and totally unexpected display of Chinese martial arts and weaponry. Rosie was so incredibly special and gorgeous, why did she have to get shot? She really needed to find out how Rosie's spinal injury recovery, under Sergei's innovative medical treatments, was progressing, despite Rosie's vehement insistence to everyone, particularly Lauren, that she wanted absolutely no contact or visitors seeing her in a wheelchair. Rosie had obviously taken her serious gunshot injury very badly; perhaps Mila, her old friend, knew more. A discussion with Svet now seemed a very distant proposition since that disastrous attempt at coming out on the triplets. It would be nice to do something right with the Dubois entourage for a change. A detailed conversation at the generous buffet table with a group of feisty female science representatives from the newly joined Bulgaria took her mind off family woes. Complimenting Lauren on her prophetic and wide ranging nuclear plan for the next fifty years, the Bulgarians seemed especially clued up on recent Russian progress with fusion, some aspects of which she needed to check out with Philippe. A mild security commotion caught her eye at the top of the palatial room. Somebody uniformed was being led out in some distress. Then two very tall and smartly dressed blonde women, with a distinctly commanding presence, began marching through the crowd of bureaucrats, catching the swivelling gazes of an array of intrigued male and female delegates. She immediately recognised one of them. How could she not, viewing the sexy ankle-booted occupant of a vivid red knee-length Prada dress, a delectable bow tying up the neckline and temptingly fastened all down the front with large white pearl buttons. Her companion was equally stunning in Versace yellow.

"Lauren, you look fantastic and the Energy Commissioner tells me you're speech was so forward thinking and visionary that he will be raising it at the next EC Presidential summit. Oh, I'm sorry, can I introduce you to Dr Katrine Henrikson. Katrine is leader of the Danish Social Alliance Party, presently holding the balance of power in their coalition. We met last night in the Alamode Hotel next door."

"Last night?